arms. … had she been *thinking* to kiss the enemy?

Who was she kidding? Jackson wasn't the enemy, even if he was part of the news media. Maybe at first she hadn't trusted him—with her background, who could blame her? But during the time they'd spent together she'd learned that there was so much more to him than his dashing looks and his news coverage.

He was a man who'd loved and lost. He was kind and generous. He went out of his way for others, even when he'd rather be doing anything else. And he had a sense of humor. The memory of his deep laugh still sent goosebumps down her arms. That was a sound she could listen to for the rest of her life—

Whoa! Slow down.

She knew that this moment of playing house would end soon—just as soon as the avalanche was cleared and they were able to plow the roads. Then they would return to reality. But for now they had their own little world within the walls of this cabin and she intended to enjoy it as long as it lasted.

And if that should include some more kisses…?

Well, she wouldn't complain.

A smile pulled at her lips.

She'd be … n
could c … r
kissing. … t
hadn't la …

SNOWBOUND WITH AN HEIRESS

BY

JENNIFER FAYE

First Published in Great Britain 2017
By Mills & Boon, an imprint of HarperCollins*Publishers*
1 London Bridge Street, London, SE1 9GF

ISBN: 978-0-263-92344-5

23-1117

Our policy is to use papers that are natural, renewable and recyclable products and made from wood grown in sustainable forests. The logging and manufacturing processes conform to the legal environmental regulations of the country of origin.

Printed and bound in Spain
by CPI, Barcelona

Award-winning author **Jennifer Faye** pens fun, heart-warming, contemporary romances with rugged cowboys, sexy billionaires and enchanting royalty. Internationally published, with books translated into nine languages, she is a two-time winner of the *RT Book Reviews Reviewers*' Choice Award. She has also won the CataRomance Reviewers' Choice Award, been named a TOP PICK author, and been nominated for numerous other awards.

For Tonya.

Thanks for being there from the beginning…
I am thankful for our friendship
and your unending encouragement. :)

CHAPTER ONE

PEACE AT LAST…

Serena Winston paused along the snowy path. Out here in the beauty of the Alps, it was so quiet. She lifted her face up to the warmth of the sun just seconds before it disappeared behind a dark cloud. Shadows quickly spread over the mountainous region of Austria.

She sighed. The sunshine had been so nice while it lasted, but the snow was starting to fall again. But she had to admit that the snowflakes had their own charm as they fluttered to the ground. It was so different from her home in sunny Hollywood.

"Arff! Arff!"

"Okay, Gizmo." Serena glanced down at her recently adopted puppy. "You're right. We better keep moving."

There was already plenty of snow on the ground. Serena's fondest wish had always been to learn to ski, but for one reason or another, she'd kept putting it off. First, it was due to the worry of injuring herself before filming a movie. Being an actress did have its drawbacks. And then, there just wasn't time to jet off to Tahoe for a long weekend of skiing—especially now that she'd inherited her legendary father's vast estate. Selling off some of his holdings was more complicated than she had anticipated.

Realizing the direction of her thoughts, she halted them.

She drew in a deep, calming breath. This holiday excursion was meant for escaping her daily pressures and refocusing her Hollywood career. There was yet another reason for this spur-of-the-moment trip, but she didn't want to think about it, either. There'd be time for problem-solving later.

When she glanced back down at her teddy bear dog, she found he'd wrapped his lead around a bush. The easiest way to fix the situation was to release Gizmo from his lead. It was no big deal. Gizmo was not one to wander off.

Serena unhooked the lead. "Stay," she said firmly.

Gizmo gazed at her as though understanding what she'd said. He didn't move a paw.

"Good boy."

Serena set to work untangling the leash from the prickly shrubbery. It wasn't an easy task. What had Gizmo been doing? Chasing something?

At last, she freed the leash. She'd have to be more careful about letting him out on the full length of the lead in the areas with rougher terrain.

"Arff! Arff!"

She watched as her little dog took off in hot pursuit after a brown-haired creature. "Gizmo! Stop!"

Serena ran after the dog. She continued calling his name, but he paid her no heed. For a little guy with short legs, Gizmo could move swiftly when he was motivated enough. And right now, he was very motivated.

Serena wasn't familiar with the terrain, as this was her first visit to the small village nestled in the Austrian Alps. This area had been on her bucket list to visit right after Fiji and right before Tasmania. With her rush to leave Hollywood, it seemed like the right time to scratch another adventure off her list.

The snow grew heavier. Between the snowflakes and trees, she spotted a road ahead. And though it appeared to be a quiet road, the thought of little Gizmo being anywhere near it had Serena pumping her legs harder and faster.

"Gizmo—"

Serena's foot struck a tree root. Down she went. *Oomph!*

The collision of her chest with the hard, frozen ground knocked the air from her lungs. She didn't have a chance to regroup before she heard the sound of an approaching vehicle. With each heartbeat, the sound was growing closer.

Ignoring her discomfort, Serena scrambled to her feet. "Gizmo! Here, boy."

She continued after the little furbaby who'd captured her heart a few months ago. At first, she hadn't been so sure about owning a dog. Gizmo was full of puppy energy and in need of lots of love.

But now she couldn't imagine her life without him. Gizmo made her smile when she was sad and he made her laugh when she angry. Not to mention, he got her up and moving when she thought she was too tired to take another step. He was there for her unlike anyone else in her life.

It wasn't like Gizmo to take off and not listen to her. She supposed that between the long flight from the States and then the intermittent snow showers that they'd been cooped up inside for too long.

The blast of a horn shattered the silence.

It was followed by the sound of skidding tires.

A high-pitched squeal confirmed Serena's worst fears.

Her heart leaped into her throat as she came to a stop.

A loud thud reverberated through the air. And then the crunch of metal sent Serena's heart plummeting down to her new snow boots.

A whole host of frantic thoughts sprang to mind. They jumbled together. The immobilizing shock quickly passed and she put one foot in front of the other. All the while, she struggled to make sense of the tragedy that undoubtedly awaited her.

As if on autopilot, she cleared the overgrown path. She scanned the quiet road. Her gaze latched on to the back end of a dark sedan. Inwardly she cringed.

And to make things worse, there was no sign of Gizmo.

Or maybe that was a good thing. She was desperate to cling to any sense of hope. She held her breath and listened for a bark—a whimper—anything. There were no puppy sounds.

Please let Gizmo be safe.

Steam poured out from the engine compartment of the crashed vehicle. The driver's side was bent around a cluster of trees. Serena's mouth gaped. Was that the reason Gizmo didn't respond? A sob rose in her throat. Was he pinned in the wreckage?

Tears pricked the back of her eyes. *Please, say it isn't so.*

Moisture dampened her cheeks. She swiped at the tears. For a normally reserved person who only cried on a director's cue, Serena wasn't used to a spontaneous rush of emotions. Realizing she couldn't just stand there, she swallowed hard and then moved forward, wondering what she would find.

On legs that felt like gelatin, she moved across the road. Realizing the driver's-side door was pinned by a tree trunk, she approached the passenger side and yanked open the door.

A snapping and popping sound emanated from the car. Serena didn't even want to imagine what that might be. Still, she glanced around for any sign of fire.

Not finding any flames, Serena knelt down to get a better look. There in the driver's seat was a man with dark brown hair. His head was leaned back against the seat. His eyes were shut. His dark lashes and brows gave his face a distinctive look. There was something familiar about him, but in her frantic state, she couldn't make any connections. Right now, she had to get this man to safety in case his car went up in flames.

Even though she'd played a nurse once in a movie, she didn't know much about first aid. The movie had been a stalker/thriller type. The medical aspects were minimal. She reached for the cell phone in her back pocket. She pulled it out, but there was no signal. This wasn't good—not good at all.

"There…there was a dog…"

The deep male voice startled Serena. His voice wobbled as though he was still dazed. She glanced up to find a pair of dark brown eyes staring back at her. Her heart lodged in her throat. Was it wrong that she found his eyes intriguing? And dare she say it, they were quite attractive. They were eyes that you couldn't help staring into and losing yourself.

The man's gaze darted around as though trying to figure out what had happened. And then he started to move. A groan of pain immediately followed.

"Stop," Serena called out. "Stay still."

The man's confused gaze met hers. "Why? Is there something the matter with me?"

She could feel the panic swelling between them. "I'm not sure." She drew in a calming breath. Getting worked up wouldn't help either of them. She drew on her lifetime of acting. "I don't know the extent of your injuries. Until we know more, you shouldn't move." Which was all well and good until the car caught fire. But she could only deal with one catastrophe at a time. "I'm going to call for help."

"You already tried that. It didn't work." His voice was less frantic and more matter-of-fact.

She swallowed hard. So he'd seen that. *Okay. Don't*

freak out or he'll panic. Without a cell signal, their choices were diminishing. And the car was still popping and fizzing. She didn't want to tell this injured man any of this. Nor did she want to admit that the dog that created this horrific event was hers. The backs of her eyes burned with unshed tears. And that her poor sweet puppy could very well be—

No. Don't go there. Focus on getting this man help.

The man released his seat belt. The only way out for him was to crawl over the passenger seat. But he shouldn't be moving around until a professional looked at him.

"Don't move," she said as he pushed aside the seat belt. "I'll go and get help."

"I'm fine." His voice took on a firm tone.

He was sounding better, but it could just be shock. What if he got out of the car and collapsed in the middle of the road? She certainly couldn't lift him, much less carry him. Even with him being seated, she could see that he was over six feet tall and solidly built. Why did he have to be so stubborn?

The man leaned toward the passenger seat.

"I'm serious. You shouldn't be moving." She swiped her hair out of her face. It was wet from melting snowflakes. It was coming down so hard that she couldn't see much past the other side of the road. "You could make your injuries worse."

As though transforming her concerns into reality, he groaned in pain. Serena's heart lurched. She automatically leaned forward, placing a hand against the man's biceps, helping to support him.

"What is it? What hurts?" Her gaze scanned his body looking for blood or any possible injury, but she didn't spot any.

His breathing was labored. "It's my leg."

"What's wrong with it?"

"I can't move it."

Not good. Not good at all.

And as if matters weren't bad enough, a white cloud billowed out from under the hood. Her heart pounded. What was she supposed to do now?

CHAPTER TWO

SERENA CRAWLED OVER the passenger seat, making her way to the driver's side. "We have to get you out of here. Quickly."

"Don't worry," the man said. "It's just steam."

She wanted to believe him. She really did. But she wasn't sure if the man was totally lucid. For all she knew, he could have a head injury or be in shock or both.

She refused to abandon him. She prayed the car didn't explode into flames before she freed him. With the man slouched over, he was in her way.

With her hand still on his shoulder, she pushed with all her might. He didn't budge. The man was built like a solid rock wall.

"I need you to sit up," she said.

"What?" His voice was a bit groggy. His gaze zeroed in on her. "What are you doing?"

"I need you to move so I can see what's going on with your leg."

"You don't know what you're doing. You're going to make it worse. Go away!"

His harsh words propelled her back out of the car. What was up with this guy? Maybe it was the shock talking.

"I'm trying to help you. Now quit being difficult."

She took a calming breath and knelt down again. "Move! Now!"

The man's dark brows rose.

It appeared her brusque words had finally gained his full attention. The man muttered something under his breath. At last, he started to move. He was almost upright when he let out a grunt of pain.

"Is it your leg?"

He nodded as he drew in one deep breath after the other.

She glanced between him and the dash. There just might be enough room for her to wiggle in there. It'd help if she had a flashlight. And then remembering her cell phone, she grabbed it from her pocket and turned on the light.

Her gaze met his. "I'm going to try not to hurt you, but we have to free your leg. Can you work with me on this?"

The man's eyes reflected his uncertainty, but then he relented with a curt nod. "Just do it. And quickly. I smell gas."

He didn't have to tell her twice. On her stomach, she moved across the butter-soft leather upholstery. When she got to the man's body, she did her best to focus on the task at hand and not the fact that when she placed a hand on his thigh, it was rock hard. The man was all muscle and—and she had work to do. At last, she was wedged between him and the dashboard with barely any room for her to move her arms.

"Can you move the seat back?"

His body shifted. "It's not working. The electrical system must have shorted out."

"Okay. I've got this."

She had to get this man free of the car and then find out what had happened to Gizmo. Her poor sweet furbaby could be hurt or worse—

Stop. Deal with one problem at a time.

Hands first, she repositioned herself. She flashed the light around. The side of the car had been smashed inward. His ankle was pinned between the car door and the brake pedal. It looked bad—real bad.

Serena drew in an unsteady breath, willing herself to remain calm when all she wanted to do was run away and find someone else to help this man. But there wasn't time for that. She could do this. She could. Serena placed her hand gently on his leg and paused. When he didn't cry out in pain, she proceeded to examine the situation. She ran her hand down his leg, checking for any major injuries. She didn't feel any. There was no wiggle room on either side. The brake pedal was digging into his flesh.

Knowing that she was going to need two hands, she held up the phone to him. "Can you hold this for me?"

He took the phone. The light was angled too high.

"Tilt it a little lower. I'm going to try to move the brake pedal. Are you ready?"

"Yes. Just do what you need to do."

Serena pressed on the brake. The pedal became stuck on his black leather dress shoe. She tried moving his foot, but it wouldn't budge.

She felt his body stiffen. Serena released his foot. He was really pinned in there. And it frightened her to know that she might not be able to free him before the car went up in flames.

She swallowed hard. "I'm going to take off your shoe and see if that will help."

"Do what you need to do. You don't have to keep updating me."

Just then she inhaled the scent of smoke. Her pulse quickened. They were almost out of time. And this wasn't the way she planned to leave this world.

Her fingers moved quickly. The shoe tie pulled loose.

He cursed under his breath.

She stopped moving. "Sorry."

"Don't be sorry. Keep going."

"But I'm hurting you."

"It's going to hurt a lot more when that fire reaches us."

"Okay. Okay. I've got it. I'll try to do this as quickly as possible."

"Do it!"

The melting snow on the top of her head dripped onto her nose. With her arm, she brushed it off. All her focus needed to be on freeing this man, and in essence herself, from this smashed-up, gasoline-leaking, smoldering car.

Serena once again worked to free his shoe from his foot. It didn't move easily and she suspected he had a lot of swelling going on. She reminded herself to focus on one problem at a time. However, at this moment the problems were mounting faster than she could deal with them.

The smoke caused her to let out a string of coughs.

"Are you okay?" Not even waiting for her answer, he said, "You should get out of here."

"Not without you."

When she moved his foot again, she heard the distinct hiss of his breath. He didn't say anything and so she continued moving his foot. At last, his foot slipped past the brake pedal.

She pulled back. "You're free."

There was perspiration beading on the man's forehead. It definitely wasn't hot in the car. It was more like freezing. Her maneuvering his foot must have hurt him more than he'd let on. She felt really bad adding to his discomfort, but she had no other way to free him.

"Now," she said, "let's get you out of here."

She eased out of the car and attempted to help him, but he brushed her off. The smoke was getting heavier.

"I've got it," he said. "Just move away from the car."

"Not without you." She stood just outside the car.

"Quit saying that. Take care of yourself."

She wasn't backing away. If he needed her, she would be there. The popping and fizzing sounds continued. Her gaze darted to the hood where the smoke was the heaviest. Her attention returned to the man.

Hurry. Please hurry.

She wondered how bad the damage was to his left leg. It suddenly dawned on her that he most likely wouldn't be able to walk on it. But what choice did they have as they were stuck in the middle of nowhere. It was becoming increasingly obvious that no one used this road—at least not in the middle of a snowstorm. And who could blame them, she thought, glancing around at the snow-covered roadway.

Right now, she just wanted to find Gizmo and head back to the cabin. *Gizmo.* Where was he? Her heart clenched with fear. *Please let him be safe.*

It took her assistance to get the man to his feet. Or in his case, his one good foot. He'd finally had to relent and lean on her shoulder. Between hopping and a bit of hobbling, she got him to the other side of the road, a safe distance from the car.

"Thank you," he said. "I don't know what I'd have done if you hadn't come along."

"You're welcome."

"My name's Jackson. What's yours?"

In the daylight, she recognized him. The breath hitched in her throat. He was trouble. Make that trouble with a capital *T* and an exclamation point. He was Jackson Bennett—the god of morning news. She turned away.

He was on the airwaves for three hours each morning in American homes from coast to coast. People quoted him. And quite often his name trended after a particularly stunning interview.

The producers of his show had been in contact with her agent a few times to set up an on-air interview, but each time the logistics hadn't worked for one of them. She couldn't be more grateful about that now. Still, she couldn't breathe. There was a definite possibility that he'd recognize her.

This was not good. Not good at all.

In her mind, he was the enemy—the press. All of her carefully laid plans were in jeopardy. She was surprised he hadn't recognized her already. Would her different hair color and lack of makeup make that much of a difference? She could only hope. After all, who came to the Alps and expected to run across an award-winning movie star from the States?

Regardless, there was no way she was voluntarily outing herself. She'd worked too hard to flee the paparazzi and everything else related to Hollywood, including her agent. It was best that she kept their encounter brief. Not only was she over men, but Jackson was a professional newsman. With enough time, he was bound to sniff out her story.

"Mae. My name's Mae." It wasn't a lie. It was her middle name.

"Mae?" He gazed at her as though studying her face. "You don't look like a Mae."

Oh, no!

"Who do I look like?" The words were out before she could stop them. She wanted to kick herself for indulging in this conversation that had a distinct possibility of blowing up in her face.

He continued to study her. "Hmm… I'll have to give that some thought."

There was a large rock nearby. She brushed off some

of the freshly fallen snow. "Sit here and wait. I'll be right back."

"Where are you going?"

Gizmo's name clogged in her throat. She'd never be able to get the words out. She swallowed hard. "I… I have to check on something."

"It's too late to save the car."

She turned to find fire engulfing the hood. If Gizmo was there—if he was trapped—she had to help him. Serena quickly set off for the car, before she could talk herself out of her plan.

Jackson was shouting at her to stop, but she kept going. She would be careful—as careful as she could be. She could feel Jackson's gaze following her. She didn't care what he thought. If Gizmo was hurt and needed her, she had to help him.

Serena rushed through the thickening snow to the car. She carefully made her way down over the small embankment. All the while, she kept an eye out for any sign of her buddy. Between the snow and the wind, there was no sign of his little footprints.

With great trepidation, she turned toward the place where the car was smashed against the trees. Could he be in there?

She rushed over and bent down. She reached out to sweep away the snow from around the front tire, but for the briefest moment, she hesitated. Her whole body tensed as she imagined the ghastly scene awaiting her.

She gave herself a mental shake. With trembling hands, she set to work. And then at last, most of the snow had been swept away. There was no Gizmo. She took her first full breath. It didn't mean he was safe, but it was a good sign. And right about now, she'd take any positive sign possible.

She turned in a full circle, searching for him. She even

ventured the rest of the way down the embankment. There was no sign of him. The crash must have spooked him. How far had he run? And how long would he last in the extreme conditions? She repeatedly called his name.

Between the thickening clouds and the heavy snow, visibility wasn't great. With the deepest, most painful regret, she realized she couldn't help Gizmo. A sob caught in her throat. The backs of her eyes stung. She couldn't fall apart—not yet. She had to get Jackson to safety and then she'd return to continue her search for Gizmo. The car continued to smoke and smolder, so she scooped up some armfuls of snow and heaped them on the hood, hoping to douse the flames. She then moved to the side of the car and, catching sight of a bag in the back seat, she retrieved the large duffel bag.

She returned to the rock where the man was still sitting. "I need to get you out of this weather."

"What were you doing?"

"What are you talking about?"

"Just now. You were searching for something." And then his eyes widened. "That dog. He's yours."

Once more her eyesight blurred with unshed tears. She blinked repeatedly. She nodded.

"It almost killed me." The man's deep voice rumbled.

Serena's chin lifted and her gaze narrowed in on him. "And you might have very well killed him."

As though her pointed words had deflated him, the man had the decency to glance away. His anger immediately dissipated as the gravity of the situation sunk in.

"Are you sure?" he asked. "I tried to miss him."

"I called him and I searched around, but I didn't find any sign of him."

"And just now, when you returned to the car, were you looking under it for your dog?"

She struggled to keep her emotions in check. She nodded. It was the best she could do.

"I'm sorry." His tone softened. "I'd never intentionally hurt an animal."

"It's not your fault. It's mine. I let him off his leash. I should have known better."

"Maybe he's okay. Maybe he got lost."

She shook her head, wishing Jackson would be quiet. He was attempting to comfort her, but it wasn't working. Aside from seeing Gizmo alive and healthy, nothing would soothe her pain and guilt.

She couldn't let herself think about Gizmo any longer. She had to take care of Jackson. And the way he was favoring his leg, there was no way she would be able to get him back to her cabin without a little help. Her cabin was a ways from here. And it was situated in a secluded area. That was why she'd chosen it. It was far from prying eyes and, most important, the press.

But now, well, the location wasn't ideal to obtain medical aid. But she was certain that once she got ahold of the rescue services, they'd send someone to get Jackson medical treatment.

With her thoughts focused on getting help, she turned to Jackson. "I have a place. But I think you're going to need some help getting there."

"I'll make it." He stood upright. He'd barely touched the ground with his injured leg when his face creased with obvious pain.

"Are you ready to concede now?"

His gaze didn't meet hers. "What do you have in mind?"

"I'm going to look for a tree branch that you can use as a cane. Between my shoulder and the tree branch, hopefully we'll be able to limp you back to the cabin."

"Cabin?"

"Uh-huh. Is that a problem?"

"Um. No. I won't be there long."

A smile pulled at her lips at Jackson Bennett's obvious disapproval of staying in a cabin. He had absolutely no idea that it was a two-story log home with just about every creature comfort you could imagine. But Jackson was right about one thing: he wouldn't be staying with her for long. Once she had phone service, he'd be on his way to the hospital and out of her life.

CHAPTER THREE

"Arff!"

Jackson Bennett glanced around. Was it possible that the dog the woman was so worried about had been unharmed? He hoped so.

He squinted through the heavy falling snow. Where was the dog? Maybe if he caught it, he'd be able to pay the woman back. They could part on even terms. He hated feeling indebted to anyone. If only he could locate the source of the barking.

"Arff! Arff!"

He glanced around for some sign of Mae. Maybe she could find the dog. But it appeared she was still off in search of a makeshift cane for him.

Jackson got to his feet. With difficulty, he turned around. There beneath a tree, where the snow wasn't so deep, stood a little gray-and-white dog. It looked cold and scared. Jackson could sympathize.

"Come here," he said in his most congenial tone. "I won't hurt you."

There was another bark, but it didn't move. The dog continued to stare at Jackson as though trying to decide if Jackson could be trusted or not. Jackson kept calling to the dog, but the little thing wouldn't come near him.

Jackson smothered a frustrated sigh. How did he gain the dog's trust?

He again glanced around for Mae. How far had she gone for the walking stick? A town on the other side of the Alps? Italy perhaps?

He considered shouting for her, but then he changed his mind. If he frightened the dog, they'd never catch it. And it wasn't fit for man or beast in this snowstorm.

Jackson turned back to the dog. If only he had a way to coax him over, but he didn't have any dog treats. And then he thought of something. He'd missed his lunch and had grabbed a pack of crackers to eat in the car. Would a dog eat a cracker?

Jackson had no idea. His experience with a dog consisted of exactly seven days. And it hadn't gone well at all.

Once the dog had made a mess on the floor, chewed one of his mother's favorite shoes and howled when his mother put him in the backyard for the night, she'd taken the dog back to the shelter. Jackson remembered how crushed he'd been. He'd begged and pleaded for his mother to change her mind. His mother had told him that it was for the best and sent Jackson to his room.

He banished the memories to the back of his mind. Those days were best forgotten. His life was so much different now—so much better. He didn't have a dog and, for all intents and purposes, he didn't have a mother, either. It was for the best.

He pulled the crackers from his dress shirt pocket. He undid the cellophane and removed one. It consisted of two crackers with cheese spread between them. He hoped this would work.

"Here, boy."

The dog's ears perked up. That had to be a good sign.

The pup took a few steps forward. His nose wiggled. Then his tail started to wag.

"That's it. Come on."

The dog's hesitant gaze met his and then returned to the cracker. The pup took a few more steps. He was almost to Jackson.

Jackson lowered his voice. "That's a good boy." He laid the cracker flat on his hand and took a wobbly step forward. The dog watched his every move but held his ground. Jackson stretched out his arm as far as it'd go.

And then the dog came closer. After a few seconds of hesitation, he grabbed the cracker. Jackson caught sight of the blue sparkly collar on the dog's neck. Something told him that this was most definitely the woman's dog. The flashy collar was in line with the woman's rhinestone encrusted cell phone and her perfectly manicured nails.

As the dog devoured the cracker, Jackson knew this was his moment to make his move. Balancing his weight on one foot, he bent down. He lunged forward to wrap his hands around the little dog.

The dog jumped back and Jackson lost his balance. He reached out to regain his balance, but he'd moved too far from the large rock. He instinctively put his weight on his injured leg. Wrong move. He swore under his breath.

"What in the world!" came the beautiful stranger's voice.

It was too late. She couldn't help him. His injured leg couldn't take the pressure of his weight. It gave way. He fell face-first into the snow.

Jackson sat up with snow coating him from head to toe. He blew the snow from his mouth and nose. Then he ran a hand over his face. At that moment, he felt something wet on his cheek. He opened his eyes to find the dog licking him. *Ugh!*

"Aww...you found him." A big smile bloomed on the woman's face. If he thought that she was beautiful before, she was even more of a knockout when she smiled. "You're such a naughty boy for running off. Come here, Gizmo."

"Gizmo? What kind of name is that?" Jackson attempted to get to his feet. He failed.

The woman's brows drew together, but she didn't move to help him. "What's wrong with his name?"

Jackson sighed. "It's a bit cutesy for a boy, don't you think?"

"Cutesy?" Her green eyes darkened to a shade of deep jade.

"Never mind." What did he care what she named her dog? If his head wasn't pounding, he would have kept his thoughts to himself. He would have to make a mental note to tread carefully going forward. Without Mae's help, he hefted himself to his feet.

In the meantime, she picked up the dog and brushed snow from Gizmo. "We need to get you home and in front of a fire. You poor baby."

As Jackson brushed himself off, he couldn't help but watch how the woman oohed and aahed over the dog. What amazed him the most was how the dog was eating up the attention as though it knew exactly what she was saying.

Mae turned to Jackson as though an afterthought, holding out a stick. "Here you go."

He accepted the sturdy-looking branch. Somehow it made him feel like some sort of Paul Bunyan figure. Although his suit and dress shoes would definitely suggest otherwise.

"How in the world did you find Gizmo?" she asked.

Jackson couldn't actually admit to having done much of anything, but if she wanted to give him partial credit, who was he to reject it. After all, if he hadn't thought of the crackers in his pocket, the dog might have run off again.

"We sort of found each other. And he likes the same crackers as I do."

"Crackers?"

"Yes. I have some in my pocket. They were supposed to replace my lunch, but I got distracted when I turned on the wrong road and my GPS wouldn't work out here. Anyway, I forgot about them."

She nodded as though she understood, but there were still unspoken questions in her eyes. "I hate to say it, but the snow's not letting up. If anything, it's getting heavier." She frowned as she glanced upward. "I threw a bunch of snow on the fire when I was looking for Gizmo. I think it doused it. If not, this heavy snow should take care of it." She turned to him. "Are you ready to hike out of here?"

"I don't see where I have a choice."

"I've got to carry Gizmo because the snow is starting to get too deep for his short legs. And I'll take your bag as you'll need all your energy to move on your good leg. But you can put your arm over my shoulder to balance yourself. Hopefully between that and the cane, you'll be able to make it back to the cabin."

"Sounds like a plan."

He got a firm grip on the stick and placed an arm over her shoulders, trying not to put too much pressure on her. He felt guilty that he couldn't even relieve her of his bag, but she was right, anything more would unbalance him. His ankle was really starting to throb now that the adrenaline was wearing off.

She glanced over at him. "Thank you for finding Gizmo."

"You're welcome."

Were those unshed tears shimmering in her eyes? But in

a blink, they were gone. And he wasn't sure if he'd imagined them after all.

At least, they were now even. He glanced over at his snow angel. She was the most beautiful woman he'd ever laid his eyes on. It was hard to miss her stunning green eyes. They were unforgettable and strangely familiar. But that was impossible, right? After all, she was here in Austria and he was from New York City.

But the more he thought about it, he realized that she spoke with an American accent. Now, that he found interesting. What was an American woman doing in Austria at Christmastime? Did she have family here? Or was it something else? Perhaps it was the journalist in him, but he was curious about her story. And then he wondered if she might have an interesting story—something to humanize the holiday segment that he'd flown here to film.

He assured himself that it was professional interest—nothing more. After all, he was off the market. Ever since his wife passed away, he'd kept to himself. No one could ever fill the empty spot in his heart and he had no desire to replace his wife, not now—not ever.

Their progress was slow but steady. He felt bad for holding her back. "Why don't you go on ahead?" he suggested. "You've got to be cold."

"No colder than you. And I'm not leaving you out here. You don't even know where my cabin is."

"I can follow your tracks—"

"No. We're in this together."

Boy, was she stubborn. Even though it irked him that Mae was out here in the frigid air on his account, a small part of him admired her assertiveness. She would certainly be a tough nut to crack during an interview. Those were the interviews he enjoyed the most. The ones where he had to work hard to get the interviewee to open up—to get to the heart of the matter.

A lot of his peers would disagree and say that an interview should flow smoothly. But he wasn't afraid of confrontation—of setting matters straight. But being stuck on the morning news cycle, he didn't get to do many meaty interviews—certainly not as many as he would like.

They continued on in silence. And that was quite all right with Jackson. His head hurt. No, it pounded. But that pain was nothing compared to his ankle. However, he refused to let any of that stop him.

He clenched his jaw as he forced himself to keep moving. It was very slow progress, but one step at a time, he was moving over the snow-laden ground. The snow had seeped into his dress shoes. At first, his feet had grown cold. Then they had begun to hurt. Now they were numb.

He sure hoped they got to their destination soon. Freezing to death might make a big news story—but he wasn't that desperate for headlines.

He glanced once more at Mae, but she'd pulled up her hood with the fluffy white fur trim, blocking the view of her beautiful face. "Is it much farther?"

"It's just over that rise." She turned her head, sending him a concerned look. "Do you need to rest?"

"No." If he stopped now, he doubted he'd be able to move again. "I can make it."

"Are you sure?" There was a distinct note of doubt in her voice.

"I'm sure." His teeth started to chatter, so he clenched his jaw together.

Attempting to keep his thoughts on anything but the unending cold, he glanced at the woman next to him. He was torn between being angry at her for causing the accident by letting her dog loose and being grateful that she was some sort of angel sent to rescue him.

Then guilt settled in. How could he be upset with someone who was so concerned for him? She may have been irresponsible with the dog, but she'd cared enough to help him. He couldn't forget that. Perhaps this was the twist in the story he'd come to Austria to tell. Perhaps he could attribute her actions to the holiday spirit. Maybe that was stretching things, but he liked the sound of it. He knew that angle would tug on the heartstrings of his viewers. But it wouldn't be enough to garner the attention of the television executives—the same people who had passed him over for the evening news anchor role.

He stared straight ahead. There indeed was a slight hill. In his condition, it seemed more like Mont Blanc. But between the thick tree limb that Mae had located for him and her slim shoulders, he would make it.

Hopefully this cabin came equipped with a landline. He had to get out of here. This wasn't a vacation for him. He was on assignment and his film crew was due to arrive tomorrow. He'd arrived early to scout out some special settings for his Christmas-around-the-world series. This accident would definitely put a crimp in his plans, but by tomorrow he'd be back on track. He refused to let his ankle and various minor injuries hold him back—not when there was work to be done.

He didn't know how much time had passed when the cabin at last came into sight. He paused for a moment, catching his breath. But only for a moment and then he was moving again—pushing through the pain. Between the snow and his injured leg, this walk was a bigger workout than he normally experienced at the gym.

His body was giving in to the cold and he stumbled. "We need to stop."

She narrowed her gaze. "Are you quitting on me? Are you a quitter?"

"I'm not a quitter." What was wrong with her? "Can't you see that I'm injured?"

"I think you're being a wimp."

"Wimp?" He glared at her. Anger warmed his veins. He'd been wrong about her. This woman wasn't an angel—not even close. She was rude and mean.

He'd show her.

He kept going.

One slow, agonizing step after the other.

CHAPTER FOUR

At last.

Serena's gaze zeroed in on the large log cabin. Any other time, she'd stop to admire how picturesque it looked with the snow-covered roof and the icicles hanging around the edges. But not this afternoon. With the thickening snow and the added weight from supporting Jackson, her back ached and her legs were exhausted. Still, her minor discomforts were nothing compared to Jackson's injuries.

She felt bad for being so mean to him back there. But angering him enough for him to prove her wrong was the only way she knew how to keep him going—how to save his life.

If he'd stopped, she'd have never gotten him moving again. Pain and fatigue were deeply etched on his handsome face. And there was no way she was letting her favorite morning news show anchor become a human Popsicle.

Still, she had to temper her sympathy. If she let herself become too involved with this man, she'd end up paying a steep price. Her last romance had cost her dearly.

Her thoughts turned to Shawn McNolty—Hollywood's rising star. He'd also costarred in Serena's latest movie, which was set to release over the holidays. During the filming, their agents had contrived for them to be seen together to get the public buzzing about a potential romance. But as time went on, Shawn had convinced Serena that instead of putting on a show they could start a genuine romance. He had been so charming and attentive that she'd convinced herself that taking their romance from the big screen to real life could work.

And everything had been all right, or so she'd thought, until she overheard Shawn talking to one of his friends. They'd been out to dinner and she was just returning from the ladies' room while they were standing in the waiting area. Shawn was telling his friend that his arrangement with Serena was working out much better than he'd planned. The longer he spent escorting Serena around town, the more promo he got. The more headlines he received, the more movie scripts came his way. And the best part was Serena didn't even have a clue. He prided himself on being that good of an actor. The memory still stung.

He wasn't the first man to date her in order to further his acting career, but she'd soon realized with those other men that the relationship was one-sided at best. But there was something about Shawn that had caught her off guard. Maybe it was his dark, mysterious eyes or his warm laugh that made her stomach quiver or the way he looked at her like she was the only woman in the world for him. Whatever it was, she'd convinced herself to let go of the past. She'd been sure Shawn was different—that he'd truly cared about her.

Maybe that was why she hadn't suspected something was up when he continually demanded that they go out instead of chilling at her Beverly Hills mansion. He always insisted that they stop and pose for the paparazzi, saying that it was good publicity for their upcoming film. The list of suspicious activities went on—activities that at the time she'd refused to see, but later it had all made sense. The pieces had all fallen into place when she overheard his words at the restaurant. Shawn McNolty had used her for his personal gain.

But he wasn't the only actor in this relationship. Not wanting a public confrontation, she swallowed her heated words and pretended that she hadn't heard a word he'd said about her. Serena didn't even remember what she'd ordered for dinner that last night or how she made it through the meal before she pleaded a headache and took a cab home. The rest of the evening was a blur.

Finding out that her romantic relationship was nothing but a sham was followed by a voice mail from her agent telling her that she'd been turned down for not one but two serious award-contending roles. At that point, she had nothing keeping her in California. She'd needed some downtime. A chance to unplug and regroup. That was the moment when her plan to go off the grid had been born.

With the aid of some temporary hair dye left over from Halloween, she'd switched her honey-blond hair to red. She'd been told by her housekeeper that she was practically unrecognizable without her distinctive eye makeup. Add a ball cap and nondescript jeans, and her disguise had been complete. She'd marched right out the door and jumped in a cab bound for the airport.

And now, even though she had the best of intentions, she knew taking this journalist into her home would end up decimating her serene escape from reality. Jackson may not be on the same level as the paparazzi who would climb the trees outside her Hollywood home, but as soon as he recovered, he'd want something from her—just like Shawn.

Unless she drove Jackson directly to the hospital. It would be what was best for all of them. And her rented all-terrain vehicle was sitting in the driveway. If she could make it to the road, the rest would be slow going, but she was confident she could make it, at least to the nearby village. It may not have a hospital, but there should at least be a doctor. Right?

When they reached the vehicle, she stopped. "Just give me a second."

"What are you doing?"

"Looking for my keys." She pulled off her glove and reached in her coat pocket. Her fingers wrapped around the keys. "Okay. Let's get you seated." She brushed some of the snow from around the door. When she pulled it open, the man sent her a puzzled look. "Come on. We have to get going before the snow gets worse."

His gaze narrowed. "You know how to drive in this much snow?"

Not really. A few times, she'd driven when she was in Tahoe, but it hadn't been in a snowstorm. Still, these weren't normal circumstances.

"I… I've done it before."

He looked at her, then the vehicle and finally at the rise up to the road. He shook his head. "No way. I'll wait here until the authorities can get me."

"But—"

"Arff! Arff!"

Gizmo started to wiggle in her arm. "Okay, boy."

"I think he agrees with me. We should go inside."

"We can't." When the man's eyebrows rose, she added, "I mean, you need medical attention."

"I'll be fine. Unless we get in the vehicle and end up in another accident."

She worried her lip. She was out of reasons not to take this journalist into her home. She quickly inventoried the cabin's contents to make sure there wasn't anything lying about that would give away her true identity. There were the contents of her wallet, but he wouldn't see that unless she gave him reason to be suspicious of her—like standing here in the snow, making him wonder why she didn't just take him straight inside.

Serena inwardly groaned.

Stubborn man.

"I know I'm a stranger," he said. "But I promise you no harm."

She wasn't afraid of him. At least, not in the manner that he thought. But at this point, he was either an excellent actor or he hadn't figured out her true identity. Perhaps the hair dye, Strawberry Temptation, and lack of makeup worked as well as her housekeeper had said.

"Arff! Arff!"

She couldn't fight them both. "Well, don't just stand there. Let's go inside."

Serena again let Jackson lean on her shoulder. Trying to get him up the snowy, icy steps was quite a challenge. She wasn't sure her shoulders would ever be the same again. But at last, they made it.

She helped him into the warm cabin and shut the door on the cold. She normally loved snow. But not this much, this fast. And not when it left her snowbound with a member of the press.

She helped him take off his gloves and wool dress coat. He was totally soaked. And ice-cold. His teeth chattered. The only way to warm him up was to strip him down. She started to loosen his tie.

His hand covered hers. "I… I think you're pretty and all, but…but I don't move this fast."

He thought she was coming on to him? She lifted her chin to set him straight when beyond his bluish lips and chattering teeth, she noticed a glint of merriment in his eyes. He was teasing her. That had to be a good sign, right?

"I'm glad to see your sense of humor is still intact, but if you don't get out of these wet clothes, you're going to get severe hypothermia." She attempted to move his hand, but he wouldn't budge.

"I know how to undress myself."

"Fine. Take everything off. I'll get you some blankets." Seeing him standing there leaning all of his weight on his good leg, she knew he was close to falling over from pain and exhaustion. "Let's move you closer to the fire."

She once again lent him her shoulder. Lucky for both of them, the couch was close by. Once he was seated and loosening his tie, she worked on getting a fire started.

A few minutes later, she returned to the great room with her arms piled high with blankets. Jackson sat on the couch in nothing but his blue boxers and socks. Heat immediately rushed to her cheeks. She was being silly. This was an emergency and it wasn't like she was a virgin.

"Something wrong?" he asked.

She knew she was blushing and there was nothing she could do to stop it. She averted her gaze. "Here you go."

She set the blankets beside him. One by one, she draped them over him. That was better. But she couldn't get the image of his very lean, very muscular body out of her mind.

She swallowed hard. "You forgot your socks and they're soaked. I'll get them—"

"No. I can do it." There was obvious weariness in his voice and his eyes drooped closed. "Stop…"

She ignored his protest and set to work. She removed the sock from his good leg. His foot was scary cold. She held it between her hands, trying to get the circulation going. It didn't work.

She glanced up at her unexpected guest. His eyes were still closed. Next, she worked the sock from his injured leg. His ankle was swollen and an angry mess of red and purple bruises.

"Is something the matter?"

His voice startled her. "Um, no." She had to tell him something. "It's just that your feet are so cold."

"They'll be fine."

"It could be frostbite. You weren't exactly dressed to hike through a blizzard. Can you feel your toes? They are awfully pale."

"They have that pins-and-needles sensation."

Holding his feet in her hands wasn't going to be enough help. She grabbed a basin of lukewarm water for him to soak his feet in. He put up a fuss, but eventually he gave in to her ministrations.

When Jackson's feet had sufficiently warmed up, he settled back on the couch. "How does it look?"

The horrible purple-and-red bruise was on both sides of his ankle. The inside wasn't as bad as the outside, but the ankle was a mess. And it was swollen to the point that she couldn't see his ankle bone.

"I think it's broken," she said as though she had any clue about medicine.

"Are you a doctor?" he asked.

"Me? No." Heat swirled in her chest and rushed up to her face. She knew where this conversation was headed.

He arched a brow as he studied her face. "I have the strangest feeling that we've met before. Have we? Met before, that is?"

"No. I don't believe we have."

She knew for a fact that they'd never crossed paths. For the most part, her life was limited to Los Angeles while she knew his work kept him based in New York City. And if they had met, she wouldn't have forgotten. The man was drop-dead gorgeous, and he had the sexiest deep voice. He was the only reason she tuned into the morning news show.

And now he was here, in her cabin, in nothing but his

underwear. But it couldn't be further from a romantic interlude. He was a member of the press and she was a Hollywood star in hiding. Once he figured out who she was, he'd broadcast it to the world. The thought made her stomach roil, especially after the mess she'd left behind in California.

"Hmm… I don't know where I've seen you, but I'm good with faces. It'll come to me."

Not if she could help it.

She retrieved a towel that she'd grabbed while gathering the blankets for Jackson. She called Gizmo over and dried him off. Then she situated him on a chair near the fire with an extra blanket. The puppy immediately settled down. With one eye closed and one partially open, he looked at her as though to make sure she didn't go anywhere.

"I won't leave you." She petted him and then kissed the top of his fuzzy head.

She got to her feet and turned to Jackson. "I'll call emergency services. They'll be out in no time to take you to the hospital and deal with your car."

"I'm sorry to be such a bother."

"It was my fault, or rather my dog's. Anyway, everything turned out okay. Except for your ankle…and your car." She moved to the phone on the desk.

When she'd checked in at the leasing office, they'd warned her that cell service was spotty in the mountains so they'd installed a landline. She picked it up and held the cordless phone to her ear. There was no sound. She pressed the power button on and off a few times, but there was still no dial tone. *Great!*

She could only hope she'd get a signal with her cell phone. She hadn't in the couple of days she'd been here, so why would today be any different? But she refused to give up hope.

With her cell phone in hand, she headed for the door. She paused to slip on her boots.

"Where are you going without a coat?" Jackson asked.

"Out on the porch. The phone lines must be down due to the storm, so I'm going to see if I can get a cell signal outside."

He didn't say anything more. She noticed this was the first time she'd headed for the door without Gizmo hot on her heels. Today's adventure had wiped him out. He hadn't budged from the chair. In fact, at one point she'd heard Gizmo snoring. He was so sweet and she felt so blessed that he was safe.

She paced from end to end of the large porch. There was no signal at all. She held it above her head and craned her neck to see if that helped. It didn't.

She lifted on her tiptoes and waved it around. Nothing. She leaned out over the large wooden banister. Snow fell on her phone and her arm, but there was still no signal. There had to be something she could do.

Her gaze moved to her rented all-terrain vehicle. Maybe she could go get help. But then she noticed how the snow was piled up around the tires. She glanced into the distance and she couldn't even see the line of trees at the end of the smallish yard. Who was she kidding? She'd never even get out of the driveway.

With a heavy sigh, she turned back toward the door. Chilled to the bone, she rushed back inside. She brushed the snow from her arm.

"Well?" Jackson's weary voice greeted her.

"Do you want the bad news? Or the bad news?"

He arched a dark brow. "Is that a trick question?"

"Not at all. So which shall it be?"

Was that the beginning of a smile pulling at his lips? Serena couldn't quite be sure. And then she conjured up the image of him smiling like he did each morning on television when he greeted the viewers. He was so devastatingly sexy when he smiled—

"Did you hear me?" Jackson sent her a funny look.

She'd lost track of the conversation, but she knew that he was waiting on her news. "The bad news is that there's no phone service whatsoever."

"And the other bad news?"

"We're stuck here. Together."

His handsome face creased with frown lines. "And exactly how long do you think we'll be snowbound?"

She shrugged. "Your guess is as good as mine. They did warn me when I rented this place that should there be a snowstorm, it would be quite a while until they dug me out considering I'm off the beaten path."

"Just great." He raked his fingers through his thick brown hair. "I can't be stuck here. I have a job to do."

Did he mean reporting that he'd found her? Serena didn't want to believe he was like the paparazzi. She wanted to believe that Jackson Bennett had integrity and honor. But she couldn't trust him. She couldn't trust anyone—including her own judgment. She always wanted to see the best in people. And that had gotten her into trouble more times than she cared to admit.

Still, she didn't want him to worry. "I promise you that as soon as possible, I'll get you medical attention. And I'm sure soon people will be looking for you."

His eyes widened. "Do you know who I am?"

What was the point in keeping it a secret? "You are Jackson Bennett. You're the face of *Hello America*."

A pleased look came over his face. "And I'm here on assignment. I have a camera crew flying in to help me film some Christmas segments."

It was on the tip of her tongue to ask him if she was to

be included in one of those segments, but she caught herself just in time. If he could be believed, he didn't recognize her. "I can promise you, they aren't getting through the storm."

"Is it getting worse?"

She nodded.

He muttered under his breath. "I can't just sit here."

He went to stand up. As soon as his injured foot touched the ground, his face reflected the pain he felt.

"Sit back down. First, I think I should bandage your ankle and then you can sleep. When you wake up, help should be here." She sincerely hoped so, for both of their sakes.

This luxury cabin may come with a fully stocked pantry and fridge, but something told her it would be lacking on first-aid items. She'd have to be inventive.

CHAPTER FIVE

JACKSON BLINKED.

It took him a moment to gain his bearings. That hike had taken more out of him than he'd expected. After Mae had bandaged his ankle, she'd helped him into a pair of sweatpants and a long-sleeved T-shirt he'd packed in his bag, her cheeks pinking prettily all the while, and settled him on the couch with pillows and blankets. She'd then insisted that he get some rest.

As time went by, there were very few spots on his body that didn't hurt. He didn't want to think of what would have happened to him if it wasn't for Mae. The mental image of his car going up in flames sent cold fingers of apprehension trailing down his spine.

Mae tried to act tough, but he'd watched how she fussed over her dog. She was a softy on the inside. In fact, he was willing to bet there was a whole lot more to Mae than being an angel of mercy. So what exactly was her story?

And what was she doing in this isolated cabin?

Jackson's gaze followed the stone chimney of the fireplace up, up and up until he reached the impressive cathedral ceiling. He took in the balcony and could only imagine what the second story must be like. Okay, this place was much more than a cabin. It was a luxury log home at the least and more like a mansion.

Was Mae staying here all by herself?

The place was much too big for just one person. Oh, and her dog. How could he forget Gizmo? She'd be lucky if the dog didn't get lost in here.

He gave himself a mental shake to clear his thoughts. He had a lot more important things to worry about than this woman's extravagance. He had to find a way to salvage his career—his stagnant career.

Ever since his wife passed away, his job was what got him up in the morning and helped him through the days. The nights were a different matter. He was left with nothing but memories of the only woman that he would ever love. When she'd died, he didn't know how he'd go on. In the beginning, breathing had taken effort. His existence had been an hour-to-hour proposition. And then he'd progressed to day by day. That was when he'd sought refuge in his work—going above and beyond for a good story.

His work was the sole reason he was in Austria. It was the second Christmas since he'd lost his wife, and he couldn't stay in New York City. He didn't want to be invited to friends' holiday celebrations. He didn't want tickets to Christmas programs in theatres. He wanted to be alone, but no one seemed to understand.

He may not be able to totally escape the holiday, but at least in Austria it would be on his terms. Jackson took in the towering pine tree in front of the two-story windows. And when his gaze landed on the boxes of decorations, he realized that he'd been taken in by a Christmas zealot. He sighed. This was just his luck. The sooner he got out of there, the better.

Speaking of his beautiful hostess, where had she gone? He paused and listened. Nothing. Was she napping? If so, he couldn't blame her. The afternoon had been horrific and stressful, not to mention the hike over mountainous terrain with him hanging on her shoulder. He'd tried not to lean on her too much, but at times, she was the only thing keeping him from falling face-first in the mounting snow.

He glanced to the spot where the dog had been lying on a blanket. Even he was gone. That was strange. He was just there a moment ago—right before Jackson had closed his eyes to rest them.

Jackson decided it was best that he go check on things. He saw his makeshift cane close by and grabbed it. His gaze moved to his bandaged ankle. He'd be lucky if it wasn't broken, but he wasn't going to think about that now.

With a firm grip on the cane, he lifted himself up on his good leg. What he wouldn't give now for a set of crutches. He turned himself around, finding the cabin even larger than he'd originally imagined. This place could easily fit three or four families.

Just then Mae appeared with her arms full of clothes. "What are you doing up?"

"I was wondering where you'd slipped off to."

"Well, when you fell asleep, I decided I should move my things out of the master suite to one of the upstairs rooms."

"Upstairs? But why? I'll be out of here in no time."

Mae moved to an armchair and laid her clothes across the back of it. "About that, I don't think either of us is going anywhere anytime soon."

"What? But why?"

"The snow hasn't stopped."

He half hopped, half limped his way to the door and looked out. The sun was setting, not that it was visible with the snow clouds blanketing the sky. But evening was definitely settling in. And Mae was right. The snow, if anything, had gotten worse. There were several new inches out there since they'd arrived at the cabin.

"It doesn't look good," he grudgingly conceded.

"Don't worry. I have plenty of food."

She might be sure of that fact, but he wasn't. It wasn't like they were in a cabin in a highly populated ski resort. This place was miles from the closest village, and from what he could tell, there were no neighbors close by.

He settled on the edge of the couch. "Um, thanks." He wasn't sure what else to say. "But I don't want to put you out. I can take the room upstairs."

From across the room, she sent him an I-don't-believe-you look. "On that leg? I don't think so." She started to pick up the clothes again. "I have dinner under control."

Come to think of it, he was hungry. Jackson sniffed the air, but he didn't smell anything. "What is it?"

"I hope chili will do."

Chili sounded good on such a cold evening. "Sounds great. Do you need help in the kitchen?"

She shook her head. "There's nothing to do but open a couple of cans and warm them up."

Open cans? Was she serious? He did his best to eat healthy. When your career involved standing before the cameras—cameras that picked up every shadow and wrinkle—you learned to drink lots of water and avoid food out of a can.

"Is that a problem?" her voice drew him from his thoughts.

"No. Thanks for taking me in and feeding me. I will pay you back."

She shook her head. "That's not necessary."

She had a point. Anyone who could afford a place this extravagant didn't need a handout. Far from it.

"Are you staying in this massive log home by yourself?" He vocalized his thoughts before he could register how that might sound.

Her brows arched. "I am." She paused as though trying to decide what to say next. "It's all they had left when I arrived."

So this trip was spur-of-the-moment. He found that interesting. To his surprise, he was finding most everything about this woman interesting. That hadn't happened to him since…since he'd met his wife.

Not that his interest in Mae was remotely similar to the way he felt about June. He supposed that it was only natural to feel some sort of indebtedness to the person who saved your life. That had to be it. For all he knew, he'd hit his head in the accident. It sure hurt enough to have struck something.

"Sorry. I didn't mean to be nosy," he said. "I guess it's just the nature of my job."

Just then Gizmo came running into the room.

"Gizmo, stop." Mae had a horrified look on her face.

Jackson couldn't help but wonder what had put that look on her face until the little dog stopped in front of him with something pink hanging from its mouth.

"Gizmo!" Mae rushed forward.

The dog dropped a pink lacy bra at Jackson's feet. He glanced up to find Mae's face the same shade as the delicate bra. Jackson couldn't help himself. On one leg, he carefully maneuvered himself closer to the floor so he could pick up the piece of lingerie.

He straightened just as Mae reached him. A smile pulled at his lips as he held out the bra. "I believe this is yours."

"Quit smiling." She snatched the very alluring bra from him. "It isn't funny."

"Your dog has an interesting sense of humor."

"He's a klepto. That's all." And then realizing that she was still holding the bra in front of him, she moved it behind her back.

"You have good taste." He knew he shouldn't have said it, but he couldn't resist a bit of teasing.

The color heightened in her face. "If you're done critiquing my lingerie, I'll take my clothes upstairs."

She turned promptly. With her head held high and her shoulders rigid, she moved to the armchair. For some reason, he didn't think she would be so easily embarrassed. After all, earlier today she was not afraid to call the shots, including stripping him down to his boxers and then dressing him. But just now, he'd witnessed a vulnerable side of her. *Most intriguing.*

"Pink looks good on you," he called out.

She turned and gave him a dirty look. It was at that point that he burst out laughing. In that moment, he forgot about all his aches and pains. He couldn't remember the last time he'd laughed without it being on cue. It felt good. Real good.

Mae gathered her clothes and strode over to the steps leading to the second floor. A smile lingered on his face as he settled back on the couch. He figured he'd be less of a bother here as opposed to anywhere else.

Gizmo returned to the room. He hefted himself onto the couch. He settled against Jackson's thigh and put his head down. Jackson never bothered with dogs, but maybe Gizmo wasn't so bad after all. He ran his hand over the dog's soft fur. At least, Gizmo had a sense of humor. Unlike his human counterpart.

This was not the quiet solitude that she'd imagined.

Serena busied herself in the kitchen, trying to put together dinner. But all the while, her thoughts were on Jackson. He was not what she'd expected. He was more down-to-earth. And his eyes, they were—dare she say it—dreamy. She could get lost in them. And his laugh, it was deep and rich like dark French roast coffee.

Realizing that she was in dangerous territory, she halted

her thoughts. Maybe she had fantasized about him being the perfect man one too many times while watching his morning show. And now that he was here in her cabin, she was having a hard time separating fantasy from reality.

And her reality right now was preparing an acceptable dinner. For someone who spent very little time in the kitchen because of a constant string of diets, she was pretty pleased with the appearance of dinner. Even Jackson couldn't complain. She hoped…

She glanced down at his tray to make sure she hadn't missed anything. There was a freshly warmed bowl of chili straight out of the can. A spoon and napkin. A glass of water because she didn't know what he liked to drink. But there was something missing. A man his size that had been through so much that day would have a big appetite. Should she add a salad? Nah, it would take too long. And then she decided to add some buttered bread.

When it was all arranged on the tray, she turned toward the door. She just hoped he still had his leg propped up on a pillow. If she could get him moved to the bedroom, she wouldn't have to trip over him in the living room. And maybe then she'd be able to get back to the quiet time so she could do some more work on her screenplay.

Since she'd arrived in Austria, the words had been flowing. Well, maybe not flowing, but they'd been coming in spurts. Sometimes those spurts consisted of an entire scene or two. But other times, she struggled to write a sentence, much less a paragraph. She wondered if that was how it worked for all writers or if it was just because this was her first script.

Serena paused at the doorway. Recalling her monthly indulgence of visiting the local drive-through for a bowl of chili, she realized they would top the bowl with diced onion and cheese. Perhaps she should do the same. The chili did look a little blah. Serena returned to the kitchen island.

By the time she chopped up the onion, her eyes were misty. Maybe the onion wasn't the best idea, but she wasn't wasting it, so she tossed it on. And then she topped it off with a handful of sharp cheddar. She returned the remaining onion and cheese to the fridge. It was then she noticed some fresh parsley.

Gizmo strolled into the kitchen. He came right up to her. He still had a sleepy look on his face.

She knelt down to fuss over him. Her fingers ran over his downy soft fur. "Hey, sleepyhead, you finally woke up."

"Arff!"

She loved the fact that he spoke to her as though he actually understood what she was saying to him. Sometimes she wondered if he understood more than they said dogs could understand. It was almost as though he could read her mind.

Serena washed her hands before rinsing off the parsley. Then she began to chop it up. She glanced over to find Gizmo lying in front of the stove with his head tilted to the side and staring at her.

"What are you looking at?"

"Arff! Arff!"

"I'm not making a big deal out of this. I would do this for anyone who was injured and needed my help." It didn't matter that Jackson was drop-dead gorgeous and when he laughed, he made her stomach dip like she was on a roller coaster.

She assured herself that she wasn't going out of her way to impress Jackson. She wouldn't do that. After all, she was Serena Winston. Daughter of two Hollywood legends. Heiress to the Winston fortune and an award-winning actress. She didn't need to work to impress any man.

Except that Jackson didn't have a clue who she was. That should be a relief, but it made her wonder if she wasn't pretty without her normal layer of makeup. Or perhaps the strawberry blonde hair didn't work for her. Maybe it was true what they said about blondes having more fun.

What was she doing? She yanked her thoughts to a stop.

Now, because she liked the looks of the parsley and not because she was trying to impress the influential reporter, she sprinkled it over the bowl.

She caught Gizmo continuing to stare at her with those dark brown eyes. "Would you stop looking at me like that?"

Gizmo whined, stretched out on the rug and put his head down. That was better.

Serena again grabbed the tray and headed for the door. Time to go wait on Jackson. She assured herself that no matter if he smiled at her or not, she would drop off the food and leave. After all, he was enemy number one—the press.

CHAPTER SIX

He was so comfortable—so relaxed.

And, best of all, he was no longer alone.

Mae was right there, next to him. So close. So temptingly close that he could smell her sexy and flirty perfume. It was the perfect mix of spice and floral scents. As though it had cast a spell over him, he gazed deep into her eyes.

He reached out, pulling her toward him. He ached to feel her lips pressed to his. There was just something about her—about her strawberry blonde hair that turned him on.

"Jackson," she called out to him.

He loved the way she said his name. It was all soft and sultry. He moaned in eager anticipation of where this evening was going to go.

"Jackson."

"Mae." He couldn't bring himself to say more. Why waste time on words when he could show her exactly how he was feeling—

Suddenly, he was jostled.

"Hey, Jackson. Wake up."

His eyes flew open. The bright light from the lamp on the end table caused him to blink. Wait. What was she doing standing there with a tray of food? They had just been snuggled together on the couch.

He blinked, trying to make sense of everything. And

then it all came crashing in on him. He'd dozed off again. Fragmented images of his dream came rushing back to him. Not only had he been dreaming, but he'd been dreaming about Mae. He uttered a groan.

A worried look came over her face. "What's the matter? Is it your ankle?"

He hurried to subdue his frustration. What was wrong with him? He had absolutely no interest in Mae. None whatsoever!

He glanced up at her. The look on her face said that with each passing moment she was becoming more concerned about him. What did he say? His still half-asleep mind struggled to find the right words.

"Um… I just moved the wrong way. It's no big deal."

She consulted the clock on the mantel. "You can have some more painkillers. I'll go get you a couple."

Mae set the tray down on the coffee table and rushed out of the room. He didn't argue, because he needed a moment or two to pull himself together. He shifted until he was sitting sideways on the couch, keeping his foot propped up. Realizing he hadn't eaten since breakfast, he reached for the plate of bread.

At that moment, there was a shuffling sound. And then a fuzzy head popped up over the edge of the couch. Without invitation, Gizmo hopped up on the couch. This time he didn't immediately settle down for a nap. His tail swished back and forth.

So the little guy wanted to make friends? Jackson smiled. It'd been a long time since he'd briefly had a dog. And nowadays, his life wasn't conducive to keeping a pet. But that didn't mean he and Gizmo couldn't be friends.

He sat still as the dog paused and sniffed the bandage on his leg. And then the pup continued up the edge of the couch. Jackson was all ready to pet him when the dog became distracted by the food. Before Jackson could move the plate, Gizmo snatched a slice of buttered bread. For a dog with short legs, he sure could move swiftly.

"Hey. Stop."

Gizmo didn't slow down. He jumped off the couch. Just as Mae returned, Gizmo rushed past her. The dog was a blur of gray-and-white fur.

A frown settled on Mae's face. "What did you do to Gizmo?"

"Me?" Jackson pressed a hand to his chest. "Why do you think I did anything?"

"Because I know you don't really like him."

He didn't like Gizmo? Was that really how he came across? Maybe that was why the dog chose the bread over him. The thought didn't sit well with Jackson. He would have to try harder with the little guy—even if he was a bread thief.

Mae crossed her arms, waiting for an answer to her question.

Jackson's gaze met her accusing stare. "I promise you that I didn't do anything to him."

"Then why was he running out of here?"

Obviously she'd missed the piece of bread hanging from the little guy's mouth. Well, who was he to rat Gizmo out? It wasn't like it was going to score him any points with his very protective owner.

"I don't know. Maybe he heard something." Jackson shrugged. And then he held up three fingers. "Scout's honor."

Her stance eased. "You were a Boy Scout?"

"I was." He studied her, surprised by the glint of approval in her eyes. "I take it you approve?"

"I... I guess. I'm just surprised, is all."

For that moment, he wanted to gain her approval. "I was in the Scouts for a number of years."

"You must have enjoyed it."

"I don't know about that. Some of it, sure. But as I got older, I wasn't that into it. But my mother, she insisted I remain a member."

"Your mother? But why?" And then Mae pressed her lips together as though she hadn't meant to utter that question. "Sorry. You don't have to answer that."

He didn't normally open up to people about his past. He glossed over the important parts and left everything else unsaid. But for some reason, he felt like he could open up to Mae. "I was just six when my parents divorced. My father moved on, remarried and had another family. And so he wasn't around much. My mother felt that I needed a male role model. She worried that she wasn't enough for me. And so she enrolled me in Scouts so I could learn to whittle wood and make campfires. You know, all of the stuff that turns a boy into a strong, responsible adult." Now, it was time to turn the tables on her. "And were you a Girl Scout?"

She shook her head. "My, um, parents, they weren't much into me taking part in group functions."

He arched a brow. "I thought all parents wanted their kids to interact with others."

Mae glanced down. "They…they were overprotective."

"Oh. I see. Well, it appears you didn't miss out on anything by not learning how to build a fire. And think of all the calories you saved by not eating all those s'mores and roasted marshmallows."

He was attempting to make her smile, but she was still avoiding his gaze and she definitely wasn't smiling. There was more to her childhood than she was willing to share.

Something told him she hadn't had it easy—even if this luxury log home said otherwise.

"You better eat before it's cold," Mae said.

"What about you? Where's your food?"

"Oh, I'll eat in the kitchen." Her gaze strayed across the plate on his lap. "I see you already ate some of the bread."

"I guess I was hungrier than I thought. Thanks for this."

"It's no big deal. I'm sure your wife did things like this for you all of the time."

"Actually, she didn't. She came from old money and never learned to cook. By the time we met, she had her life the way she wanted it, and so for us to work, I had to fit into her life."

Mae's mouth gaped and then as though catching herself, she quickly forced her jaw closed.

"I see I surprised you with that admission." He sighed. "I guess I surprised myself in a way. My mother was a lot like my late wife. She had her life and I had to fit into it—but I didn't do a very good job. I always thought when I grew up that I would end up with someone who was the exact opposite of my mother. And I convinced myself that June was different. After all, she had money. She didn't need mine. And she was cultured. My mother was anything but cultured." Why was he rambling on? He never opened up about his private life with anyone. "But you don't want to hear all of that."

"Actually, it's nice to know that my life isn't the only one that isn't picture-perfect."

So he was right. She had skeletons in her closet. He wondered what they might be, but he didn't venture to ask. They'd shared enough for one evening.

His steady gaze met hers. "You've been great. I don't know what I'd have done without you. I won't forget it."

Her cheeks filled with color. "It's not that big of a deal."

"I promise that I'll find a way to pay you back." When she went to protest, he said, "I was thinking that once I'm mobile I could treat you to dinner in the village."

This time her gaze did meet his. "I… I don't think that would be a good idea."

Okay. He may have been out of the dating scene for a number of years, but he was pretty sure that wasn't how the conversation was supposed to have gone. Perhaps he hadn't stated it properly.

"I know this place is really nice, but you can't spend all of your time here alone. And I'll be staying in the area until after Christmas, so I'd like to pay you back in some manner. I just thought a friendly dinner might be nice. If you change your mind before I leave tomorrow, I'll give you my phone number."

There, that was much clearer. Surely she wouldn't object now. Would she?

"Thank you." She sent him a small smile. "That's a really nice offer, but you don't have to feel like you owe me anything. After all, if it wasn't for Gizmo, we wouldn't be here."

She did have a point, but he had a feeling she was just using that as an excuse. Did she really find him that repulsive? He wasn't used to a woman rejecting his offer for dinner—not that he dated, but he did have business dinners and he was never without female companionship for those.

Mae was different. Very different. And that made him all the more curious about her. If only they had phone reception, he'd do an internet search on her. After all, he was a reporter. Research was a part of his daily routine. Sure, he had people to do it, but he liked to do a lot of his own research. He liked learning all sorts of new things.

There was only one problem. He didn't know her last

name. Was that just an oversight on her part? Or had she purposely withheld it?

"Well, I'll let you eat. I need to go check on Gizmo. He's being suspiciously quiet." She turned to walk away.

"Hey, you never said what your last name is."

"I didn't, huh?" And with that she continued toward the kitchen.

He was staying with a mystery woman who had no lack of funds but guarded her privacy above all else. What had happened to make her so secretive? Or had she always been that way?

The bed started to vibrate.

Serena's eyes opened to find that morning was upon them. But for the life of her, she couldn't figure out what was causing the vibration and it was getting stronger. Was it an earthquake?

Gizmo started to whine. She couldn't blame him. She was used to earthquakes, or rather she was as used to them as you could be when you were a California native. The truth was they always put her on edge. But she hadn't expected to encounter them in Austria. Unless this was something else entirely. Whatever was happening, it wasn't good.

She hugged Gizmo close. "It's okay, buddy. We'll be okay."

Serena scrambled out of bed. She threw on her fuzzy purple robe and headed out the door. Her feet barely touched the staircase.

By the time she reached the first floor, the vibration had stopped. She found Jackson out of bed. He wasn't wearing a shirt, giving her an ample view of his bare back with his broad shoulders and tapered waist. A pair of navy pajama bottoms completed the sexy look. She mentally urged him to turn around.

Instead, he remained with his back to her. His hand was gripped firmly to his makeshift cane as he gazed out the window next to the front door.

Perhaps he hadn't heard her enter the room. "What was that?"

He at last turned, giving her a full view of his muscular chest with a splattering of hair. "I'm not sure, but I'd hazard a guess that it was an avalanche."

Realizing that she was staring at his impressive six-pack abs, she forced her gaze to meet his. "That…that was way too close for my comfort."

"Mine, too," Jackson said matter-of-factly.

She was impressed that he was willing to make such a confession. In her experience, men never admitted to a weakness—least of all her ex-boyfriend. Men were all about putting on a show of how macho they were.

And somehow she'd imagined Jackson, with his bigger-than-life personality, to be full of bravado. Instead, she found him relatable. In that moment, she liked him a little bit more—probably more than was wise considering his means of making a living.

"How far away do you think it was?" she asked, trying to keep her attention on something besides Jackson's temping, naked chest.

"I don't know. The power is out, too."

"Don't worry, we have a generator. The realty people showed me how it works."

He glanced down at his leg. "I'd like to get out there and take a look around, but I'm not as mobile as I'd like to be."

"Speaking of which, you should be in that bed, resting your leg."

He shook his head. "I was going stir-crazy."

"I take it you're not one to sit around."

"Only if I'm doing research for a news story. But seeing as how there's no internet and no phone service, that idea is out."

She was thanking her lucky stars for the lack of communication with the outside world. "I'm sure we'll be able to get you out of here today. Your first stop should be the doctor's or the hospital to have your leg checked."

Jackson glanced back out the window. "The snow is getting lighter, but there's got to be at least three feet of it out there. If not more."

"What?" It wasn't nearly that bad when she'd taken Gizmo outside last night, but it was more than her pampered pooch could appreciate. He definitely enjoyed his California sunshine. But then again, a lot of hours had passed since then.

Serena rushed over to the window to have a look. Jackson wasn't exaggerating. There were no signs of their footsteps from the prior evening. Between the snow and wind, any trace of them had been swept away.

She turned back to Jackson to find him staring at her instead of the snow. Heat swirled in her chest. She was used to having men stare at her, so why was she having such a reaction to Jackson looking at her now?

And then she realized that in her hurry to find out what had caused the massive tremors, she'd rushed downstairs without running a brush through her hair. Unlike his sexy appearance, she must look quite a mess.

How did men wake up looking good? It was frustrating because her hair was always going in far too many directions and sticking straight out in other places. And then she started to wonder if she had drool in the corners of her mouth. A groan started deep inside, but she stifled it. But the heat rushing to her face was unstoppable.

Just then Gizmo moved to the door and started to bark. She made a point of turning away from Jackson as though to talk to the dog. With one hand, she petted Gizmo. With the other hand, she ran her fingers around her mouth. She finally breathed a little easier.

"It's okay, boy. I'll take you out in a minute."

"Out? Where?"

"Lucky for me this cabin is fully prepared for anything. There's a snow shovel on the side of the porch."

Serena dressed quickly and then fired up the generator. She stuffed her feet in a pair of snow boots that she'd picked up in the nearby village upon hearing the forecast. And then she put on her coat and pulled a white knit cap over her mussed-up hair.

After attaching Gizmo's leash, she turned back to Jackson. "After I take him out and shovel for a bit, I'll get you some breakfast."

"You don't have to."

She shrugged. "I'm going to need some breakfast after I shovel out the driveway. Or at least start on it. Suddenly that driveway looks very long."

Jackson's face creased with frown lines. "You shouldn't do all of that shoveling."

"Really? I don't see anyone else around here to help dig us out."

A distinct frown formed on his handsome face. "I should be doing it."

"And how exactly would you manage to shovel snow on one leg?"

"Maybe the sun will melt it."

"When? A month from now?"

He sighed. "Okay. I'll help you."

"No, you won't." She glared at him, hoping he'd understand her level of seriousness. "You'll stay right here."

Not about to continue this pointless argument, she let herself out the door. The snow was light but the wind was still gusting. She could imagine that many of the mountain roads would be impassable and she didn't even want to think of how the avalanche would delay Jackson's departure.

At least if she got the vehicle and the driveway dug out, once the roads were opened, she could get him to the village. She just had to hope that would happen sometime today. The longer they spent together, the harder it was to keep her true identity a secret.

CHAPTER SEVEN

He felt like a caged tiger.

Moving between the window and the couch was making his ankle throb. His conscience wouldn't allow him any peace. He shouldn't be inside this cozy cabin while Mae was outside doing all of the hard work. He felt awful. He'd never had a woman take care of him—not even his wife.

When he'd first met June, she'd been a model and he'd been at the fashion show to do an interview. It was back when he just did spotlight interviews for an evening entertainment show. She was delicate and spoke with a soft voice. She was kind and thoughtful—the exact opposite of his mother.

And in no time, he'd fallen for her. In just a few short months, they'd been married amid her family's protests. With both of them driven by their passion for life and work, their futures were on the rise. Fueled by his determination and June's encouragement, he'd taken on the anchor chair of *Hello America* within six months of their marriage. It appeared that nothing could stop them.

And then a few years later, she'd received the life-altering diagnosis—she had cancer. He clearly remembered that day at the doctor's office with an overhead light flickering, the slight sent of antiseptic in the air and June's muffled cry. Jackson's gut knotted as the memories washed over him.

That day was when all their dreams and plans had fallen to the white tiled floor and shattered into a million sharp, jagged pieces.

He'd dropped everything as they'd embarked on the fight of their lives. He'd needed to make sure she was always taken care of, whether it be surgery, a treatment or just being at home recovering from the side effects of her treatments. He'd turned his life upside down and inside out—not because he had to but rather because he wanted to be there for June.

He had her favorite magazines on hand for her to thumb through, her favorite flavored water, chicken broth and movies. He'd never minded. He would have done anything for her. Just the memory of everything she'd endured because of that horrible disease made his stomach turn.

And as much as he'd loved June, he could see now that she was so different from Mae. June never would have waited on him like Mae had the night before. But that was not exactly fair. Because June didn't know how to cook, she would have called for delivery service.

As for shoveling snow, June hadn't believed in physical labor. It was the way she'd been raised, with a silver spoon in her mouth. And as luxurious as this cabin may be, June wouldn't have voluntarily come here. She liked touring the small villages, but she preferred staying in the city or at the ski resorts. He'd never had a problem with her choices because when she had been happy, he'd been happy.

But maybe there was more to life. A different way of being. Maybe happiness didn't have to be a one-sided venture. A bit of give-and-take sounded appealing—

Stop! What was he going on about this for? It wasn't like he would ever see Mae and her glorious strawberry blonde hair after he got away from here. It still bothered him that he couldn't place her face. You'd think that a knockout like Mae would stick out in his memory. Maybe it was the accident. He didn't say anything to Mae because he didn't want to worry her, but that had to be the source of his headaches and his fascination with her.

In the three years, five months and eleven days that he'd been with June, he'd never willed her to be anything other than what she was—the woman that loved him. When she'd looked at him, the love had shone in her eyes. No one had ever looked at him that way. Their relationship may not have been perfect, but they'd found a way to make it work.

He jerked his thoughts to a halt. What was the matter with him? Why was he comparing June to Mae?

While Mae was nothing like June, there was something about her—a vulnerability that drew him near. She'd been wounded in the past and was leery of trusting him. They had that in common—the lack of trust. After having loved with all his heart and losing June so quickly, he was wary of letting anyone get close to him. Until now, he hadn't given much thought to how he kept people at arm's length. Maybe it was something they both needed to work on.

Jackson made his way to the kitchen. He may not be any help outside, but he could still whip up a mean breakfast. He pulled open the fridge door to find the shelves loaded with food. Wow! This place was certainly well stocked, or else his beautiful hostess had bought a lot of food for just herself and her dog.

Leaning on one leg tired him quickly, but he refused to give in. He would have a lovely meal ready for Mae. She deserved it. He just wished it would ease his guilty conscience, but preparing breakfast with bacon, eggs, hash browns and pancakes did not even come close to the task of shoveling all that snow.

But thanks to Mae's efforts, he'd soon be getting out of here. The storm was almost over and the road would be opened. And none too soon because he still had to film the segments for the holiday special. He had no idea where his crew was, but they were resilient. He was certain they would have hunkered down for the storm. And as soon as the cell phone service was reestablished, they'd make contact.

However, the holiday special was bothering him. He was better than puff pieces. He wanted to do more substantial segments—the type of investigative reporting that they featured on the evening news. But before he could do that, he had to get a story that would grab the network bigwigs' attention.

He thought of the avalanche. That was a story, but without something more like hikers or skiers trapped, it wouldn't go anywhere. Instead of playing where-in-the-world-is-Jackson? he needed to be tracking down a headline-making story—

"What smells so good?"

He turned from his place at the stove to find Mae standing in the doorway. But she was frowning, not smiling like he'd envisioned. "What's the matter? Did you hurt yourself?"

"The problem is you. You shouldn't be in here hobbling around."

"I figured you'd work up an appetite."

"I told you I would make food when I came inside."

"And I thought I would surprise you. So...surprise." He grinned brightly, hoping to lighten the mood.

And still there was no smile on her face. It bothered him because she was so gorgeous when she smiled. He remembered how hard it used to be to make June smile when she got in one of her moods. But he'd always persevered until he won out and eventually June would smile at him. Because when he'd said his wedding vows, he'd meant every single word. He would not get a divorce like his parents. He would not fail.

But Mae was not June. Why should he care if she smiled or not?

"Go sit down. I'll finish this," she said.

"It's done. I just have to put this last pancake on the plate. By the way, your fridge was well stocked. I hope you don't mind that I helped myself."

She washed up and then followed him to the kitchen table. "No. I was worried that it would all go bad. So thanks for helping me to put it to good use."

Once they were seated at the table next to a bank of windows, Mae's gaze skimmed over all the serving dishes heaped with food. "Who's going to eat all of this?"

"Arff! Arff!"

They both laughed at Gizmo's quick response.

"It appears that Gizmo worked up an appetite, too," Jackson said.

"I don't know how that could be when he spent the entire time sitting on the porch. He refused to get off it, even after I shoveled out an area in the yard just for him."

Gizmo yawned and whined at the same time.

They both smiled at the animated pooch. Maybe Gizmo wasn't so bad—at least when he wasn't running loose and causing car accidents.

As they each filled their plate, Mae asked, "So what had you so distracted when I walked in?"

"Distracted?" It took him a moment to recall what she was talking about.

"You had a very serious look on your face."

"Oh, I was thinking about work."

"Aren't you supposed to relax? Isn't this a vacation?"

He shook his head. "I came here to work."

Was it his imagination or did Mae's face visibly drain of

color. "Um, what's your assignment?" And then as though she realized that she might be prying, she said, "Sorry. I don't mean to be pushy."

"It's okay. I'm doing a Christmas special. You know, a sort of Christmas around the world. I already did one in Ireland, Japan and now Austria. Well, that depends on if I ever find my camera crew after this storm." He glanced out the window. "Hey, the snow is just flurries now."

"That's good, because let me tell you, there's a ton of snow out there." She sighed. "You know, I've worked up such an appetite that I could eat all of this food."

"Go ahead."

She shook her head. "I can't."

"Sure you can. In fact, I can make more."

"Don't tempt me. But really, I can't."

"Don't tell me that you're dieting."

She shrugged. "Okay. I won't tell you."

"What does someone as beautiful as you have to diet for?" He wanted to tell her that she could stand to put on a few pounds, but he didn't dare. He didn't want her to take it the wrong way.

"So I fit in my clothes. But I think I can squeeze in a little more after that exercise this morning." Her gaze met his. "You're a really good cook."

He continued to stare into her green eyes. "I've had a lot of experience."

He didn't bother to add that after his parents divorced, his mother wasn't around much as she had to bounce between two and sometimes three jobs to make ends meet. And so he did the bulk of the cooking. And then with June, she didn't know how to cook and so he'd taken on the role as he enjoyed creating delicious meals that were healthy and nutritious.

"If your job on television ever falls through, you could become a chef."

He smiled at the compliment. "Thanks. I'll keep that in mind. It might come in handy."

Now what was she supposed to do?

Serena stared out the window at the snowy landscape. They still hadn't plowed open the road and there was no way that she could drive through three feet plus of snow. She would have to have a monster truck with chains on the tires and even then she doubted that she'd make it out of the driveway.

With a heavy sigh, she accepted that there was nothing she could do for now. Instead of wasting her energy worrying about Jackson's presence, she needed to concentrate on writing a screenplay.

This was her chance to make a name for herself that had nothing to do with her looks or the legacy her two famous parents had left her. And time was running out because sooner than she'd like, she had to return to Hollywood to begin filming her next movie. The contract had been inked months ago and to back out at this late date would tarnish her name in the industry, not to mention the penalties she'd be subjected to for failure to perform.

But most of all, she took pride in standing by her word. When she said she'd do something, she did it. So not only would she do the movie, but she would also get this screenplay written over the holiday break—before she went back and faced the public scandal of her life.

She wanted to find a place on the second floor to write—away from Jackson. But she was still worried about him. His injury was serious, and he was overdoing things. Try as she might to keep him in bed, he never stayed more than five minutes at a time.

There was a desk with a lamp in the corner of the great room and that was where Serena took a seat with her laptop. This was one of those five-minute periods where Jackson was in the bedroom with his foot up. Gizmo was lying on a padded bench next to the window, watching the snow blow around in between snoozes. Now was her chance to get some work done.

She opened her laptop and after she logged in, her script popped up on the screen. She quickly read over what she'd written last night before she went to sleep. It didn't sound too bad, but something was missing. She just couldn't put her finger on what it was. Perhaps if she kept going, it would come to her. She hoped.

Serena's fingers moved rapidly over the keyboard. This screenplay might not be a serious drama, but it wasn't slapstick comedy, either. It was filled with heart. For now, writing about a warm family with a central love story and a happily-ever-after made her happy. It was about a loving but complicated family that she wished she'd been a part of. In the future, she intended to work on screenplays with more serious scenarios.

She paused and smiled. Perhaps writing an award-worthy screenplay wasn't as important as writing the story of her heart. Who knew, maybe it'd be prize-worthy after all. It might be a little zealous, but wasn't that what dreams were meant for?

For now, she'd chosen a shopaholic heroine and her large, boisterous family. Her ex-boyfriend needed a wife to keep his wealthy grandmother from writing him out of her will and leaving it all to her favorite pet charity. The hero was all about getting the money and pretending to be what his grandmother wanted him to be that he missed the point that money couldn't make you happy. And the heroine had to learn that a bigger wardrobe and a larger apartment wouldn't change who she was and that she hasdto accept herself, blemishes and all.

The more Serena typed, the more she worried whether she was going in the right direction with the plotline. Still, she kept pushing forward one word at a time—one sentence after the next—

Knock. Knock.

She jumped. She'd been so involved in her script that she hadn't heard anyone approach the door. Gizmo must have been sound asleep, too, because it wasn't until the knock that he starting barking as he scrambled to the door.

Serena jumped to her feet. "Gizmo, quiet."

The pup paused to look at her as though to ask why in the world he would want to be quiet when there was obviously an intruder on the premises. Immediately he went to his growl-bark, growl-bark stance.

"Who is it?" Jackson asked from behind her.

"I'm just about to find out—if I can get Gizmo to settle down." She bent down and picked up the dog.

The pup gave her a wide-eyed stare but at least he quieted down. With him securely in one arm, she opened the door. She couldn't help but wonder if it was another stranded person. "Can I help you?"

It was a man in a red snowsuit with a white cross on the left side. "I stopped to make sure you are okay." He spoke English with a heavy German accent.

"We are." She noticed how Jackson limped over to stand behind her. "Are you with the leasing company?"

"I'm not. I'm with the emergency crew working on clearing the avalanche, but they let us know that an American woman was staying here, and that you are by yourself, which I see you're not."

Jackson cleared his throat. "They must have cleared the road."

Serena peered past the man, looking for his vehicle in the freshly shoveled driveway. There was no vehicle. Maybe he left it on the road, but she didn't see it there, either. Surely the man didn't walk here. This cabin was in the middle of nowhere and this wasn't the weather for walking.

The man lifted his sunglasses and rested them on the top of his head. "Actually, I'm getting around on my snowmobile."

As the wind kicked up, Serena said, "Why don't you come inside?"

They moved back and let the man in the door. The man stepped forward just enough to close the door against the cold air. He was shorter than Jackson and had a much more stocky build. His face was tan, as though he spent a lot of time outside, and his eyes were kind.

The man cleared his throat. "The avalanche was bad. It has a stretch of road shut down until we can get equipment in to clear it." The man glanced around. "I see they got the power fixed."

"Not yet," Serena said. "It's a generator."

The man nodded in understanding. "They are hoping to get the power restored to this area sometime today."

Since this man seemed quite knowledgeable about their situation, she asked, "Do you know how long it will be until the road is open?"

He shook his head. "I have no idea."

"The thing is, Mr. Bennett here was in a car accident and I need to get him to the doctor—"

"I'm fine," Jackson interjected.

A concerned look came over the emergency worker's face as he turned to Jackson. His gaze scanned him. "I'm trained in first aid. Why don't you sit down on the couch and let me look at you. We can call in an emergency helicopter if we need to. It'll be tricky under these conditions but not impossible."

Jackson frowned. "I told you I'm fine."

"And I would like to see this for myself." The emergency worker gave him a pointed look.

They continued to stare at each other in that stubborn male fashion. It was really quite ridiculous. Why did Jackson have to be so stubborn?

Serena stepped forward. "Jackson." When he didn't look at her, she tried again. "Jackson, let him look at you. I'd feel much better if he did."

At last, Jackson turned to her. "I told you not to worry."

It was on the tip of her tongue to tell him that she did worry about him, but she stopped herself just in time. What in the world had gotten into her? She barely even knew this man. He might be amazingly handsome and she might be able to listen to his rich, deep voice for hours on end, but she had sworn off men. So she would be fine admiring Mr. Jackson Bennett via her television because that was as close as she planned to get to him once they could get away from this cabin.

Serena could feel both men staring at her. Heat swirled in her chest, but she refused to let that stop her from being honest—or at least partially honest. "I'd feel a lot better if someone who knew something about medicine would have a look at you. That was a bad accident. You have a lot of bruising. And your ankle doesn't look good."

Jackson sighed. "All right. If it's really that important to you."

"It is."

Jackson limped toward the couch.

"I'll be right back," the emergency worker said. "I have medical supplies on my snowmobile."

Serena followed Jackson. He sat on the couch and put

his injured leg up on the coffee table. She knelt down on the floor and set Gizmo next to her. Finally, the pup had settled down. She didn't know what had gotten into him. He was usually friendlier. After all, he'd taken to Jackson.

She reached for the makeshift bandage.

"What are you doing?" Jackson asked.

"Taking off the bandage so he can have a look at you."

"I can do it."

She'd already started undoing the knot that she'd made to hold everything in place. "Just relax." She continued to struggle with the bandage. "I almost have it."

"It might be easier if you use scissors."

She didn't respond. The truth was that he was right, but when she was around him, her thoughts became jumbled. And when she touched him, her heart raced. What was it about this man that had her reacting like she was once again a schoolgirl with a crush on Jeremy Jones, the school's up-and-coming rock band singer?

She'd never felt this rush of emotions when she had been with Shawn. Sure, she'd enjoyed their time together, but she hadn't felt like it was anything special. Maybe she should have realized it was a sign that things weren't right. But she'd never been in love before, so she didn't know how it should feel. And now she never would know, because she was avoiding men—unless they unexpectedly crashed into her life.

Finally, the knot gave way. She made quick work of undoing the bandage. As much as she'd wished his ankle had healed quickly, it remained a kaleidoscope of colors from purplish black to red and some pink. What a mess.

Just then the door opened and Gizmo once more went into guard dog mode. Serena followed him to the doorway, where he had the emergency worker pinned to the door. Serena rushed over to pick up Gizmo.

The man had his hands full of medical supplies. If she were to go by looks, it appeared this man knew what he was doing. And that would be good for all of them because she was so far removed from a nurse that it wasn't even funny.

"I'm sorry," she said. "He's not normally like this." When Gizmo started barking again, she said firmly, "Gizmo, stop." The dog didn't even bother to look at her as he kept a close eye on the stranger. "I'll just go put him in the bedroom."

Fifteen minutes later, Jackson had been all checked out. The emergency worker said that he didn't believe Jackson's injuries were life-threatening, but he was certainly banged up. If Jackson wanted to be evacuated, he'd call in a chopper. Jackson adamantly declined, saying that with the avalanche there were others in more need than him. And Serena promised to keep a close eye on him.

With Jackson in a proper bandage, the emergency worker packed up his stuff and walked away. Just as he opened the door, the light bulbs brightened, signaling that the electricity had been restored.

"Thank goodness," Serena said. "Things are starting to look up."

"I'll be back to check on you tomorrow." And with that the man left.

Serena closed the door. "Sounds like I better let Gizmo out before he scratches the door. I don't know what's up with him."

"He's just protective of you."

"Then how do you explain him taking to you?"

"Oh, that's easy, I bribed him." An easy smile pulled at Jackson's lips.

Serena's stomach dipped. Okay, it was official, he was much cuter in person than he was on television. And if she didn't get him out of here soon, he might worm his way past her defenses. But would that be so bad?

After all, they were on two different coasts. Surely with all those states between them and their busy schedules, they'd never lay eyes on each other again.

She shook her head. Obviously she wasn't used to the solitude. Everything would be fine. She would stick to her resolution of no men. Soon the plows would open up the road and Jackson would be on his way out of here.

"What?" Jackson's eyes filled with confusion.

"Hmm..."

"You shook your head. Why?"

"Nothing." She hunted for a legitimate answer to his question. "I should have figured that you would resort to bribing."

"It wasn't my idea." Jackson said it as though it were the undeniable truth. "Gizmo stole my bread last night and well, I didn't rat him out and we've been friends since."

"And it only cost you a slice of bread?"

Jackson smiled and her stomach once again did that funny dipping thing. "Yeah, I guess it was worth sacrificing part of my dinner."

"And that would explain why he wasn't very interested in his." She planted her hands on her hips. "I don't want him eating human food so if you could refrain from feeding him in the future, I would appreciate it."

"I'll try, but no promises." When she arched a brow, he added, "Hey, he's sneaky."

"Uh-huh." Was it possible that this journalist was truly a big softy at heart?

The thought stuck with her as she went to turn off the generator. She really wanted to dislike Jackson. It would make this arrangement so much easier, but the more time she spent with him, the more she liked him.

CHAPTER EIGHT

THE DAY SLIPPED by very slowly.

Jackson didn't know what to do with himself. He wasn't good at sitting still and yet his ankle, though most likely not broken, was still severely bruised and swollen.

He picked up his cell phone from the coffee table. He put in his passcode only to find that there was still no signal. So much for them getting the cell tower fixed today…or whatever was causing the disruption in service. He knew he shouldn't complain. With the avalanche, everyone had much larger concerns.

He tossed the phone back on the coffee table and sighed.

Mae glanced up from her laptop. "Do you need something?"

"Yes. I mean, no."

"So which is it?"

He limped over to her desk. "I'm just bored, is all. I'm not used to having time on my hands. Usually I don't have enough hours in the day to get things done. Today I don't have enough things to do."

"I understand. My life is usually very hectic. That's one thing I love about being here. No one can bother me and I can make my own schedule."

"So what has you so busy on the computer for hours on end?"

"This, oh, well…it's nothing."

Was it his imagination or did her cheeks take on a shade of pink? His curiosity grew. She closed the laptop and stood. He couldn't take his eyes off her as she stretched.

"You don't strike me as a shy woman. So what has you blushing when I asked about what you were working on?"

Her fine brows drew together. "And you are not on the job. I'm not one of your stories. You don't have to keep pushing until you get all of the answers."

Realizing that he'd overstepped, he held up both hands. "Sorry. I guess this sitting around is really starting to get to me. I think I've read every magazine on the coffee table at least twice."

"Then I can put you to work." Her eyes lit up as though she'd come up with the perfect answer.

He was intrigued. He'd love to spend some productive time with Mae. Perhaps his abundance of enthusiasm should bother him, but he chose to ignore the telling sign. "What do you have in mind?"

"I'll be right back." She took off upstairs.

Gizmo got up from where he'd been napping on the couch. When he yawned, he let out a little squeak. Jackson found himself smiling. Gizmo walked over to him. Jackson petted him and scratched behind his ears.

"You're not so bad. In fact, you're kind of cute."

"Arff!"

Jackson couldn't help but laugh. "You know, if I didn't know better, I'd say you knew what I was saying."

"Arff! Arff!"

"Sounds like you two are having quite a conversation," Mae said as she descended the stairs with her hands full of bags.

"And what is all of that?" He had a feeling he didn't want to know, but the reporter in him needed the answer.

"This is what we're going to do this evening. And if you do a good job, I'll let you roast some marshmallows over the fire tonight."

He couldn't help but laugh again. He tried to remember the last time he'd laughed this much and failed. Was there such a time?

He didn't think so, as June had been more reserved. She was quiet in public. She would say that it was the way she was raised, but he knew the truth—she was painfully shy. Still, she hadn't let it stop her as a fashion model. Each day she did what was expected of her. And although it took a lot out of her to get in front of the cameras, she'd pasted on a smile and never missed a photo shoot.

But there had been times when she'd let her hair down and unwind when they were in bed. Then she'd been all his. And there had been nothing shy about her then. He could make her laugh, moan and make all sorts of unladylike sounds—

Jackson squelched the memories. He wanted to be present in this moment. He took in Mae's smile. It lit up her face and made her eyes sparkle, but it was more than that. How did he say it? It was like when she smiled the world was brighter. It filled him with a warmth, and he never wanted to let that feeling go. It healed the cracks in his broken heart, making him feel whole again.

"Can you make your way over here?" she asked as she set the bags down in front of the Christmas tree.

And then he put it all together. He shook his head. "I don't do Christmas trees."

Her eyes widened. "You don't celebrate Christmas?"

"No. Not that. I celebrate it—or I used to. But I never did the decorating." The truth was, with busy work schedules that often conflicted, neither he nor June were home long enough to worry about it. Instead, June would hire professionals to come in and decorate their tree. It was always different each year. Different color. Different theme.

Mae stood there with a puzzled look on her face. “Why wouldn’t you decorate your tree? Doesn’t it look rather sad and pathetic without ornaments?”

“It had ornaments. I just didn’t put them on.”

“Why not?”

“There wasn’t enough time.” That seemed to be the theme of his life. There were so many things that had been skipped over or missed because there wasn’t enough time. And now time had run out for him and June.

“You have to make time for the important things in life. My father used to always put off things and then he died.” There was a slight pause, but before Jackson could say a word, she continued. “I don’t want to miss the good things in life because I’m too busy. Life is too short.”

It was as though she understood exactly what he’d been through, but that was impossible. He kept his private life private. “I’m glad you’re taking advantage of life. You’re right, it is too short.”

She reached into the bag and pulled out a box of ornaments. She proceeded to attach a hook and hang it on the tree. “See. Nothing to it. Come on. Decorate it with me. I already strung the lights the other night.”

But it was more than the fact that he didn’t have experience at trimming a Christmas tree—everything about the season would remind him of June. It would be a painful reminder of all that he’d lost. Christmastime was the time of year June loved the most. It was when she was at her best—when they had been at their best.

“Jackson?” Mae’s voice jerked him from his thoughts.

He shook his head. “I don’t think this is a good idea.”

“Sure, it is. After all, it’s almost Christmas.”

“But this is your tree, not mine.” He knew it was a lame

excuse, but he just couldn't bring himself to admit the truth—he felt guilty celebrating without June.

"For as long as you're here with me, it's our tree. Yours, mine and Gizmo's." At that point, the dog's ears perked up. Mae turned to her pup and said, "Isn't that right, boy?"

As if on cue, Gizmo barked. Spontaneous laughter erupted in Jackson. These two seemed determined to cheer him up. And it was working.

He normally wasn't that easily amused, but being around Mae and her dog was bringing out a whole new side in him. And he honestly didn't know what to make of it—what to make of the way Mae made him feel.

This isn't a good idea.

It'll be fine.

The conflicting thoughts piled one on top of the other. But it came down to the fact that Serena felt sorry for Jackson. How could a man who appeared to have everything miss out on the spirit of Christmas?

To her, Christmastime was going beyond your normal comfort zone in order to lend others a helping hand. She tried to do it year-round, but filming schedules usually upended her best efforts to visit the soup kitchen during the rest of the year.

She'd been doing it for years now. At first, she'd done it in defiance of her father, who'd said that no Winston should be pandering to others. How she was related to that man was beyond her. They disagreed about most everything. When she was young, she used to wonder if they'd mixed up the babies in the hospital nursery. She'd even said it once to her father—he hadn't taken it well, at all.

But the more time she spent at the soup kitchen, the more she liked the people there. She soon learned that her attendance wasn't so much about what she could give them but rather what they gave her. They reminded her that there was so much more to life than money and contracts. Because in the end, it was about love and kindness.

Of course, none of those people knew her true identity, either. She'd always wear a wig and dress in baggy T-shirts and faded jeans that she'd picked up at a secondhand store. She'd quickly learned just how comfortable those casual clothes could be—

"And what are you thinking about?" Jackson asked as he placed a hook on a glass ornament.

What would it hurt to share her thoughts? After all, they were living here together for the foreseeable future. It wasn't like she was going to open up and spill her whole life story.

"I was thinking about what I would be doing now if I were at home."

"Let me guess, shopping at the mall. Your arms would be full of shopping bags with gifts for your family."

She shook her head. "Not even close."

He blinked as though shocked by her denial. "Hmm… let's see. You'd be on holiday on a cruise ship."

"Although I like the way you think, that's not it."

He shrugged. "Okay. I give up. What would you be doing?"

"Working in a soup kitchen."

He didn't say anything, but the shock was quite vivid in his eyes. And he wouldn't stop staring. He made her want to squirm, but she held her ground.

"Why are you looking like I joined the circus?"

He visibly swallowed. "I'm sorry. I think what you do is great. It's just that I'm not used to people around me being so giving with their time. Everything in my world is rush-rush."

Surely he couldn't be that impressed. She'd watched his

show regularly and knew that he attended fund-raisers. "And if you were in New York, what would you be doing?"

He shrugged. "Not much."

"But it's the holidays. Come on. Maybe you'd be attending some prestigious event."

He shook his head. She glanced into his eyes and noticed how the light in them had dimmed. And then it dawned on her that the look in his eyes was one of pain and loss. His wife had died a while back. And now that she thought about it, she hadn't glimpsed any photos of him at the various gala events since his wife had passed away.

So he knew what it was like to lose someone close—just like she'd lost her father. Even though her parental relationship had been complicated, it didn't mean that she hadn't loved him.

"My…my wife," Jackson said, drawing Serena from her thoughts, "she was always busy with one charity group or another. I don't attend the fund-raising events now—not without her."

The way his voice cracked with emotion didn't get past Serena. She recalled how he and his wife had appeared inseparable. It seemed like every Monday morning there were photos of them on *Hello America.* Serena recalled how they always looked so happy—so in love. It was obvious that he was still in love with her.

Serena's gaze immediately sought out his left hand. No ring. And then realizing what she was doing, she glanced away. There may no longer be a physical link to his wife, but in his heart, he would always love her. The proof was in the pain reflected in his eyes and the catch in his voice when he spoke of her.

"I'm sorry for your loss." And now she understood why he wasn't anxious to decorate the Christmas tree. It probably reminded him of his wife and their holidays together.

"If you don't want to help me, that's okay. I'm sure celebrating Christmas alone isn't easy."

He continued putting hooks on the ornaments. "I lost her a couple of years ago." He paused as though that was all he was going to say. "At first, after she died, I didn't know how I was going to go on. We did everything together. She even traveled with me when I did travel segments for the morning show."

"Did you two make it to Austria? Is that why you're here?"

He shook his head. "She didn't like snow. I had the option of picking the places for the Christmas segment. And I wanted something different—a place without memories."

Serena was surprised that he was opening up to her. It made her feel guilty for keeping so much of herself a secret. But a part of her liked having him treat her like a normal human being and not like a superstar or a part of Hollywood royalty.

Her parents had had the most notorious, glamorous love story on- and off-screen. There was even a movie about their stormy, passionate relationship. Serena had never watched it and never planned to. She'd been there for the real thing and that had been enough for her. Real life was never like the lives portrayed on the big screen. In fact, in her case, reality was as far from glamorous as you could get.

Serena was lost in the past when Jackson spoke.

"What about you? Why aren't you with your family?"

This was her moment to solidify whatever this was growing between them. Dare she call it a friendship? She glanced at him. At that moment, he looked up and their gaze caught and held. Her heart beat wildly. Friendship wasn't exactly the only thing she was feeling where he was concerned.

No other man had ever made her feel this way. Sure there were gorgeous on-screen heroes. But she never let herself get caught in those romances. Growing up in a Hollywood family, she knew that love was fleeting at best. And then she'd met Shawn. It'd been after her father's death and perhaps her defenses had been down. Whatever the reason, she'd let him into her life. And what a mistake that had been.

But she wasn't going to repeat that mistake by making another one with a world-renowned television journalist. With all her effort, she glanced away. She turned to climb the ladder to place the ornament high up on the tree.

"Aren't you going to share?" he asked.

She did owe him an answer. It wasn't fair to expect him to open up when she wasn't prepared to do the same. "My father died last year. I don't have a reason to be home."

"I'm sorry." There was a pause as though he was considering what to say next. "What about your mother?"

"She's off on a Caribbean cruise with her latest boyfriend." She didn't bother to add that the aforementioned boyfriend was Serena's age. "My mother was never very maternal or traditional."

Jackson didn't say anything. He probably didn't know what to say because he'd had the idyllic childhood and the picture-perfect family. She was happy for him, but sad for herself. Some would say that it made her a stronger person, but she just thought it made her more cynical about life.

Jackson moved to the ladder to hand her another ornament. "Mae, I'm sorry."

She turned to tell him that he didn't have to be sorry. But before she could tell him, she dropped the Christmas ball. It fell to the floor and Gizmo let out an excited bark. He'd been waiting all this time for something to play with.

"No, Gizmo."

But it was too late. The dog chased the ball under the ladder. She moved too quickly. She'd never know if it was her sudden shift in weight or Gizmo running into the ladder, but the old wooden ladder swayed. Serena reached out, but there was nothing to grab onto. The ladder tilted to one side.

Serena started to fall. A shriek tore from her lungs.

And then her body crashed into Jackson's.

His strong arms wrapped around her. "It's okay. I've got you."

"Gizmo?"

"Is fine."

She turned her head to thank Jackson and that was when she realized just how close they were. She breathed in his scent—a mix of soap and pure masculinity. It was quite a heady combo.

For a moment, neither spoke. They didn't move as they stared deep into each other's eyes. It was just as well that he didn't say a word, because she'd have never heard him over the pounding of her heart. In fact, it was so loud that it drowned out any common sense.

She was in the arms of Jackson Bennett—her morning eye candy. He was the man that she had had a secret crush on for years now. How was it possible that it took them both traveling to Europe for their paths to cross? When people said that life was stranger than fiction, they were right.

And then his gaze dipped down to her lips. He was going to kiss her. The breath caught in her throat. She'd always wondered what it would be like to be kissed by him. And this was her one and only chance to answer that question.

With the Christmas lights twinkling in the background, Serena's eyes drifted closed. Letting go completely of the ramifications of her actions and just giving in to what she wanted, she leaned forward. His lips pressed to hers.

The kiss was slow and tender. After being unceremoniously groped in the past by eager suitors, this cautious approach caught her off guard. As the kiss progressed, she realized that Jackson was unlike any of the other men in her past.

She wondered what it would be like to have a real relationship with a mature, self-assured man like Jackson. While she could never picture herself long term with Shawn, she could envision a life with Jackson—marriage, kids, the whole nine yards!

The image was so real—so vivid that it startled her.

She pulled back. Her eyes fluttered open. As soon as his gaze met hers, heat rushed to her face. She felt exposed and vulnerable.

She knew that there was no way he could read her thoughts, but that didn't ease her discomfort. Of all the men to imagine a future with, Jackson wasn't the right one. He still loved his late wife.

Jackson didn't say a word as he lowered her legs to the floor. He went to straighten the ladder before he retrieved the Christmas ornament from Gizmo. And all that time, Serena stood there trying to make sense of what had just happened.

That kiss had been like a window into the future. But how was that possible? She immediately dismissed the ludicrous thought.

But she was left with one question. Now that they'd kissed, how did they go back to that easy, friendly coexistence? Because every time her gaze strayed to him, she'd be fantasizing about what would have happened if she hadn't pulled away.

CHAPTER NINE

THE NEXT MORNING, Jackson made his way to the kitchen. He yawned. He'd been restless most of the night. All the while, he'd been plagued by memories of the kiss. It had been an amazing kiss. The kind of kiss that could make a man forget his pledge of solitude—forget the risk he'd be taking with his heart if he were to let someone get close.

Even knowing the risks, there was a part of him that wished it hadn't ended. Chemistry like that didn't happen every day. In fact, he'd be willing to bet that it only happened once in a lifetime.

His thoughts had circled around all night, from how much he wanted to seek out Mae and pull her close to continue that kiss to wondering why he'd let his resolve weaken. What had he been thinking to kiss Mae? And what did that say about his devotion to June?

He still loved June. He always would. That acknowledgment only compounded his guilt.

And now what must Mae be thinking? She hadn't seemed interested in him. In fact, in the beginning he wasn't even certain that she was going to let him seek shelter from the storm in her cabin. But had that kiss complicated their relationship?

He paused at the kitchen doorway, not sure what to say to her. Perhaps it was best to act as though the kiss had never happened. With that thought, he pushed open the door.

An array of cereal boxes sat on the table next to an empty bowl and fresh orange slices. It appeared Mae had been up early that morning. He wondered if she'd had problems sleeping, too. He scanned the kitchen but didn't find any sign of her.

Gizmo came wandering into the kitchen.

"Hey, little guy, where's your momma?"

For once, the pup didn't say anything. Instead, Gizmo yawned. It appeared no one in the cabin had slept well. Maybe it was just from being cooped up for so long. But he knew that wasn't the case. It was the kiss…

Every time he'd closed his eyes, Mae's image had been there. It wasn't right. He shouldn't have done it. He shouldn't have gotten caught up in the moment.

He knew that June was gone and was never coming back, but he'd promised to love her forever. He also recalled how June had made him promise to move on with his life—to love again. The painful memories came flooding back.

June had been so unwell and yet her last thought had been of him. He hadn't kept his promise—at least not until now. Not that he was going to pursue Mae. He just couldn't move on as though June had never been a huge part of his life. How could he put his heart on the line again?

The grief of losing June had cost him dearly. The thought of being so vulnerable again had him withdrawing from friends and social settings. Until Mae…

She made him remember how things used to be—think of how things could be if he'd let himself go. She made him feel alive again. He shook his head to clear his thoughts, but it didn't work. Mae was still there in the front of his mind.

With a sigh, he sat down at the table and filled the bowl with corn flakes. He didn't really have an appetite, but his stomach growled in protest. Perhaps some food would help his attitude.

He glanced down to find Gizmo had wandered off, leaving Jackson alone with his thoughts. The cabin was quiet. As he stared out the window, he was pleased to find the sun was out. Today would be the day when he was able to get on with his life. He knew the thought of leaving here should bring him a sense of relief but it didn't.

The truth was, he'd really enjoyed the time he'd spent with Mae. She had a way about her that put him at ease. Maybe it was because they'd each shared a recent loss or the fact that neither had a loving, devoted mother. Whatever you wanted to say, they shared a special connection. One he wouldn't soon forget.

But Christmas was only a week away and if he didn't get this last segment shot, it'd be too late to air. The slot would get filled and everyone would move on.

If only he could put a special spin on this segment, something more than Christmas in a quaint village in Austria. He knew what they'd already planned would pull on the viewers' nostalgic heartstrings, but his thoughts needed to be on the head honchos in the front office. He only had until the first of the year to prove that he was the man for the evening news slot.

Jackson heard the kitchen door creak open. He turned expecting to find Mae, but instead it was once again Gizmo. He strolled back into the kitchen with something in his mouth. Jackson smiled and shook his head. That dog was forever stealing things. He wondered if Mae would find everything the dog had stolen before she left here. Well, he could help her out this time.

He got up and approached Gizmo. "Hey, boy, what do you have there?"

The dog tried to get around him, but Jackson blocked him. That definitely wasn't a dog toy in his mouth, and this time it wasn't a pink lacy bra, either. The memory of that piece of lingerie combined with the kiss last night heated his veins—

No. Don't go there. It was a onetime thing. Let it go.

He knelt down to pet the dog. Luckily his ankle was starting to feel a bit better with the aid of over-the-counter painkillers. Still, he kept his weight on his good leg.

His fingers wrapped around what appeared to be Mae's wallet. "Give it to me."

Gizmo clenched tighter and started to pull back. He gave a little growl, all the while wagging his tail. Gizmo's head shook back and forth as he tried to work the wallet away from Jackson.

"You're a strong little guy, aren't you?"

Gizmo let out another little growl as his tail continued to swish back and forth.

Well, this was one game of tug-of-war Jackson didn't want to lose.

"Let go." No such luck. "Gizmo! Stop."

Suddenly, Gizmo let go.

Not prepared for the dog's sudden release, Jackson fell backward. He lost his grip on the wallet as he tried to catch himself. He landed squarely on his backside.

Gizmo didn't tarry. He turned to make his escape. Jackson sat on the floor and watched as the dog pushed the swinging door open with his nose.

Jackson couldn't help but smile and shake his head. He wondered if this was what it was like having small children. He would never know since he and June were never blessed with any. It was yet another thing that they'd put off too long—another dream that would never be fulfilled.

He went to pick up Mae's wallet when he realized that it had come open and some of the cards had scattered across the tile floor. He picked them up and started putting them in the wallet when he noticed the name on them: Serena Winston.

He immediately recognized the name. How could he not? Serena Winston came from a legendary family. He'd tried repeatedly to interview her, but for one reason or another, it had never worked out.

This had to be some sort of mix-up. The Serena Winston on these cards couldn't be the famous actress. But if that was the case, why did Mae have them? He held the California driver's license closer. He studied the similarities. If Mae were to be a blonde and add makeup—

His mouth gaped.

It was her. The driver's license read: *Serena M. Winston. Serena Mae Winston?*

Jackson sat there stunned. He'd thought that they'd formed a friendship. He'd trusted her with intimate details of his life, but she hadn't even been honest about her name—at least not her whole name.

Everything started to fall in place, such as her ability to lease this luxury cabin for herself and her dog. She'd been hiding in plain sight with her strawberry blonde hair and lack of makeup. He'd never seen any photos of Serena Winston with reddish hair. She was known far and wide for her honey-blond strands. And it explained what had happened to her—how she was able to drop off the radar.

His thoughts circled back to how he'd believed that they were beginning to trust each other. Then there was that kiss—the kiss he hadn't been able to forget no matter how hard he tried. Well, he no longer had to worry about it. Obviously, it had been all one-sided. All the time, she'd been playing him for a fool.

Anger warmed his veins. He didn't like to be lied to. His gut knotted at the thought of her laughing behind his back. He wished this was some sort of dream because he'd liked Mae—a woman who didn't even exist. Why couldn't just one thing in his life go his way?

He stuffed her cards back in the wallet. He got to his feet. With the breakfast dishes and food long forgotten, he headed out of the kitchen to find his hostess. The jig was up and he intended to tell her.

He'd just reached the living room when his cell phone rang. At last, the cell tower had been fixed. But it couldn't have been worse timing. The only person he wanted to speak to was Mae—erm, Serena. But he didn't see her at the desk working on her laptop. Nor was she on the couch. He could only guess that she was upstairs. And he wasn't sure his ankle was up for that particular challenge.

The buzzing of his phone would not stop. He withdrew it from his pants pocket and checked the caller ID. It was his agent. And it wasn't the first time Fred had called. There was a long list of missed calls. He must be worried about Jackson disappearing, especially at such a pivotal time in his career.

Jackson's gaze returned to the grand stairs leading to the second floor. The phone vibrated in his hand. He sighed and accepted the call.

"Jackson, thank goodness. What happened to you?"

"I was involved in a car accident."

"Accident? Are you hurt? Did you injure your face?"

Leave it to Fred to get to the heart of his concern—Jackson's marketability. "My face is fine."

"You're sure?"

"Yes."

"Well, where are you? The crew has been looking for you. They aren't sure what to do."

"I'm snowed in." He headed for Mae…erm…Serena's desk in the great room to drop off the wallet. "And you'll never believe who rescued me…"

CHAPTER TEN

THE KISS MEANT NOTHING.

Nothing at all.

That was what Serena had been telling herself ever since last night, when she'd fallen into Jackson's more-than-capable arms. What had she been thinking to kiss the enemy?

Who was she kidding? Jackson wasn't the enemy, even if he was part of the news media. Maybe at first she hadn't trusted him—with her background, who could blame her? But during the time they'd spent together, she'd learned that there was so much more to him than his dashing looks and his day job.

He was a man who'd loved and lost. He was kind and generous. He went out of his way for others, even when he'd rather be doing anything else. And he had a sense of humor. The memory of his deep laugh still sent goose bumps down her arms. That was a sound she could listen to for the rest of her life—

Whoa! Slow down.

She knew that this moment of playing house would end soon—just as soon as the avalanche was cleared and they were able to plow the roads. Then they would return to reality, but for now, they lived within their own little world with their own rules and she intended to enjoy it as long as it lasted.

And if that should include some more kisses?

Well, she wouldn't complain. An impish smile pulled at her lips.

She'd been kissed by a lot of leading men, but none of them could come close to Jackson. That man was made for kissing. Just the memory of his lips pressed to hers had her sighing. It hadn't lasted long enough, not even close.

And now, instead of kissing that handsome man, she was doing his laundry. Something wasn't right about that. But she was proud of herself for being able to take care of herself. Neither of her parents knew how to work a washing machine much less the dryer. They'd always been dependent on domestic help.

Serena learned early on that if she wanted true privacy, she had to be self-sufficient. And to be honest, she was never quite comfortable with people waiting on her. Maybe it was the time she'd spent serving food at the soup kitchen—seeing people who barely made it day to day—that had opened her eyes to the extravagances that her parents took for granted.

Whatever it was, she'd learned to do everything for herself except cooking. She had yet to master it. But she could clean the bathroom and iron her clothes.

It was only recently when her filming schedule became so out of control that she'd taken on a housekeeper. It was only supposed to be temporary, but Mrs. Martinez was so sweet and in desperate need of work that Serena kept her on.

Sometimes Serena missed doing the laundry. She found it relaxing. But doing Jackson's laundry had extra benefits, like the lingering hint of his cologne on his laundered shirts. She stood in the master suite next to the closet sniffing his shirt. If he were to walk in now and catch her, she would die of mortification. She was acting like some teenager—

There were footsteps followed by Jackson's voice. Was he talking to Gizmo? But she didn't have time to contemplate the answer as she was still clenching his shirt.

Not about to be caught acting like a lovesick puppy, she stepped into the closet and slid the door shut. She had to hunch over in order to fit. Why couldn't this closet be a walk-in? But no, it had to be long and skinny. And there was a hanger digging into her shoulder blade. She started to move when the metal hangers jingled together. She froze in place.

What was she doing in here?

Plain and simple, she'd panicked.

What was it about Jackson's presence that short-circuited her thought process? She never had this problem with any other man in her life. Jackson was unique.

She was about to open the door and step out when she heard her name mentioned. The breath caught in her throat as she strained to catch what he was saying about her.

"I'm serious. Serena Winston saved my life."

There was a pause. He must be talking on the phone. That meant the cell service and internet were back online. She didn't know if that was a blessing or a curse. She supposed she would soon find out.

"Don't you dare say a word. I told you that as my friend, not my agent." A pause ensued. "Because I told you not to. Just leave it be."

Serena smiled. Jackson was protecting her privacy. He was a bona fide hero in her book.

"Hey, Gizmo." Pause. "No. I was talking to the dog."

Oh, no. If Gizmo realized she was in the closet, he would put up a fuss. No sooner had the thought passed through her mind than there was the sound of pawing at the door. Serena didn't move. She didn't so much as take a breath. She just prayed that Gizmo would get bored and move on.

"Arff! Arff!"

"Are you serious? She's all over the headlines?" Another pause. "I don't need to check it out." Pause. "Yes. I know this scoop could make a difference in my career, but it's not worth it to me."

Serena smiled broadly and pumped her fist, banging her hand into more hangers. *Jingle. Jingle.* She reached up, silencing the hangers. The last thing she needed was for him to catch her lurking in his closet. She didn't even want to imagine what she must look like. This was easily the most embarrassing moment of her life—and if Jackson caught her, it would be even worse.

"Arff! Arff!"

Scratch. Scratch. Scratch.

"Stop…No, not you. I was talking to the dog. Listen, I've got to go take the dog out." Pause. "I don't know." Pause. "As soon as they plow open the roads."

Jackson's footsteps could be heard approaching the closet. "There's nothing in there, boy. Come on. I'll take you out."

Jackson's footsteps faded away.

Serena cautiously exhaled a pent-up breath. She opened the closet door a crack to make sure the coast was clear. It was. She quickly exited and stretched. Her muscles did not like being hunched over for so long.

Not wasting too much time, she hung up the shirt, closed the closet and exited Jackson's bedroom. She glanced toward the front porch, where she saw him through the window. His ankle must be feeling a lot better if he could put on a boot and go out in the snow. That was good, right?

For some reason, the thought of Jackson being mobile didn't make her happy. Soon he'd be leaving her. And now that she knew she could trust him, she wanted him to stay.

The only question she had was whether he'd known who she was all along. If not, what had tipped him off?

She carried the now-empty laundry basket back to the laundry room just off the kitchen. As she placed it on the floor next to the dryer for another load, she realized that this place, even though it was quite large, was very homey. She'd never felt relaxed at her home in Hollywood.

And then she realized that perhaps it wasn't the structure around her but rather the people in it. Gizmo was new to her life and they'd immediately bonded. And now there was Jackson. She felt guilty for not trusting him sooner. Perhaps it wasn't too late to make it up to him.

She returned to the great room and was about to sit down at her laptop when she noticed her wallet sitting on the corner of her desk. How in the world had it gotten here? And then she noticed the distinct bite marks in the black leather. Gizmo. He was the one who'd given her away. *That dog.*

Just then the front door swung open. Gizmo raced into the room as though he were being chased. He stopped and shook himself off. Serena couldn't help but smile. This dog did not like snow.

"What's so amusing?" Jackson asked.

"Gizmo. He doesn't like the snow. At all."

"Give him time. It might grow on him."

Somehow she didn't think that would be the case. She glanced down at the wallet with bite marks. She supposed it was a little late to come clean considering Jackson knew the truth about her.

"I see you found the wallet," Jackson said. "I rescued it from Gizmo. I think he was planning to hide it."

"He is a bit of a thief. You better watch your stuff." How did she say this? Did she just apologize for keeping her true identity a secret? Would he understand?

Jackson said something.

"Hmm..." She'd been lost in her thoughts and hadn't caught all he'd said.

"I said your secret is safe with me."

It wasn't until her gaze met his dark, pointed stare that she knew she was in trouble. He was angry with her for keeping her identity from him. She didn't know what to say to undo things.

"I... I'm sorry," she said, but the words didn't seem to faze him. "I have a hard time trusting people."

"Do you know that there's a search on for you? It appears that your fiancé is heading it up. His face is all over the media sites begging for information about your whereabouts."

Her hands balled up at her sides. How dare Shawn act like he cared? It was all a show—just another way for him to benefit by linking himself to her.

"He's not my fiancé. We were never engaged—not even close."

Jackson's brows rose. "That's not what all of the tabloids are saying."

"Shawn would do anything for headlines, including feeding false information to the press. He doesn't like me, much less love me. I'm just a stepping-stone to his goals."

"Really?" Jackson sounded skeptical. "Why don't you tell people the truth about him?"

"Do you think they'd believe me? Anything I say will be twisted and blown up into an even bigger scandal. I just want it to all die down and go away. I want him to go away. I wish I'd never met him."

Jackson wore a puzzled expression. "And that's what you're doing here—hiding until the story dies?"

"In a manner of speaking." She didn't actually consider it hiding, but she wasn't going to argue semantics with him.

"From what my agent was telling me, the story is growing with every day you're gone." He raked his fingers through his hair. "It might be good to let someone know that you're alive and safe. Some tabloids have even surmised that you're dead. Others think you've been kidnapped."

"Seriously?" She shook her head and sat down at the desk. "Can't people mind their own business?"

"Is there anything I can do to help? Perhaps my agent could release a statement to put everyone at ease—"

"No. No statement."

"Okay. So what? You're just going to suddenly reappear one day?"

"Something like that."

She pulled up the tabloids on her laptop. The headlines were ridiculous. And below the headlines was a photo of a distraught Shawn. Her stomach churned. When was that guy going to get on with his life? She would give him this much, he was a great actor. Because if she didn't know that he was lying, she might have believed his show.

Unable to take any more of the lies and sensational journalism, she closed the laptop. "Listen, I'm sorry I wasn't up-front with you."

"I understand. At least now I do. When your driver's license fell on the floor, I wasn't very happy with you."

"I… I don't know what to say. I came here to be alone and then I thought—oh, I don't know what I thought. I should have told you, but I hadn't worked up the courage. It isn't easy for me to let people into my life."

He nodded as though he understood. "You've lived your

entire life in front of the cameras. You don't know who you can trust. And with my occupation, I'm sure that didn't help things."

"You're right. It didn't. I was afraid that once you found out who I was, you would make me a headline on your morning news show."

When frown lines bracketed his eyes, she knew that she'd said too much. That was the thing about letting people get close. She wasn't sure how much to say and how much to hold back. At least when she was acting in front of the camera, she had printed lines to follow. She didn't have to figure out what to say, how much to say and when to say it.

That was another problem that kept her from seeking the spotlight. She was awkward in public. It would seem odd to most considering who her parents were and what she did for a living. But when she was in front of the cameras, she got to pretend that she was someone else—someone brave and ready to say their piece. However, Serena Mae Winston was a private person who struggled with the fame that her family lineage and job brought her.

Jackson cleared his throat. "I know we haven't known each other for long, but do I strike you as someone who would go behind someone's back to make a headline?"

"No." The look on his face said that he didn't believe her. "I mean it. I know we haven't known each other for long, but I… I trust you." He had no idea how hard that was for her to say.

His stance eased, as did the frown lines on his face. "Then maybe we should start over."

"Start over?"

He nodded. Then he approached her and held out his hand. "Hi. I'm Jackson Bennett. The face of *Hello America*."

She placed her hand in his and a warm sensation zinged

up her arm. Her heart palpitated faster than normal. "Hi. I'm Serena Winston. I'm an actress who is trying to have a normal, quiet holiday."

"I'm happy to meet you, Serena—"

Just then there was a loud rumbling sound. It woke Gizmo from his nap on the couch. He started to bark as he ran to the door. Jackson and Serena followed.

"What do you think it is this time?" she asked.

"It's definitely not another avalanche. This is a much different sound." Jackson listened for a moment. "I think they are opening up the road."

"Really? We can get out of here?"

"You're that anxious to get rid of me?"

"I didn't say that, but we need to get you to the doctor to see if you did any serious damage to your leg."

"Do you really think I could walk on it if I had?"

"Is that what you call the motion you make?"

"Hey, I'm trying here."

"I know. I just worry that you're trying too hard and that you're going to do permanent damage to yourself."

As they were standing there next to the window talking, a red-and-black snowmobile cut across the front of the yard.

"Looks like that guy from the emergency crew is back to check on you," Serena said.

"I'm fine. You all need to quit worrying about me."

"If you were fine, you would walk normal."

Jackson grunted and limped over to the couch while Serena waited for their visitor to make it to the door.

CHAPTER ELEVEN

SHE WAS RIGHT.

But that knowledge didn't make Serena happy.

The official diagnosis was in. Jackson's ankle was fractured. Even the doctor was surprised that Jackson was able to get around as well as he had been. As it was, the doctor had set him up with a walking boot.

"We shouldn't be here," she said as they stood at the edge of the town square. "You should be at home resting your leg."

Jackson turned and stared into her eyes. "Have you ever been to a Christmas market?"

"Arff!"

Jackson smiled and gazed down at Gizmo. "I wasn't talking to you, boy." Jackson's gaze rose until it met Serena's again. "I was talking to you."

"Um, well, um…no. But I'm not exactly dressed for it."

His gaze skimmed over her white coat, red scarf and faded jeans. "There's nothing wrong with what you're wearing."

She lifted a hand to her hair. "But I didn't do anything with my hair."

"You look cute with a ponytail. It suits you. You worry too much. You're beautiful just the way you are."

The way Jackson stared so deeply into her eyes made

the rest of the world fade away. In that moment, it was as if just the two of them existed. He was staring at her like—like he wanted to kiss her.

Her gaze lowered, taking in his very tempting mouth. The thought of once again being held in his very capable arms and feeling his mouth pressed to hers was quite tempting. Was it possible that he was the first man to like her just the way she was?

Her father had always been disappointed in her. It didn't matter if it was her choice in movie roles or if it was the style of her haircut. She'd never gained his approval and then he'd died on her before anything could be resolved between them. One minute he was giving her a hard time about not aligning her romantic relationship with her career. And the next, he was lying on the floor, dead, from a massive heart attack. That was it. No time for "I love yous" or "goodbyes." It was just over—in a heartbeat.

Maybe that was why she let herself become involved with her leading man. Shawn was great-looking and he could say all the right things, but she soon learned that it was all a show. He was constantly acting, being whoever he needed to be to impress people—to get a leg up in the Hollywood world.

But Jackson didn't want anything from her. Not even an interview. He was the first man who'd ever been comfortable with who he was without having to put on a show for the public, which surprised her. After all, Jackson's career was about projecting a certain image for the public, but here he was with scruff on his jaw and his hair a little ruffled by the breeze and he wasn't the least bit worried about his appearance.

She liked being treated like a real person instead of a star. A smile lifted her lips. She liked Jackson. He was so different from the other men who had passed through her life.

"I don't know what's going through your mind," Jackson said, "but whatever it is, I approve. You should smile more often."

Just then Gizmo saw another dog. Being the friendly sort, he wanted to go visit. He started to run, but after walking in a circle, his leash was now wrapped around Jackson and herself. So when Gizmo ran out of length, the leash yanked them together.

Her hands pressed upon Jackson's very firm chest. She had to crane her neck to look into his eyes. It was then that his gaze moved to her lips. He lowered his head and immediately claimed her lips.

His kiss was gentle and sweet. It made her wish that they were back at the cabin where the kiss didn't have to end—where they could see where it would lead. Because she realized that their time together was almost at an end. Jackson would have to get back to the project that he'd flown to Austria to do, and she needed to add some serious word count to her screenplay if she wanted it ready for her agent when she returned to Hollywood. It would hopefully give the paparazzi something to talk about besides her scandalous love life.

"Arff! Arff!"

Their lips parted and they turned to Gizmo. He jumped up, placing his front paws on Jackson's good leg.

"I think someone wants to be picked up," Serena said.

"That might be easier if he hadn't wrapped us up in his leash."

"Maybe someone shouldn't have released so much of his leash."

Jackson's eyes widened. "You're blaming me for this?"

"I'm not blaming anyone. I certainly don't mind being tied up with you."

His brows rose. "Oh. You don't, huh?"

When Jackson leaned in for another kiss, Serena pressed her hand to his chest. "How about you hold that thought until later?"

"Later?" He started to frown but then his eyes widened as he caught her true intention. A broad smile lit up his face. "I think that can be arranged."

More and more people continued to arrive at the market. No wonder Gizmo had changed his mind about wandering off and instead wanted to be held. He was not used to such a crowd. The Christmas market really drew in the people. But who could blame them? This was the most wonderful time of the year.

Jackson quickly untangled all three of them. "There. Now shall we go explore?"

"Are you sure you're up for this? The doctor did say that your leg will tire quickly with that boot on."

"Stop worrying. I'm fine. I'll let you know when I get tired."

"You promise."

"I do."

"What about Gizmo?"

"Let him walk for a bit. That pup has more energy than anyone I know. And then when we get home, he'll sleep instead of getting into more mischief."

"That sounds like a good plan." She smiled up at him. "I like the way you think."

"Well, if you like that wait until you find out what I have planned for later."

She couldn't help but laugh at his outrageous flirting. Things between them were so much different now—so much easier since he knew the truth about her. If only she had known how good it could be between them, she would have told him sooner.

They strolled through the Christmas market locally known as Christkindlmarkt. The thing Serena loved most was sampling all of the local delicacies—from sipping mulled wine to devouring *kiachl*, somewhat like a donut with cranberry jam. Serena had never tasted anything so delightful. Jackson enjoyed the *raclette brot*, a type of bread with warm cheese. And of course Gizmo had to sample most everything, too. So much for her rule about not feeding him human food. After all, it was the holidays. Everyone deserved a treat.

"Are you enjoying yourself?" Jackson asked.

"I am." In the background a brass band played holiday tunes. And overhead, strands of white twinkle lights brightened the night sky. "This place is amazing. And I can't bring myself to stop sampling all of the delicacies."

"I know what you mean. I'm full, but I just have to try one more thing."

They both laughed. The evening was perfect. No one recognized her with her strawberry blonde hair pulled up in a ponytail and lack of makeup. Here in Austria, she was just another person on the arm of a very handsome gentleman.

And then he reached out and took her hand in his. His fingers threaded through hers quickly and naturally as though they'd been doing it for years. Her heart leaped in her chest.

This man, he was something extraordinary.

And Serena knew in that moment, in the middle of the Christmas market, that her life would never be the same.

He couldn't stop smiling.

Jackson sat in the passenger seat as Serena pulled into

the driveway of the cabin. She'd chatted the whole way home from the Christmas market. He was glad he'd suggested they go. Not only was it a scouting mission for his segment for his morning news show, but it also had been their first official date.

Serena put the vehicle in Park and turned off the engine. "And we're home."

"Hey, what happened to your smile?"

She shrugged. "It's just that all of the magic of the evening disappeared."

"Ouch." He grasped at his chest.

"What's the matter? What hurts?"

"My ego. You just pierced it. I'm wounded."

"Oh." She smacked his shoulder. "You had me worried. I thought something was seriously wrong with you."

"There is. You just said the magic has ended."

"You know what I meant. The music. The festive mood. The amazing food. I loved the evening."

"And you don't think my company can compare?"

Serena's green eyes widened. "What exactly are you implying?"

"Forget twinkle lights, I'm thinking of setting off some fireworks tonight."

Her mouth lifted into a smile that made her eyes sparkle. "I don't know. Do you think you're up to it?"

"Let me give you a preview." He leaned forward and pressed his lips to hers.

His kiss was gentle and restrained. He wouldn't push her, but he needed to extend the invitation. It'd been a very long time since he was with a woman. His gut tightened at the thought of living up to Serena's expectations.

But he didn't have long to contemplate because she kissed him back with undeniable desire, which soothed his worries. As their kiss deepened, a warmth flooded his chest. The cracks and crevices in his heart filled in. In that moment, he no longer felt like a shell of a man. He felt complete and eager to step into the next stage of his life. Whatever that may be.

Serena pulled back. "We should go inside. It's getting cold out here."

They both turned to find out why Gizmo wasn't whining to go inside. The pup was sound asleep in the back seat. Jackson couldn't help but smile.

"So he really does run out of energy once in a while."

"It's hard to believe, but it does happen. Isn't he so cute?"

"He is…when he's sleeping."

"Hey." She swatted at Jackson's arm. Then a worried look crossed over her face. "You do like Gizmo, don't you?"

He knew by the serious tone of her voice that him bonding with her dog was nonnegotiable. Someday she'd make a good mother. Unlike his mother who'd taken his dog away from him.

"Oh, no," she said. "You don't like him."

"What? No. I mean, yes, I do."

"But you frowned when I asked you about it."

"That wasn't why I was frowning. I swear. I didn't even realize I was frowning."

He was going to have to do better to keep his thoughts from being so obvious on his face. Considering his job, he was normally quite adept at it. But either Serena could read him better than most or he felt so at ease around her that he didn't think to hide anything.

And now he had no choice but to share with Serena that painful moment in his childhood. He'd never told anyone about it—not even his wife. It was a part of his life that he'd blocked out—until he'd met Serena and Gizmo.

"I was just thinking about the past. I had a dog once. He was rambunctious and I was young, about seven years old. Long story short, he got in lots of trouble and a week later, my mother took him back to the pound."

He remembered clearly how his mother had told him to stop crying. He wasn't a sniveling wimp. If he was strong, if he was a man—unlike his father who ran off at the first sign of trouble—then Jackson would be fine. He didn't need a dog.

He'd been so young at the time that his priority was not letting his mother down. He wanted her to be proud of him more than anything else in the world—even more than having his puppy.

"I can't believe it," Serena said. "Your mom took your dog away."

He nodded. "But it's okay."

"What's okay about it? She got it for you, but seven days later she took it back to the shelter."

"It was my fault. I didn't take care of Rover like I'd promised."

"You were only seven. How responsible can a seven-year-old be?"

Jackson shrugged, realizing that even after all this time he was protecting his mother. "It doesn't matter. It was a long time ago."

"But it still bothers you, so it matters."

He pulled back and reached for the door handle. "I don't want to talk about this."

Serena didn't say anything as he walked away. By the rigid line of his shoulders, she knew the evening had been ruined. And it had held such promise.

CHAPTER TWELVE

WHAT HAD HAPPENED?

Serena had been trying to make sense of what had happened to their perfect evening ever since Jackson had withdrawn from her. That had been last night and now, not quite twenty-four hours later, he was still unusually quiet.

Had she misread everything last night?

Impossible. There was no way she'd misread his kisses—his very stirring kisses. Those kisses had left promises of more to come. Oh, he had been into her just as much as she had been into him. So where had it all gone so wrong?

Or was it for the best to put a halt to their desires? After all, every man that she'd let get close had hurt her. Why should Jackson be any different?

But the truth was, she wanted him to be different. She wanted him to be the exception to everything she knew about men—that they were critical, careless with their words and didn't believe in love for love's sake but rather for what it could do for them and their careers.

"Hey, what has you so deep in thought?" Jackson's deep voice stirred her.

At last he was talking to her. A smile came to her face. Maybe she was making too big a deal of things. Perhaps he'd just been tired last night. After all, the doctor did say that the boot on his ankle would tire him out.

"I was just thinking about what I'm working on."

"I'm sorry to interrupt." Jackson had a mug in each hand and held one out to her. "I just thought you might like this."

"Oh, coffee. I always like coffee."

"It's not coffee."

"It isn't?" She accepted the mug and glanced into it to find little marshmallows and hot chocolate. "Thank you."

"I just thought that with it snowing again this might be fitting."

"It is." She took a sip of the milky chocolate. It was perfect. "This is the best hot chocolate I've ever had."

He smiled proudly. "Thank you."

"Is this from a packet? If so, I have to make a note to buy some when I get back to the States."

He shook his head. "It isn't from a box. I made it."

She took another sip and moaned in pleasure. "How did you make it?"

He eyed her up as though trying to decide if he should divulge the information. "Can you keep a secret?"

"Definitely. I just have to be able to make this again. It's that good."

"Well, while we were at the Christmas market yesterday, I bought some chocolate."

"Why don't I remember this?"

"Because you and Gizmo were at the stall with the gourmet dog biscuits. Anyway, that's my secret."

"So you melted chocolate into milk."

"Not just any chocolate but dark chocolate. However, you can't tell anyone. It's our secret."

She smiled, liking the idea that they shared confidences. "I can't believe you are so good in the kitchen." And then she realized that he might not take her words as a compliment. “It’s just that you are so busy. I don’t know how you find the time.”

“I don’t have a busy social calendar, not anymore. Anyway, once you learn how to cook, it’s like riding a bike, you never forget.”

“I wouldn’t know.”

“You mean you can’t ride a bike?” The look on his face was one of unimaginable horror.

“No. I mean, yes, I can ride a bike. It’s the cooking that I never conquered.”

“Did you ever try?”

She nodded. “I’ve attempted to teach myself without success. My mother can’t cook, so she obviously didn’t show me. And my father thought that cooking was a waste of time. That’s what he paid people to do. So he forbade me from spending time in the kitchen when instead I could spend the time taking voice lessons as well as dance and acting classes.”

“Sounds like you had a very busy and educational childhood.”

She shrugged. “It was what it was.” Her childhood was a mixed bag of extravagance and neglect. She was certain she wasn’t the only Hollywood child to have the same experience. “How did you become so good in the kitchen?”

“Come to the kitchen with me and I’ll tell you.”

“The kitchen, but why?”

“Because you’re going to have your first cooking lesson.”

She struggled to keep her mouth from gaping. After she recovered from her surprise, she said, “You don’t want to do this. I’m pretty sure I can burn water if left alone.”

He smiled. “I think you’re better than you give yourself credit for.”

“I wouldn’t be so certain.”

"Come on." He reached out and took her free hand. He tugged until she got to her feet. "After all, you can make chili."

"You know that it was out of a can."

"Still, you didn't burn it. That's a start."

"I must admit that I can handle a microwave."

"Good." They moved to the kitchen. "Now you have to pick—red or white?"

"Wine?"

"No. Sauce."

She liked them both. "Paired with what?"

"Pasta and…" He opened the freezer and searched inside. "How do you feel about shrimp?"

"I love it." She was so thankful that he'd given up on the idea of teaching her to cook. She was hopeless. But with Jackson cooking, this was going to be a delicious dinner.

"Good. Now what sauce would you prefer?"

"White." She couldn't help but smile. She'd never been in the kitchen with a man where his sole interest was in preparing her dinner. In fact, no man had ever cooked her dinner. Her smile broadened.

"Well, what are you doing standing over there. Put your hot cocoa down and wash up. You have work to do."

"Me? Cook?" This was not a good idea. Not at all.

"Uh-huh. In fact, you can do it all yourself. I'll supervise."

Her stomach plummeted. So much for the delicious dinner that she'd been envisioning. "Are you sure you want to ruin dinner? I'm good with watching."

"You'll never learn to cook that way. Trust me. This will work."

She had absolutely no illusions about this cooking adventure turning out to be anything but a disaster. Still, it was sweet that Jackson wanted to help her. She just hated the thought of disappointing him.

Why exactly did he elect himself to teach Serena to cook?

Because it was easier than discussing his background. That was one thing about June, she never prodded him for answers. But Serena was the exact opposite. She was most definitely the curious sort. He wasn't sure how to deal with her.

For so long now, he'd been fine with leaving the past alone. But being around Serena had him reexamining his life. It all made him uncomfortable. The more he thought about things, the more he questioned his choices.

He didn't like the uneasiness filling him. Before he'd arrived in Austria, he'd had a plan—a focus. His life was to revolve around his work. Now he didn't know if that was the right path for him.

What he needed now was to get away from here—away from Serena. He'd be able to think clearly and he could go back to—to what? His lonely condo in New York? His workaholic tendencies?

No matter what his life may be lacking, it was better than the alternative—loving and losing. Once down that road was enough for him. He was better off alone.

He shoved all these thoughts and questions into the box at the back of his mind. Tomorrow his camera crew would arrive. And he doubted that his life would ever intersect Serena's again. Although, the thought of not seeing her again settled heavy in his chest.

"Where do I start?" Serena's voice jarred him from his thoughts.

"You'll need to rinse the shrimp under some water and remove the tails. And while you do that, I'll put on a pot of water for the pasta."

He couldn't believe that no one had ever taken the time to teach her to cook. He felt bad for her. It made him wonder what kind of a childhood she'd had.

"Were you left alone a lot as a child?" The question was out of his mouth before he realized that it was none of his business. He placed the pot on the burner and turned the heat to high. "Never mind, you don't have to answer that."

She glanced over at him. "Is this my friend Jackson asking or is it Jackson Bennett, king of the morning shows, who wants to know?"

Ouch! That comment hurt more than he was expecting. "I promise nothing you share with me will show up on my show or in the press. I'd like to be your friend."

She rinsed off another handful of colossal shrimp and set them aside before she turned back to him. "I'd like that. It's just that I never had anyone in my life that I could completely trust."

"That must have been rough."

She shrugged. "I dealt with it. I learned pretty quick that I could only count on myself."

"Still, that's not right. A kid should have someone to turn to—someone to rely on."

Serena arched a brow. "Are we talking about me or you?"

Jackson realized that he'd let his emotions get away from him. It was just that he felt a strong connection with Serena. It was something that he'd never felt with June or anyone else in his life.

He cleared his throat. "Why don't I give you a hand?"

He moved next to her at the sink and started removing the tails of the shrimp. Why did he keep opening himself up to her? He knew better. The real Jackson Bennett was a man with flaws and scars. He would never add up to the vision she gained from watching him on television.

Serena was used to men who had it all together—looks, careers and charisma. He was the shell of the man he used to be. Cancer had more victims than those carrying the disease. It could suck life right out of the people around it—grinding hopes and dreams into smithereens. And sometimes leaving in its wake a broken person.

"Do you cook a lot?" Serena asked.

He shrugged as he swallowed hard. "As much as I can. It's the only way I've found to make sure that I fit into my suits." He reached for a couple cloves of garlic. "Eating out is tempting, but then I start putting on the pounds that I can't lose even when I go to the gym."

"I totally get that. They say the camera puts on ten pounds but that was before high definition. Now it adds fifteen pounds and amplifies any wrinkles or blemishes. So if you can show me an easier way to watch the scale, I'm all for it."

Jackson placed a clove of garlic on a cutting board. He showed her how to put the flat side of a chef's knife on the clove and with her palm press down on it to remove the skin. She did the same with the other clove. Then Serena minced the garlic before chopping some fresh parsley and tomatoes that they'd picked up at the market.

"Jackson?"

He'd just added butter to the skillet. "Yes?"

"I thought I was supposed to cook the meal."

She was right. He'd just gotten so caught up in his thoughts of the past that he'd been moving around the kitchen on automatic. "You're right. Sorry. It's just habit." He stepped to the side of the stove. "Okay, then. Here. Take the handle. You'll want to swish it so the butter coats the bottom of the pan."

She did as he said.

"Now add the garlic." He talked her through the process of adding the shrimp, the fresh parsley and a little seasoning. Jackson inhaled the savory aroma. "Smells wonderful."

He added the angel-hair pasta to the pot of boiling water, gave it a stir and lowered the temperature.

"You're cheating," Serena said.

And then he realized he should have let her do all the steps. "But it's so much easier when we work as a team. Trust me, you're doing the hard part."

"What do I do next?"

"Turn the shrimp."

He hovered just over her shoulder, watching her every move. He told himself that he was just trying to be an attentive mentor, but the truth was he was drawn to Serena like a magnet. There was something so appealing about her and it went far deeper than her natural beauty. There was a tenderness—a vulnerability—about her. And she made him feel as though he were her equal—as though they were perfectly matched for each other.

"Jackson." Serena waved a hand in front of him to gain his attention. "The shrimp's pink."

Pulled back from his thoughts, he blinked and quickly took stock of where dinner stood. He told her to drain the shrimp and set them aside. Then they added more butter, flour, milk, chicken broth and seasoning to the pan. Then the most important part—the cheese. She added lots of mozzarella and Parmesan. In the meantime, Jackson drained the pasta.

They worked well together. Really well. It was like they'd been doing it all their lives. And he wasn't sure what to make of it. Perhaps he'd isolated himself too much since his wife's death and now he was overreacting to Serena's presence.

Oh, who was he kidding? He was falling for this woman—

this award-winning actress. And he had no idea what to do about it.

"Do I add the tomatoes now?" she asked.

"Yes. And the shrimp. And make sure you remove it from the heat."

He wasn't sure where this evening was headed, but he sure was hungry now. And his hunger had absolutely nothing to do with the amazing Alfredo shrimp pasta they'd just created.

CHAPTER THIRTEEN

DINNER HAD BEEN PERFECT.

The company was amazing.

Jackson couldn't recall the last time he'd had such a wonderful evening. And now Serena leaned back on the couch with Gizmo on one side of her and Jackson on the other. The glow of the fireplace added a romantic ambience to the room. And when Jackson settled his arm around her, she didn't resist.

Was it wrong that he wanted this night with her? He knew that it would be a fleeting moment. After all, he was going to head back to New York as soon as his work was completed.

But there was something special between them. He wasn't ready to put a label on it. Not yet.

"And what has you so deep in thought?" Jackson asked, noticing he wasn't the only one staring reflectively into the fire.

"I don't know."

"It wouldn't happen to be that masterpiece you've been working on every spare moment you get, would it?"

"You'll laugh if I tell you."

Jackson pulled back so he could look at her. "Why do you think I would do that?"

She shrugged. "It's what has happened in the past."

"Not by me."

"True." Serena worried her bottom lip. "I shouldn't have said that. You've been so kind to me, helping me in the kitchen and visiting the Christmas market even though you really didn't feel up to it. Those are things other men in my life would never have done. I shouldn't have made such a thoughtless remark."

"It's okay." He once again settled next to her.

"Can I have a do-over?" When he nodded, she said, "I was thinking about my script."

"You're writing a television show?" He wanted to know more about her. Everything about her fascinated him. "Have you always been a writer?"

Serena didn't say anything. He willed her to open up to him because she was like a mystery. The more he knew about her, the more he wanted to learn.

Her gaze met his. "I've always been a reader. When I was younger, I would write, but then my father found out and told me that I was wasting my time."

"I'm sorry he smashed your dreams."

She shrugged. "I shouldn't have let him. But I was young and easily swayed."

"I take it you're not so easily swayed these days."

"I'd like to think not. Time and experience have a way of changing a person."

"And in your case, I think you've made the most of your experiences."

She arched a brow at him. "You think you know me that well?"

A small smile teased his lips. "I think you are an amazing woman with a big heart. You love your puppy and you take in injured strangers."

Color rushed to her face. He couldn't believe someone as beautiful as her hadn't been complimented on a regular basis. But he couldn't deny that she was adorable with the rosy hue in her cheeks. Not that he was thinking of starting anything serious with her.

It was time he changed the subject before he said too much and made them both uncomfortable. "So what are you writing? A family saga? Or a paranormal series?"

"No...ah, actually, it's a big-screen movie." She paused as though expecting him to say something, but he quietly waited for her to finish. "A family saga with a central romance."

"That's great."

"You're just saying that."

"No. I'm not. I read some every day. Mostly biographies but I also enjoy some suspense. I think anyone that writes has a precious gift."

This time she shifted on the couch until she could look him in the eyes. "Do you mean that?"

"I do. I'd like to read it, if you'd let me."

She shook her head and sat back on the couch. "You can't. It's not finished."

"How about when it's finished?"

"That's the thing. I'm stuck. I've tried different endings but nothing I've tried seems to work."

"Give it time. Don't force yourself. If you relax, the answer will come to you."

"Do you really believe that?"

"I do. It works for me. When I'm working on a segment. I like to do a lot of my own writing."

"Thanks." She turned her head and smiled at him. "I really appreciate your support."

He lowered his voice. "Just know that you can always talk to me—about anything. I care about you."

Serena's heart jumped into her throat. She turned her head to say something, but words failed her. Her gaze met his dark eyes. He wanted her. It was right there in his eyes. They were filled with desire.

When he lowered his head, she found her lips were just inches from his. Her heart beat faster. Should she do it? Should she make the next move? Meet him halfway?

Perhaps actions did actually speak louder than words. She leaned forward, claiming his lips with her own. They were smooth, warm and oh, so inviting.

Jackson shifted on the couch so that he was cupping her face. Her arms instinctively wrapped around his neck. The kiss deepened. There was no hesitation—no tentativeness. There was only passion and desire.

It seemed so right for them to be together. It was like she'd been looking for him all of her life. He accepted her as she was and he hadn't tried to change her.

Jackson leaned back on the couch, pulling her on top of him. Her hands shifted to his chest. Beneath her fingers she felt his strapping muscles. Her heart fluttered in her chest as her body tingled all over. She'd never felt this way with a man before—not even close.

Thoughts of Jackson's approaching departure crowded into her head, but she forcefully shoved them away. If all she had after this vacation were memories, she wanted them to be good ones. She wanted them to be so good that she would recall them with a smile when she was a little old lady.

She was beginning to realize the greatest gifts in life were the good memories. She wanted to make exceptional memories with Jackson. She needed him to remember her, because she would never ever forget him. Not a chance.

Jackson took the lead with their kiss. Exploring, taunting and teasing. Her body pulsed with lust and desire. Beneath her palm, his heart beat hard and fast. Oh, yeah, this was going to be an unforgettable night—

Something cold and wet pressed to her cheek. *What in the world?*

Serena pulled back to find Gizmo standing up on his back legs with his nose next to hers. A curious look reflected in his eyes as though he was thinking: *What did I miss? Huh? Huh?*

Simultaneously Serena and Jackson let out a laugh. Gizmo looking pleased with himself.

"Arff! Arff!"

With a smile on his face, Jackson said, "I think we should take this into the bedroom."

Serena's gaze moved between her two favorite males. "I think you're right."

Once they got Gizmo settled on his dog bed, Jackson took her hand in his. She led him to the bedroom where they could explore these kisses in private.

CHAPTER FOURTEEN

SERENA COULDN'T SLEEP.

She was too wound up—too happy.

For a while now, she'd been watching Jackson sleep. His face was so handsome and he looked so peaceful. He was so much more than the alpha image he projected on television. There was a gentleness to him—a compassion that broke through the wall around her heart.

This evening had been more amazing than she'd ever thought possible. And as she watched Jackson draw in one deep breath after the other, she had a light-bulb moment. She realized the reason she couldn't finish her screenplay.

Her mind started to play over where she'd left her heroine bereft after the black moment with the hero. Until now, everything Serena had tried to bring the couple back together had felt hollow and empty. And that was because she didn't know what it was like to fall in love.

Until now...

She was falling in love with Jackson Bennett—the man who greeted America with a smile and a mug of coffee every weekday.

And he was the inspiration she'd needed to finish the script. Perhaps this was a whole new start to her life. She knew that she was jumping too far ahead and she had to slow down.

After all, Jackson had said that he cared about her—not that he loved her or that he was falling in love with her. Maybe that was the line he handed all his women. She didn't want to believe it because he just didn't seem like the type to go casually from one relationship to the next.

Was that how her heroine would feel? Or would she be confident that they could overcome their biggest obstacle? The questions continued to whirl through her mind, but she kept them relegated to her script. She would figure out where her relationship with Jackson went later—preferably after she got some sleep.

But for now, she had a mission. She gently slipped out of bed. There was a distinct nip in the air. She threw on clothes as fast as she could. All the while she kept glancing over her shoulder to make sure she hadn't disturbed Jackson. His breathing was deep and even.

Holding her breath, she tiptoed out of the room, closing the door behind her. The fire had died off in the great room and a definite chill was in the air. Gizmo lifted his head and looked at her. He didn't make any attempt to move from his oversize cushion with his blue blanket and his stuffed teddy he used for a pillow. She turned on a lamp next to the couch. Gizmo gave her a curious look as she made her way to the fireplace to rekindle the fire. But apparently it was too cold or he was too tired to beg her to take him outside. She couldn't blame him.

With the fire started, she fussed over Gizmo before gathering her laptop and moving to the end of the couch closest to the fireplace. With a throw blanket over her legs, she opened her laptop and set to work. For the first time in quite a while, her fingers moved rapidly over the keyboard. When the words came to her without a lot of effort, it was like magic. It was as though the story had taken on a life of its own. The characters were speaking to her and all she had to do was type out the words.

She didn't know how much time had passed but the sun was just starting to come up when she typed *The End* and pressed Save for the last time. She shut her laptop, set it on the coffee table and then laid her head on the backrest of the couch with a satisfied smile, her heavy eyelids drooping closed.

Quack. Quack.

Jackson's eyes opened at the sound of his alarm. His assistant, who was fresh out of college, had decided to play a trick on him and had reset his phone to various obnoxious sounds. A duck for his alarm, an old car horn for his phone and other random, off-the-wall sounds. What she didn't count on was him liking them. They were easy to distinguish from everyone else's cell phone. And best of all, it made those around him smile. So he'd left the tones as they were.

He wondered what Serena thought of his quacking alarm. He opened an eye and glanced over to find the bed empty. Serena was gone. He ran his hand over the pillow and mattress, finding her spot cold. Apparently she'd been gone for quite some time.

He sat up and looked around the room, but there was no sign of her. What did her absence mean? Did she regret their lovemaking? Did he regret it?

The reality of their actions sharpened his sleep-hazed thoughts. He'd made love to another woman. He sunk back against the pillows. Maybe it was a good thing that Serena had gone. He wasn't sure he'd be good company right now.

He'd broken his word to himself. He was moving forward—starting something—leaving the memories of his wife behind. Guilt slugged him in the gut. What would June think?

No. He couldn't go there. Right now, he had to straighten things out with Serena. He had to tell her that they'd made a mistake. But if Serena hadn't spent the entire night, did that mean she wasn't looking for a relationship? Could it be that easy?

The only way to find the answer was to find Serena. He quickly showered and dressed. His film crew was picking him up this morning. And while out and about, he'd arranged to rent another vehicle that he'd pick up some time that day.

He exited the master suite and Gizmo came running up to him. "Shh…"

Gizmo moved to the front door. Jackson glanced around, expecting Serena to be hot on Gizmo's heels, but she was nowhere to be found. Jackson grabbed his coat and the leash. Gizmo was so excited that he kept stepping in front of Jackson, almost tripping him.

"Arff!"

A distinct grunt soon followed.

Jackson put his finger to his lips. "Shh…"

Gizmo's tail continued to rapidly swish.

Jackson tiptoed over to the couch and there he found Serena curled up in a ball beneath a little blanket that didn't even completely cover her. She'd rather freeze on the couch than be snug in bed with him?

The thought dug at him as he rushed to the bedroom to grab a blanket from the bed. He draped it over her. With a sigh, she snuggled to it.

Jackson stared down at her very sweet face. She looked almost angelic as she slept. He wondered what she was dreaming about. He doubted that it would be about him. Not that he wanted her to dream of him.

No matter what Serena said, she still didn't trust him. Her sleeping out here was proof of it. And why should she when he acted without thinking? He had nothing to offer her.

"Arff!"

He had to take Gizmo out before Serena woke. It would be so much easier if they didn't speak—not just yet. He had to get his thoughts sorted. He needed time to find the right words to say to her—to salvage their friendship. Serena was a very special person and he hated the thought of completely losing her from his life.

CHAPTER FIFTEEN

THE CABIN WAS QUIET—too quiet.

Serena utilized the printer on the desk in the great room and spent most of the day proofing her script. But the reason she'd rushed in and immersed herself in editing the script had more to do with filling in the silence around her. She was amazed at how quickly she'd gotten used to having Jackson around. And how much she missed him when he was gone.

Warning bells rang in her head. She was getting in deep—perhaps too deep. It wasn't like Jackson was asking for her hand in marriage. Not that she wanted him to drop down on one knee. She just wanted to know that he cared for her—and his feelings for her were more than a passing fancy.

Her gaze moved toward the window. Evening was settling in and snow had begun to fall. Big fat flakes fluttered about before piling on top of the many feet of snow. And Jackson was out there somewhere on these mountain roads. She wished he'd taken the four-wheel drive like she'd insisted. But he'd assured her that he would be fine. If he was so fine—why wasn't he home yet?

She gathered the pages she'd been working on and put a rubber band around them. With a deep breath and a bit of trepidation, she carried the script into the master suite.

Jackson had requested to read it. Why should she resist him? After all, if she wanted it to be produced into a movie, a lot of other people would have to read it.

She stopped in front of the king-size bed. She lowered the pages that she'd been clutching to her chest. The pages still had her corrections on them, but they were clean enough for Jackson to read.

Her gaze moved to the title page. Letting Jackson read this would be more revealing than making love to him—at least that was the way it felt in that moment. They weren't just words on a page, they were an intimate piece of her. Her empty stomach roiled. She swallowed hard.

Without giving it any further thought, she placed the manuscript at the end of the bed. Then she turned and headed for the door as fast as her legs would carry her. She knew that if she didn't leave quickly she would chicken out and take back the pages.

Just then a set of headlights streamed in through the windows. Jackson was home. She smiled and Gizmo ran to the door barking.

"It looks like I'm not the only one anxious to see Jackson, huh, boy?"

Gizmo turned to her and wagged his tail before he turned back to the door to continue barking.

Serena glanced at the clock on the fireplace mantel. She would have to let the little furbaby get the first greeting. She was needed in the kitchen. She'd prepared dinner to the best of her ability and it was just about to come out of the oven.

Time to get it over with.

Jackson had played out this scene in his mind more times than he cared to admit. None of it ended well. But he couldn't put it off any longer.

He opened the door, not sure what to expect. Gizmo jumped up on him with his tail swishing back and forth. Jackson had him get down so that he could step inside and close the door.

Then Jackson bent over to pet Gizmo's fuzzy head. "Hey, boy, I'm happy to see you, too."

Maybe he should reconsider getting a dog. It was really nice to come home to somebody. But it was Serena that he wanted to see. Where was she?

He'd been thinking of what to say to her all day, to the point where he'd been distracted during taping. It'd made for a very long day with many retakes. And he'd ended up frustrating his crew. He'd apologized and blamed it on his ankle. He wasn't ready to tell anyone about Serena. They'd make more of the situation than he wanted.

He'd just shrugged off his coat and hung it near the door to dry when he heard footsteps behind him. He turned and there was Serena looking all down-to-earth in faded jeans, a red sweater and her hair pulled up in a ponytail.

There was something different about her. It took him a moment and then he realized that she'd changed her hair back to its former blond color—at least close to it.

"You changed your hair?"

She smiled and nodded. "I thought it was time that I got back to being me."

He didn't know what that meant. Did it have something to do with her creeping out of his bed during the night? Was she sending him some sort of message? If so, he wasn't sure he understood.

"It looks nice." That was not what he'd planned to say, but he was caught off guard.

"And you are just in time."

"For what?"

"Dinner. I cooked again."

"Oh. Okay." Why was she acting all nice? He thought she would be angry at him for rushing things last night. Instead, she was cooking for him. What had he missed?

"Don't look so worried. It came out of a box and I followed the directions." She sent him a puzzled look as though she didn't understand why he was acting strange. "I set the table in the kitchen, but we can eat in here if you'd prefer."

"Serena, stop it."

Her eyes widened. "Stop what?"

"Acting all nice. Like nothing happened."

"Oh. You mean last night."

"Yes, last night. Don't act like you forgot."

"How could I forget?"

At last, they were getting somewhere. "Well, say it."

"Say what?"

Was she going to make this whole thing difficult? Was he going to have to drag every word out of her mouth? One thing was for sure, if he didn't know it before, he knew it now, Serena was so different from June. When June was angry, he knew it. With the outside world, his wife had been reserved. With him, not so much. Thankfully they hadn't argued much.

But Serena for some reason was masking her displeasure. Instead of telling him the problem, she was hiding behind a friendly but cool demeanor. He didn't like it. He'd rather face the problem and then move on. So if she wasn't going to do something about it, he would.

"Say what you're upset about. Don't hide it."

She worried her bottom lip. "That's strange, because I'm usually a much better actress. It's nothing for you to worry about."

"Of course I'm worried. It involves me." He stopped

himself just short of saying that if there was a way he could make it up to her he would.

That was how he used to handle June. Then again, maybe that was how June handled him. He wasn't so sure anymore. The more time he spent with Serena, the more clarity he was gaining on his past. Maybe it hadn't been as perfect as he wanted to remember.

She sighed. "I don't want it to ruin dinner. We can talk after we eat."

He did not understand this woman. She wanted to eat first and then argue? Who did things like that? Before he could ask her, she'd headed into the kitchen.

He sighed and shook his head. He might as well as get comfortable. This was going to be a long evening. He headed for the master suite to take off his suit jacket and tie.

When he entered the room, he flipped on the overhead light. He kicked off his shoes and loosened his tie. He really didn't have any appetite. He'd been tied up in knots all day.

He sat down on the bed and his hand landed on paper. He glanced down to find a ream of paper. He picked it up and read the top sheet: *Life Atop The Ferris Wheel* by Mae Ellwood.

Jackson removed the rubber band and flipped to the last page. The last line read: *The End.* She'd finished it? But last night she'd said she was stuck.

He dropped the pages to the bed and headed for the kitchen. He plowed through the door and came to a stop when he found the kitchen aglow with a candle in the center. Dishes were set out and dinner was awaiting him. But it was the woman wearing the great big smile that drew and held his attention.

"Dinner's ready. I hope you brought your appetite."

"I, uh, sure." But he couldn't eat, not yet. There was one thing he had to know. "Did you get out of bed last night to go work on your script?"

The smile slipped from her face. "Is that what's bothering you?"

"Of course it is. Imagine how I felt when I woke up alone and the spot next to me was cold, as in you never slept there."

She approached him. "I'm sorry. I didn't think. Well, actually I did a lot of thinking. That's why I couldn't go to sleep. I realized what I was missing for the ending of the script and I had to go write it out while it was fresh in my mind. I was afraid that if I went to sleep I would forget parts of it."

He breathed his first easy breath all day. "So you didn't leave because you regretted what happened between us?"

The smile returned to her face. "No, silly. I don't regret any of it."

He reached out and drew her to him. She melted into his embrace as though they'd been doing it for years. He planted a kiss on her lips. She immediately kissed him back.

As his lips moved over hers, each muscle in his body began to relax. He had no idea until now how worked up he'd been. And it'd all been over a screenplay.

Serena pressed a hand to his chest and pulled back. "Are you ready to eat?"

He really didn't want to eat at the moment. He'd be more than happy to keep kissing her. But he knew this meal was a big deal. And he was proud of her for going outside her comfort zone and cooking dinner—even if it came out of a box.

"Sure. What is it?"

"It's baked mac-'n'-cheese. Is that all right?"

"Sure."

"And there was some bread that I picked up at the market."

"Sounds good to me." After they were settled at the table, Jackson said, "So I saw the manuscript on the bed. Did you leave that for me?"

She nodded. "Did you change your mind about reading it?"

"Definitely not." He took her hand in his. "Thank you for trusting me with it."

"Thank you for caring enough to read it."

Tonight Serena would sleep and he'd stay up. He loved to read and the fact that Serena had penned this script made it all the more special. No matter how much he tried to deny it, Serena was special. He just didn't know what to do about his growing feelings for her and his nagging guilt over letting go of his past.

CHAPTER SIXTEEN

THE FOLLOWING EVENING, Serena paced back and forth in the great room. Gizmo was right behind her, pacing, too. Back and forth they went, from the staircase to the front door. If she stopped, Gizmo stopped. He always did sense when something was bothering her.

She stopped and looked down at the dog, who sat down and looked up at her. "What are we going to do? We can't keep pacing. It's not helping anything."

"Arff!"

"Sorry. I'm too worked up to sit."

If only she had something to take her mind off Jackson's impending critique of her script. But now that the script was done, she didn't have anything else planned for the trip. If only she knew how to knit or crochet, she'd have something to do with her hands.

Instead, all she could do was wonder if Jackson had liked the story line. He'd left that morning while she'd still been asleep. And now he was home, but he hadn't even mentioned one word about the script. He could have at least given her a clue if he liked what he'd read so far.

Jackson exited the kitchen.

Serena stopped pacing. Instead of barraging him with questions about her script, she calmly asked, "Do you need help with dinner?"

"No. It's all under control."

Should she ask the question that was teetering on the tip of her tongue? But what if he didn't like it? What if he hated it? Her stomach plummeted.

Forgetting that he was still in the room, she resumed pacing. In time, hopefully the activity would work out some of her nervous tension. Because she'd resolved not to ask Jackson about the script. She would not. It was for the best.

"Anything on your mind?" Jackson asked.

She stopped and looked at him. Was he reading her mind? Or was this his way of toying with her? Well, she wasn't falling for it.

"No," she said as normally as possible. "Is it time to eat?"

"Actually it won't be ready for a while. I thought we could do something in the meantime."

Her gaze narrowed. "What did you have in mind?"

"You'll see. Dress warm. We're going outside."

She didn't know what he was up to, but it obviously had nothing to do with her script. "Don't you have something else you need to do?"

He paused as though considering her question. "Hmm… the meat is marinating. The potatoes are prepped. And the salad is ready. No. I have everything done."

She frowned at him. How could he forget about her script? Was it that forgettable? Disappointment settled in her chest. "Maybe you have something to read?"

A smile pulled at his very kissable lips. "I don't have anything urgent—"

"Jackson!" Every bit of her patience had been used up.

"Oh. You mean your script?" he said it innocently enough, but the smile on his face said that he'd been playing with her this whole time.

"Of course I mean the manuscript. I thought you wanted to read it."

"I did."

"You did? You mean read the whole thing already? I just gave it to you last night."

"I know. And it's your fault that I didn't get any sleep."

"You stayed up all night and read it?"

He nodded, but he didn't say a word. There was no smile on his face. There was no clue as to what he thought of her script. He was going to make her drag it out of him.

"And…" She waved her hands as though pulling the words from him.

"And…I think…that…"

"Jackson, say it. If you hated it, just say so."

"I love it."

"What?" Surely she hadn't heard him correctly. If he loved it, why did he make it so hard for her to get an answer out of him?

"Serena, you're very talented. Your words are vivid and emotional. I could see the entire story play out in my mind."

Her heart was pounding with excitement. And a smile pulled at her lips. "Really? You're not just saying that to be nice, are you?"

"Do I look like a nice guy to you?"

"Well, yes, you do. So I have to be sure. Because if you didn't like it, you can tell me. I can take it. I might cry myself to sleep, but I can take it."

He laughed. "So much for the calm and cool Serena Winston that graces the covers of all the glossy magazines. This uncertainty and nervousness is a whole new side of you."

"Jackson!"

"Okay." The smile slipped from his face. "Yes, I'm serious. You are a talented writer and I would like to interview you—"

"No." She didn't know how he could take such a nice compliment and ruin it in the next breath, but that was exactly what he'd done.

"You didn't even let me finish."

"You don't need to. I thought you were different. I thought you were my friend. But you're just like the others, you want something from me."

He frowned at her. "I don't know who you spend your time with, but I'm not like that. If you had let me finish, I was going to say that I could do the interview and it would be about your writing. We could start spinning the story of your screenplay and then you'd have producers and directors pounding down your door to get their hands on it."

"Oh." She wanted to believe him. She wanted to think that he wasn't after her to help further his career, but she'd trusted people in the past and they'd turned against her. "I don't think so. I want this screenplay to sell on its own merits and not the fact that I'm famous. I need to know that I can do it on my own."

His eyebrows rose. "You do know what you're turning down, don't you? I can do the interview according to your rules. I don't have to touch upon your personal life… unless you want me to."

"I… I don't know."

"Will you at least consider it?"

She sighed. "I guess. But don't get your hopes up."

"I won't. But don't dismiss the fact that you can present yourself to the world as something more than an accomplished actress."

She nodded. "I hear you. I'll consider it."

"And while you do that, I have a surprise for you. Now, go put on your warmest clothes."

"You were serious about that?" When he nodded, she asked, "What do you have in mind?"

"You'll find out as soon as you change. Hurry."

Sled riding.

Serena felt like a kid again. There was a hill beside the cabin that ended in a small field. They'd been outside for an hour. She hadn't laughed this much in a very long time, if ever. Even Gizmo was having fun riding down the hill. He took turns riding on her lap and then on Jackson's.

At first, she wasn't sure about taking Gizmo on a sled. But the hill wasn't too steep. And her pup seemed perfectly fine with it. Jackson didn't go down the hill as much as her because walking up the incline with the boot on his ankle was a hard and slow process for him. At least he'd thought ahead and had wrapped a bag around his leg to keep it dry.

Serena felt bad that he couldn't enjoy sledding as much as her, but he insisted she keep going and Gizmo had barked his agreement. Jackson had even brought along a thermos of his amazing hot chocolate. And as the sun set, she couldn't think of anyplace she'd rather be.

After they took a seat on an old log, she turned to him. "Thank you for this. Would you believe I've never been sledding before?"

"Never?"

She shook her head.

"I thought you said you went to Tahoe."

"Later. As an adult. By then I spent most of my time in the lodge." She took a sip of hot cocoa. "When I was a kid, I didn't know what snow was. My father hated it. And my mother, well, she had her own life."

"I'm sorry. I grew up in New York, so we had snow often."

"Did your parents take you sledding?"

He shook his head. "My father left when I was seven. And my mother was always working. When she wasn't working, she was blaming me for my father leaving."

"That's awful. It must have been so hard on you. I'm so sorry."

He stared off into the distance. He didn't say anything for the longest time. She didn't push him. Maybe it was time that she opened up more about herself.

She drew in a deep breath to settle her nerves. "I know what it's like to have a rough childhood. Though most people wouldn't guess it because my family had money and fame. A lot of people think that money equates to happiness. I can testify that it doesn't. Sometimes I think the more money you have, the unhappier you are."

She chanced a glance as Jackson to see if he was listening.

Jackson cleared his throat. "My father was a doctor. But when he split, he was terrible at paying my mother what he owed her. She had to fight and beg for every check. And when they did arrive, they were always months late."

"Do you still speak to your parents?"

He shook his head. "I haven't seen my father since I was nine or ten. He remarried and that was that. As for my mother, she never did stop blaming me for her marriage breaking up. I send her a check once a month to make sure she's taken care of."

"You send her money, but you don't visit?"

"It's better that way."

"Where does your mother live now?"

"In New York."

"So you live close to each other, but you never see each other?"

Jackson turned to her. "Why are you making it out like it's all my fault? My mother could just as easily track me down. My address is on every check I send—checks that she promptly cashes."

Serena knew she probably should mind her own business and keep her thoughts to herself, but she knew what it was like to lose a parent—a parent that she had unresolved issues with.

"I understand that it's tough for you, but talking as someone who recently lost a parent, I have regrets. There are so many things that I wish I had told my father. He may have annoyed me and he may not have been the perfect parent, but he was the one that was always there for me. While my mother was off moving from one younger man to the next, my father was home every night. He cared about what I did. I didn't always agree with him—okay, I rarely agreed with him—but I believe that everything he did, he did because he loved me. He just didn't know how to tell me. As a result, I never got to thank him or tell him..." Her voice cracked with emotion. She cleared her throat. "Tell him that through it all...I loved him, too. That chance was stolen away when he had a massive heart attack. Now, all I'm left with are memories and regrets."

Jackson wrapped his arm over her shoulders and pulled her close. He leaned over and pressed a kiss to the top of her head. "Neither of us have had an easy time when it comes to family. But I'm sure your father knew that you loved him."

"Just as your mother knows that each check is your way of saying that you love her?"

"Something like that."

Serena felt as though she was finally getting through to him. She shifted so that she could look into his eyes. "Tell her. Tell your mother how you feel before it's too late."

He shook his head. "It is too late. Anything that was between us ended a long time ago."

"A parent and child's love is forever."

"Maybe in some cases. But not in ours. I'm just a reminder of how her life went wrong."

"Will you at least think about it?" She knew she had no right to ask it of him, but she didn't want him to end up with nothing but remorse. And when he did realize the error of his ways, she didn't want him to talk to a cold tombstone that couldn't talk back.

"I will, if you'll agree to that interview."

Her lips pressed together into a firm line. One thing had nothing to do with the other. Nothing at all.

"Listen," Jackson said, "I know you don't like hiding who you are. I think the real you is pretty special. Don't let people steal that away from you. Stand up for who you are and what you've created."

He made a good point. It had felt so good washing out that temporary red dye from her hair, even if it all didn't come out. But was what he was asking of her the right move? Could she trust him to do the right thing? She'd heard him talking on his phone when he didn't think she was around, and he was hungry for a big story to propel his career even higher.

The only way to know was to ask. She worried her lip. If he was on the up-and-up, he would take her question as a sign of doubt in him. And if he was stringing her along for a big story, he'd never admit it. So where did that leave her?

Her heart said to trust him. He'd never hurt her. But her mind said to be cautious. She'd been burned before by people that she thought she could trust. She wished there was an easy way to figure out whom she could trust and whom she couldn't. If her past was any indication, she wasn't a good judge of character.

Jackson's gaze met hers. "I can see that you're struggling with the decision. What if we do the interview and I give you the decision of whether to air it or not?"

In his gaze, she found honesty and so much more. Her heart pounded out its decision, overruling her mind. Sometimes she overthought things.

She pulled off her glove and held out her hand. "You have a deal."

He removed his glove and wrapped his warm hand around hers. "It's a date. Tomorrow evening after my last day of filming, I'll have the crew stop by and film it for us."

"And they won't mind? You know, staying late and doing this?"

He smiled. "When they find out who I'll be interviewing, they'll be falling all over themselves to help out."

"But they won't tell anyone?"

"Not if you don't want them to. I've worked with this crew for a long time. They are a good bunch."

Serena thought about it for a moment. "If they could just keep it quiet until after the New Year that would be good."

He lifted her hand to his lips. "It's a deal."

He kissed the back of her hand. And then he leaned over, pressing his lips to hers. She approved of the way he sealed deals. They might have to do a lot more negotiating in the future.

CHAPTER SEVENTEEN

In a strange twist of fate, that car accident had been a blessing.

As the thought crossed his mind, Jackson wondered if he should have had the doctor examine his head as well as his ankle. But if not for the accident, he most likely never would have met Serena. Instead of looking forward to Christmas, he would be looking for ways to avoid the holiday.

Just as promised, the next evening, Jackson's crew showed up at the cabin to film the interview. Jackson wasn't sure what to expect of Serena. He knew that she was professional, but he also knew how nervous she was about her new venture into script writing.

Instead of dressing in the latest fashion and wearing her signature eye makeup, she'd dressed modestly in a cream-colored sweater and matching pants. Her blond hair was twisted in back and pinned up. Wisps of hair surrounded her face, softening the style. And though she did wear makeup, it was light and just enough to accentuate her beauty. She looked perfect.

They'd previously agreed on a list of questions and Jackson followed the script, even though it was in his nature to venture into unknown territory. But out of respect to

Serena, he stuck by their agreement. That was until the very end…

"Why have you decided to make this move from in front of the cameras to a place behind the scenes?"

Serena's green eyes momentarily widened as she realized it wasn't one of the preapproved questions. But he hadn't been able to help himself. He found this question to be paramount.

Like a professional, she had taken the question in stride. "I wouldn't say this is a permanent move. I've already signed on for an upcoming movie."

"That's great. I'm sure your fans will be relieved to hear the news. I know I am." It was the truth. He loved her movies. They'd helped get him through some of the toughest days of his life after his wife died. "But what drove you to try something new?"

"Actually, writing isn't new for me. The part that is new is sharing my words with the world. I think that writing is as close to magic as you can get—bringing life to a page. And I've found that I love putting words on the page."

And now that the interview was over, it was time Jackson worked a little magic of his own. He sent the interview over to his agent. He wanted Fred to have the interview edited and polished just the way it would be done if it were to air on *Hello America*.

His agent immediately phoned. As they talked, Fred got him to admit that if Serena did go through with releasing the interview to the public that it would help not just her but him as well. His agent begged him to release it or let him do it. Fred swore that this was what they needed to rocket Jackson past the other applicants for the national evening news spot.

Jackson told his agent to calm down. This interview

wasn't for him—no matter how much his career could use the boost. He'd truly done the interview with altruistic intentions. And he'd made his agent promise to have the raw footage cut and cleaned up. Then he was to forward it back to Jackson so he could play it for Serena, who still hadn't made her mind up about airing it.

"Phone me as soon as it's finished," Jackson said to his agent.

"Are you sure we can't just use some of it? I mean, come on, she's been missing for almost two weeks now. It's all the media is talking about."

"No. And don't you dare leak her location or you'll be fired."

His agent laughed. "You'd never do that. We've been together since the beginning—"

"Fred, I'm serious. Don't do anything that we'll both regret."

"Don't worry. I've got your back."

"And you'll get the footage back to me by tomorrow night?" Jackson really wanted to present it to Serena for Christmas. He was certain she would be so impressed by the results that she'd gladly release it.

"I'll do my best," Fred said. "But you have to realize that most people are already on Christmas holiday."

"Surely you know someone you can trust to turn this around quickly."

"Well…there is someone, but he's not cheap, especially with this being the holiday."

"Money isn't an issue."

"I'll give him a call."

"Thank you," Jackson said. "I'll owe you."

"And I'll collect." His agent laughed.

As Jackson disconnected the call, he knew that Fred would in fact collect on that favor. Usually it was to get

Jackson to make an appearance at some stuffy dinner that he wouldn't want to attend. But Jackson would deal with the ramifications later.

Right now, he was feeling optimistic about the final cut of the interview. Serena was a natural in front of the camera. Her face had lit up when she was talking about her script. And he'd never had so much fun interviewing anyone.

"What has you smiling?" Serena stepped through the doorway after taking Gizmo for a short walk.

"I'm just happy, is all." He stood next to the window, staring out at the snowy evening. "Do you think it always snows this much?"

"I have no idea, but I like it. It puts me in the holiday spirit." The smile slipped from her face. "I suppose now that your work is done here you'll have to head back to the States."

He reached out and wrapped his arms around her waist. "Are you saying you're already tired of me?"

"I could never get tired of you. I was just wishing you could stay for Christmas. After all, it's just in two days."

"That soon?" When she nodded, he said, "Well, if you were to twist my arm, I might consider staying. After all, my flight isn't until the day after Christmas."

Instead of smiling, she frowned.

"What's the matter?" he asked. "I thought you wanted me to stay."

"I do. That's not it. I just realized that I don't have anything for you—you know, Christmas presents." Her eyes reflected her concern. "Do you think it's too late to head into the village to shop?"

"Yes, I do. They close early in the evenings." He could see his answer only compounded her distress. "Hey, look at me." When she glanced at him, he said, "I don't need any presents. I promise. I have everything I want right here."

He drew her close and placed a quick kiss on her lips.

Serena pulled back. Her eyes opened wide and then a big grin filled her face.

"Oh, no," he said.

"What?"

"You have a look on your face that worries me. I have a feeling I'm not going to like what you say next."

"You can stop worrying. I just got an idea for a new screenplay."

"That's what you were thinking about when I kissed you?"

She shrugged and looked a little sheepish. "I can't help when inspiration strikes."

"Uh-huh. And what is this idea?"

She shook her head. "I'm not telling you. You'll have to wait and read it."

"Really? That's all I get for being your inspiration?"

"Well, maybe if you kissed me some more, you might get something you do like."

Now she was talking his language. "How about we take this to the bedroom?"

"I think that would be a good idea."

The next morning, Serena woke up early.

Jackson was still sound asleep, but that wasn't surprising as he'd had a late night—a very late night. Serena smiled as she recalled the night she'd spent in his arms.

She knew their time together was quickly running out. But she was wondering about relocating to New York, once filming for her next movie wrapped up, of course. After all, she could stand to take a break from movies, and she hadn't yet signed up for anything after this next film. If writing screenplays didn't pan out for her, she could try Broadway. Actually, that was another item on her bucket list. Why put off until tomorrow what she could do today?

The more she thought about the idea, the more she liked it. She just wondered what Jackson would think of the idea. After all, it wasn't like they had to move in together. She could get her own place. They could go slow and see where things were headed.

Slow? Like they'd taken things so far? It sure hadn't been very slow, but she wouldn't change any of the events that got them to this point—well, that wasn't exactly true. She could have avoided the whole Shawn debacle. And she was certain that Jackson would have preferred to skip the accident. But at least he was safe and they were happy together.

She slipped out of bed and put on her fuzzy robe. She quietly padded out of the room and headed for the desk. Her mind was buzzing with thoughts of New York and ideas for her next screenplay. She wanted to get started on notes for it. She decided it was going to be a holiday rom-com.

She opened her laptop and typed in the password. She paused as she realized this would be her second romance. What was up with that? She always thought she would work on a serious drama that dealt with tough issues, but for some reason, it was matters of the heart that spoke to her. Jackson's image came to mind and she smiled. He'd definitely had an influence over her.

And then she realized what she could give him for Christmas—herself. She could wrap up a piece of paper that said something about her being New York–bound. She liked the idea. She just hoped that he would, too.

But first, she had to get some writing done. When her computer booted up, it automatically loaded to her email.

It was one thing to skip town and not take calls, but totally sealing herself off from life was another thing altogether. As long as she kept up on her emails and listened to her voice mails, she let herself buy into the illusion that she was on top of things.

The top email in her inbox was from her agent. There was a high-priority flag. Her agent really needed to take some time off and enjoy the holiday. After all, it was Christmas Eve.

The subject line caught and held Serena's attention:

Call me ASAP! Damage control needed!

Damage control? For what? She hadn't been in town for days. There was no way she could have done anything to require such a message. And then she noticed that there was an attachment.

Her agent wasn't an alarmist, so dread was churning in her empty stomach. Her finger hovered over the open button. She knew that once she looked at it that it would cast a cloud over this wonderful holiday season. Was it so wrong for her to want this bit of heaven to last just forty-eight hours more? Besides, who would be looking at the tabloids over the holiday?

She closed her email and opened a new word processing document. She put the email out of her mind and instead concentrated on the idea that had come to her last night while she'd been kissing Jackson.

One of the hardest things for her to write was the opening line. It carried so much weight. It had to snag the viewer's attention. It had to set the tone for the entire movie.

And so Serena typed out a sentence that would be read as part of the heroine's thoughts…

This was to be a Christmas unlike any other.

It was okay. It gave an idea of what was to come. But it didn't pop. It wouldn't stand out and make the viewers forget about their popcorn and soda. Nor would it draw them to the couch to sit down and find out what happened next.

Her mind wandered back to her Christmas present for Jackson. Her mind started playing over all of the various messages that she could write. It could be a long letter, explaining what their time together had meant to her and how she'd been able to regain her trust in her judgment and in men. But that seemed like too much.

Perhaps she should tell him how much fun she'd had with him and that she didn't want it to end. Something like: This wasn't an ending but rather a beginning.

And then she realized the best route was the simplest one. Nine little words would tell him everything he needed to know.

She opened a blank document and started to type. She played with the font size and the color until she ended up with:

My ♥'s in New York...
so I'm moving there.

She made it so the font filled the page and then she printed it. She searched the desk until she found an envelope. Now all she needed was to dress it up. After all, it was a Christmas present of sorts.

But she had no wrapping paper. She would have to be inventive. Her gaze strayed to the Christmas tree and latched on to the red velvet bows attached to the end of random branches. One of those would be perfect.

And so she decorated the envelope and placed it beneath the Christmas tree. Now she couldn't wait for Christmas. She hoped this present would make him as happy as it did her.

CHAPTER EIGHTEEN

ALONE AGAIN...ON Christmas Eve.

Instead of getting upset over finding the spot next to him empty, Jackson just smiled. He knew last night when Serena got her stroke of genius that it wouldn't be long until she headed to the keyboard to start her next screenplay.

He was proud of her for following her dreams, even though she didn't know for sure how they would turn out. She may be famous, but she was known for her acting, not her writing. There was no guarantee that any production company would get behind her screenplays. But he was excited to know that his interview might help pave this new road for her.

He grabbed his phone to see if his agent had sent him the interview. His fingers moved over the screen until he pulled up the email with the attached video. A smile pulled at his lips. After they'd talked on the phone, Jackson had followed up with an email. He made sure to tell his agent to add music at the beginning as well as some visual narrative. Nothing was to be overlooked. This was that important to him.

Jackson played the video. It was just as he'd imagined—no it was better. And the most striking part was Serena Winston. She was a star, even when she wasn't on the big screen. Beyond her undeniable beauty, there was an air about her—the kind that princesses and queens possessed.

The bedroom door creaked as it opened. Jackson pressed Pause on the video. Then he turned off his phone. There was no way that he was letting her see it. Not yet. This was special and it was his Christmas gift to her.

Serena poked her head inside. "Morning, sleepyhead."

Gizmo squeezed past her, ran into the room with his tail wagging, jumped on the cushioned bench at the end of the bed and then hopped on the bed.

"Arff! Arff!"

"He's been waiting for you to get up. It seems that Gizmo approves of you, which is saying something because he doesn't take to many people. Usually he hides."

Gizmo rushed up to Jackson and before Jackson could move fast enough, Gizmo licked his cheek. "Yes, Gizmo. I like you, too. And it's okay, sometimes I want to hide from people, too." After wiping the wet kiss from his cheek, Jackson turned his attention back to Serena. Their gazes met and he smiled. "I don't even have to ask what happened to you. I can see by that glint in your eyes that the writing is going well."

"It is. And this screenplay is going to be even better than the first one."

"It better be."

"Why do you say that?"

"Because I was the inspiration, remember?"

Her cheeks grew rosy. "I remember." And then she pulled a white pastry box from behind her back. "I have a surprise for you."

His empty stomach rumbled its anticipation. "And what have you been up to besides writing?"

"I drove into the village."

"Did you sleep at all?"

She nodded. "But I'm an early riser."

"You couldn't have gotten much sleep."

She shrugged. "That's what coffee is for. And that reminds me. I picked up some more dark chocolate while I was in the village. I don't know if it's as good as what you bought at the Christmas market, but it was all I could get at that hour of the morning."

He arched a brow. "I take it you really like the cocoa?"

"Oh, yes. What could be better? Chocolate and fresh pastries."

He climbed out of bed. "You don't have to convince me." He threw on some clothes and headed for the door. He paused to place a kiss on her lips. "Well, what are you doing standing there? We have some cocoa to make."

It didn't take long until he had the milk warmed and the chocolate melted into it. With two steamy cups and a box of pastries, they returned to the great room. Serena had started a fire while he was taking care of things in the kitchen. And she'd thought to turn on the Christmas tree lights. It was a very cozy setting, even if the cabin was quite large.

She turned to him on the couch. "Do you know what the best part of a chilly morning is?"

"There's a best part?"

She smiled and nodded. "Snuggling together under a blanket."

He reached for the throw on the back of the couch and snuggled it around Serena before draping what was left over his legs. Gizmo decided it was a good idea and joined them on the couch.

"You know I could get used to this," she said.

Jackson leaned toward her and pressed his lips to hers. He didn't say it, but he could get used to this, too. This relationship was so different from the others in his past.

Serena was more than willing to meet him halfway, like her thoughtful trip to the village for breakfast food or her attempt to cook dinner, even though it was a struggle. It didn't matter to him if she'd burned the food, he'd have still loved it, just because she put herself out there for him.

He deepened the kiss. She tasted sweet like chocolate and it had never tasted so good. His hand cupped her face. He never wanted to let her go.

And yes, he knew that their time together was almost at an end. He had a flight back to New York in less than forty-eight hours. When he'd flown to Austria, he hadn't wanted to come. He'd been fully focused on his career and he'd wanted to be any other place but the Alps, where no news ever happened. Instead he'd found something more important—happiness.

He pulled back so that he could look into Serena's eyes. "Do you know how happy you make me?"

She smiled at him. "How happy is that?"

"So happy that I think I want to give you your Christmas present right now." When she frowned, he realized that they'd agreed to forgo presents. "Listen, I know we said that we weren't going to exchange gifts, but this is special. And I hope you really like it—"

"But we can't open gifts."

"Why not?"

"It's not Christmas morning."

"Oh." He hadn't realized that she was a stickler for tradition. And he really didn't want to wait. "Can you make an exception just this once?"

"I suppose." A big grin lit up her face. She looked excited, like a little kid on Christmas morning after Santa left a sled full of presents under the tree. "I got you a present, too."

He struggled to keep from smiling. "You broke the agreement."

"You broke it first."

"True enough." He smiled at her, causing her stomach to dip. "I think you're really going to like my present."

"Open mine first—"

"Not so fast. Maybe we should flip for it."

"Or maybe you should be a gentleman and let the lady go first."

He sighed. "I guess you have me there." He motioned with his hand. "Okay. Go ahead."

She smiled in triumph. "You're really going to like it. The present is under the tree."

He turned but he didn't see anything. "Are you sure?"

"It was right there." She stood and walked over to the tree. She got down on her hands and knees. She looked all around, even under the tree skirt. "It's not here." And then she turned around. "Gizmo."

The dog's ears lowered and he put his head between his paws.

"Don't look so innocent. It's not going to work this time." Serena got to her feet. "Gizmo, how could you do this?"

The pup let out a whine.

Jackson didn't want to see the whole day ruined. "It's okay. It'll turn up. I can give you my present."

"No." And then, as though Serena understood how bad her response sounded, she said, "I'm sorry. I'm just frustrated. I have to find your gift. I can't believe this happened. That dog is such a thief."

Jackson laughed. "I can't argue with that."

"Please help me look for it."

"What am I looking for?"

"You'll know it when you see it. It has your name on the front."

Jackson got down and looked under the couch and then he checked under the armchair. "You know, you could make this a new tradition—hunting for your Christmas present. I'm sure Gizmo would be glad to help."

"Oh, no. When we get back to the States someone is going back to doggy school. Huh, Gizmo?"

He whined and put his paw over his head.

Jackson chuckled. "I'd like to help you, buddy, but I think she means business."

And sadly, he wouldn't be around to see Gizmo's transformation from an ornery puppy to a well-behaved dog. But more than that, Jackson was going to miss Serena. She was a ray of sunshine in his otherwise bland and gray life.

But before all of that, he had his present for her. While Serena was off searching the kitchen, Jackson pulled out his cell phone to forward her the video. Luckily they'd been talking over lunch yesterday about how to keep in touch and she'd given him her email—*GizmoPuppy007@mymail.com.* He smiled at the address. He didn't think he'd ever forget it—or her.

"I have it."

Serena ran into the great room, waving the envelope around.

"Where did you find it?" Jackson asked as he stood next to the Christmas tree.

"Under the bed. I also found my wallet. I didn't even know that it was missing…again. I must have put it down when I got back from the bakery and he found it. I also found my hairbrush and one of your socks. He had quite a collection."

"Well, bring it over here." When she approached him and held out the sock, he smiled. "Not that."

She dropped the sock on the floor. "Did you mean this?"

"Yes." He snatched the envelope from her fingers.

She automatically grabbed for it, but he held it out of her reach. "Hey, that wasn't fair."

"Ah...but see, it has my name on it." He pointed to where she'd scrolled his name with a red pen.

"But..." The protest died in her throat. What was she going to say? That she was having an attack of nerves? How would that sound? "Oh, go ahead."

She didn't have to tell him twice. He jabbed his finger into the corner of the envelope and started to rip the seam open. Talk about an overgrown child.

He pulled out the folded piece of paper. His face was void of expression as he read it. His gaze moved to her and then back to the paper. For the longest time, he didn't say anything.

"I don't understand." His eyes studied hers.

Was he serious? She didn't think it was that hard to understand. But if he really needed her to break it down for him, she could do it in three words. "I love you."

Jackson took a step back as though her admission had dealt him a physical blow. "No, you don't."

AKA, he didn't love her back. And by the horrified look on his face, he didn't want her moving to New York, either. Her heart plummeted down to her toes. She blinked repeatedly. She would not cry in front of him. She moved to retrieve the note from his hand, but he took another step away from her.

With his back against the tree, he said, "You can't love me. It's too soon."

Each denial that passed by his lips was like a dagger stabbing into her fragile heart. Her vision blurred.

She blinked away the unshed tears and then summoned a steady voice. "I think what you mean to say is that you don't love me."

"I… I…"

"Save it. The truth is written all over your face."

"I tried to tell you that I wasn't ready for a relationship."

"Was that before or after we made love? Or perhaps when you offered to do this interview? Because I never heard those words. You made it seem like—well, it doesn't matter because I obviously read everything wrong."

"I never meant to hurt you. You've been great. I really appreciate everything you've done—"

She glared at him. "Stop with the kind words." The last thing she could stand now was him being all nice to her. He was yet another man who took what he needed from her heedless of her feelings. "The truth is you think that the time we've spent together was a mistake. One you wish you could forget."

"Serena, I…" He hesitated as he stared at her, seeing that she meant business. "Okay. You're right. I did things and said things that I shouldn't have done. Our time together was great. You're great. But it can't last. You've got to understand. I still love my wife."

The words were pointed and drove straight into her heart. For a moment, she couldn't breathe. So this was it. There was nowhere to go from there. She struggled to keep it all together. She forced herself to take one breath and then another. The last thing in the world she wanted was for him to see just how deeply his words had hurt her.

Serena reached for the note she'd written him and finally snatched it out of his hand. "Now that we've cleared the air. You should go."

She didn't need him to stay and make this worse. There was no way she could compete with a ghost. The ghost would win every time because he could switch up his memories to make his late wife perfect.

And Serena was anything but perfect. Hence, the misguided note in her hand. She clenched her fingers, crunching up the paper.

"Please don't take this personally." Jackson's voice was low. He took a step toward her. "Your note, it was the sweetest, most generous gesture that anyone has ever done for me. Someday you'll find the right man to share that note with. I'm sorry it wasn't me."

Her heart clenched in her chest as she shook her head. "Don't say any more. You're making it worse. Just go."

"You want me to leave now?"

"Yes." She wasn't sure how much longer she could keep her emotions in check. She'd made such a mess of everything.

"Serena, we don't have to end things like this."

"I don't want to work this out. It's not like we're in love. We need to go our separate ways. Now." And then, because she didn't trust herself to keep her rising emotions in check, she said, "I'll be in the kitchen until you're gone."

Gizmo, as though sensing her distress, had moved to sit at her feet. She bent over and scooped him into her arms. With her head held high, she walked away. After all, she was a Winston—Winstons knew how to maintain their composure—even when their dignity and their hearts had been shredded.

Once in the kitchen with the door shut, she set Gizmo down on the floor. There were no happy barks and no tail wagging. He moved over to the table where Jackson's chair was still pulled out. He settled on the chair and stared at her with those sad puppy eyes.

"Stop looking at me like that," she whispered, feeling

guilty for the mess she'd made of all their lives. "Jackson was never going to stay anyway."

Gizmo whined and covered his head with his paw.

Great. Now even the dog was upset with her. You'd think Gizmo belonged to Jackson instead of her. It looked like she wasn't the only one to let down her defenses and fall for the sexy New Yorker.

Serena moved to the window and stared out at the sunny day. The cheeriness of the weather mocked her black mood. She clung to her dark and stormy emotions. It was so much easier to be angry with Jackson than to deal with her broken heart.

She didn't know how much time had passed when she finally plunked down in a chair opposite Gizmo. By then, the pup had dozed off. She was thankful. She didn't think she could take any more of his sad face.

Her phone buzzed. Certain that it was just a friend wishing her a merry Christmas, she leaned over and retrieved it from the kitchen counter. The screen showed that she had four new emails.

Two from friends, one from her agent and one from Jackson—that was strange. What would he send her?

She checked the time stamp, finding the email from Jackson had been sent some time ago—before she'd made an utter fool of herself. What could it be?

And then she recalled him mentioning something about a Christmas gift. Could this have something to do with it?

She hesitated before opening her email. Maybe it would be best to get it over with now. But when she went to click on the email from him, the screen jumped as more graphics loaded. Instead of Jackson's email, the email from her agent opened. Before she could close it, her gaze skimmed over Jackson's name. How would her agent know anything about Jackson being here with her?

The more she read, the worse she felt. Her stomach churned when she got to the end of the email. Jackson had broken his word and had used her interview to further his career. Here she was throwing herself at a man who felt nothing for her and, worse, had lied to her. Once again, her poor judgment had led her into trouble.

She rushed out of the kitchen to confront Jackson, but he was nowhere to be found. When she moved to the window, she saw his rental car pulling out of the driveway.

She told herself it was for the best. There was no way he could undo the fiasco with the video. Right now, it was out there for all the world to see. But even worse than that was the fact that she was in love with a man who didn't love her back.

So much for a merry Christmas…

CHAPTER NINETEEN

THE OUTLINE OF the cabin filled his rearview mirror.

Jackson turned onto the mountain road and headed for the nearby village, hoping that there would be a vacancy. It was Christmas Eve. The village might be full of people visiting for the holidays. If so, he'd keep driving. There was nothing keeping him here.

He told himself he would be fine, even though he felt anything but fine. After all, he hadn't come to Austria to start a relationship. How dare she accuse him of leading her on? He hadn't. He wouldn't. He had made his situation clear to her. Hadn't he? Suddenly he wasn't so sure those words had made it from his thoughts to his lips. When he held Serena in his arms, it was so easy to forget about everything but kissing her.

Just then his phone rang. It was his agent. He didn't really want to talk to him, but it would be best to tell him that the deal with the interview was off. He put the man on speakerphone.

"Hey, Fred, I was about to call you."

"She loved the video, didn't she?" Before Jackson could respond, Fred said, "I knew she would. That's why I took the liberty of releasing it before people got too distracted with Christmas."

"You did what?" Surely Jackson hadn't heard him correctly. He wouldn't go public with the video after Jackson told him how important Serena's privacy was to her.

"Don't worry. It's trending. It's going to hit a million views anytime now—"

"Fred, I told you not to do this!" He was shouting now and he didn't care.

"Relax. I've got your back."

"You're kidding, right? I told you how important this video was to me."

"Of course it's important. That's why I had the best people in the business polish it up before I released it. And let me tell you, after it aired on your network, the video went viral. People are talking about it on every media platform. You're a hero. You found Serena Winston."

"And what about her? Do you know what you've done to her?"

His agent's voice took on an angry tone. "I didn't do anything to her. She should thank me for her name being on everyone's tongue."

"And did you ever stop to think that if she worked that hard to disappear she might value her privacy?" Serena was going to be so hurt and he'd already done so much damage. He had to do something to fix this.

"Give me some credit. I didn't tell anyone where she is." Fred's voice drew him from his thoughts. "What is up with you? I thought you wanted to do whatever it took to land that evening anchor position? Where is the thank-you?"

"There isn't going to be one. I told you the interview was to be kept under wraps—"

"Wait. You're upset about her, aren't you?"

"No."

"You are. You don't care about the tape being leaked—you care that Serena Winston is upset. What has gotten into you? Where are your priorities?"

"You want to know my priorities? My priority is keeping my word—without it I'm nothing. And I gave Serena my word that I would keep that interview confidential until she decided if or when to go public with her screenplay. And now, thanks to you, everyone and their grandmother knows about Serena's project—a project that she wasn't ready to take public."

"But this will help both of you—believe me, this is all going to work out. And I didn't tell you the best part. The network executives tuned in. They loved the interview and they want you." When Jackson didn't respond, Fred asked, "Did you hear me?"

"I did. And I don't care. This isn't about me. It's about Serena."

"And she's going to thank you—"

"No. She isn't." Jackson's hands clenched the steering wheel until his knuckles turned white.

"Wow! I've never heard you go off the handle like this."

"If you thought I'd be happy using someone I care about to further my career, you don't know me at all."

"I thought I did. You used to always be so calm and take everything in stride. What has happened to you? It's Serena. She's gotten to you."

"No, she hasn't." Besides, he'd messed things up with her. If he'd had any hope of ever making things right with Serena—this was the final straw.

"Oh, I get it. You're in love with her, aren't you? That's why you're so upset."

He may not be able to do anything about Serena's anger toward him, but he could make sure his agent never leaked a video again.

"Fred, you're fired."

Jackson disconnected the call. He pulled off the quiet mountain road. He got out of his vehicle and just started pacing. He had so much pent-up energy and he just needed to wear it off.

Because there was no way Fred was right. He was not in love with Serena. Sure, he thought she was great. And she had opened his eyes to a life without June, but did that constitute love?

Erase. Erase. Erase.

Serena sat at her desk trying to work on her rom-com screenplay but nothing she wrote was the least bit entertaining. Her heroines were snappy and her heroes were being mulish. It was a disaster.

Her muse was on strike.

And worse yet, her heart was broken. Splintered into a million painful shards.

What had she been doing letting herself get so close to a man who was obviously still in love with his late wife? She should have gotten the hint by the amount of times he'd mentioned June—the love of his life.

And then there was the leaked video. Now that she'd calmed down, she realized it wasn't the disaster she'd originally imagined. Her agent had sent a follow-up email letting her know that there had been numerous read requests for her script.

Jackson may not love her—it had been written all over his face when he'd read the note she'd given him for Christmas. And then he'd tried to gently wiggle out of the idea of them continuing their relationship when they returned to the States.

Even so. He never struck her as a liar or a man who went back on his word. She'd been in the industry long enough to know there were a hundred and one different opportunities to leak a video to the public—

Serena drew her thoughts up short. What was wrong with her? Why was she making excuses for him?

Because whether she wanted to admit it or not, she couldn't hate a man for loving his late wife. It wasn't his fault that someone had laid claim to his heart before Serena had met him.

And perhaps she'd read more into things than she should have. There appeared to be plenty of blame to go around. She thought of talking to him—of setting things straight—but she didn't have his phone number. And at this point, she was probably the last person that he'd want to speak to.

Maybe a year or two from now, when this evening was a distant memory, she'd bump into him during one of her business trips to New York. It would be awkward at first, but perhaps they could get coffee. Maybe they could find their way back to being friends.

A tear splashed onto her cheek. Gizmo rushed over and settled on her lap. Her hand automatically stroked his back, but all she could think about was Jackson and how friendship with him would never be enough.

CHAPTER TWENTY

HE LOVED HER.

He loved her laugh, her smile, and her so-so cooking.

He loved everything about her.

Jackson had thought about nothing else since Serena had tossed him out of her life. And though he hated to admit it, his agent was right. His reaction where she was concerned was way over the top. If that interview had been with anyone else, he would have dealt with it in a more businesslike, more restrained manner. But this interviewee was so much more than a pretty face—she was a breath of fresh air in his otherwise stale life.

And because he'd been too busy trying to impress her, he hadn't slowed down long enough to think about how letting her interview out of his possession could end up being a mess. Jackson paced back and forth in his rented room in the village. He raked his fingers through his hair.

He'd made a gigantic mess of everything. But he refused to give up hope on rectifying his relationship with Serena. After all, wasn't Christmas the season of hope and forgiveness?

He loved Serena Mae Winston.

Not the Hollywood star.

Not the up-and-coming screenplay writer.

But he loved the woman who struggled to cook pasta,

who was brave enough to climb in a wrecked car to save a total stranger and who didn't take any gruff from a less than stellar patient.

He grabbed his phone but then realized that he didn't have her phone number. He swore under his breath. What had he been thinking? He should have gotten it a long time ago. Wasn't that one of the first things guys asked for when they were trying to pick up women? It just went to show how long he'd been out of the dating world.

Left with few options, he started typing her a brief email. He had no idea if she would even open it, but he had to try. His thumbs started moving rapidly over the screen of his phone.

Mae. Yes, that's the name of the woman who first caught my attention. It's the name of the person I've come to admire and care a lot about—more than I realized until now.

I guess it's true what they say about not realizing what you've got until it's gone. I made a HUGE mistake and for that I apologize. I wish I could undo so many things, but I can't.

I promise you that I will not take advantage of any opportunities that come my way because of the leaked video. All I want is a chance to show you how sorry I am for not realizing what a precious Christmas present you had given me.

I love—

Erase. Erase.

He didn't want to say too much without seeing her—without being able to gaze into her eyes. He wanted her to see how much she meant to him.

He concluded the email with a simple: Jackson.

His finger hovered over the send button. He reread each

word, evaluating its meaning and wondering if he could do anything to make the email more powerful. He knew he was overthinking everything. But this message was all he had at this point.

He knew that she would see the subject line before she pressed Delete. And he only had two words for it.

I'm sorry.

His gut was telling him that this wasn't the right way to do things. He could do better. The cursor moved back and forth between Send and Delete.

He pressed Delete.

He needed to woo her over and an email wouldn't do it. This was going to take him pulling out all of the stops. He had to show Serena how much she meant to him.

It was still early—before noon. Perhaps there would still be some shops open. With a plan in mind, he rushed out of his rented room, down the steps and out the door. The sidewalks were busy with people bustling around with last-minute shopping before the big day.

A group of young people stopped on the sidewalk to sing to a growing audience. Jackson got caught up in the lurkers. He paused to listen to their harmonious and joyful voices. It wouldn't have been so long ago when he would have walked right past such an exhibition, unmoved and uncaring. But he was beginning to see all the wonderful things around him when he slowed down and paid attention.

After their first song, Jackson continued down the sidewalk. Thanks to his visit here with Serena, he remembered a few of the stores in the town square. He just hoped they were still open.

His first stop was the florist. He picked out every long-stem red rose and for double the usual delivery fee he was able to have them sent to Serena right away. He attached a note:

This is only the beginning...
J

The singers were still entertaining people as Jackson made his way to the jewelry store. He was going to get Serena a real Christmas present. One that was all wrapped in shiny paper and tied up with a red bow. It would be a gift that told her exactly how he felt about her.

The jewelry store had exactly what he had in mind. And his plan was taking shape. On his way out of the store, he knew what else he needed in order to get Serena's full attention.

CHAPTER TWENTY-ONE

READING WAS GOOD.

They said that it could be an escape from reality. And right now, Serena needed to escape from the mess she'd made of her life. After all, no way did an actress and a television journalist belong together. Just the thought of it would have made her father roll in his grave.

Serena focused on the words on the page. Her eyes scanned the sentence and then the next. By the time she got to the third sentence, she'd forgotten what she'd read in the beginning.

And so she returned to the beginning of the paragraph, intent on reading this reference book on writing screenplays. She really did enjoy writing her first screenplay and though her second had hit a snag, she was certain if she kept at it, the story would come together.

Just over the top of the book, she spotted the large bouquet of red roses that Jackson had sent her. She rested the book against her chest as she continued to stare at the beautiful blossoms nestled in a sea of baby's breath. She'd placed them on the coffee table.

She should probably just get rid of them—out of sight, out of mind. But they were so beautiful. It would be a crime to do away with them.

But it was the attached card that had stirred her interest.

What had Jackson meant by saying this was just the beginning? Had he had a change of heart? Were these flowers something that he'd planned before their big blowup? If so, he obviously didn't know that red roses symbolized unconditional love.

Her contemplation came to a halt as she heard not one, but multiple car engines. This was followed by a string of car doors closing. Gizmo awoke from his nap and started his guard dog routine of *bark-bark-howl. Bark-bark-howl.* Repeat. He took off toward the door to defend his home.

Serena tried to hear beyond the dog. It sounded like there was a whole army descending on the cabin—wait, no, not an army.

There was singing.

Christmas carolers?

Serena tossed aside her book and joined the excited Gizmo at the door. She glanced out the window to find the sun had set. Her driveway quickly filled with carolers. They were each holding a candle as they sang. And they were singing in English. Serena was impressed.

She rushed to pull on her coat and boots. Then she attached Gizmo's leash.

She picked up the barking, tail-wagging dog. "Shh…or I'm not taking you outside."

It took a moment, but he quieted down…just until she got outside with him. When he started again, she shushed him. And ran her hand over his back, hoping to calm him.

The singers were amazing. Their voices were beautiful. But what were they doing out here? It wasn't like there were houses lining the road. Dwellings were quite scattered in this particular area. Still, she felt blessed that they would come visit her.

They helped to buoy her flagging spirits. If only Jackson were here with her. She'd bet he'd really enjoy this.

But she didn't know where he was. For all she knew, he could be on a flight back to New York.

And then the group parted. It was hard to make out who was walking between them in the dark. Whoever it was, they were approaching the porch. As the person got closer, Serena recognized Jackson. Her heart jumped into her throat. What was he doing here?

She noticed that he was carrying more flowers. The backs of her eyes stung. His image started to blur. She blinked repeatedly. She couldn't believe he was here.

Gizmo wiggled and barked, anxious to get to Jackson. She wasn't the only one happy to see him. She put the dog down. Gizmo immediately ran over to Jackson, who bent down to pet the dog.

In the background, the choir continued to sing. And then Serena realized this was what Jackson had meant by the note with the flowers. He was responsible for bringing the carolers to her door.

He approached her. Their gazes met and held. Her heart started to pound.

"I'm sorry," they both said simultaneously.

Then they both gave an awkward laugh. He held the flowers out to her and she accepted them.

Serena knew she had to say more. She had to make this right. "I overreacted earlier. I was feeling insecure when you didn't like the idea of me moving to New York and I handled it badly."

"You didn't do anything wrong. I did. I totally messed up everything when you gave me that most amazing Christmas present. I panicked. And then I complicated matters by giving your video to my agent to have him get a team to clean it up and give it a polish. I wanted to surprise you with it for Christmas. But my agent got it into his head to leak the video, even though I told him not to. Anyway, he's no longer my agent."

"He's not? Because of me?" She didn't like the thought that she was responsible for someone losing their job.

"No. I let him go because I can't work with someone I don't trust."

"Do you trust me?"

"I do. It's just that I wasn't being honest with myself."

"How so?" She held her breath wondering what he would say.

"I promised June that I would move on—that I'd make a new life for myself. Before she got sick, we'd talked about having kids—a boy and girl. She wanted me to have that chance. She…she thought I'd make a good father. And so she made me promise to marry again. At the time, I would have said anything to make her happy. I didn't think that I could take a chance on love again—the loss—the pain. I didn't want to love anyone ever again. And then I met you. Do you know what you've taught me?"

Serena shook her head.

"I learned that it's a very lonely life without someone to share it with. And I don't want to hide from the truth."

"What truth would that be?"

He stepped closer to her. He reached out and stroked his fingers over her cheek. "The undeniable truth is that I love you, Serena Mae Winston."

"You do?"

"I do."

She at last drew in a full breath. "I love you, too."

He pulled her close and kissed her. It was the sweetest, most meaning-filled kiss of her life. She didn't know why it took traveling halfway around the globe to find her soul mate, but she'd do it again. At last, she felt as though she was right where she belonged.

When Jackson pulled back, he looked her right in the eyes. "Do you trust me?"

She knew what he was asking. If his career would come between them. "Do you plan to share with the world details of our private lives?"

"Only the pieces that we agree on sharing."

"Then yes, I trust you." She knew in that moment that her father had rolled over in his grave with a very loud groan, but she wouldn't let that stop her. Her father had died alone. She didn't want to end up like him. She wanted to learn from her father's mistakes.

In the background, the carolers had moved on to a slower song in German. Even though she understood only a few words, it was still a beautiful harmony.

Jackson pulled a little box from his pocket. It was wrapped in shiny silver paper with a red bow. It looked like a jewelry box. What exactly had he done?

He held it out to her. "This is for you. It is a proper Christmas present to replace the one that was ruined. I hope you like it."

Her fingers trembled slightly as she undid the ribbon and the paper. It was indeed a little black box from a jeweler's. The breath caught in her throat. When she lifted the lid, she found a black velvet box—a box bigger than one that holds a ring.

Jackson held the wrappings so that she could use her hands to open the last box. Inside was a silver heart locket. It was engraved with a beautiful design. It was delicate and attached to a thin box chain.

"It's beautiful." Tears of happiness filled her eyes. She glanced up at him. "Thank you."

"You have my heart for now and always."

"And you have mine."

"Arff! Arff!"

Jackson stuffed the wrapping paper and empty boxes in his pockets. Then he bent over and scooped Gizmo up in his arms.

Serena leaned forward and hugged her two favorite guys. “We love you, too, Gizmo.”

“Arff!”

EPILOGUE

One year later...

"I CAN'T BELIEVE you were able to lease the same cabin."

Jackson carried Serena over the threshold. "I wanted everything to be special for my Christmas bride."

She turned to look into her husband's eyes. "You didn't have to bring me to Austria for it to be special. You do that all by yourself."

Serena leaned forward and pressed her lips to his. She'd never tire of kissing him. Ever.

Jackson was everything she'd never thought she'd have. He was her best friend. He lent her an ear when she needed to vent. He offered a word of reason when she was worked up. And he was the person who filled her life with much laughter and tons of love. And she could only hope she did the same for him.

Their lives had been evolving over the past year. She'd filmed her last contracted movie and was now concentrating on her writing, which meant she could relocate to New York. Jackson had been promoted to the anchor chair of the evening news for the biggest network in the country. He had more control over the content than ever before and he was very happy. They both were deliriously happy.

"Arff! Arff!"

Reluctantly, she pulled back. Jackson gently set her feet on the floor.

Serena knelt down and ran a hand over Gizmo. "You are special, too."

"Arff!"

Serena couldn't help but laugh. "I still think Gizmo understands exactly what we say."

"I think you're right."

She straightened and walked into the great room. "I can't believe that yesterday we were with your mother next to the Pacific Ocean where we exchanged vows. And today we are in the Alps. I'm so glad you patched things up with her."

"I'm glad I'm smart enough to listen to my very intelligent wife with her wise advice."

"Aw…" She approached him and wrapped her arms around his trim waist. "You know exactly what to say." She pressed a quick kiss to his lips.

"Look." Jackson gestured toward the window. "The snow I ordered is just starting—"

"It is?" She rushed over to the window. "It is." She turned back to Jackson. "Something tells me if you have any pull with Mother Nature this will turn into a snowstorm."

"You bet. It worked well the first time around."

"You consider a car accident working well?"

He shrugged. "It brought you into my life, didn't it?"

A smile tugged at Serena's lips. "It did, but I'd prefer if you didn't get hurt this time around."

"I'll see what I can do about that. Maybe if we hide away in this cabin, you can keep an eye on me." His eyes had a playful twinkle in them.

"I think you have a good idea." She stepped farther into

the room. “Oh, look, a Christmas tree.” She turned back to Jackson. “Did you do this?”

He nodded. “I know how much you enjoy the holiday.”

“But it isn’t decorated.”

“I thought you’d enjoy doing it.” Then he pulled something from his pocket. “And I have the first ornament.”

He handed it to her. She glanced down at the cake topper from their wedding. It was a winter bride and her dashing groom; the bride was dressed in white with a hood and cape, and holding red roses. The cake topper now had a small brass hook with a red ribbon strung through it.

Serena’s gaze rose to meet her husband’s. “Did you think of everything?”

“I tried.”

She slipped off her coat and rushed over to the tree where the ladder was waiting. She climbed up to find the perfect spot for the ornament. It took her a moment to decide. “There. Isn’t it perfect?”

“Yes.” And then he started to gently shake the ladder.

“Jackson. Stop.” She held on so she didn’t fall. “What are you doing?”

“The last time you were up on that ladder, you fell into my arms. I just want a repeat.”

She frowned at him. “Stop playing around.”

“I won’t drop you. I promise.”

“That’s good, because I have a Christmas present for you. I hope you like it.”

He arched a brow. “I thought we agreed not to get each other anything since we were going to be on our honeymoon.”

“I didn’t go shopping for it. I promise.”

“So you made me a gift?” There was a look of intrigue reflected in his eyes.

"In a manner of speaking." Happiness and excitement bubbled up in her chest. "Merry Christmas, Daddy."

His eyes opened wide. "Daddy?"

The breath caught in her throat. This hadn't been planned, but she knew he wanted children. She just didn't know if he wanted them now.

Please be excited. Please. Oh, please.

Why wasn't he saying anything? Was he in shock?

"Jackson?" She snapped her fingers. "Jackson, speak."

"I… I'm going to be a dad?"

A hesitant smile lifted her lips as she nodded. "Does that make you happy?"

At last, his lips lifted at the corners. "Oh, yes. That makes me very happy. Come here, Mrs. Bennett."

She started to climb down the last couple of rungs on the ladder, but her feet never touched the floor as her husband swept her into his arms. His lips pressed to hers. He left no doubt in her mind just how happy he was about this news.

And then he pulled back ever so slightly. "What do you say we trim the tree later?"

"Why, Mr. Bennett, what do you have on your very naughty mind?" She laughed.

"As I recall, you like my naughty mind."

"Mmm-hmm…" She smiled up at him.

And with that he carried her to the master suite to begin their happily-ever-after.

* * * * *

If you enjoyed this story, check out these other great reads from Jennifer Faye:

MARRIED FOR HIS SECRET HEIR
THE MILLIONAIRE'S ROYAL RESCUE
HER FESTIVE BABY BOMBSHELL
THE GREEK'S NINE-MONTH SURPRISE

All available now!

Lying on the blanket beside Eli, Hadley didn't sleep.

She was aware of his breathing, his every movement. She tossed and turned, careful not to let her hand brush Eli's, not to let her arm nudge his. She stayed on her side and her side only. But in spite of the blankets and the sleeping bag, the floor was hard. In spite of the heater in the room, the air was chilled. To her dismay, she began to shiver.

Eli must have heard her teeth chattering because he turned around to face her. "Are you cold?"

"Yes. And I'm thinking about tomorrow, and the mom out there and the foal, and the other horses."

"World peace, and if your family's worrying?"

"My mind doesn't want to turn off."

"I think it would if you got warm. Come here."

She could tell he'd held out his arm to her.

"Come on," he coaxed. "Combined body heat will warm you up."

She didn't know if she was being stupid to try it. But she was cold. And if she was going to get any sleep tonight, she had to warm up. She moved into the crook of Eli's arm, and he wrapped it around her.

"Better?"

Oh, yes, it was better. Too much better.

* * *

Montana Mavericks:

The Great Family Roundup—

Real cowboys and real love in Rust Creek Falls!

THE MAVERICK'S SNOWBOUND CHRISTMAS

BY

KAREN ROSE SMITH

First Published in Great Britain 2017
By Mills & Boon, an imprint of HarperCollins*Publishers*
1 London Bridge Street, London, SE1 9GF

Special thanks and acknowledgement are given to Karen Rose Smith for her contribution to the Montana Mavericks: The Great Family Roundup continuity.

ISBN: 978-0-263-92344-5

23-1117

Printed and bound in Spain
by CPI, Barcelona

USA TODAY bestselling author **Karen Rose Smith**'s eighty-seventh novel was released in 2015. Her passion is caring for her four rescued cats, and her hobbies are gardening, cooking and photography. An only child, Karen delved into books at an early age. Even though she escaped into story worlds, she had many cousins around her on weekends. Families are a strong theme in her novels. Find out more about Karen at www.karenrosesmith.com.

To my veterinarians,
Doctors Brian and Jessica,
who treat my cats with expertise and caring.

Chapter One

Eli Dalton ran his hand over his pregnant mare's side. He breathed in the scents of leather, straw, old wood and the dampness from snow that had begun to fall. Worry niggled in his gut. He'd been around horses all his life, and something just didn't seem right with Amber's labor. She'd been a wild mustang, and he'd gentled her himself. He couldn't let something go wrong. He couldn't lose her foal.

Leaving her for a few moments to get some perspective, he went to the barn door and peered out. Two or three inches of snow had already fallen. Any other time, somebody else would be around to give him an opinion. Of course, this weekend of all weekends, everyone was gone from the ranch. His parents had left for Missoula for an equipment auction, and Derek, the only sibling who was still living at home, had gone with them, as had his uncle and cousins. One of his sisters, Kristen, might have been some help, but she'd flown to LA with her husband to celebrate an early Thanksgiving with him. Eli's gaze ran over the miles of fencing on the Circle D. Ranching and caring for horses had been embedded deeply in his soul from before he could remember.

He heard a noise coming from Amber's stall. She was down. He rushed to her and ran his hand over her belly…looked into her eyes. She whinnied at him, and he knew there was only one thing to do. Call the veterinarian.

"Don't you know your biological clock is ticking?"

Hadley Strickland pushed her wavy dark brown hair away from her face and glanced around the kitchen at the dishes being prepared for the Strickland clan, wondering how to exit this conversation. Her sister Tessa, who lived in LA, had a vacation home on Falls Mountain and was here for Thanksgiving, didn't hesitate to probe, question or bully. Ever since she'd found her "happily-ever-after," she was worse. Hadley was just glad her sister Claire wasn't in the kitchen right now to weigh in on this conversation as well.

Hadley cast her dark brown eyes on her grandmother Melba Strickland, who was matriarchal and grandmotherly all at the same time. But her grandmother was no help at all because she asked, "Have you dated in the past few months?"

There were so many ways to answer that question. Hadley put in long hours at the veterinary clinic where she worked in Bozeman. She often covered for other vets when it wasn't her turn in the rotation. She kept up on all the latest veterinary journals. On top of all that, she was qualifying for her pilot's license. However, the simplest answer could usually turn the subject of the conversation in another direction much faster. She didn't want anybody dwelling on her personal life.

She added cherry tomatoes to the salad she'd been fixing and said offhandedly, "I'm too busy to date."

As a small animal vet, she was thinking of expanding horizons by owning her own practice someday. But for now, if she became a pilot, she might be able to help animals at a greater distance or in the wild. She knew someday her life would come together. But she also knew it might never include romance again. Her family didn't know her secret, a secret that was embarrassing and showed how foolish a woman could be when she was wildly attracted to a man.

She could see Tessa was gearing up for another question when the cell phone attached to Hadley's belt buzzed. She kept it there from habit because she was never without it. Gratefully, she plucked it out of its case, gave a sheepish smile to her grandmother and sister and checked the screen.

"It's Brooks Smith," she murmured. He was the town's main veterinarian. She always stopped in when she was in Rust Creek Falls to check out his practice and talk to him about the latest advances in animal care. She even helped him now and then. Maybe he wanted to set up a time they could get together while she was in town. He and his wife, Jazzy, ran a horse rescue ranch, and Hadley was always fascinated by the work they did there.

She held up her finger to her sister and grandmother, indicating she was going to take the call. "Hi, Brooks," she said.

"Hey, Hadley. How are you?"

"I'm good. What's up?"

"I need a favor."

"What can I do?"

"I'm tied up on a ranch near Kalispell. Dr. Wellington, a vet working with me, quit unexpectedly, and my backup vet, my dad, just had knee replacement surgery."

Hadley knew Brooks and his dad coordinated their practices even though they were in separate locations. Brooks's dad had been gearing back, hoping to retire soon.

"What's the favor?" Maybe he wanted her to go in and check on animals at his practice.

"There's a mare in labor at the Circle D, and Eli thinks she's in trouble. No obvious signs, but he knows horses. She's down in her stall, and he's worried."

Her grandfather, Old Gene as he was called, came into the kitchen and was studying the women with a probing eye. He spotted Hadley on the phone.

"So you want me to drive to the Dalton ranch and see if he needs help?"

"That sums it up. I know it's snowing and you're spending time with your family, but Eli wouldn't put out a call without good reason."

"I have all-wheel drive. I'll be fine. Does he know you're calling me?"

"He doesn't know I'm specifically calling *you*. I told him I'd try to get somebody out there. I'll call him back and let him know. Thanks for doing this, Hadley. I owe you."

"You owe me nothing. You know, Brooks, I mostly handle small animals. Horses aren't my specialty."

"You're a vet, Hadley. That counts right now. I'll

tell Eli you're coming, and I'll text you his number in case you need it."

Drew and Benjamin, two of Hadley's cousins who were here for Thanksgiving, suddenly made an appearance in the kitchen doorway. Hosting family for the holidays, her grandparents had a full house. Drew and Benjamin were over six feet tall, and with their sudden male presence, the kitchen seemed very small.

"Are you really going out in this?" Old Gene asked.

Drew studied her with a worried expression. "This is supposed to be a monster storm. We could get a lot of snow in a short amount of time."

"Then I'd better get going," she said. "There's a mare who needs me."

And before anyone else could protest or stop her, she left the kitchen to dress in warmer clothes and boots.

Hadley veered down the lane to the Circle D, her vehicle's tires churning up snow as she drove. She'd almost been relieved to leave her grandmother's boardinghouse, and that was unusual. She enjoyed being with family. But on this visit there seemed to be pressure from her sisters, her grandparents and even her cousins to talk about her love life. She had *no* love life—with very good reason. No one knew why, and she wasn't about to reveal it. Her parents were supposed to arrive for Thanksgiving next week, and that would mean even more pressure.

Pressure for what? Finding Mr. Right when Mr. Right didn't exist? Pressure to be some woman she wasn't? Pressure to get hurt again?

She took the fork in the lane that led to the house and barn. She assumed that if the mare was having problems, that's where Eli Dalton would be. She thought about this rancher who was supposed to be one of the eligible bachelors in town. Their paths had crossed now and then, most recently at his sister Kayla's wedding. But there were so many cowboys and ranchers in Rust Creek Falls that Hadley didn't pay much attention to him. After all, she wasn't looking.

As she climbed down from her vehicle and slammed the door, complete silence surrounded her. There wasn't a creature stirring. Snow fell more heavily now, and she supposed they'd all taken cover as best they could. Montana was beautiful, but the winters could be harsh. Most humans and creatures living here knew how to survive and thrive. She was still trying to figure out the thrive part.

Opening the back door of her SUV, she grabbed her bag, closed the door and trudged to the barn. After she opened the door, her eyes adjusted to the dimmer light. As they did, she took in the scents—horses, hay, aged wood. She took a few more steps forward, and then she saw him. Eli Dalton was leaning low over his horse. She assumed it was his horse. The way he was caressing her, she saw so much caring just in the stroke of his hand. He was murmuring to her, encouraging her, and something in his tone made Hadley's throat tighten. That was silly. She'd seen a man's kindness to a horse before.

Eli's hair was dark brown, thick, and fell over his brow as he leaned forward. He knelt by the horse's back, his own back long and lean as he bent down to the horse's belly and put his ear to it. His shoulders were so broad. Although he was kneeling, she could tell his legs were long. He was wearing the requisite worn cowboy boots that looked like his favorite pair. His navy insulated vest fell open over his green-and-navy flannel shirt. He was so focused on the horse, he was totally unaware that she'd come in.

She made sure her boots made a scuffling noise as she approached him.

He looked up as if startled from his concentration.

"I'm Hadley Strickland," she said in explanation. "Brooks Smith called me to help you."

He looked torn, as if he wanted to stand and approach her, yet he didn't want to leave the horse. To help him with that dilemma, she went to him.

He held out his hand to her.

"I'm Eli Dalton. We met at Kayla's wedding briefly. In the receiving line."

As Hadley shook his hand and gazed into his eyes, her world seemed to spin a little faster. His grip was firm and warm and urged her breaths to come faster. Recognizing the red flags of attraction, she pulled her hand out of his clasp. "There was a lot of chatter and bedlam at the wedding," she murmured for something to say. "That's a wedding for you."

He gave her an odd look, and she changed the subject. "So what seems to be the problem?" She looked over the horse again from her golden-brown coat to the white blaze, from her forelock to her nose.

"I'm not sure. Amber is a wild mustang I adopted. I gentled her. I've been with her every day. I've been around pregnant horses since I was three, and I know what pregnancy and labor is supposed to look like."

"What are the signs that make you think something's wrong?"

"This is a maiden mare from what I can tell, so I know she can foal a bit early or late. She's not particularly high-strung, so I don't think she's resisting the normal process of delivery. Her udder has been swollen for the last five weeks. I've been cleaning her with warm cloths."

"And she let you?"

"She trusts me."

Hadley took that in. As she knelt beside Eli, she saw the thickened nipple. They naturally developed a thick waxy material. When the nipple got waxed, that was an indicator that the foal would be born within the next day or so. Even though Hadley didn't often handle large animals, she knew each mare was unique. All the owner could do would be to evaluate all the signs for an impending foaling.

"Will she let me examine her?" Hadley asked.

"If I stay here and talk to her, she will."

"All right, let me get my gloves on and we'll do it."

Hadley tried to forget that Eli was there as she checked signs of the rump and tail-head muscles softening. "Any changes in behavior?"

"She's been more affectionate lately and separated herself from the other horses."

"What about appetite?"

"She hasn't eaten today."

"I see you laid down straw."

"I'll switch it to shavings a few days after birth. Usually this is a natural process, but something's bothering me about it."

"Nothing specific?"

"No, but I didn't want to get in trouble with the snowstorm. It was better to have someone here to help than me not having the expertise to handle anything unusual that comes along."

Aha, Hadley thought. Eli was a planner. Rumor had it that he was steady and responsible. His attitude today proved it.

Hadley continued her examination, then stripped off her gloves and put her stethoscope back in her bag. "All we can do is wait. This could be a couple of hours, maybe more."

They both heard the howl of the wind against the side of the barn. "Maybe you should leave. Go back to the boardinghouse while you can still get out."

"Brooks is a friend, Mr. Dalton. He asked me to help so I'm here to help. I'm staying."

Eli had to be a good six foot four. She was only five foot four. He studied her with probing green eyes from her green jacket to her cowl-necked pullover sweater to her skinny blue jeans and boots. "All right," he said, "But call me Eli."

"And I'm Hadley."

He nodded. "It's good to have backup here, Hadley. Thanks for coming out. Have you eaten lunch?"

"No. I didn't think to grab anything to bring along."

"I'll go up to the house and get us something." He nodded to the horse. "We have to keep up our strength so we can help her."

"Amber, did you say?" she asked.

"Her coat's that color," he explained. "And her eyes."

A man who noticed the color of a horse's eyes. Eli Dalton was intriguing her more and more.

As Eli trudged through four inches of snow to the farmhouse, he knew he shouldn't feel hot. It was just the stress of worrying about Amber. It wasn't his blood running faster every time he looked at Hadley Strickland.

Although he'd more than noticed her when they'd crossed paths in the past, he'd never gone out of his way to chat her up. There was good reason for that. He knew her type all too well. She was educated and career-minded just as Elaine had been. His thoughts wanted to take him back twelve years, but he resisted as he always did. He had no intention of ever getting involved with a woman like that again. Since then, "serious" hadn't been on his mind.

He knocked the snow from his boots before he went into the house. Once inside, it didn't take him long. His mom always had the refrigerator stocked. After all, hungry ranch hands needed fuel. He scooped together sandwiches with thick bread and lots of meat and cheese, then slipped them into ziplock bags and put those into a grocery bag. He grabbed packets of mayonnaise and mustard from the refrigerator shelf. His mom kept plenty in there to put in lunch boxes for when they were out for the day fixing fence or other repairs. Next, he brewed coffee. When it was ready, he poured it into a large thermos, grabbed a tin of cookies, a few foam cups and paper dishes, then pushed everything into another grocery bag. Picking up both bags and the thermos, he headed out again.

In the barn once more, Eli spotted Hadley standing at Amber's stall. The mare was back on her feet.

"She's not ready," Hadley said. "I think she's trying to help herself."

"You mean let gravity help her," Eli amended.

Hadley looked at him then, her gaze locking to his.

He felt a jolt of elemental attraction that he attempted to dismiss.

"I told you I don't have a lot of experience with horses," she reminded him.

With difficulty, he transferred his focus to Amber again rather than Hadley and gave her an out if she wanted it. "I hate to tie you up here if it's not necessary."

"But you're still worried."

Apparently she could read him. He didn't like that. Over the past dozen years, he'd dated…but never seriously. He tried *not* to let women read him. Still, he answered her truthfully. "I am worried. Not only about Amber. The snow's getting deeper, and you might not be able to get out if you don't go now."

She laid her hand on his forearm. "I think taking care of a horse in labor is more important than my getting back to town."

The sincerity in her voice rocked him almost as much as the feel of her hand on his arm.

They stood awkwardly for a few moments because they both knew what Hadley staying would entail. They'd be cooped up here together, almost perfect strangers who knew nothing about each other. She pulled her hand away from him.

They might be strangers, but he was becoming more curious about her.

"Come on," he said. "Let's go into the tack room and have some lunch. Dad had that area of the barn renovated so he could use it as an office as well as a tack room. He made sure it was safe for a gas-fed infrared heater. It's not toasty, but it's warmer than the barn."

Hadley followed him to the tack room.

"Living in Montana, I'm sure you've been snowed in before." They might as well get to know something about each other.

"I have," she agreed with a nod. "If I'm at the clinic, I keep the animals company. I've always been able to entertain myself with a good book, and I carry one wherever I go."

"Do you have one with you now?" he asked as he pulled a wood captain's chair next to the desk chair.

"I have one in the SUV."

Hadley was glancing around, and Eli tried to see the tack room area through her eyes. It was orderly with saddles on sawhorses and harnesses and bridles hanging on pegs on the wall. The concrete floor, absent of straw or any debris, made the space safe for the heater. The heater kept the room between fifty-five and sixty degrees when it was running. He kept his jacket hanging on a peg behind the door. If it came to it, Hadley could use his coat as well as her own. Eli's gaze swept from the computer and flat-screen monitor on the scarred wood desk back to her.

She caught him watching her. "What?"

"I just wondered if you were cold." He reached for the bag of sandwiches to give his hands something to do. For some reason, he was so tempted to push back the waves of her hair from her cheek. That was a crazy idea.

"I'm cold-weather friendly," she told him with a smile. "Even though I spend most of my hours in the clinic with small animals, I do like to hike and cross-country ski."

He arched his brows. "Good to know."

A few minutes later he'd laid out everything he brought into the tack room and poured the coffee into the insulated cups. She looked at all of it a bit wide-eyed.

"What's wrong?" he asked.

Her cheeks reddened. "This is really thoughtful."

He chuckled. "Making a few sandwiches and brewing coffee?"

"You brought chips and cookies, too."

There was something in her voice that made him study her. "Why do you think that's thoughtful? I need to eat as well as you."

"Never mind," she said, her cheeks growing a little redder.

He handed her a sandwich. "We could be here a while. We need stuff to talk about. Feel free to spill anything you want."

Now she laughed. "It's no deep, dark secret."

Although those were the words that came from her very pretty lips, a shadow passed over her eyes. That shadow convinced Eli that maybe Hadley Strickland *did* have secrets. He waited.

"I've just come to expect men to think about themselves first."

To lighten the mood, he grinned at her. "I did. I was hungry."

She gave him a steady look. "Let's just say I think your momma taught you well."

That gave him pause. "She did," he agreed. "Though with my brother Derek, I'm not sure he had his ears open."

Hadley laughed. "He *does* have a reputation."

"You've heard about it from Melba and Old Gene? Or maybe your sisters?"

"My sisters mostly. Not that we talk about men every time we get together." There was amusement in her voice, and he wondered what they *did* talk about. Family? Their goals and dreams?

After taking a few bites of his sandwich and having a swallow of coffee, he asked, "How long are you staying in Rust Creek Falls?"

"I plan to stay until after Thanksgiving. My mom and dad will be joining the rest of the clan here." When she said it, she wrinkled her nose slightly. When she did, he noticed freckles on her cheeks. She had such a beautiful natural look.

He cleared his throat and asked, "You're not glad your mom and dad are coming?"

She looked thoughtful for a moment then shrugged. "Oh, I love spending time with Mom and Dad and the rest of my family. It's just that sometimes they gang up on me because my life isn't as settled as theirs. As long as I can keep the conversation on everybody else, we're good."

In the silence that followed, Hadley's cell phone beeped. She'd opened her coat, and now she pulled the phone from a holder on her belt. Eli couldn't help but glimpse under her coat—at her softly rounded breasts, her slim waist. She wasn't tall either. Just how well did she handle the animals she treated?

When she seemed to hesitate about answering the call or text message, he encouraged her to do it. "You'd better use your phone while you can. Service is spotty out here on the best days, and on days like this, it can cut out anytime."

She checked her phone and smiled. "It's my grandmother. She wants to know if I got here safely." Her thumbs worked the small keyboard, and then she returned to eating her sandwich.

"What did you tell Melba?"

"That I'm midwifing and don't know when I'll be back."

"And you added, *Don't worry about me*," he guessed.

"You obviously understand the protective family."

"I'm protective myself at times." After all, he was the oldest. He'd learned responsibility at a young age. He'd not only learned it but accepted it. Taking care of those around him came naturally to him.

Suddenly Hadley put her sandwich down and looked over her shoulder.

"What is it?"

She put her finger to her lips to shush him, and seemed to listen intently. Then she got to her feet and was careful to step softly toward the shelves to the rear of the tack room.

"A field mouse could have made its way in here," he began.

But Hadley paid no attention. Instead she bent over to the lowest shelf, moved a box of grooming equipment and scooped up something. When she turned around, in her arms she held a kitten.

At that moment, Eli knew he was in big trouble. Hadley Strickland standing there with a kitten in the crook of her arm was a sight that made his blood run fast and his heart increase its rhythm. Just what he didn't need—an attraction to a well-educated woman who probably considered ranch life foreign to her. He had to get his libido under control and do it *fast*.

Chapter Two

Hadley walked toward Eli, and for a few seconds he thought about backing up. But he couldn't. He was mesmerized by her and the kitten in her arms.

As she stood in front of him, she handed him the kitten. "Can you hold her? I think the mom is back there, too."

What choice did he have? Along with catching Hadley's vanilla scent that was so different from the perfumes women usually wore, besides being close enough to think about touching her hair that looked even softer than he originally thought it might be, besides staring at her lips for a nanosecond and imagining—

Coming back to reality with a jolt, he took the kitten and nestled it on his forearm. It was adorable with colors split on its face. One side was tan, the other dark brown into black. All shades from gold to brown melded in its coat.

Hadley's gaze met his, and they seemed locked in the moment. Then her focus went to the kitten. She brushed her thumb under its eye.

"She's too little to be separated from her mom, so if we make friends with one, we have to make friends with both." With that she swiftly turned and went back to the shelves. In another minute, she had another cat in her arms, a lighter tortoiseshell, one that hardly looked old enough to have a litter of kittens.

"Do you think they're hungry?" Eli asked. "There's cat food in the cupboard." He motioned to the storage units near the shelves.

"Stray cats are usually always hungry," Hadley agreed. "The little one should be old enough to eat a bit of cat food mixed with water. You haven't seen them around before?"

"Barn cats come and go. My guess is they hide whenever humans come in. If I see them, I feed them." He gave a shrug. "But I haven't seen these two before."

"They probably took shelter in here from the cold and the snow. They need to be tested, and the little one looks as if she might need eyedrops."

"We can do that," he said. "They're not going to get out of the barn now, that's for sure."

Hadley settled the momma cat on the chair. Instead of scampering away like Eli might have expected she would do, she sat there and looked up at Hadley, as if grateful for the company and the attention.

"What about the kitten?" he asked. "Should I just put her down?"

"Do you have a box and maybe an old blanket? We can make her a better bed. After she eats, she might sleep there, depending on the mom."

"You said they need to be tested. What are you testing for?"

"Feline leukemia and FIV."

"And if they have it?"

"We'll talk after they're tested. No use jumping the gun."

Eli handed Hadley the kitten, understanding that she dealt with this every day—clients bringing pets for her care, clients losing pets, clients hoping Hadley could make everything better. He found the food, then emptied a box that held old tack that needed repair. In no time, he'd created a bed with a fleece saddle pad.

Eli searched for something they could use for dishes. He borrowed the lid to a jar that held organic cookie treats for the horses. It was big enough that both mom and kitten could eat from it.

Handing it to Hadley along with a bottle of water from a case on the floor, he said, "This is the best I could do."

"This will work great. Are you sure you've never done this before?"

"There's a first time for everything."

When their eyes met, Eli thought he caught a flash of attraction in Hadley's brown gaze. He knew *he* was feeling it. Maybe it was just the idea of being cooped up during a snowstorm that made their awareness of each other so intense.

"I'll check on Amber," he said gruffly and exited the tack room to do just that.

Hadley told herself to focus on what she was doing while Eli checked on his horse. Why did her gaze want to follow him? Eli drew her eyes to him like he was a magnet and she was the weakest piece of metal. It wasn't just his broad shoulders, though they *were* broad. It wasn't his slim hips and his flat stomach under his vest, though she could imagine a six-pack under his flannel shirt. It wasn't his long legs encased in jeans that fit oh, so well. How often had she seen cowboys in jeans? Eli's jeans looked as if they were comfortable, worn white in some places. She *had* to stop sneaking peeks at him.

Focusing on the cat food and the water, she mixed it together in the lid. As soon as she lowered it to the floor, momma cat was there instantly and so was baby. Only baby seemed to be having a hard time of it. Not used to eating food from a dish? That was easily fixed.

Hadley dipped her finger into the mixture and held it to the kitten's nose. The kitten's little pink tongue snuck out and lapped at her finger. The hairs on the nape of her neck prickled, and she felt Eli's presence as soon as he was near. It wasn't his shadow. It wasn't the soapy leather scent that seemed to surround him. It was just… him. He was back and watching her.

Hadley knew about the cowboy kind. She'd dated a few. They were hardworking, but often narrow-minded, never looking at the world around them, only at the world they knew.

Eli hunkered down next to her and lifted the cat food can. "It looks like she needs a little more." He forked more food into the lid, his arm bumping hers.

Hadley poured more water from the bottle and almost spilled it. Being this close to Eli made her feel a bit shaky. How crazy was that?

"Do you really think they'll sleep in the box?" he asked.

As she turned to face him, her body was close to his.

She took in the details of his face, the lines around his eyes, the slight furrow in his brow. There was a light scar on the left side of his cheek, and her fingers suddenly itched to touch it.

No, no, no, she told herself, turning away from him. She murmured, “They might. If Momma thinks it's cuddly, warm and safe.”

Giving her attention once more to the momma cat and baby, she saw the kitten was eating from the dish now, having gotten the idea from tasting the food on Hadley's finger.

Feeling suddenly nervous around Eli, she needed something to say. “They'll probably sleep after they eat. If you put the box right near those shelves where they were, they'll probably settle there. They're creatures of habit just as we are.”

She used a bit of the water to wash her fingers, and then wiped them on a napkin. She went to her bag that she'd dropped on the desk and took out a vial of antibacterial gel that needed no water and rubbed it on her hands. Then she hurriedly left the tack room to check on Eli's mustang.

Immediately, Hadley saw that Amber didn't seem to be in any distress. Maybe Eli had been all wrong about a problem with labor. Maybe she should leave while she could.

On the other hand, she sighed at the thought of being around a whole boardinghouse full of Stricklands. Maybe the truth was that it was getting harder to keep her secret from her family. In some ways, she wanted to talk to her sisters about it. Yet in others, she still felt ashamed and foolish about a romance that had been so wrong. No one really needed to know what she'd done.

Not ever. But keeping her past romantic mistake to herself sometimes made her feel as if there was a wall between her and her family.

As she walked back to the tack room, she glimpsed Eli setting the box near the shelves. Joining him, she watched the momma cat walk toward the box and the baby follow. Momma circled a few times, hopped in and kneaded the saddle pad. Baby hopped in with her. Soon she was suckling her mom.

With a smile that made Hadley feel tingly all over, Eli studied the cats with her. Then he asked about Amber. Though she told him the mare was fine, he obviously needed to see for himself.

In the barn once more, he ran practiced hands over Amber's flanks. "She's restless, but not pushing. I don't know what happened earlier. She's even eaten a little."

"We'll keep watching her," Hadley assured him.

The gusts of wind outside suddenly became more forceful. The side door of the barn blew open, and more than one horse whinnied.

"I'll get it," Hadley said, rushing toward the door.

"Put the bar across," Eli called to her. "Or do you want me to do it?"

"I can do it," she called back. She might be short and slender, but she was strong. She worked out with weights when she could. She had to stay strong to lift animals, even though she was a small animal vet. Sometimes she had to handle German shepherds that could weigh ninety or a hundred pounds.

The vehemence of the wind pushed against the door, and she pushed back, closing it with a bang. She hefted up the plank of wood beside the doorjamb and swung it into place. She glanced toward the other end of the barn, where, luckily, the large airplane hangar-style door was securely latched. When the wind blew, the plank rumbled a little, but it wasn't going anywhere. She couldn't see out of the high windows up above. Falling snow completely blocked them.

Eli came out from the stall. "That was impressive. Do you handle elephants in your small pet practice?"

She laughed. "No, but I try not to let the big dogs run away with me. I had to lift a pregnant Newfoundland once. Ever since then, I've kept up my strength. It comes in handy at times like these."

He beckoned to the tack room. "Come on, let's finish our lunch. Maybe nibbling on those cookies will help us forget about the wind howling outside. Are you nervous being in here?"

Following him to the warmest spot in the barn, she sat in the captain's chair and watched as he poured coffee into the top of the thermos and handed that cup to her. He used a foam cup for himself.

"Nervous?" she asked. "You mean about the storm?"

"About the storm, about being cooped up in here with a relative stranger, about not knowing when you'll get out."

She motioned to the heater. "We have heat." She gestured to the cookie tin. "We have food." She pointed to the water. "We even have bottled water. That's more than a lot of people have on a daily basis. I think we'll survive. No, I'm not nervous." Though if she was really honest with herself, being this close to Eli in a confined space caused the jitters to plague her.

"How long did it take you to gentle Amber?" Conversation seemed the best way to calm them. She had to admit she wanted to know Eli better.

"It depends on what you mean by *gentling*," he explained. "It took about a week until she would come to the fence when I called. I just sat there and spoke to her in a low voice, not expecting anything from her. The next part of the gentling was treats. A hungry horse will want to get to know you faster. I ordered those organic cookies that are supposed to be good for horses. She definitely needed her share of vitamins. She took to them. I'd hold out one of those and she'd come right up. She was still skittish, but after another week or so of that, she let me touch her. First her neck, then her flank, then her nose. I would just go outside and sit with her and whittle."

"Whittle?"

He shrugged. "It's just a hobby of mine."

"So you took time out of your daily schedule to spend with Amber?"

"I did. How else was I going to get to know her, or let her get to know me?"

Hadley pulled one of the cookies from the tin to give herself something to do and something else to think about other than the sound of Eli's voice and the idea of him running a hand down Amber's flank. The cookie was chocolate chip, and she took a bite and savored it. "Great cookies."

"My mom knows how to bake."

"Melba does, too," Hadley said. "And she teaches me favorite recipes whenever I'm around her."

"Do you cook much for yourself?" Eli asked.

Hadley shook her head. "I'm rarely at my place. Mostly I pick up takeout. Sometimes on weekends I'll make a stew or soup, sticky buns or a loaf of bread. It isn't that I don't know how, it's just that I don't have time. I'm taking lessons for my pilot's license now. I have even less leisure time than before."

For some reason, Eli frowned. "A pilot's license. You sound like a woman who wants adventure."

Something about the edge to his voice told her he didn't think that was a good thing. "I don't know about wanting adventure. I just don't want my life to be static. Piloting a small plane could help me reach patients at a greater distance, even the wild horses if they need medical care. I haven't figured it all out yet. I just know I want to." Changing the subject away from her life, she said, "I understand you have cousins staying here now."

"I do, but I'm not in the mix too much. I built a cabin on my chunk of the ranch in late summer, so I have privacy when I want it. My brother Jonah designed it, and I worked on it myself."

"Did you decorate it, too?" She could imagine that it was a bachelor pad with a requisite big-screen TV, recliner, king-size bed and not much else.

But Eli answered her seriously. "My sister Kristen gave me some suggestions, but for the most part I went online and found the rest."

"You mean like stuff for the walls?"

"Why sound so surprised?" he asked with amusement twinkling in his eyes. "I like art and pottery. There's a wall hanging a friend of my mom's made. Or are you more surprised that I know how to use a computer? I'm a rancher, Hadley, but that doesn't mean I don't have other skills."

He seemed insulted when he said it, and she'd never meant for anything she'd said to be an insult. But she must have touched some kind of nerve because he definitely had withdrawn.

Taking a cookie from the tin, he stood. “If you could keep an eye on Amber, I’m going to check on the other horses. Just yell if you need me.” Then he gave her a look. “Yell if Amber needs me. I have the feeling you’re the type of woman who doesn’t need anyone.”

Leaving her sitting there with her mouth practically open, he left.

Eli had to admit he didn’t know what had gotten into him. Maybe he’d just wanted to put some kind of wedge between himself and Hadley since they’d been thrown into this situation that had seemed to produce a potent attraction. Or maybe, truth be told, he’d never put his failed relationship with Elaine in the past. He thought he’d gotten over any insecurity he might have had about not going to college or seeking a higher education. At the time, he’d told himself it was an unnecessary expense and not essential to a good life. After all, he could read on his own, and he did. He knew about subjects from inorganic chemistry to horse husbandry, and he had traveled. He’d traveled with Elaine.

When she’d left, any wanderlust he might have had went with her. Hadley, with her education and expertise and adventurous spirit, had reopened past wounds without even knowing it. It wasn’t her fault. She was who she was. The problem was—she was damned attractive. But she seemed to have an attitude that he was a cowboy, a rancher who couldn’t see farther than the end of his nose. That’s what had gotten under his skin. Granted, he was self-taught at computer skills, but he could master any program or app. He didn’t care about just barbed wire and the best boots to wear on the ranch.

He was emptying a sack of feed into a bin when Hadley called to him. "Amber is down again."

Without hesitation, he rushed to the horse's stall, wondering if this time the foal would be born or if something else was going on. He saw right away that Hadley had wrapped Amber's tail. Smart move, and he should have done it.

"Do you need the foaling kit?" he asked. He had one and kept it well stocked.

"No, I have my bag."

He could see the placental sac had broken. The pressure of Amber lying down had probably ruptured it.

"She's starting to push," Hadley said, kneeling on the straw beside Amber.

Eli knew this part of the labor. It should happen fairly quickly. If it didn't happen in an hour, then there *was* trouble.

Amber was making groaning sounds now, and Hadley was concentrating on her and what was happening. "I see it," Hadley said, and he knew she was talking about the white sac that covered the foal.

But Eli realized suddenly that this wasn't going to be a normal birth. The foal was in the breech position, hind feet first.

Crouched down beside Hadley, Eli asked her, "What's the best way to handle this?"

They both could see the hooves, and they were flexed upward toward the mare's tail. "Are we going to lose it?" he asked, his chest feeling tight.

"We are *not* going to lose it," Hadley assured him. "Breech births are more difficult, but we can still make this as natural as possible without complications."

As Amber groaned, Eli's elbow brushed Hadley's.

Their eyes locked for a moment, and he said huskily, "I'm glad you're here." He meant it, feeling something deeply comforting because of her presence. And it wasn't simply because she was a vet.

"I'm glad I'm here, too," she murmured. Then louder, she admitted, "I haven't done anything like this since an apprenticeship with a vet right after college. But I know what to do, Eli." This time Hadley pulled on gloves that reached to her elbows.

His thoughts seemed to be in an uproar until he pulled one free. "What are you going to do?"

"Just give her a little help if she needs it. Let's just see if nature takes its course. I don't want to step in if I don't have to."

He was experienced enough to know that letting nature take its course was the best route to take. Amber giving birth was a natural process. Yet he didn't want to lose either the foal or the mom.

The foal's hocks delivered, and Eli knew the foal's hips and tail would follow. Yet there seemed to be a problem, and Amber was straining hard.

Hadley murmured almost to herself, "The hips are the foal's widest part when delivery happens this way."

"Can you help? Can you get her baby unstuck?"

"I don't want to interfere too much, and I don't want to hurt either of them. I remember when Charlie did this..."

"Charlie?"

"The vet I worked with. He was seventy and had been delivering horses for almost forty years. I can picture exactly how he handled the birth. I'm going to grasp the foal's feet and just pull gently down toward Amber's hooves. That should rotate the foal's pelvis so it can pass through the birth canal more easily. Say a prayer."

As Hadley did what she said she was going to do, Eli did say a prayer. They both seemed to hold their breath as the foal slid out, making its appearance into the big wide world.

In the next few moments, Hadley removed an instrument from her bag and broke the sac surrounding the foal.

When Eli glanced at Hadley, he saw her eyes were misty. The birth of Amber's foal had touched her deeply. His throat constricted too because a miracle lay before them. What would have happened if Hadley hadn't been here?

"You saved them," he said, close enough to Hadley to kiss her.

She seemed to be eyeing his lips the same way he was eyeing hers. "You could have done the same thing," she whispered.

He got a whiff of that vanilla scent of hers that right now seemed as magical as an aphrodisiac. Shaking off the feeling and gathering his concentration, he conceded, "Maybe. But you knew what you were doing. I've only read about it."

Her eyes searched his face. "You were prepared for this?"

"I try to be prepared for everything. But I've never delivered a breech birth."

Awareness of the fact that he and Hadley seemed to be breathing in unison swept over him.

He was also aware of the way Hadley's bangs lay near her brows...aware of her high cheekbones...aware of the curve of her lips. With a supreme effort, he forced himself to focus on the situation at hand.

"They'll probably lie like this for ten to fifteen minutes," he said.

The horses needed to rest as the umbilical cord transferred a vital amount of blood from mare to foal. When that was complete, the cord would break on its own.

"I know," Hadley responded.

Her eyes were on his again, and she was close enough for their words to mix in the chilly air. Suddenly, she backed away. "Since we still have some waiting to do," she said, pulling off her gloves, "is there any more coffee?"

Now Hadley had refocused her gaze on the foal and his chocolate-brown coat. He had a white blaze like his mom.

"Do you see babies delivered often?" Eli asked.

"Mostly dogs and cats. It's been years since I was present at a foal's birth. I'm always in awe."

"Just wait until the little one starts to nurse. That's a sight to behold, too."

She nodded, her long dark hair slipping over her shoulder. "When a baby's born—dog, cat, horse—it's hard for humans not to want to step in, care for it, wipe down and cuddle it. But letting nature take its course and letting momma and baby bond is so important. Maybe that's why some women like to use midwives at home instead of going to the sterile noisy atmosphere of a hospital. Mother and baby can bond more easily."

"Could be." Eli had never really thought about that. But Hadley could be right. Hospitals, antiseptic walls, nurses and doctors could muddle up the whole process.

He would have stepped away then to go fetch the coffee for their wait, but Hadley took hold of his arm. Her touch through the flannel of his shirt caused a reaction inside him he hadn't felt for a very long time.

She said, "I'm glad you called Brooks, and I'm glad he called me. I wouldn't have wanted to miss this."

In spite of what he'd thought about Hadley earlier, he suddenly realized his attraction to her wasn't going to go away merely because he wanted it to.

Chapter Three

Hadley had amazed Eli as she'd helped deliver the foal. In spite of being short and slender, she *was* strong, and she was capable. As they'd tended the mare, they'd been huddled close. Very close. If he had leaned in, he could have kissed her.

But the enormity of the birth had prevented him from doing that. Watching the miracle had kept him grounded—grounded in what he did for a living, grounded in the satisfaction of raising horses, grounded in the knowledge that Hadley was an expert in her field.

As they sipped their coffee on stools, watching momma and foal rest, he asked, "Where did you go to school?"

"Colorado State. It was a good experience."

"Have you been in Bozeman since vet school?"

"I have. They've been good to me at the practice.

There are three vets, so we rotate and we can each get time off. That's how I was able to come here to Rust Creek Falls for Thanksgiving."

"Delivering a foal came back to you. Maybe you should expand your practice," he suggested.

She looked over at the colt. "Actually, doing this has revved up my interest in larger animals again. One of our vets specializes in farm and ranch animals. I might tag along with him more often."

She gestured to the lid that had come from the cookie jar. "I noticed those organic cookies for the horses."

"I try to keep up with the healthiest feeds and herbs that help temperaments. I keep everything as natural as possible," he confirmed.

"You use herbs for temperament?" she asked.

He nodded. "I mix them in with the feed. I've picked up a thing or two over the years."

He wasn't sure why he'd just made himself sound a lot older than she was. But he didn't think he was. He was thirty-five.

"How old are you?" Eli asked her.

"Thirty-one. Why?"

He shrugged. "I just wondered."

She narrowed her eyes. "Did you think I was younger or older than that?"

Releasing a long breath, he knew he'd backed himself into that corner. "I plead the fifth. No matter what I say, it will be wrong."

She laughed, and he liked the sound of her laughter.

Suddenly their attention was taken by Amber. Apparently the rest period for the mare was over. She stood and the umbilical cord broke.

Hadley quickly stood, too, as did he.

Arm to arm, they watched as the foal, on shaky legs, rose to its feet. Again, Eli could almost feel Hadley's emotions as she watched mother and baby bond.

Sometimes in the past, he'd had to guide the foal to its mom's nipple. But this foal found it easily. His momma nudged him a little and accepted him.

Eli knew they weren't out of the woods yet. The placenta still had to be delivered. If that didn't happen in about four hours, the risk of infection in the mare was greater. Once again he was glad that Hadley was here. Standing close together, shoulder to shoulder, arm to arm, he was disturbed by an attraction to Hadley that he now had to acknowledge.

But acknowledging it didn't mean he was accepting it. He stepped away. "I'm going to see what's going on outside."

He felt Hadley's gaze on his back when he went to the barn door. To his dismay, he couldn't get it open.

Hadley glanced his way. "What's the matter?"

Instead of going to the back door near the tack room this time, he went to the bigger door and tried to slide it on its tracks. He managed only a few inches when snow fell in. Lots of snow.

"We're snowed in," he announced.

Hadley came hurrying to the door, looked outside and gasped. "There has to be twenty inches out there."

"Close to it," he agreed, accepting the situation for what it was. After all, he did live in Montana.

Hadley began pushing some of the snow away. She looked almost frantic.

"What are you doing?"

"I have to get out. It's still snowing. There will be

even more in a little while. I'll never be able to get back tonight."

Earlier, she'd sounded reconciled to the fact that she'd be here awhile. But maybe she hadn't considered an overnight stay. Was she panicked *because* of their attraction?

"Would that be so awful?" he teased, hoping to ease her anxiety.

Then he saw a multitude of emotions flash through her eyes. Panic. Maybe even a little fear. What was *that* about?

"I can't be cooped up with you," she said, kicking at the snow again but only managing to have it stick to her jeans and her boots.

He wasn't sure what made him do it, but he took her by the shoulders and turned her toward him. "Hey! You've got to relax. I have power bars stowed away in the tack room, peanut butter, canned stew and bottled water. As you said earlier, we have more than some people."

Just then, the lights in the barn blinked out.

"Oh, no," she said. "The electricity."

To reassure her, he gave her shoulders a little squeeze. "The space heater is run by gas, and I have battery-powered lanterns. Not to mention a butane stove to warm the stew. We're not going to freeze or go hungry. This could be one of those times when you have to roll with the punches."

"Oh, I've rolled with plenty of punches," she insisted, looking almost angry about it. She jerkily pulled away from him.

He couldn't understand her withdrawal and couldn't

help but take it personally. Apparently being cooped up with a cowboy wasn't her cup of coffee.

"Look," he said, "you don't have anything to fear from me. I'll be the perfect gentleman." He raised his hands in a surrender gesture. "I won't touch you. Promise."

Then he pushed the door to the outside world closed again before any more snow could fall in. When Hadley didn't say a word, he left her standing there as he returned to Amber and her foal.

Hadley stood in a far corner of the barn, cell phone in hand, trying to get a connection. She was upset with herself and upset with the situation. Eli wanted her to roll with the punches. She'd certainly done that in the past. But for some reason, it was harder to do it now.

She tried again to connect with Melba or her sister. But her texts wouldn't go through. She was glad she'd texted after she'd arrived. At least her family knew she was safe here.

Safe?

Oh, she was sure Eli would be the perfect gentleman because he said he would. From everything she knew about him he was steady, reliable and kept his word. Not only that, but from their conversation, she'd gleaned the fact that he wasn't narrow-minded like some cowboys. He seemed to have a wealth of knowledge about many subjects.

The bottom line was that she was attracted to him and didn't want to be. Worse, she was cooped up with him in an almost intimate situation. The birth of that foal had *made* this situation intimate. She'd felt it when the baby was born and she and Eli had gazed into each other's eyes. They both valued that momma and colt the same way. That had made Eli even more attractive to her. And when the colt had stood on wobbly legs and gone to his momma, she was so touched she could have cried.

Trying to get a grip on the situation, she told herself she could handle her attraction to Eli. All she had to do was ignore it. She knew how disastrous instant attraction could be. She'd lived with the regrets that had come from it. Attraction had caused the biggest mistake of her life.

Still, she knew she'd offended Eli, and she needed to apologize. She just didn't know the best way to do it.

For a while, Eli had been closeted in the tack room, coming out now and then to check on Amber and her colt. Whenever he did, his face softened just looking at them. But as soon as he turned away, he was stoic again.

She had to fix this. They would be stuck here together until tomorrow. She'd accepted the situation for what it was—she was snowed in with Eli. But this awkwardness between them was her fault, and she had to remedy it.

Thinking about the best way to approach the sexy rancher, first she checked on the momma cat and kitten. The kitten was nursing, and its momma looked content. Hadley hoped they were both healthy. When she left, she'd take them to Brooks's clinic.

Noticing the tin of chocolate chip cookies, she remembered she and Eli had eaten only a few. They'd be delving into the rest for supper. She checked her watch, glowing in the darkness of the barn. It was almost suppertime. Eli had set one battery-powered lantern near

Amber's stall and another in the tack room. He had a third he could carry wherever he went.

She glanced around the tack room. Eli had mentioned a butane-powered stove. Maybe they could warm water for hot tea. She always carried tea bags in her purse. It was a habit she'd started in college when she'd had a mug warmer in her room. She still carried that mug warmer in her SUV, but it wouldn't do any good if she couldn't plug it in. But a portable stove would be a means to mediation. She decided a peace offering might be the best way to start conversation again with Eli.

Rooting in her purse, she found the small plastic bag she kept the tea bags in. Taking her courage in hand, she walked to Amber's stall. Eli was sitting on a stool watching the mare. It was actually hard to see him because he wasn't right by the lantern.

He must have heard her footsteps because he turned toward her. "They seem to be doing well," he said in an even tone.

"Yes, they do," she agreed, not knowing how to begin. It seemed she was as bad at apologies as being cooped up with Eli. She wiggled the plastic bag in her hand. "I have a few tea bags. I thought maybe we could warm water on the stove. Even weak tea would be something to warm us up."

He studied her in the shadows. She noticed his jaw lose some of its rigidity, and his stance relaxed some. "Hot tea sounds good. I'll see if I can rustle up a pot to use."

She followed him to the tack room and watched as he took out the portable stove and fired it up. Then he opened the cupboard and dug around inside. He produced not only a small saucepan but canned beef stew.

"When I spend time down here with an ailing horse, I make do with whatever supplies are around. How do you feel about beef stew from a can?"

"If we can warm it up, it will be great. If we can't, I'll leave the beef stew to you and I'll take the power bar."

Opening another upper cabinet, he took out the box of power bars. "We can sit in here for a spell. If you're cold, you can wrap up in a saddle blanket." He gestured to a man's suede jacket hanging on a peg behind the door. "Or put that on, on top of your coat."

"I'm fine," she assured him, imagining the feel of Eli's coat around her, his scent enveloping her.

He handed her the saucepan. "If you want to start the water, I'll find a flashlight. We might need that, too. The lantern batteries could run out."

As Eli left the tack room, Hadley realized that he was a planner and apparently thought ahead, always prepared with plan B.

She set the water to boil and glanced over at the momma cat and kitten. They stayed cuddled together in the bed Eli had made.

When he returned to the tack room with two flashlights, Hadley said, "I'll have to feed momma again when we're done. She needs nourishment to be able to nurse her baby."

From somewhere Eli had found two more foam cups. Hadley dropped a tea bag into each. "I hope you like orange spice. That's all I have."

"Orange spice is fine. My mother has a whole cupboard full of everything from chamomile to Earl Grey."

Again Eli had surprised her. Men didn't usually notice that kind of thing. "You're a tea drinker?"

"It's not always my choice," he admitted. "But whenever Mom wants to talk, she pours us both a cup of tea. In a sense, I've learned what I like and what I don't."

From the cabinet he pulled out a jar of peanut butter. "We can always slather peanut butter on the cookies."

With a smile, she suggested, "I think beef stew and plain cookies will be fine."

Once the water for the tea was poured, Eli popped the top of the beef stew can and dumped it into the saucepan. He found a few utensils in a drawer and used a fork to stir the stew. The light from the lantern was bright in the dark room and played over Eli as he prepared their dinner.

She handed him a cup of tea. "It should be brewed. You don't want it to get cold."

"It will feel good going down."

Every time Eli spoke, his deep voice seemed to mesmerize her. She found herself staring at his face, the creases around his mouth, his firm jaw, his lips. She didn't know why, but she got the feeling that he was a sensual man, not afraid of touching.

She quickly shut down that thought and took a sip of her tea. It was hot and did feel good going down. Now was the time to apologize.

However, just as she was about to open her mouth, and probably put her foot in it, he looked away, down at the stew. "I think it's ready," he said, and she wondered if he'd been studying her face as carefully as she'd been studying his.

He'd found only one bowl in the cupboard. It had a black stripe around the outer rim and was chipped here and there. "We'll have to eat out of the same bowl," he told her gruffly. "Or you can have the bowl and I'll eat out of the pot."

"Whatever suits you is fine with me." After all, she *could* roll with the punches, couldn't she?

After a quick glance at her, he said, "You take the bowl." He produced a glove from somewhere, and when he sat on the desk chair, he laid it on his thigh. Then he propped the pot on that.

They ate for a few minutes in companionable silence, hearing only the sounds of the wind against the barn, the soft whinnies of horses stirring in their stalls, the creak of the timbers overhead as the roof absorbed the cold.

Finally, she moved restlessly on the stool and worked up her nerve. "Eli, I'm sorry about earlier."

"Earlier?" he asked as if he didn't know what she was talking about.

"I never meant to give the impression that I thought—"

He cut in. "That you thought I was just a cowboy. That I only knew how to rope a steer. That I didn't pay attention in school because my life was only here on the ranch."

She wasn't sure what to say to all that.

As if he'd never intended to say what he had, he sighed and ran a hand through his thick hair. "I guess we all have preconceived notions."

She was cognizant of the fact that he didn't mention what his might be about her.

He did add, however, "Just so you know, I ran track. I could have had a scholarship to college."

"You didn't want to go?" There was no judgment in her voice. She seriously wanted to know.

"I had other things on my mind then. And, no, I didn't see the need. One year passed into two and then three. My parents depended on me, and I'd made a life here."

He wasn't saying what had happened in those years after high school, and she really had no right to pry. She certainly didn't want him asking *her* personal questions.

After Eli had finished his stew, he set the pan on the desk. Hadley passed him her bowl, and he set that on top of the pan. She couldn't help but slip her phone from her pocket and check it.

"There's still no signal," she said with disappointment.

"Your family knows you're here." His tone was reassuring.

She shook herself free of the notion that her family was worrying about her. "Old Gene and Melba know I can take care of myself. I don't think they'll worry. What about *your* parents?" she asked him.

"They'll have watched the weather reports for here from Missoula. They'll know what's happening. I've often handled the ranch on my own, and they know everything will be taken care of."

"Because you're the dependable one?" Hadley asked.

"Something like that," he said with a nod. "I'm the oldest, so I've probably always had more responsibilities than the others."

She could easily see that.

"Ready for that cookie now?" he asked with a smile that made him look rakish and charming, even handsome. At first she'd thought his face was too craggy to be handsome, but she'd been wrong. And now with a bit of beard stubble shadowing his jaw, he was downright sexy. Way too sexy.

"A cookie sounds good," she said, noticing the husky tone in her voice. Eli Dalton made her insides quiver.

The cookie tin was sitting on the desk. Removing the lid, he smiled at her. "There's only one. Do you want it?"

"We can split it," she suggested.

He took it from the decorative tin, and she couldn't help but notice his long fingers and large hands. Those hands had been so gentle on Amber.

As if he'd caught her watching him, he said, "I washed up a bit ago. I let snow melt and added dish detergent."

"I wasn't thinking that—" Her voice broke off because she didn't want to tell him what she had been thinking. That the touch of his hand on her skin would be a pleasurable thing. She was hoping he couldn't see her blush in the dusky barn.

He didn't question her further. Rather, he broke the cookie in half and gave her the larger piece. That said something about him, too. Not only that he was a gentleman, but that he might often be self-sacrificing. No. She was reading too much into a simple gesture. No man she had ever known had been self-sacrificing, and certainly not the one she'd gotten entangled with.

"What's wrong?" Eli asked.

She took a bite of the cookie. "What makes you think something's wrong?"

"You were frowning. Not just a simple frown, but a deep one."

"Just thinking about something in the past I'd rather forget," she said truthfully, then finished the cookie and the rest of her tea. Her thoughts pushed her away from Eli. "I'm going to check on Amber."

Once she was on her feet, she didn't want to seem rude, so she asked, "Are you going to name the colt?"

"I'm going to wait until tomorrow so I can see him better in the light. I like to let the babies name themselves."

She liked that idea. In fact, she liked a lot about Eli Dalton.

Eli watched Hadley walk away with the third lantern, wondering what had unsettled her again. He took the empty cookie tin and the dirty pan to the counter. There he poured in the soapy mixture he'd made from the melting snow. That would have to do until morning or whenever someone plowed them out. That's what it was going to take. He could probably forge a path through to the house, though it would be foolish in a blizzard. If he'd been more prepared, he would have tied a length of rope from the door of the house to the barn as a guide rope. But there was really no reason why he and Hadley couldn't stay in the barn comfortably until morning. Then they could decide if they wanted to venture to the house.

He wondered if the snow was still coming down. He didn't want to attempt to open the door and have it get jammed in the snow, letting cold air in. But there was another way he and Hadley could check on the outside world to see what was happening.

When Eli returned to Amber's stall, Hadley was standing there watching momma and baby.

"This is a sight you can never get tired of," she said.

He felt that connection again with Hadley because she understood the bonds between mother and baby. "I know," he agreed. Then he said, "And I know another sight that's spectacular, too. Come with me to the hayloft." He picked up the lantern Hadley had carried to the stall.

She glanced over her shoulder at him. "Seriously?"

"I don't have a secret lair up there," he promised her. "I just want to show you something."

"Famous last words," she mumbled under her breath, and he had to grin. Just what kind of men had she been associating with?

"We'll have to feed the horses, and I want to make sure everything's locked up for the night first," he explained. "This will be the first step in doing that. Come on."

"Do I need to bring anything with me?" she asked, trailing after him.

"Nope. Just your sense of wonder."

When he stopped, turned around and studied her, he could see she had no idea what he meant. But she followed him, and that meant she trusted him…a little.

Making sure the loft ladder was steady, he asked, "Do you want me to go up first, or do you want to climb first?"

"You go first," she said. "You know where you're going."

Easily he climbed the ladder to the hayloft, still holding the lantern. He was used to doing it. Once there, he waited for her.

She climbed up more slowly, careful each booted foot was steady as she took the next rung. As she reached the top of the ladder, he held out his hand. She hesitated only a moment, took it and held on until her feet were firmly planted in the hayloft and the straw there. Holding her hand like that, he felt more than a little warmth zing up his arm. But when she was balanced, she quickly let go.

She looked around, and he could tell she was trying to compute what he wanted to show her. Bales of hay and a few farm implements sparsely dotted the hayloft. He went to the doors. They were made like shutters, two halves coming together to form the door closing. Now he unlatched the left side and let it swing open. Then he did the same thing on the right. The snow had stopped for now, but the wind still blew. The sight beyond the barn was worth the frigid rush of air.

When he beckoned to Hadley, she stepped closer, finally realizing what he wanted her to see. Under the moon glow, the landscape was pristine, white as far as the eye could see. Fir trees rose up in the distance against a blue-black sky.

"What a view!" Hadley said with awe in her voice. "This is what Christmas dreams are made of."

"Or a cowboy's winter dream," Eli said softly. "The snow causes problems, that's for sure. It's going to take us a while to dig out. We'll even have to get the corral clear so we can exercise the horses. But I wouldn't give up moments like this to live anywhere else."

One moment they were standing in the straw looking out over the snow-covered landscape, and the next they were gazing at each other. Understanding seemed to pass between them once more, and something even more potent. Hadley's face was tilted up to his. He'd set the lantern on the floor a couple of feet away so it wouldn't ruin their view of the outside. He couldn't see much, but he could see the sparkle in her eyes, the look on her face that said maybe, just maybe, she was thinking the same thing he was—that a kiss right now could be something special. He wanted to reach for her, pull her close. But if he did and she didn't want that, or if he did and she suddenly got scared, they still had the rest of the night to spend together. He wanted her to trust him, and a kiss right now could end that possibility before it even started.

A cold gust of wind suddenly blew their way, and Hadley shivered. That was a signal.

He couldn't refrain from touching her, though, so he gently placed his hand on her shoulder. "Come on. I don't want you to get colder than you are. We can go back to the tack room and warm up. I just thought you needed a little entertainment tonight."

"That view is better than a movie," she assured him, turning toward the ladder.

After he secured the doors to the hayloft, he said, "Maybe I should go down the ladder first. I can make sure you don't fall."

"I can get around on my own quite well," she protested a bit defensively.

"All right," he said. "Go on. I'll follow you."

She gave him a look that was cautious, no doubt because he'd given in so easily. He watched as she tried to figure out how to maneuver herself over that top rung of the ladder from the hayloft. Finally, she got down on her knees and eased onto the first rung backward.

"Maybe I *should* have let you go first," she muttered.

"Hindsight is twenty-twenty," he said amiably.

In the light of the lantern, he could see her glare. Ignoring it, he held the ladder steady until she was halfway down. Then he maneuvered onto it and climbed down after her.

When he'd reached the barn floor, too, she said, "You

mentioned we have to feed the horses. Any special feed for Amber?"

"It's made up in the bin next to the large one. It's a special mix that should suit her well for the next couple of weeks."

Apparently Hadley was going to help him. She easily found the bin, scooped the feed into a bucket and took it to Amber while he fed the other horses. When he passed the birthing stall, he told her, "I'll lay out blankets in the tack room. Hopefully that will be enough cushioning so we can sleep. Are you okay with that?"

"We can be thankful for the heater," she said, not expressing what she thought about the blankets.

Following the trend of her thoughts, he added, "And we can be thankful that we have friends and family out there who will see that we get dug out as soon as possible."

"And if we aren't dug out tomorrow?" Hadley asked in a low voice.

"If we're not dug out by noon, I'll get to the house somehow and figure out how to get you there, too."

But Hadley didn't look reassured by his words, just worried. "What if the snow starts again?"

"It has to stop sometime." He could see her eye roll from the light of the lantern he carried. He asked seriously, "Wouldn't you rather think about the best rather than the worst?"

"I would, but that doesn't mean the best is going to happen."

There was something about Hadley that told him she'd been through a crisis that had colored her view of men and maybe even the world. The question was—would she let him get to know her well enough to find out her secret?

Chapter Four

Hadley knew it made sense that she and Eli would bunk down together in the tack room/office where the heater was located. But the situation was still awkward. She'd be sleeping in here practically side to side with Eli! He'd gathered all the saddle blankets he could find, and now she helped him spread two of them across the floor. He'd found a sleeping bag tucked on a shelf. He'd unrolled that, opened it and laid it over the blankets.

Looking around the tack room instead of looking at him—because he drew her gaze to him much too often—she said, "This room looks a lot newer than the rest of the barn."

"This was an old barn, so we added on the tack room/ office, and that other small room for tools. It works well. We don't have to worry about the heater causing condensation in the rest of the barn."

"And it keeps the moisture from your tack."

"Exactly." He went to the shelves again and produced an orthopedic pillow. "Dad uses this when his back's bothering him. You can have it for under your head."

"What about you?"

"I'll use my vest."

"Should I keep my coat on?"

"We'd be better off under a blanket letting our body heat combine. You can use your coat as an extra covering or under you for more padding."

Letting their body heats combine?

"Eli—" she protested almost breathlessly.

"Look. I know this isn't the ideal situation. But we're both going to have our clothes on. It's not as if this is a romantic overnight escapade."

No, it wasn't. But as she studied Eli, she knew it could be. Oh, not tonight. They'd both set boundaries. But he was a hunk and she was a red-blooded woman, though that red blood had turned cool over the past few years. Yes, she'd told everybody she was too busy to date, but it was so much more than that.

"Do you need a power bar before we bunk down?" he asked.

"No, but we should check mom and foal at intervals."

"The heater's on a timer, and it will go on and off. That always wakes me. I'll make sure I check them."

"I can take my turn."

"No need if you're sleeping. But if you're awake, you're welcome to."

Eli had left a lantern switched on and placed it on the desk. Taking his jacket from the peg behind the door, he put it on, then carried the other lantern out into the barn to make one last check. She was sure he wasn't checking only momma and baby, but the other horses, too. The wind had picked up again. It buffeted the tack room addition as if it was trying to push it into the main part of the barn. But she knew the construction was solid. Anything the men in this family did would be solid.

While Eli was gone, she wandered around the tack room, running her hand over the leather saddles, realizing what good condition everything was in. Even the stirrups were clean. This family obviously knew how to run a ranch and keep it in good shape. Maybe she was just trying to distract herself because she didn't want to lie down on that floor and wait for Eli. That was too reminiscent of—

She put the thoughts out of her head.

When Eli returned to the tack room, his jacket looked wet. Melting snow shone on it by the light of his lantern.

"Did you try to go outside?" She looked down at his boots, and they were wet, too.

"*Try* is the operative word. About half of me got out the door. There's just no point even attempting it. The blowing snow is icy."

"Do you have snowshoes?" she asked, nervous because she couldn't imagine how they would ever make their way to the house if they had to.

"I have a pair, but they're up at the house. We have a snowmobile, too. Sometimes we need it to get out to the cattle. We'll have to take it all into consideration by noon tomorrow if no one's here to plow us out."

To distract herself from being snowbound with Eli, Hadley peered into the box where momma cat was sleeping, her baby tucked in beside her. She noted, "They don't seem the least bit perturbed about all this."

"You have to remember that they don't always know

where their next meal's going to come from, at least momma cat doesn't. She takes food when she can find it. She takes comfort when she can find it."

Hadley thought about that. "I guess you're right. Cats live from moment to moment. Maybe we'd be better off if we did the same."

"We're trying to do that tonight," he suggested, looking at their makeshift bed. "Are you ready to call it a night? I have to wipe down my jacket, but go ahead and get settled. I'll be there in a minute."

By getting settled, she supposed he meant taking off her hat, jacket and boots. The jacket was first. She decided to lay it long ways under her to provide more comfort. The fleece would go only so far, but she'd take what she could get. She'd worn double socks inside her boots, so her feet shouldn't get too cold. Besides dressing for the cold, she really hadn't thought about what she was wearing when she'd driven out here today. So her jeans and a long-sleeved sweater in multiple shades of blue weren't exactly her best garments. But what did that matter anyway? She was going to be rolled up in blankets on the floor.

As Eli dried off his coat, he asked, "Any nighttime routines?"

"What? Like covering my face with a blue mask so nobody would recognize me, yet it would make me glow in the morning?"

He was quiet a few moments and she didn't know why, but apparently he'd been thinking over what he was going to say. "I can't imagine you'd need a blue mask to glow in the morning."

She was speechless. She was rarely speechless. "That's an awfully nice thing to say."

"It's not just nice, it's true. You have that kind of face. When that foal was born, you glowed like the sunrise. That's the way I picture you in the mornings."

To get the subject away from *her* and his words that made her almost breathless, she sat down on the floor on the bedroll they'd made and asked, "What's it like, living with extra guys in the house?"

"When a fire burned down Uncle Phil's house, he and his five sons weren't just looking for a new house, they were looking for a fresh start. They came here to regroup."

"So your uncle has five boys?"

"Yep. Zach, Garrett, Shawn, Booker and Cole. They sure filled up our house again. I mean our family house," he added. "I'm just glad I got my place done so I'm out of the mix."

"You don't enjoy being with them?"

"They're all good guys, and yes, I like them. We can talk about ranching all day and all night. But I have more experience, and I guess I just look at life differently than they do. Take my brother Derek for instance. He's at one extreme. He wants to have fun every weekend, nights, too, if he's not too tired. Me, on the other hand, I look at the work—that comes first. I make sure I have that done, all of it, before stepping out. Zach, Garrett, Shawn, Booker and Cole are somewhere in between. But sometimes when I'm with them, I just feel a lot older, like I don't belong there."

"They make you feel that way?"

"Oh, no. They never would."

Eli set the lantern on the floor beside the bedroll and then lowered himself beside her. She hadn't covered up yet, but now she did. Yes, she had all her clothes on, but the blanket gave her another layer of protection.

In the next few moments, they settled themselves side by side with at least six inches between them. Silence wound about them like a web that was almost claustrophobic as they lay there. Hadley broke it by asking, “So do you think your uncle wants to buy a ranch around here?”

“He already has an eye on a place similar to the Stockton family property—Sunshine Farm—and he’s looking into it. He and his sons like Rust Creek Falls. They like the way it made a comeback after the flood. It could have just disintegrated into nothing like some small towns do. But the people here really rallied, and volunteers came from everywhere to help. That’s how Brooks Smith met Jazzy. She was one of those volunteers. They make a great couple. When you see them together, you just know they belong together.”

“I agree with that. Their passion is their work,” Hadley mused. “They have that in common.”

Eli agreed. “What more could they ask for?”

“I think Jazzy wants a family,” Hadley suggested.

“That will come.”

Would it, Hadley wondered? The older a woman got, the harder it could be to get pregnant. That’s what her sisters had been ribbing her about, and she knew there was some truth in it.

Thinking about that, she was hopeful she’d fall asleep, but during the first couple of hours of lying on the blanket bedside Eli, Hadley didn’t sleep. She was aware of his breathing, his every movement. She tossed and turned, careful not to let her hand brush Eli’s, not to let her arm nudge his. She stayed on her side and her side only. But in spite of the blankets and the sleeping bag, the floor was hard. In spite of the heater in the room, the air was still chilled. To her dismay, she began to shiver.

Eli must have heard her teeth chattering because he turned around to face her. "Are you cold?"

"Yes. And I'm thinking about tomorrow and how we're going to get out of here, and about the mare out there and the foal, and the other horses."

"And world peace, and if your family's worrying?" She heard his soft laughter.

"My mind doesn't want to turn off."

"I think it would if you got warm. Come here."

She could tell he'd held out his arm to her.

"Come on," he coaxed. "Combined body heat will warm you up."

She didn't know if she was being stupid to try it. But she *was* cold. And if she was going to get any sleep tonight, she had to warm up. She moved into the crook of Eli's arm, and he wrapped it around her.

"Better?"

Oh, yes, it was better. Too much better. Being this close to him sounded alarm bells in her mind because she was attracted to him. Taking a deep breath, she managed, "I am warmer."

"Good. Then don't move. Let's talk about something that isn't in your head or on your to-do list."

"Like?" she asked, wondering where he was going with this.

"Like…tell me your favorite building in the whole world."

It was an odd question, but she went along with it.

"That depends on what it's used for, or whether we're looking at it just for architecture."

"All in all."

"Probably the Louvre in France. What's yours?"

"The Smithsonian Air and Space Museum. As a boy I wanted a piece of my own moon rock."

She laughed. "Did you go on camping trips, look up at the sky and learn the constellations?"

"Sure did. Whenever Mom could, she bought us books on our favorite subjects. One of mine was astronomy. Kristen liked the classics, plays mostly. They made her into the actress she is. What did you read about most as a kid?"

"Do you know the author Zane Grey?" Hadley asked.

"Of course I do. He lived in Arizona for a while, and wrote about Oak Creek Canyon."

"Exactly," she said. "One of the most beautiful places on the planet."

And so it went. Hadley soon realized Eli wasn't like most cowboys, or even like his dad. Charles Dalton was a man of few words. Eli could easily paint pictures with his words, especially of his antics with his brothers and sisters when they were young. That made her laugh. Before she knew it, she was comfortably snuggled into his shoulder and falling asleep.

When Eli awakened, he felt totally disconcerted. He was practically hugging Hadley, and her cheek was against his chest. They'd both been up several times during the night, checking on Amber and the foal. When one moved, the other knew it, so they hadn't taken turns, they'd just gotten up together. It had been intimate in an odd way, but not as intimate as the way they were tucked together now.

The last time they'd checked on the horses, it had been 4:00 a.m. Gazing up at the frosted window, he realized it was morning.

He reached for his phone that he'd laid beside their blankets. It was almost 9:00 a.m., much later than he'd ever slept.

Hadley stirred. As he studied her, he realized she was much more vulnerable asleep than awake. Awake, she always seemed to have her guard in place. He wondered whether it was just around him, and knew he had to resist the urge to find out.

However, when her eyes flew open and she looked up at him, her brown eyes stunning, her pretty face so tempting in the morning light, he couldn't help but lean closer to her.

"We overslept," he murmured. "It's almost nine."

The momma cat and kitten were curled up and sleeping, snug against Hadley's hip. She couldn't move and didn't seem to want to. "We have to feed the horses," she said, but she still gazed up at him.

"We do," he agreed. He didn't move either. It was as if they were being drawn together by a magnetic force, one stronger than he'd ever felt before. He could see in her eyes that she felt it, too. Their body heat had kept them warm throughout the night. Now he felt as if a furnace had been turned on high in the room.

"Hadley..." he said, and leaned in even closer so she'd realize his intent.

She gave a little sigh, lifted her chin a notch and waited. If she'd given any indication she didn't want him to kiss her, he would have thrown off the blanket and rushed into the barn. But her lips parted slightly, and he decided real time and the real world didn't mean much right now. They were closeted in their own world where the only thing that mattered was their attraction to each other.

Eli was taken by surprise when his lips brushed Hadley's. Just from that simple touch there was heat and a potent desire he didn't know if he'd ever felt before. He didn't know what he'd intended, but he got more than he bargained for. When his tongue swept her bottom lip, she responded. Her hand went to his neck, her fingers tunneling in the hair at his nape. His arm curved around her tighter. As his tongue touched hers, sparks became a roaring fire. He slanted his mouth to gain better access. His tongue darted against hers, probing and stroking. She gave as good as he did.

He wasn't thinking. He was only feeling, sensation after sensation, when a noise punctured the sensual haze that surrounded them. He couldn't make sense of it at first because all of his attention was on this amazing kiss. But then the hum became a growl and then a churning, and he realized someone from the outside world was coming to their rescue.

The only problem was, he didn't know if he wanted to *be* rescued.

Either his break in concentration affected Hadley, or she, too, was aware of the noise coming from what had to be a snowplow.

"I guess we'd better—" She started to sit up.

"I'd better open the door so they know we're in here," he said.

And before Eli knew it, they'd scrambled apart and gotten to their feet. Hadley scooped up the kitten, folded her into the crook of her arm, and was petting her as if her life depended on it.

When he was unsettled like this, the way he handled it was by action. So he said, "I'll go meet them," though he didn't know who "them" was. All he knew was that whoever was running those snowplows had saved him and Hadley from either a mistake or a terribly awkward situation. What had led him to kiss her like that?

He was still asking himself the question when he shoved his arms into his jacket and wrenched the door open so hard, the wood squealed. But he still couldn't push it open more than six inches. He'd left his Stetson on a peg near the door. Now he grabbed it, pushed it through the opening and waved it outside. They should see a black hat against all that white snow.

And they did. As he watched, he recognized Old Gene running the snowplow. Hadley's grandfather drove the machine practically up to the door. Levi Wyatt, Hadley's sister Claire's husband, jumped down from the other side of the snowplow with a shovel in his hand. Gene could get only so close to the door, but Levi soon shoveled a path the rest of the way so Eli could push the door open.

Behind him, Eli was aware of Hadley. She'd come out of the tack room and shut the door, probably to keep the kitten and her momma inside. Knowing her, she'd probably fed them, too.

Soon both Gene and Levi were in the barn checking on them.

"So I see the two of you survived," Old Gene said, as he first looked at Eli and then at Hadley.

"Amber had her foal," Hadley said in way of explanation. "Momma and colt are doing just fine. I want to help Eli feed the horses before I get out of here, and I have to take the momma cat and kitten along. Can I get around anywhere in town?"

Levi gave her an odd look, as if he knew she didn't spend most nights in a barn with a practical stranger. "Main Street in town has been cleared. Some plows are working on the side streets."

Gene seconded that with a nod. "You should be able to get to the clinic and back to the rooming house."

"You don't have to help me feed the horses," Eli said. "I know you want to get going."

"It will take me a few minutes to shovel out her car," Levi said. "So you don't have to rush if you want to make sure everything's okay in here before you leave."

"I'll find you a box for the cat and kitten," Eli told her. Without meeting her gaze, he went to do just that.

He needed time to think, time to remember, time to figure out exactly how Hadley Strickland had mixed up his thoughts and his feelings until he didn't know which way was up.

As soon as Hadley was closer to town, she phoned Brooks. To her surprise, he was at the clinic. "I stayed overnight," he said. "We had a couple of patients I wanted to make sure were okay."

"Jazzy was alone at the ranch?" She thought about the horses there as well as his dad, who still needed care.

"A part-timer who helps with the horses stayed with Jazzy overnight. My wife is quite capable, you know."

"I know," Hadley admitted. "It's just with the blizzard and the electricity out, it's tough to be alone on a night like that."

"I talked to her this morning, and everything's fine at the ranch. Where are you?"

"Since you're at the clinic, I'm on the way to you. I have a momma cat and a baby who have to be checked out and tested. They were in Eli's barn."

"So you were there overnight?" His voice held more than that simple question.

"I was. The mare and foal are doing well, and Old Gene and Levi came to plow us out. I'll be at the clinic in about five minutes."

And she was. She was able to park along the street but had to climb over a snowbank holding the box with the cat and kitten. Brooks must have seen her coming though because he came out and took the box. Everywhere she looked she saw mountains of snow. The street was cleared, and the walk around the clinic was shoveled or snow blown. She was sure Brooks had taken care of that.

Once inside the clinic, Brooks said, "Let's get these two tested, then we'll see what else we can do for them." Brooks took them into an exam room, and she stayed with them as he got the samples he needed.

While she was with her own furry clients in Bozeman, she tried to keep busy waiting for test results. But here, all she could do was pet the two cats and think about Eli. Not only think about Eli, but think about that kiss. She supposed it was natural when two people were attracted to each other—and they certainly were—for something like that to happen. They'd been in close contact for hours, sleeping cuddled together for body heat. The attraction had just suddenly walloped them both. At least she guessed that's what had happened. She'd protected herself so carefully for so long, never letting her guard down, never letting an attraction take over again. But yesterday, watching the birth, finding the cat and kitten, being cooped up in that room with Eli, somehow she'd become vulnerable again. She couldn't let that happen. She really couldn't.

When Brooks returned to the exam room, he was smiling. He was an attractive man, over six foot. He was lean and broad-shouldered with dark brown eyes that usually had a twinkle. But nothing about him made her heart go pitter-patter. Nothing about him attracted her the way Eli did.

"What's the verdict?" she asked, and realized she was holding her breath.

"They're clear, both FIV and feline leukemia. But I agree that the kitten could use eyedrops. And they both need a flea treatment. Is Eli going to keep them? The baby requires more care than running around a barn."

"I don't know what he'll do. I suppose I could call him. Maybe since we're not in the midst of a blizzard, I can reach his cell."

Brooks must have noticed her tentative tone because he asked, "Didn't you two get acquainted while you were there?"

"We were caring for the horses," she said, almost defensively.

Brooks's eyebrows arched. "I didn't mean to suggest otherwise, but you must have had time to talk. You're a good judge of character. You know how to take care of human clients as well as the furry ones. Didn't you get a read on Eli?"

Oh, she'd gotten a read on him okay. At least she thought she had. But then really, what could you get to know in just a few hours?

"I like the way he handled his horse," she answered, noncommittally. "But I'll give him a call and see what he wants to do about the cats."

Brooks gave her an odd look and then a nod as he left the exam room.

She took out her phone. Eli answered on the second ring.

"Hadley," he said. "You got back to the clinic okay?"

There was that protective note again. She wasn't sure if it bothered her or reassured her.

"Yes. Brooks was here. He tested the cat and kitten, and they're clear of FIV and feline leukemia. But the little one needs eyedrops. I guess I'm calling to find out what you're going to do with them. You can't really let the kitten just run around loose in the barn."

"I suppose I could keep them in the office in the barn."

She thought about it. "You really should do that until the flea treatment works."

"Flea treatment?"

"Even in winter they can have fleas and ear mites. I'll give them a treatment that will take care of that, but you really need to give it forty-eight hours. You don't want to drag the fleas somewhere else."

"No, I certainly don't. Okay, in the office it is."

"Are you going to come pick them up?"

"I can do that. How long will you be there?"

Brooks could show Eli what to do, but she knew he probably wanted to get back to his ranch, too. "I can stay until you get here."

"I've been shoveling and snowblowing since the lane was opened. I'll take a break from that and come get them. I should be there in about fifteen minutes."

"See you then."

As the call ended, Hadley stared at her phone. She wondered if seeing Eli again would be an awkward reunion.

The kitten meowed, breaking into her thoughts, and she cuddled it next to her body. But her thoughts returned to the one subject that had dominated her mind for the last hour: Eli's kiss.

The best kiss of her life.

Chapter Five

Hadley heard the door to the clinic open and close. In the exam room with the momma cat and kitten, she waited for the knock on the door. It came.

Brooks opened the door a crack in case the cats were exploring on the floor. He immediately noticed she had kept them on a blanket on the table. “Eli’s here,” he said with a grin.

She supposed Brooks was just being his cheery self and she tried not to read anything into that grin.

Eli must have been right behind him because Brooks stepped aside and there the rancher was. He seemed even taller and more broad-shouldered in the exam room than he had in the barn. It made sense, she supposed. The exam room was smaller than the tack room. She always used logic when she was disconcerted or unsettled.

“I’m sorry to bring you out in this snowy mess,” she

apologized. "I didn't want to coop them up in a crate here if I didn't have to."

"No problem." When Eli came closer to the table, she felt a few sparks lighting her nerve endings. Maybe they came from remembering his hand on her face, the touch of his long fingers, the sensuality of his kiss. The room was getting warmer, and that wouldn't do at all.

"You said they tested clear?" he inquired, but his gaze was on her, not on the cats.

"They did." The kitten stood up when she saw Eli as if she remembered him.

She scrambled over to him, meowing, and he picked her up. "You're going to have to stay in the tack room for a day or two," he told her. He looked at Hadley. "Momma cat, too?"

"You'd better. Do you have any other cats around the barn?"

"I haven't seen any others. My guess is with this snow, none will go wandering either."

"Are you going to leave these two in the barn permanently?" She was having a problem keeping her mind on the conversation when Eli's gaze was locked on hers.

"I haven't decided yet. Maybe Mom will want them up at the house."

"Is she a cat person?"

"We've always had cats around the place. I just imagine Dad with a big bloodhound sitting by his side on the porch if he retires. But I don't think he'd like that picture."

"Probably not," she agreed. From everything she'd heard about Charles Dalton, he'd be active on the ranch until the day he died.

Why couldn't she stop looking at Eli? His gaze

seemed to tether to hers. Trying to shake off the pull she felt toward him, she grasped at the nearest thing. The eyedrops. She held them tightly in her hand. "These are the eyedrops for the kitten. I thought we could give her the first dose together," she explained, covering up her nervousness. "Two hands are always better than one, so if you could get someone on the ranch to help you, that would be great. You'll have to give her the drops twice a day."

She showed him the small bottle and pointed to the instructions. "Just squeeze one drop into each eye. I'll hold her while you manage the bottle to see how fast the drops flow out."

"I have a feeling you're going to make this look easy when it's not."

"It *is* easy…once you do it a few hundred times."

He chuckled. "All right. I'm ready. I suppose the object of this is to do it quickly so she doesn't squirm away."

"Exactly." As she held the kitten, Eli let the drop fall into first one eye then the other. The kitten meowed loudly in protest. As soon as Hadley set her down on the table once more, she ran to her momma.

Eli ran his hand down the momma cat, and again Hadley noticed the gentleness of his touch, the way he brushed his fingers through the cat's fur. This time she grabbed a package from the counter and showed it to Eli. "These are a snack that will boost their immune systems. Give momma about ten each day. Baby can have two or three. Break them up for her."

"I'll take good care of these two," he assured her.

Hadley gave him a long look. He might want to take

care of them, but he was a busy rancher, and she wondered if he'd forget them.

Apparently Hadley didn't hide her doubt. "I really will," he said again. "I just have to figure out the best way to do it."

He was about to pick up the box that she'd carried the cats in, but Hadley stopped him. "We have cardboard temporary carriers here. Let me get one of those for you. It will be much easier that way. The handles lock together, and you won't have to worry about the cats getting out."

Before she reentered the exam room a few minutes later, she took a deep breath. After she opened the door, she noticed that Eli was studying a chart on the wall while he carried the kitten in the crook of his arm.

He turned toward her. "You seem to be at home here."

"I've helped Brooks out a few times, so I know where things are."

"Since the receptionist isn't at the desk, should I pay you?"

Anne Lattimore, Brooks's receptionist, was snowed in. She'd called him and said she'd get here as soon as she could. But as far as Eli paying Hadley...

"Don't worry about paying today. Brooks will bill you for this office visit and the testing."

"You made an overnight house call, so I expect to pay you for your time, too."

"I was doing a favor for a friend. It was *my* time. I'm not going to charge for it."

"Hadley—" His voice was a husky, low protest.

She tried to ignore the way his voice seemed sensual and...intimate.

"Seriously, Eli. All I did was supervise."

"And probably save the colt," he concluded. "I named him Coco, by the way, because of his color."

In spite of her resolve not to fall under any man's spell ever again, she took a few steps closer to him. "It was an experience I won't soon forget."

They gazed into each other's eyes, knowing the birth of the colt had been the beginning of something else. However, Hadley didn't want to acknowledge that. Needing to keep her hands busy, she broke eye contact and opened the carrier on the table. Then she scooped up momma and set her inside. When Eli did the same with the kitten, his hand brushed hers. They looked at each other again as if not knowing what to say.

He closed the carrier and then picked it up, hesitating only a second before going to the door.

Hadley walked him out to the reception area.

There he said, "I guess I'll see you around."

Hadley nodded but suddenly couldn't respond. Seeing Eli again would be a pleasure. But that was a pleasure she was going to deny herself.

When Hadley returned to the boardinghouse from the clinic, she was met with hugs and kisses.

"Are you all right?" her grandmother asked.

"Did you freeze while you were out there?" her sister Claire inquired, looking her over.

"You'll have to tell us all about it," Old Gene suggested with a wink.

Hadley ignored that wink. Realizing she'd had little sleep and the adrenaline that had rushed through her when she was around Eli was ebbing, she was suddenly very tired. Oh, she'd gotten a few hours of sleep last night in Eli's arms. But the rest of yesterday and this morning had been exhausting, and she didn't think she was ready to face this crowd of family inquisitors.

Her sister Claire must have seen that because she said to the group, "Why don't we let Hadley get her bearings, change clothes, maybe even rest a bit. Then she can come down and have a snack with all of us."

While Melba and Old Gene seemed to agree, and Levi tended to his and Claire's daughter, Bekka, Claire spirited Hadley away up the stairs to the room where she was staying.

Once inside, Hadley flopped on the bed and said, "Thank you."

She sat there for a few seconds until Claire asked, "Well?"

"Well, what?"

"Well, aren't you going to tell me what happened?"

"Nothing happened. I delivered a foal. End of story."

"I hardly think so," her sister asserted. "I know what Eli Dalton looks like. He's hot."

Hadley kept silent.

"Not only is he hot, but you were cooped up with him for hours, and not only for hours, but overnight. Are you going to tell me again that nothing happened?"

The *nothing* that had happened had been a very surprising kiss. The other *nothing* that had happened had been her cuddling in Eli's arms. But she wasn't about to reveal either of those to Claire, just as she wasn't going to reveal what had happened in Las Vegas three years ago.

"Nothing happened," she said again, trying to make her sister believe it. "Eli felt the birth wasn't going right. That's why he called Brooks and Brooks called me. So

I went out there. At first nothing seemed amiss, but as the mare began to deliver, we saw it was a breech birth. I had to give it a little assistance. We had a lot of time waiting around, and then being snowed in. We couldn't even get the barn doors open, not until we were plowed out this morning."

Claire gave her a long, level look. "I think you're leaving something out."

This was her sister after all, so Hadley grudgingly gave her something. "I will admit, Eli Dalton isn't what I expected. He's different from other cowboys I've met."

"How so?"

"He's self-taught, but knowledgeable in many subjects. He has a wide range of ideas. He doesn't seem mired just in his own thoughts or in a narrow point of view."

"Like other cowboys you've met?"

"Right."

"And just how many cowboys have you dated?"

Hadley shrugged. "A few."

"There's something you're *not* telling me. There's something that's kept you from seriously dating for a very long time. Don't you think you should spill what that is?"

Claire had this fine habit of making Hadley feel guilty. Yet Hadley knew once she let the cat out of the bag, so to speak, she could never live down her impulsive mistake. Her family would pounce on it. They'd want to fix it. They'd want to fix *her*. They'd want to hook her up with somebody eligible so she could settle down and begin the life they wanted for her.

But she wasn't exactly sure of the life she wanted. She didn't want to be poked or pressured or coddled…

or looked at as a foolish woman who'd leaped into a situation without using her head. She just wanted to be treated like a normal woman who was finding her way.

"Claire, I'm fine. I have nothing to say. Everybody's dating habits are unique."

"Are you going to date Eli Dalton?"

"No. The subject never came up." Just because when they touched, she tingled. Just because when he kissed her, she swooned. Just because his gaze on hers made her feel like melting… No, the subject had never come up.

"There is something I didn't tell you," Hadley revealed.

Claire was all wide eyes and smiles now.

"I found a momma cat and kitten. I took them to the clinic and had them cared for, and Eli took them back home with him. The Circle D now has a momma and kitten as residents."

Claire swatted Hadley's arm. "Go get a shower and change. I'll pave the way for you downstairs and tell everybody that nothing happened."

"Thank you," Hadley said sweetly as she went to the shower. She knew Claire was frustrated with her, but she also knew as sisters they'd get through the frustrations. When Hadley returned to Bozeman in less than two weeks, she would no longer have to worry about spilling a secret she didn't want her family to know.

"I always thought Hadley Strickland was kind of standoffish."

Eli loved his brother Derek. He even liked him most of the time. But maybe not right now. They were sitting in the kitchen of their family home on Wednesday since the house was closer than his cabin. He'd just stopped in for a mug of coffee to warm him up before he continued checking fence lines that might have been damaged with the snow. Derek had come in about the same time.

"What do you mean she's standoffish?" Eli asked. "How do you even know her?"

"I've chatted her up," Derek admitted. "Weddings are a good place for that," he said with a wink. "But she acted all guarded, like I'd stepped on her toes or something."

"Did you try to ask her out without even having a conversation first?"

Derek gave a little shrug and a wicked grin. "Maybe."

His brother thought he could pretty much date any woman he wanted. Therefore, he figured there must be something wrong with Hadley if she wasn't interested in him.

"She's a smart woman, bro. She probably saw through your…charm."

Eli could see Derek was about to protest.

The truth was, he himself had seen a reserve around Hadley. In his experience, that kind of reserve usually came from having been hurt in a past relationship. In spite of himself, he wanted to know more about Hadley's past relationships, and more about the woman herself.

His past serious relationship had affected *him*. Out of high school, he and Elaine had dated for two years. Two years where he'd had dreams of owning his own ranch someday, building up a herd, having a family. But she'd broken his heart because she'd wanted a career in Chicago. She'd expected him to leave the ranch where he'd grown up, leave his family, friends and his heritage. He'd known then she'd never have the time and space in her life for what was important to him. He'd ended the relationship. That was the only thing he could have done.

That had been twelve years ago. Oh, sure, he'd dated since then, but not seriously. Never seriously.

In a flurry of movement, his mother came into the kitchen. She was plump with gray curly hair that framed her face. Spry and energetic, she always had something planned for her day. Today he saw baking pans were greased and floured on the counter. He also noticed that she'd set out a couple of pie plates. That gave him an idea.

She came over and gave him a hug. "I haven't seen you for a couple of days. Where have you been keeping yourself?"

"There was lots of snow to shovel, and I had to make sure the cattle had feed."

"I suppose you did," she said, going to the sink and washing her hands. "But I also heard that you have a cat and kitten living at your place. What's that about?"

"They were living in the barn office, but since I have to put eyedrops in the kitten's eyes, it seemed best to keep them at my cabin."

His mother arched a brow. "Permanently?"

"I don't know yet."

Derek cut a glance his way, then went to the refrigerator for the carton of milk.

"Are you baking pies today?" Eli asked his mother.

"Probably tomorrow morning. I'm baking a couple of cakes today. With Thanksgiving coming, we'll need those cakes and I can freeze them. And the pies… I imagine everyone here will lay into them as fast as I bake them. It's just a matter of what you want—apple, pumpkin, chocolate cream?"

Eli didn't care what pies his mother made. They were all good. "Do you think you'll have an extra?"

She picked up the flour canister and brought it to the counter. "You want to take one to your cabin?"

"No. It's a thank-you present for Hadley Strickland. She wouldn't take any money for helping with Amber. I thought a pie might be a nice gesture."

Now his mother gave him the same probing look that Derek was giving him. "I suppose it could be. What kind do you want to take her?"

"Apple would do just fine."

His mother gave a nod. "Your favorite, too. That's convenient if you want to share."

Eli could say he would or wouldn't. On the other hand, he considered the best thing to do in this situation was just keep his mouth shut.

The next afternoon, carrying the basket his mother had insisted he use to hold the pie, Eli went to the door of Strickland's Boardinghouse. A minute or so after he knocked, Melba herself came to the door.

When she saw him, she was all smiles. "Hello, Eli. It's good to see you. I thought I might have a stray guest coming in for the holidays."

"From what I hear, you have a houseful of family."

"Yes, I do, and it's wonderful. What have you got there in the basket?"

"This is a thank-you gift for Hadley. Is she here?"

"She's up in her room with that e-reader of hers, reading veterinary journals." She shook her head. "I thought this would be a vacation for her."

"That's why I particularly want to thank her. She cut into her downtime to help me out."

"Come on in out of the cold," Melba invited, motioning him inside. "I'll go get her."

Eli felt a bit ridiculous standing in the foyer with the basket until Hadley came running down the stairs. Then he didn't much care how he looked. She was dressed in black leggings and an oversize blue-and-black tunic sweater. Although it was roomy, it hugged her when she moved. He had to smile at the furry slippers with embroidered paw prints.

When she saw him glance at her slippers, she said, "What can I say? I have a pet theme going on."

As she approached him, he felt as if he needed to rid himself of his coat. Instead he held the basket out to her. "That's an apple cranberry pie to thank you for your help. I wish I could say I baked it, but that was my mother's doing."

Hadley smiled at him. "So is the pie from you or your mother?"

"Oh, it's from me, and Amber."

Just then Bekka, Claire and Levi's three-year-old, came running into the foyer and threw her arms around Hadley's legs. Afterward, she turned and headed for the kitchen, where Eli could hear babies crying. He supposed they were Tessa and Carson's twin babies.

"Things are a bit noisy here," Hadley told Eli with a smile. "That's why I was in my room."

"Do you want to take a walk so we can talk?" he asked. He hadn't intended the invitation to spill out, but it seemed like a good idea.

"Sure. Just let me take the pie to the kitchen and I'll grab my boots and coat."

He couldn't tell from Hadley's expression if she was glad to see him or if the stroll would be anything more than a walk down the street. Just what did he expect from the walk except frostbite?

He was still contemplating that when Hadley met him at the door. After they went outside, she pulled gloves from her pockets and slipped them onto her hands. At the base of the steps, she asked, "East or west?"

"Let's go west. It looks as if the sidewalk's completely clear that way."

Some of the mounds along the curb were four feet high, but the pavement cut a swath through the snow that was just wide enough for the two of them to walk. Their arms brushed as they breathed in the cold and walked half a block in silence.

Finally, Eli broke it, knowing exactly what he'd expected from this walk. "We should talk about that kiss."

After a few footsteps, she cut a glance at him and asked, "You mean at least three kisses, don't you?"

He wasn't going to quibble. He thought about it as one long kiss, but they had come up for air twice.

"I see you're a detail person," he teased, not feeling as light as he sounded.

Her boots crunched on snow that had fallen from the mounds alongside the walk. "It was the situation we were in," she claimed. "That's all. I mean, haven't you kissed someone before because you were excited or relieved or..."

She seemed to run out of words, and he filled in for her. "Or very attracted to them?"

When he turned toward her, she looked troubled. Just what was going through her head? What held her back from telling him what she was feeling? Something was. He knew it in his gut.

He was absolutely certain of it when she suddenly changed the subject. "Has your household returned to normal? Everyone back safely from Missoula?"

So she wasn't going to talk about their attraction. He'd try again later. "They're all back. With cousins helping out, the workload is lighter. It's what I like most about ranching—the teamwork."

"Teamwork," she repeated. "I've mostly flown solo."

"But you said you cover for the other vets."

"I do. But the truth is, I have more of a relationship with my furry patients than with the other veterinarians."

"That's telling," Eli said before he thought better of it.

"Telling about what?" Hadley asked defensively.

Just because she wasn't going to be open with him didn't mean he couldn't be open with her. "I think that says you believe you don't need anyone else and no one else needs you."

She vehemently shook her head. "That's not true. My sisters count on me."

"But do you count on them?" he asked.

She went silent.

He stopped and faced her. "Hadley, I didn't mean that as criticism. Self-sufficiency is a wonderful thing. But now and then it's okay to admit you need somebody, don't you think?"

"I think *you* think we know each other better than we do."

He realized immediately she was distancing herself

again. "Two people confined together for a day can get to know a lot about each other."

She didn't dispute that as they came to the end of the street. But he could see she didn't move to cross either way. So he turned to face her. "What are you afraid of, Hadley?"

It was probably the wrong thing to say because her shoulders squared, her chin went up and there was fire in her eyes. "I'm not afraid of anything."

She was full of bravado, but he didn't think it had any substance behind it. "And you believe that kiss was just about being thrown together unexpectedly."

"Sure. I mean— You're a sexy guy, Eli."

"And you're a sexy woman, Hadley."

She looked startled for a moment as if she might not believe him. He took advantage of her surprise. "But you don't want to talk about any attraction between us."

She blinked. "No, I don't. There isn't one. I mean, there's nothing between us."

He gave her a long probing look, then he took a step closer to her. "No attraction between us?"

She had that deer-in-the-headlights look, and he almost felt sorry that he was trying to prove a point. But he wanted to know what made Hadley tick. He wanted to know why she wouldn't admit to the attraction.

As he leaned a little closer, she sucked in a breath. The cold air must have shaken her back to reality because she said, "I have to get back to the boardinghouse. I'm going to babysit Bekka this afternoon while Claire runs errands."

"And the others won't be around?"

She shrugged. "Everybody has something to do."

She'd turned back toward the boardinghouse and

he did, too, walking beside her once more. “Do you like kids?”

“Sure I like kids. I’m just not as aware of my biological clock ticking as some women. And my sisters, my grandmother and even my mother don’t understand that.”

“You have a lot you want to do and see,” he suggested, feeling a sinking sensation in his stomach.

“Exactly. Once I get my pilot’s license, all sorts of opportunities might open up for me.”

“And you don’t want to be tied down.”

She looked him directly in the eyes. “No, I don’t.”

Though she said the words, and she said them with some vehemence, he didn’t quite believe her. Yet he knew from experience that a woman with dreams and goals like Hadley had would bring only heartbreak to a man like him.

They walked until they reached the steps to the boardinghouse. There Eli said, “Enjoy the pie.”

“I will. Thank you for bringing it, and thank your mom, too.”

That crazy devil inside his head made him say, “You can thank her yourself sometime. You’re always welcome at the Circle D.”

Hadley looked as if she wanted to respond, but she didn’t. She just gave him a fake smile, a wave and went up the steps and inside.

Eli felt as if more than the door to the boardinghouse had closed behind Hadley. She’d built a fence around herself with no gate. It was obvious she wasn’t letting any man jump over that fence into her corral.

The night they’d spent together and that kiss were now only shadows from the past.

Chapter Six

The following day, Eli was grooming a bay gelding when he heard the barn door open and someone called, "Hello? Eli?"

"Over here," he called back, surprised to hear Hadley's voice.

She came down the walkway to him and said, "Derek told me you were in here."

"I'm surprised to see you," Eli said honestly.

"The pie was delicious. I was going to write your mom a note, then I thought I'd just come by and check on Amber and Coco."

Write his mom a note? Did anybody do that anymore? Apparently Hadley had some of the old-fashioned girl in her.

"Maybe the momma and the kitten, too," Hadley added, looking around the barn toward the tack room.

"I took the cats to my cabin," he explained. "That seemed better than leaving them alone in here. And there's too much activity at the main house. I was afraid they'd get scared and confused. When I went online and checked cat care and kittens, I read they do better in a confined space with someone around."

"You're right about that," she agreed, looking impressed.

"You can come over to my cabin and check them out after you examine Amber and Coco."

For a moment he thought he saw a panicked look in Hadley's eyes, as if that wasn't what she'd expected at all. But then she seemed to bolster herself and put on her most professional voice. "That will be fine." Going to the stall with Amber and the colt, she let herself inside.

Eli admired her confidence and her caring. In fact he admired so many things about her.

"Does he nurse vigorously?" Hadley asked.

"Like there's no tomorrow," Eli responded with a grin.

"I should draw blood," Hadley said. "How do you feel about that?"

Eli knew if she did, lab results would tell him whether there was any infection or anemia. "That's fine," Eli agreed, knowing it had to be done.

"Temperature, heart and breathing rates are good," Hadley told him as she assessed Coco.

"They've bonded well."

"I can see that," Hadley said.

"He follows her no matter where she moves."

"What are you feeding her?" Hadley asked.

"Alfalfa hay. I've been keeping the stall cleaned out and dry. She lets me handle him," Eli said. "I've been rubbing him all over, touching his mouth and nose."

Hadley glanced at Eli. He held her gaze. He could feel that vibration between them, that attraction that had led to their kiss and the awkwardness afterward. No matter what she said, he had a feeling her visit today had more to do with that attraction between them than a thank-you for the pie or checking on Amber and the foal.

"Did you tell Brooks you were coming out here?" he asked.

"I did," she said. "I called him before I came. I didn't want him running out here unnecessarily. I like to finish what I start."

That was interesting. Did that mean she wouldn't start something unless she could finish it? Another reason for her backing away from him. She'd be driving back to Bozeman soon.

Hadley didn't seem to mind his watching her. She worked quickly and competently, careful she didn't scare Amber or pose any threat. New moms could be protective even if they'd been calm during the whole pregnancy and before. Eli watched carefully, too, because he knew Hadley wasn't used to working with horses.

"You're becoming an expert with larger animals."

"I'm always looking to expand my résumé," she joked. Then she said, "Imagine flying into herds of wild animals, helping the horses that roam the ranges without proper care."

"You'd figure out how to give them care?"

"Sure would. Everything from vaccinations to helping them heal from injuries."

"Have you ever seen them in the wild?"

"I have…in the Big Horns. I went with some friends when I was in college. They were so majestic standing on the ridge above us as if they were greeting us. That was my first glimpse of them. How about you?"

"I spotted a herd in Colorado." He wasn't going to go into it. That was during his Elaine days. "I'm going to check and make sure everything's secure here, then we can go over to my cabin."

It took some effort for him to walk away from Hadley rather than going into that stall with her. But he didn't want to crowd Amber, and he didn't want to crowd Hadley. He imagined she could be even more skittish.

Fifteen minutes later Eli opened the door to his cabin, saying, "Home sweet home."

Hadley wasn't sure why she'd driven out here today. Sure, she'd told herself she wanted to thank Eli's mom and check on the horses. But deep in her heart, she knew her purpose had more to do with seeing Eli again. She was testing her reaction to him. Maybe she wouldn't feel that "zing" when he looked at her. Maybe she wouldn't remember their kiss in vivid detail. Maybe the attraction would have disappeared. Part of her hoped it had. The other part…

Eli had driven them from the barn in his truck, and Hadley had struggled to find conversation. Not because they didn't have things to talk about, but because Eli seemed to take up all her breathing space. Whenever she was around him, she felt breathless. She could try fooling herself, but there was no denying it. Their attraction was still there.

Now as he welcomed her into his home, she realized this was much more than just a cabin. Eli had said he'd decorated it himself with his sister's help, and it was well-done. Huge beams crisscrossed the ceiling with a loft at the far end and stairs leading to it. A stone fireplace was the center point of the room, and the rustic furniture with red Native American upholstery was mostly grouped about that. Bay windows surrounded the dining area, where there was a table large enough for four. Shiplap lined all the walls along with a wall hanging in cream, red and black. The same colors were featured in the rug on the wood floor.

"No flat-screen TV?" she asked, surprised.

He laughed. "I mostly stream on my laptop. I have a bigger monitor set up in the bedroom that I can always swivel toward the bed."

The mention of his bed had her seeing visions in her mind that had nothing to do with the holidays or sugarplums.

All of a sudden the kitten barreled down the steps, half jumping and half falling as it went. It came straight to Eli and rubbed on his jean-clad leg.

Hadley laughed out loud.

"I've named her," he said. "She's Winks, and her mom's name is Whisper because she travels more quietly and not as rambunctiously."

Eli was holding Winks now, and the kitten was rubbing her head against his coat.

The momma cat, Whisper, started down the stairs now, too, obviously checking on her offspring and following the voices. Hadley held her arms out for the kitten. "Can I have a look at her?"

"Sure," he said, shrugging out of his jacket. "The eyedrops are working."

Hadley unzipped her jacket and sat on the sofa with the kitten before her on the narrow, bench-like table where a coffee table book on the Southwest lay. Her focus was on the kitten as she examined her, but she couldn't help glancing around, too. Eli's floor-to-ceiling bookshelves near the dining area were filled. Just from looking at the spines, Hadley could tell he owned books on every subject imaginable.

"I would love to have a place like this someday," she said, meaning it.

"Where do you live now?" he asked, sitting on the sofa beside her. He wasn't too close, but close enough that she was aware of every inch of him from the thick hair on his head—he'd taken off his Stetson after they'd come in—to his jean-clad thighs and worn boots.

Her thoughts scrambled, and she had to reassemble them to answer his question. "I rent the first floor of a house in town. I wanted somewhere convenient to the clinic."

"So if you take off someplace, you can leave it easily behind."

There was no censure in Eli's voice, yet she felt it was a little crisp, or maybe just the truth. "I suppose that's true. I never meant it to be permanent. I'm not there very much. What about you? Did you have a place before you built this?"

"I lived with my parents to save money and because we really are all a team. Then it was time I had a place of my own."

"How do you feel living apart from them? That had to be a change."

"It's a good change for all of us...and for Derek, too. I think when I was in the house he always felt I was looking over his shoulder. I never meant to give him that impression, but being an older brother and all that..."

"And your parents? How did they feel about your moving out?"

He gave her a questioning look as if he figured there was more behind her question than a simple answer. And maybe there was. When she'd been away at college, she'd known her parents had missed her, and they still hoped she wouldn't go that far away. But she wasn't sure where she wanted to settle. At least not anymore. She'd been willing to follow Justin Corrigan anywhere. Now she didn't think she'd give any woman the advice to do that.

Eli's voice brought her back from thoughts she'd rather forget. He said, "It's not like I'm in the next state. I'm still on the ranch, and I'm sure they're happy about that. Dad's getting older and he can't do what he once did, although he won't admit it. I can shoulder some of that for him. You know it's not something you put into words, but he knows I'm here when he needs me."

Yes, Eli was the dependable one. She shouldn't even put him in the same category with Justin. But after the fiasco with the veterinary pharmaceutical rep, she put all men in that category.

Whisper had insinuated herself between Eli's legs. Now she wound around Hadley's and then jumped up on the coffee table with her kitten. Hadley automatically checked her over, liking the care they both had been given.

Eli's voice was husky as he said, "I found an old wicker wash basket and filled it with a fleece blanket. That's up in my bedroom, and they seem to like that the best, at least for sleeping when I'm not here. When I'm home, they're down here with me."

"Have you ever had pets?"

"Not in the way you mean," he said with amusement

in his voice. "There were always the horses and foals, and learning to get to know each one of them as they were born. Cats ran around the barn, and for a while Derek and I took care of a couple of goats. We were about ten. How about you?" he asked. "There had to be a reason why you became a vet."

"There was. I had a dog, the most adorable mutt that Dad had found along the road. He was my best friend for about five years. But then cancer took him. After it did, I decided the best thing I could learn to do was take care of animals. I find them homes when I can, so I haven't taken any home with me yet. My hours aren't conducive to having a pet, but I'd like to someday."

"The same way you'd like to have your own house?"

"You make it sound like a far-off dream."

"Isn't it?"

"Possibly. My sisters and my mom, and even my grandmother, seem to want me to make all my life decisions right now, and then be done with it. I don't feel that way. I'm still exploring each one as it comes along."

Eli thought about that. "Until you find exactly what you want."

As she gazed into his eyes, the sparkle there teased her into believing she wanted something entirely different from what they were talking about.

His voice was low when he said, "Hadley."

She knew what he wanted, and she knew what *she* wanted. Yet her past experience told her being attracted like this wasn't a good thing. She couldn't be impulsive. She couldn't be reckless. When she'd been both three years ago, her heart had been broken.

"Don't you feel it?" Eli asked, bringing her back to the moment.

"What?" Her voice was a mere whisper.

"The electricity."

"I'm leaving after Thanksgiving weekend," she reminded him.

"I know," he said solemnly. "But a kiss isn't a commitment."

She knew full well a kiss wasn't a commitment. She also knew that vows might not even be a commitment. So she did the only thing she could do. She stood and then she said in her most professional voice, "Whisper and Winks look good. You're doing a good job with them, Eli. I never expected you to—"

"Take cats into my house?" He was joking with her, but the joking didn't reach his eyes. She could tell he was thinking about what had almost happened on the sofa. So was she, but she couldn't dwell on it. She couldn't even entertain the thought of anything starting with Eli.

With her emotions in turmoil, she headed for his door.

He followed her, and they were outside on the way to the car when a snowball slammed Eli in the chest. He turned and spotted Derek grinning from ear to ear. Not only Derek, but four other good-looking men with him.

Shaking his head, Eli brushed the snow off his coat. "Hadley," he said, "these are some of my cousins—Garrett, Shawn, Booker and Cole. Along with another brother, Zach, they've been living here with my uncle Phil."

Hadley had heard the story about these Dalton brothers and their dad. A raging brush fire had burned down the family ranch, taking most of the animals and tragically, their mother. These Daltons, instead of splitting apart, had managed to stick together. They'd decided to come to Rush Creek Falls to start over.

Derek piped up, "Zach was staying here until he placed an ad in the *Rust Creek Falls Gazette* to seek a wife."

Garrett added, "He ended up falling in love with Lydia Grant, who'd worked at the *Rust Creek Falls Gazette.* They're living in a cottage on a ranch on the outskirts of town."

"I think my grandmother told me that they'll marry in the spring," Hadley said. News and gossip traveled quickly in Rust Creek Falls.

Eli's cousin Booker stooped down, scooped up snow and made another snowball. "So how about a real snowball fight, cuz?"

"Don't you boys have chores to do?" Eli asked with a mock scowl.

"All done," Shawn answered, making another snowball. "And I would imagine since Hadley here is a born-and-bred Montana girl, she'd go for a little snowball fight, too." He wiggled his brows at Hadley.

When had she last had some fun, real fun? And these young men seemed like they knew how to have it. She quickly put on the gloves that had been stuffed in her pocket, scooped up snow, made a missile out of it and tossed it at Booker. He tossed a snowball back, and it whacked her in the shoulder.

Eli said, "Hadley, if you don't want to do this—"

She made a nice rounded snowball and fired it at *him.* That must have done it for Eli because he entered into the fray. Soon snowballs were flying, and they were plowing through the snow after each other. In no time their coats were splattered with white and their cheeks had turned red.

Eli said to Hadley, "How long has it been since you've built a snowman?"

"You mean a snowwoman, don't you?"

Booker said, "Uh-oh. I'm out of here. Let *them* argue about women's rights."

The others mumbled and headed back toward the barn.

"They deserted," Hadley said after they'd gone.

Eli merely shrugged. Then he looked around at the snowbanks. "We could do this one of two ways. You could build a snowwoman and I can build a snowman, or we can try to build a snow horse."

Hadley laughed at that compromise. "A snow horse it is."

For the next half hour that's what they did. And when they were finished, Hadley was rightly proud of it, too. They'd used an evergreen branch for the horse's tail, and Hadley had woven together some branches to wrap around its neck.

"How about some hot chocolate?" Eli asked Hadley. "It will warm you up before you have to drive home, and you can thank my mom in person for that pie."

She could have passed up the hot chocolate, but she really did want to thank his mother for the pie. So she agreed. "Warming up a bit would be nice."

Shaking the snow from their coats and boots, they piled into the truck and drove to the ranch house.

Hadley had a contented feeling she hadn't experienced for a very long time. Maybe it was from expending physical energy, or maybe it was because of enjoying sitting beside Eli in companionable silence. Hard to know.

Eli parked near the wide front porch. As soon as Hadley entered the Dalton house, she was encompassed by its feeling of warmth. It was because of the cozy furniture, the rugs on the plank flooring, the little touches that made a place a home. There was an aerial photograph of the ranch on one wall, along with knickknacks that Hadley imagined the children had given to their parents over the years.

As Eli escorted Hadley into the kitchen, she caught sight of Rita Dalton at the stove, stirring something in a huge soup pot.

"Hi there," Eli's mother said, her eyes lighting up. It was obvious she liked to have company.

"Hi, Mom. Remember Hadley? She was at Kayla's wedding."

"Of course I do. Melba talks about you all the time."

"Uh-oh," Hadley said. "My grandmother's as honest as they come. I'm not sure I want to know what she said."

"Come on, let me get you some hot chocolate and we can talk about it. Derek and his cousins ran through here a little while ago, but they didn't stay. You'll keep me company for a while, won't you?" she asked her son.

Eli raised his brows at Hadley, and she gave a little nod. He answered his mother, "Sure, Mom," and took off his coat. Hadley did the same, and Eli hung both of them on pegs near the back door.

"You have a lovely house, Mrs. Dalton."

"I've been working at it for years. I should."

Hadley liked Eli's mother already.

Eli started for the cupboard and was about to pull down a box of hot chocolate mix, but his mother went over to him and said, "Not that stuff. I know you and Derek use it when you want something quick. I'm going to make the real thing. Get a saucepan for me."

"She melts chocolate into it and uses cream," Eli said to Hadley in a conspiratorial voice.

"I'm going to have to build another snow horse to burn off calories," Hadley decided.

"Nonsense," Rita protested. "You could use a few pounds, just like most women your age. Oatmeal raisin cookies to go with that hot chocolate?"

Hadley laughed again. "You make it hard to resist."

"The boys never do. Kayla and Kristen..." She wiggled her hand. "Sometimes they do. I'm making a pot of vegetable soup for supper tonight, but it will be fine on simmer. I imagine your sister Claire makes that, too."

Mostly everyone in town knew Claire worked at the boardinghouse and helped in the kitchen. She'd turned from a woman who hadn't cooked into a woman who cooked really well under their grandmother's tutelage. "This time of year is great for stews and soups and baked bread."

"I have a recipe for a cinnamon loaf Melba has been asking me to give her for years, but I keep telling her it's a family secret," Rita said with a wink.

Eli took the cookie tin over to the table and pointed to a chair for Hadley. He took the seat across from her. Rita turned from the saucepan at the stove and eyed the two of them with a smile.

Hadley could see that Eli gave his mother a shake of his head that was almost imperceptible. Still, Hadley caught it. Just what did that mean? That his mother shouldn't get any ideas about the two of them? That would certainly be best.

Nevertheless, as soon as the hot chocolate was made, Rita brought it to the table and poured it into three mugs. "I'll have some with you, but I'll forgo the whipped cream. I just happen to have some that I whipped up this morning. I was going to use it on apple cobbler tonight, but I can whip up more."

And before Hadley had any say in the matter, Rita had spooned two good tablespoons onto her hot chocolate. As it floated on the top, the scent of the chocolate and the warmth of it made Hadley feel…almost weepy. How could that be? Was she so unused to being around a man and being treated kindly that this was the result?

Apparently thinking the silence had gone too long, Rita said, "We'll soon be putting up a Christmas tree. How do you feel about Christmas, Hadley? Everybody has their own take on the holiday."

That was a thought-provoking question. She'd had reasons the past few years to work on the holiday. She still enjoyed choosing presents for loved ones, but the sparkle of Christmas just wasn't the same anymore. So she said, "I believe Christmas is for children."

"Oh, you do? Are you busy tomorrow?" Rita asked.

"Mom," Eli warned.

"Shush, boy," Rita said. "I'm talking to Hadley. And before you say whether you're busy or not, I'll tell you why I'm asking. We're having a big volunteer day at the community center tomorrow. We're filling food baskets for needy families. If parents feel they can provide for their children, they're more likely to make Christmas happier for their kids, don't you think?"

"I'm sure that's true," Hadley said. "Is there a toy drive, too?"

"Yes, there is, and not just store-bought toys. People actually make things for the children—crocheted stuffed animals, wooden trucks and trains, even old-fashioned games like painted checkerboards. No child in this town should be without a smile on Christmas morning."

"That's a wonderful idea, and I'd like to help. What time should I be there?"

Derek clapped Eli's shoulder as they passed the old-fashioned hitching post outside the Ace in the Hole later that night. "Ready for this viewing party?"

Eli's mind wasn't on viewing the latest episode of *The Great Roundup*, a cowboy/adventure reality show that his cousin Travis had signed up for. Brenna O'Reilly, another resident of Rust Creek Falls, was also participating. Rather, he was remembering each of his encounters with Hadley Strickland. The one that replayed in his mind the most was their kiss.

He glanced up at the wood-burned sign for the Ace in the Hole and the neon red sign with an ace of hearts playing card over the door. This bar could be a rough-and-rowdy cowboy hangout, depending on the clientele that particular night. There had been occasional rumbles and fights, but tonight couples would be attending to watch the latest episode of *The Great Roundup*. When he visited his cousin Trav during filming in July, Trav—Ben Dalton's son—and Brenna O'Reilly seemed to really be on the road to romance.

Eli opened the bar's old screen door with its rusty hinges and then the heavy wood door. Tonight no country tunes poured from the jukebox. Instead, the TV blared loud and clear. Booths lined the outer walls while wooden tables with ladder-back chairs formed a square around a small dance floor. A few cowboys played pool in the far back. As Eli glanced around, he briefly took in the framed Old West photos and those of local ranches that hung on the walls. Studying the wooden bar lining the right side of the room and its dozen bar stools, he spotted Hadley's cousins sitting there. He could see in the mirrored wall reflecting rows of glass bottles and customers at the bar that Hadley wasn't with them.

Eli spotted several couples he knew at the tables, among them his cousin Zach with his fiancée, Lydia. From two booths, Zach's brothers, Shawn, Garrett, Booker and Cole, waved Eli and Derek over.

They joined their cousins. Seated next to Booker, Eli opened his jacket but didn't shrug out of it. He wasn't sure how long he was going to stay.

When a waitress came rushing over, Eli ordered a beer while Derek, who'd sat across from him, requested scotch neat.

Booker elbowed Eli. "Did you ask the pretty vet for a date?"

Eli didn't particularly want his cousins poking into his private life. "Why are you asking?"

"Derek told me to."

Derek grinned at Eli. He couldn't possibly know what they were talking about because of the high volume level of the TV and the cheers that were rising from the crowd during the latest challenge on the show.

Eli just shook his head at both men and turned toward the TV. One of the challenges this week *was* cheer-worthy. He'd heard all about it during the preview that aired at the end of last week's episode. He watched as Brenna and his cousin Travis fought with all they were worth to win as the host timed them. It was easy for Eli to catch up with what was happening. The couple had to bring up a wooden box from the bottom of the pond. They dived over and over until together they hefted the box to the surface of the water. Swimming as fast as they could, they sputtered to shore and dragged the box to a spot where they could work on the locks. Apparently they'd earned keys before Eli had arrived. He could tell the couple's hands were shaking as they inserted a key in one of two padlocks and then focused on the other padlock.

Booker nudged Eli again. "*Are* you going to date Hadley? I've heard you haven't had a serious romance in years."

"*Serious* would be rough with Hadley living in Bozeman."

"So you've thought about it."

"I've thought about *her*," he admitted, then turned to the big-screen TV. "Now let's see if Trav can win this."

"He'll need Brenna's help," Booker said philosophically.

They watched as Brenna and Trav pulled a burlap bag from the box, untied the knots and then dumped the puzzle pieces onto a board provided for them. Eli decided that romantic relationships were just like that puzzle. All the pieces had to fit and make the perfect picture.

The Great Roundup had given him something to think about.

Saturday morning, Eli had been passing by the community center and decided to stop in. That was all there was to it, he told himself as he opened the door of the building and went inside. The center was bustling. He knew many of the people there, and they waved to him or said hello as he made his way through volunteers who were sorting food or boxing up items. One corner of the room was obviously dedicated to toy collection.

It didn't take him long to spot Hadley, not with that glossy, dark brown hair falling down her back, black leggings that disappeared into tall leather boots and a deep purple turtleneck sweater that dipped below her fanny. He noticed everything about this woman every time he was around her, though he still told himself he didn't want to.

His mother waved at him from a table across the room, and she pointed to Hadley and winked.

He knew he was playing right into his mom's hand. She wanted him to settle down so she had grandbabies. Or maybe she just wanted him to be happy.

Wasn't he happy? He had work he liked and family, a house of his own and now pets to share it. Still… His gaze returned to Hadley.

When he approached her, she smiled and then gave him a perplexed look. "What are you doing here?"

"I had errands. I had to stop at the feed store, so I thought I'd look in here and lend a hand if it was needed."

Lorna Babcock, a frizzy-haired sixty-year-old, called to him from the toy center. "Hey there, Eli. You here to help? We can use some strong arms to carry boxes."

"Wherever I can fit in."

"Just find yourself a spot. I'll call you when we need someone to haul."

"Do you need help?" he asked Hadley.

"Sure do. I need ten boxes pretty much filled evenly with everything I've got here, from the canned beans to the fruit cocktail. That would be great if you could carry them over to that corner that's going to be the distribution center. Someone there is labeling everything and tagging with names."

"I'm on it," Eli said. Taking off his jacket, he went to hang it on the portable coat hanger. When he returned, Hadley gave him a look that he did his best to ignore. He wasn't wearing anything different from any other day—a flannel shirt, jeans and boots. But when she looked at him, he felt she was assessing all of him. Did women do that?

She quickly looked away, her eyes darting to the canned goods in front of her. Because he didn't want to embarrass her or himself, he started a different type of conversation. "Sometimes I see Rust Creek Falls as an extension of ranch living. The town pulls together just like my family does."

"I heard about how all the residents helped each other after the flood. The town has made a remarkable recovery."

"Even the newcomers have made that happen," Eli said as he boxed a jar of peanut butter next to a bag of rice. He nodded to the table next to them. "That's Hudson Jones, who married Bella Stockton. Bella's a longtime resident. When Hudson and his brother Walker were newcomers, Hudson donated electronic tablets to the elementary school so the kids could learn better. There are a lot of Secret Santas that no one knows about."

"Secret Santas?" Hadley asked, looking for clarification.

Now he realized he messed up and he shouldn't have opened his mouth. But he had to explain. "Sure, people who give without anybody knowing they do it. The result is everybody's life is made better. It's just like these food baskets. They don't seem like much, but they could get a family through a couple of weeks. That's important in these times."

Hadley stopped sorting canned goods and gave him a curious look. She asked perceptively, "Are you a Secret Santa?"

"That word *secret* goes with Santa for a reason," he responded, not answering her one way or the other. But there was a warm look in her eyes, and he realized he couldn't fool her. But he wasn't going to say more either.

Suddenly Lorna was charging toward him and Hadley.

"Uh-oh," Eli said. "Lorna's on the move."

"Is that bad?"

"It means she's going to ask us to do something for her."

Marching right up to them, the older woman said, "I need a favor." She didn't wait for them to ask what, but went on, "Jazzy Smith has asked for ten of the food baskets to give the residents she knows who would not want to be on an official list. But Brooks is tied up with a rancher outside Kalispell, and she's caring for his dad after surgery and can't pick them up. I need somebody to deliver them."

"I can deliver them," Hadley volunteered. "But I walked over here. I'll have to go get my SUV."

Before he caught his tongue, Eli said, "My truck is right outside. We can go together. I've never gotten a firsthand look at the Smith Rescue Ranch."

"It would be easier with two of you doing it," Lorna decided for them.

Hadley was looking unsure, as if his idea troubled her. However, she conjured up a smile. "We'll have ten of these ready in a few minutes," she told Lorna.

But Eli heard the uncertainty in her voice. Was this volunteer jaunt going to be awkward?

Chapter Seven

On the drive to the Smith Rescue Ranch, it didn't take long for Eli to realize that Hadley looked and acted uncomfortable. He didn't have Derek's charm with the ladies. He only knew how to be honest. "You know," he said, "you should have vetoed the idea of us doing this together if you didn't want me to come along."

"I hated to refuse Lorna," she answered. "She thought she was doing a good thing."

That answer wasn't to his liking, but he didn't think Hadley was pushing him away just for the heck of it. There was something at the bottom of her reasoning.

"Are you a people pleaser?" he asked.

Out of the corner of his eye, he saw her study him. "Yes, I am."

"Care to tell me why?" For some reason, he didn't think people pleasing came naturally to Hadley; rather something had taught her to do it.

She was quiet for a few beats, but then she answered him. "I was bullied in elementary school. I was pudgy, short and an easy target. I was the last one picked for anybody's games. If I answered in class too often, I was made fun of. So I learned from that. I tried not to capture anybody's attention. I kept my mind on my schoolwork, increased my brainpower whenever I could, but didn't let others know about it. That paid off in high school because I earned a scholarship that helped with college."

Although he knew he should keep his eyes on the road, there wasn't any traffic and he gave her a long, appraising male look. "You're too pretty to fly under the radar now."

Her gaze met his for a second before he turned his attention back to the road. "That's not a line," he assured her. For once she didn't say anything, though he didn't know if she believed him. Whether he should prod or not, he did. "Did the bullying affect your adult life?"

"I might want to please the people I care about and those who care about me. But overall, the bullying made me bolder as an adult. I push the limits now more and I stand up for what I believe in. In fact, now sometimes I'm too impulsive."

"Like when you kissed me back?"

She didn't hesitate to say, "Exactly like that."

They rode in quiet for the next mile, but then she asked him, "How did your childhood affect *your* adult life?"

He gave a shrug. "I told you, being the oldest made me feel responsible for everybody. I felt my parents depended on me to be the practical, steady one."

"Don't you get tired of that? Don't you ever want to break out and just have fun?"

"I find ways to do that now and then."

"The Daltons do have a reputation with women."

He gave her a sharp look. Then he realized that was probably true. Derek certainly did. Jonah was married now, but he'd done his fair share of dating. Eli had to admit he had, too. Only, after Elaine he hadn't been serious about it.

He glanced over at Hadley. He knew her well enough to know she didn't want to be anybody's conquest. And, from her body language, he also realized the subject was closed…for now.

Hadley felt bad about the silence between her and Eli on the rest of the drive to the ranch. But she hadn't known what else to say. The Daltons were all sexy men who could date whomever they wanted to date. And Derek and Eli, according to the gossip, hadn't seemed serious about anybody they'd dated. Not recently anyway. That told Hadley they were out for a good time.

Yet Eli didn't seem like a carefree Romeo. Still, after the hard work he did, maybe on the weekend he just wanted an outlet like many men did. It was impossible to know.

As she and Eli walked up to the front door of Jazzy and Brooks's home, she wished she could relax around Eli more. She wished—

No, she didn't. She'd stopped wishing. She knew better than to dream about hearts and flowers, and a romance that could last forever.

She reached the door first and knocked. When Jazzy

answered, she looked frazzled. Her hair was mussed, and she appeared tired.

After Hadley and Eli had stepped inside, she asked Jazzy, "Are you okay?"

Jazzy gave her a weak smile. "I've got to admit taking care of one recalcitrant patient is harder than caring for a whole stable of horses. Brooks's dad thinks he should be better already." She shook her head and then looked at Eli. "Maybe you could talk some sense into Barrett, man-to-man, because he's not listening to me. I think he might already be regretting the decision to move in here with me and Brooks. Brooks has tried to talk to him, but father-and-son communication..." Jazzy shook her head again. "Sometimes that just doesn't work so well. Barrett thinks Brooks is being condescending, and Brooks thinks Barrett is just being stubborn."

Hadley saw how worried Jazzy was about it, so she sought to reassure her. "This might not be about you and Brooks at all. It could just be that Barrett's worried about losing his independence."

Eli immediately agreed. "Men like my dad and Brooks's dad—they need to think they control at least their own world if not everybody else's. Didn't Barrett try to arrange your marriage to Brooks?"

Now Jazzy laughed. "He was a huge part of why we married. But I've got to admit, Brooks and I do belong together."

"Then maybe what you need to do," Eli suggested, "is to make Barrett feel he's more in control."

"And how do I do that?" Jazzy asked.

"I'm not sure," Eli told her. "But I'll think about it

while I'm unloading the baskets. Where do you want me to put them?"

Jazzy pointed to a corner of the living room. "Over there would be good for now. We'll be delivering them soon. While you do that, I'll make coffee. Hadley, do you want to help?"

Hadley didn't know what kind of help she'd be making coffee, but it was obvious Jazzy wanted to talk to her. So she followed her into the kitchen.

Jazzy took out a coffee canister. "Grab the milk from the refrigerator, would you?" she asked Hadley as she dumped the water into the coffeemaker. "So tell me, how do you like Eli?"

Hadley unzipped her jacket and groaned. "Not you, too."

"What do you mean, not me, too?"

"My sisters asked all kinds of questions, and Claire and Tessa aren't easy to stonewall. My grandmother wasn't too subtle either."

Jazzy eyed her before she took a small pitcher from the cupboard and poured milk into it. "From what I've heard, Eli is a good guy, loyal to his family and friends. You certainly would want that quality in a guy you dated, wouldn't you?"

Hadley gave it serious thought because this was Jazzy who was asking, and they'd become friends. "I would want that quality in a guy, but I'd want an adventurous spirit, too. I'm not sure Eli has that." She didn't mean to be that blunt, but she knew Jazzy would push as much as Claire or Tessa if she didn't give her honest answers.

After Jazzy set the milk pitcher on the table, she asked Hadley, "Do you know that Eli used to be a rock climber?"

Hadley's eyes widened in surprise.

"And he took trips to the Mexican ruins and the Alaskan glaciers. But that was when—" Jazzy stopped. She might have even stopped on purpose to force Hadley to ask questions.

All right, well, now Hadley did have some questions. "Go on," she encouraged her friend. "What were you going to say?"

Jazzy shrugged. "I go out with friends now and then. I don't just see horses and Brooks."

Hadley gave her an understanding smile.

"When we go to the Ace in the Hole, I hear talk... from the girls and from the people they know. The talk always seems to turn to the guys."

"So what did you hear about Eli?"

"Out of high school, he dated Elaine Nixon. She worked for a local insurance office. They were serious, and she had an adventurous spirit, and it seemed he did, too, back then. Together they'd find the best travel deals at slow times at the ranch. They dated for two years. They took a few jaunts to Mexico, and as I said, they visited the Alaskan glaciers, too, by helicopter. She'd go with Eli when he went rock climbing, and he taught her a lot about it. But then Elaine left town to take a job in Chicago because she was tired of small-town life. Rumor has it, she wanted Eli to go with her. But that wasn't what he wanted. Apparently after she left, his adventurous spirit just seemed to fade away."

Hadley heard noise coming from the living room and realized it was Eli bringing in the baskets. Her conversation with Jazzy ended, giving her a lot to think about as she took mugs from a mug tree and lined them up on the counter.

* * *

Eli knocked on the door of Barrett Smith's suite and heard a gruff, "Come in."

When he opened the door, he saw Barrett in a recliner, his leg propped up on a pillow. He was a barrel-chested man with gray hair and ruddy cheeks. Eli knew he was about six feet tall, but in the recliner he looked shorter and older.

As soon as Brooks's dad saw Eli, however, he grinned and sat up a little straighter. "Good to see you, boy. What are you doing here?"

"I came over with Hadley Strickland to drop off some baskets from the community center. Jazzy's going to distribute them to people who don't want their name on an official list."

"I get that. Some folks want to keep their pride. How's your dad?"

"He's good."

"I heard Hadley tended to your mare. I wish I could have done that for you. I've tended to Dalton horses for years."

Eli had known Barrett Smith since he was a boy. "I figured you probably miss what you like to do. That's why I stopped in to tell you Amber and her foal are doing really well. Hadley was great. She helped with the breech birth."

"She did, did she? She's like Brooks, up-and-coming vets when I'm on my way out."

"Do you *want* to retire?" Eli asked.

Barrett pointed to his knee encased in loose sweatpants. "I don't know as if I have a choice. If I had my druthers, I'd still be working part-time. We'll see what happens. I might sell my place and my practice and just help out Brooks when he needs it. I'll tell you one thing. I don't like feeling like an invalid."

"I know you don't. Nobody does. But you *are* one, at least for a short while. It hasn't been that long since your surgery."

Barrett frowned and looked down at the knee again. "I suppose you're right. That's what Jazzy and Brooks keep telling me. But I feel like I should be doing more. I hate just sitting here watching TV."

"You know, don't you, the more you fight it, the longer it's going to take to get better? Why don't you just let Jazzy pamper you? It isn't just for your benefit. That will make her feel like she's helping you."

Barrett looked like he was going to seriously consider Eli's words. He pointed to the armchair beside his recliner. "Sit down for a few minutes. Talk to me about what matters—ranching, animals, your family. I hear you have a houseful."

Eli spent the next fifteen minutes or so keeping Barrett company. The older man seemed starved for some talk and opinions about what was happening in Rust Creek Falls.

When Eli left Barrett with the promise to visit again soon, he returned to the living room, where Hadley and Jazzy were talking. They stopped when he came in, making Eli suspicious. Were they talking about him?

He motioned to Barrett's suite. "I had a few ideas while I was in there with him that could help all of you."

Jazzy was altogether interested. "Tell me."

"First of all, get one of those portable intercom systems, or a walkie-talkie. Let him call you when he needs you instead of your checking on him so often. That way he wouldn't feel like such a burden."

Jazzy was already nodding. "That's a great idea. I don't know why we didn't think of it."

"Because you're in the middle of the situation," he said. "I also noticed that once he started talking, he didn't want to stop. I think he's starved for a little companionship. You've got to remember, he was treating clients all day, as many as he could fit in. So he had lots of people interaction as well as pet action."

"And what can I do about that?" Jazzy asked, worried.

"Invite a couple of his friends in to play checkers or cards."

Listening up to now, Hadley chimed in, "I bet Old Gene would enjoy a visit and a game with him. In fact, he might like a break from everybody at the boardinghouse. It sure is noisy there. And my grandmother doesn't need his help with so many people around."

"Those are both great suggestions," Jazzy said. "It's serendipitous that you two dropped off the baskets." She gave her attention to Eli. "You've never taken a tour of the barns and the horses. If you want to, now's a great time. My part-time helper, Darby Conrad, is out there now. She can answer any of your questions. So can Hadley, for that matter. She's been here often enough to know most of the horses and our routine."

Eli glanced at Hadley. "Do you have time?"

"I'm not on the clock. Sure, I have time."

The path to Jazzy and Brooks's barn still had a layer of snow. Hadley's boots made impressions as they walked, but that wasn't what held her rapt attention. It was the cowboy next to her. She cast a covert glance at Eli. After her conversation with Jazzy, she had trouble seeing him in a different light. He was a rock climber? He'd explored Mexican ruins and Alaskan glaciers? He hadn't mentioned traveling during their snowbound time together. Yesterday, he had mentioned the wild horses he'd seen in Colorado. With Elaine?

He wasn't one of those silent-cowboy types. Yet she had the feeling that he was a very private person. Certainly she respected that. She'd become private about her personal life. And just like her, she was sure there was a reason he was quiet about his, too.

"There are two barns," she explained, giving him another considering look.

"I can see the one has long pens attached that separate the horses," he noted. "That's essential for wild mustangs, and I guess it would be good for horses who have been abused, too."

"Until they learn to trust," Hadley agreed.

When they walked into the larger of the two barns, Eli said, "I can tell this is a new barn. The smells are different than in a decades-old one."

"Tradition means a lot to you, doesn't it?"

"It does. I learned from my dad before I could talk, I imagine the same way he learned from his. Handing down a legacy is important, and caring for the land and the animals the best way possible. Family customs matter, too."

The door to the barn was propped open, and they walked along the stalls. Eli seemed to gravitate toward a stall with the nameplate Gypsy.

"Jazzy told me about Gypsy the last time I was here," Hadley explained. "She's a fairly new rescue who was left to starve when the owners moved away and abandoned her. She's sweet and wants to trust, but she's afraid."

He looked at her. "I thought you didn't relate to horses so well."

"Not that I don't relate. I just haven't cared for them the way I've cared for small pets. I feel more confident with other animals because I've had more experience with them. But I like horses."

He must have accepted her response because he didn't challenge it. Instead, he had his eyes on Gypsy. He didn't approach the horse, or even reach out his hand. He just stood there quietly appreciating the Appaloosa, then he started a conversation with the horse. "You know, don't you, that everybody here wants to take care of you. They won't abandon you. They'll feed you and water you and groom you. Soon you'll remember what it's like to run across a field and enjoy it, or to carry a human on your back who wants to know you, not use you."

Hadley watched, amazed, as Gypsy turned her head toward Eli, then she lifted it and her eyes seemed to study him.

"You were meant to have a good life," he told her, and she took a step toward him.

He waited a beat, then he slowly lifted his hand and held it out to her. She sniffed at his fingers. He let her, not attempting to do more than just get to know her. Finally, she nosed his palm. He ran his hand up her neck and under her mane.

Jazzy had been making progress with Gypsy and so had Brooks. But the mare was still skittish around them. With Eli, however, she'd already seemed to have given her trust. He'd made a connection so quickly. Hadley was impressed again with his gentleness and his horse-whisperer tendencies.

She stayed where she was so as not to disturb their communication, but she asked, "How did you learn to communicate with horses?"

"There's nothing magical about it," he said in the same low voice he'd used to talk to Gypsy. "Once upon a time there was a Native American who lived in a hut not far from our property's boundary line. He lived meagerly with the bare essentials. But that's all he wanted. I used to sit and listen to his stories. He knew everything there was to know about horses. I followed him around and split wood for him. In exchange, Joe made me fried bread. He spent some time with our horses, too. He died when I was in high school, but I'll never forget what he taught me."

"What was that?"

"That nothing's more important than patience, observation, a gentle voice and a kind hand."

"He sounds like a wise man."

"He was."

Hadley would have liked to have found out more, but just then the barn door opened and Darby Conrad barreled in. She was blonde and tall and had enough energy for two Energizer Bunnies. She was young, in her early twenties, and when she spotted Eli, Hadley saw her flip her hair and widen her eyes. She was in flirt mode, that was obvious.

She walked straight up to Eli and extended her hand. "Hi there. I'm Darby Conrad. Who are you?"

Eli's lips twitched with amusement, and Hadley thought he gave Darby one of those male appraising looks. "Eli Dalton is the name. I'm a friend of Brooks's. I understand you work here part-time."

"I do. I wish I could give it more hours, but I help my mom in her hair salon." She held up her hands, and her nails were painted bright pink. "I know it seems a little odd to have a manicure when you work in a barn, but it helps keep my nails in shape." She sauntered a little closer to Eli. "I suppose you love horses, too? Everybody around here does. I have a quarter horse named Moses. I barrel race with him."

"Do you participate in any rodeos?" Eli asked, as if he were interested.

At that, Hadley felt left out, so she wandered away. She went down the line until one of Jazzy's favorite horses, Clementine, a beautiful Chestnut, stuck her head over the stall in Hadley's path.

Hadley stepped up to the horse and rubbed her neck. She suddenly felt as if she were back in high school, and one of the popular cheerleaders had sneaked into the conversation that she was having with one of the boys in her class. One of the boys whom she wished would think of her as more than just a classmate. It was silly, really, that Darby could make her feel that way. But her time with Justin and the consequences of it had done a number on her self-esteem. At least in the way she related to men. She was overly careful now and much too guarded. She understood that, but she didn't know how to get beyond what had happened. Most of all, she didn't know how to trust again because of Justin's lies.

She didn't know how long she stood there thinking about it, everything that had happened, and why she couldn't seem to get beyond the past to find a future.

She heard the back barn door open and shut, but she stayed where she was.

Soon Eli came up beside her. "Why did you wander away?"

"I didn't want to intrude." As soon as she said the words, she wondered if that was the truth. Or was the problem deeper than that? No, she couldn't have been jealous!

"You wouldn't have intruded," Eli insisted. "Nothing was going on. We were just talking about her latest rodeo."

"You're blind if you don't think anything was going on. Darby was flirting and you were flirting back."

"I was just having a conversation," he protested.

Deciding to take the bull by the horns, so to speak, Hadley focused on him instead of the horse. "Can you be honest with me about something?"

"Sure, I can be." He sounded certain.

"Were you attracted to Darby?"

He mulled over the question for an instant, but then he shrugged. "Not nearly as much as I'm attracted to *you*."

That comment made her speechless, and she didn't know what to say to it. But she had to come up with something, and she had to come up with it fast. So she fell back on the first thing that floated into her mind. "We'd better get back to town before Lorna sends out a search party."

"You could call her and tell them you're going to be delayed," he suggested, still with that calm, cool manner he had that frustrated her.

"And why am I going to be delayed?"

"I'd like to make a stop at my brother Jonah's office.

I thought you might like to go with me. His architect office is a refurbished Victorian. It's quite impressive. I thought you might like to see it."

"And you need to see him right now?"

"He just got back from a business trip. I know Mom would like him and his wife, Vanessa, to come to dinner, and I thought with a face-to-face meeting I might be able to convince him better than in a text or over the phone."

"He doesn't see your parents much?"

"Ever since Uncle Phil and his boys moved in with us, Jonah has kept out of the commotion. I can't blame him. There are usually lots of conversations going on and not enough time to talk to any one person. Do you know what I mean?"

"Sure do. It's like that at the boardinghouse right now." She thought about seeing Jonah's office, and then she said, "I really do like Victorians. The boardinghouse has lots of nooks and crannies."

"Melba's place is a gem…not only for its architecture but for the news that's generated there."

"For sure. I can't help but hear gossip. I can't be around my grandmother or my sisters without getting an earful."

Actually, Tessa, Claire and her grandmother wanted to pull her into the drama and romance in Rust Creek Falls, and there had been a lot of it. But Hadley kept herself removed as much as she could. It wasn't easy. And truth be told, she *was* interested in everything that happened here. How could she stay removed from lovers who had found each other? Claire and Levi had renewed their marriage, and Tessa had found true love with Carson.

She was still thinking about that a half hour later as Eli drew up in front of a beautiful Victorian house. She hopped out of the vehicle before he could come around and open her door. But there was a giant snowbank to climb over to get to the sidewalk. Eli saw that. His long legs easily topped it. Once he was on the sidewalk, he offered her his hand. "I can help you climb over, or I can lift you over."

The idea of being lifted in Eli's arms actually made her giddy. That's exactly why she said, "I'll take a hand in climbing over." Still, that didn't work out exactly as she'd planned.

Eli took both of her hands. As she gazed into his eyes, the brim of his Stetson shaded his face. Somehow her booted foot sank into the snow mound. She would have lost her balance and fallen, but Eli's large hands caught her around the waist.

"Easy," he said, his voice deep and husky.

Easy. It would be so easy to fall into her attraction for him. She concentrated on extricating her foot from the snowdrift, but as she did, she leaned forward and practically slid down the other side. Eli caught her, his arms going around her, holding her tight against him. She lost any desire to breathe. When she looked up at him, she knew what he wanted, and she wanted it, too. He was warmth and all man, and his sizzling sexuality just seemed to encompass her. *Remember Justin*, a warning voice in her head yelled at her.

Oh, she remembered Justin.

And Eli must have seen the ghost of that memory on her face because he leaned away. "What's wrong?"

Clamoring for the first viable excuse, she glanced around. "We're on a public sidewalk. You know Rust

Creek Falls. Everyone will talk." She pulled out of his embrace and righted herself in her boots, standing firmly on solid ground once more.

"They'll only talk if there's something to talk about. Is there, Hadley?" Eli stood there, tall, handsome and questioning as he waited for her answer.

Chapter Eight

For a few moments, Eli thought Hadley was going to be honest with him and tell him there was something between them that other people would notice and maybe even talk about. But he saw the exact moment when she decided that wouldn't be a good idea…that being too vulnerable around him wasn't even a possibility.

Taking a step back, she acted as if he hadn't even asked the question. "This is attractive," she said, turning toward Jonah's office. She took a few paces toward the steps. "Coming?" she asked.

He gave her a long, steady glare. "You didn't answer my question."

This time instead of evading him, she responded, "I don't think that's a conversation to have in the cold on a public sidewalk."

"Meaning we'll have that conversation sometime in a warmer spot?"

"We'll see," she said, and he knew she meant it.

Apparently she still hadn't made up her mind about him, though what there was to decide he didn't know. He suspected Hadley Strickland didn't give her trust easily, and he wanted to know the reason why. She'd been right. That definitely *wasn't* a conversation for a public sidewalk.

He led the way up the steps to the porch, and she followed him. After he opened the doors into the foyer, he immediately spotted his brother sitting at a desk to the left in his office.

From the doorway, Eli asked him, "Are you busy?"

"Not too busy for you," Jonah said, standing. "This is a surprise."

"Jonah, I don't know if you know Hadley Strickland."

Hadley stepped up to shake Jonah's hand and studied Eli's brother, who was six feet tall with dark hazel eyes. As usual, he was wearing a dress shirt and jeans with his boots.

"I think we've met in passing," Hadley said. "I've admired your wife's mural at the resort more than once."

Eli wasn't surprised. Everyone in Rust Creek Falls knew of the mural that depicted the history of the town. Vanessa's painting graced the lobby of the restored Maverick Manor.

"I'll tell Vanessa you've admired it," Jonah said. He addressed his brother again. "And how are you enjoying living in your new house? Are you finally settled in?" He looked at Hadley. "This guy bought his furniture piece by piece. It took a while for him to get it furnished."

"I wanted to be comfortable," Eli protested. "And I am."

"It's a beautiful house," Hadley said.

"You've seen it?" Jonah asked with a raised brow.

"Hadley's a vet," Eli explained. "Amber had her foal and a little trouble. We also found a cat and a kitten, so I took them in and she came in to check on them."

"You have pets?" Jonah rolled his eyes then shook his head. "I shouldn't be surprised. There wasn't any doubt you'd put down roots here."

"And now you have, too," Eli pointed out. Jonah had spent years in Denver, till he met Vanessa.

"Yes, I have."

"I couldn't imagine living anywhere else," Eli confided, but then he remembered how his desire to stay here to ranch, to appreciate the land, had separated him from the woman he thought he'd loved.

"Now that I'm back, I can't imagine it either," Jonah agreed.

"Even though Vanessa and I haven't been to dinner lately, I do talk to Mom, you know. She said you'd be helping the Bonners with some repairs."

"That's in my plans for tomorrow," Eli said.

"You do good work, Eli. Lots of elderly folks are glad you're around."

At that Hadley gave him a questioning look, but he didn't explain.

"Speaking of Mom… She wanted me to ask you and Vanessa to come to dinner. I figured you couldn't shut me down face-to-face."

Jonah motioned to his desk. He had blueprints and papers stacked there. "I'm not avoiding the family," he said. "I'm just busy. Vanessa has been, too. She was awarded a commission to paint a mural in a hotel in Denver. She just got back."

"Can you come over Monday night for dinner? Uncle Phil and his sons are going into Kalispell. It would just be me and Derek and the folks."

"I'll check with Vanessa. That sounds like a good idea. We'll be there for Thanksgiving, but I'm sure it will be bedlam."

"Do you want to give Mom a call after you check with Vanessa about Monday night?"

"Sounds good," Jonah said. He smiled at Hadley. "It was nice seeing you again."

A few minutes later they were back in the truck. Hadley fastened her seat belt and asked Eli, "So you're helping the Bonners?"

"Do you know them?"

"My grandmother does. When I'm here and we go to church, she usually manages to talk to all her neighbors. If I remember correctly, Mrs. Bonner had a stroke about six months ago."

"That's right. She's recovering, but her husband worries about her."

"Grandmother told me that they couldn't afford to have many renovations done."

"That's why I'm helping them," he admitted.

"And Jonah said you do good work, which means you've helped others. So you *are* a Secret Santa, too." There was a twinkle in her eye and amusement in her voice.

"You could call me that if you want, but I just help people who need it. There are lots of older folk who can't afford someone to do the work and don't have kids who can do it for them."

"Tell me why you do it."

He shrugged and started up the truck. "I'm not the most educated man in the world, but I've got skills. It's good karma to share them." He wouldn't have told Hadley about the work he did. That just wasn't his way. But now that she knew—

"So if you know the Bonners, would you like to come along with me tomorrow? If you've got something else on your schedule, I understand."

"Nothing on my schedule. Not unless I get another emergency call from Brooks. If I come with you, is there something I can do to help?"

"Can you cook?"

"I wouldn't be my grandmother's granddaughter if I didn't know how to cook."

"Maybe you could bring fixings along to make a meal. I'll tell the Bonners we'll provide dinner. That would be a treat for them. They don't get that many visitors, so I'm sure they'll enjoy our company, too."

"I like that idea. I like it a lot. Thanks for inviting me along, Eli."

"Maybe I have an ulterior motive," he replied as he pulled away from the curb. "Maybe when we're not on a public sidewalk, and we're someplace warm," he added as he cast a heated glance her way, "we can have that conversation you avoided."

The next day as Carl Bonner invited Hadley and Eli inside the small home, Hadley remembered what Eli had said yesterday. He couldn't imagine living anywhere but Rust Creek Falls. He was a man with roots. Did he stay because of the ranch and his family's land? Did he stay because he liked Rust Creek Falls? Did he stay because the small town was familiar, or maybe it was simpler than all that—he stayed because his family and friends were here.

Hadley thought about her own life in Bozeman. Tessa and Claire no longer lived there. She alternated her life with her husband from California to Falls Mountain. Hadley's parents were in Bozeman, but their lives were busy and hers was, too.

Eli was carrying grocery bags, and so was Hadley. Seeing that, Carl said, "It looks as if you brought enough supplies for a week's worth of meals. I don't need no charity." The man was easily in his seventies with a white mustache and a balding pate that sported a few white strands.

"It's not charity," Hadley assured him. "I just thought after Eli does a little work, we can all use a home-cooked meal. I'm going to make a beef, noodle and tomato casserole. How does that sound?"

"That sounds just fine," Carl said with an answering smile. "I thought you were going to do something fancy with all those bags."

Suddenly Jill Bonner appeared in the doorway from the kitchen. She was using a four-pronged cane and didn't look the steadiest on her feet. Her husband went to her and helped her to an armchair in the living room.

"Do you remember Hadley Strickland from church?" he asked his wife.

"Oh, of course I do. Melba talks about you all the time," Jill told Hadley. She had snowy-white hair that looked like a halo around her head. She was thin, and her cardigan sweater looked oversize on her small frame. She was wearing sweatpants and a top that looked easy to pull on and off.

Hadley went to her and crouched down beside her chair. "Before I start supper, how would you like a cup of tea?"

"You don't have to go to any bother. Carl makes fine tea."

"I'm sure he does, but he's probably going to want to supervise Eli, don't you think?"

Jill gave a little giggle and said in a low voice, "You know how men operate, don't you?"

All too well, Hadley thought. "Let's just say my dad and grandpa would do the same." She leaned toward Jill conspiratorially. "Do you think he'd like some apple cobbler for dessert tonight?"

"That sounds grand," Jill assured her. "Is yours as good as Melba's?"

"I doubt it," Hadley said with a laugh. "But I'll make a good attempt, and I'll put together a salad so no one can say we didn't have our vegetables."

"The tea kettle's on the stove," Jill explained. "And the mugs are on the counter. We don't bother putting them away."

"I'm sure I'll find everything without a problem."

Eli said, "I'll just put these groceries in the kitchen then go get my tools and we'll get started."

The next few hours sped by. Hadley made tea for her and Jill, then started supper. Afterward, she and Jill talked. They had a lot to talk about—from her grandmother and grandfather to events at church to Hadley's practice in Bozeman. Jill even showed Hadley how she managed to crochet, telling her it was good therapy for her hand that was still a little weak from the stroke. She made mistakes but she could correct them.

Hadley wished all of life was like that. Correctable.

After they all sat down to dinner, Hadley learned that the Bonners had a son who was living in Portland.

"We wish he'd move back here," Jill said honestly. "Not so he can take care of us, but just so we can keep company with him in the time we have left. I'm sure your parents feel the same," she said to Hadley.

Hadley didn't know. She'd rarely talked to her parents about anything like that. But she bet Eli had spoken with his parents about it. His family bonds were one of the reasons he was so grounded and knew where he belonged.

Hadley had made sure she cooked enough food that the Bonners would have leftovers. After dinner, Eli helped her clean up while Carl showed Jill the improvements Eli had made to the bathroom.

While Eli plucked a dish from the drainer, ready to dry it, he told Hadley, "Carl's pleased with the repairs. I'm going to come back next week and build a ramp for the back steps. And you did a great job with supper. They should have enough for a couple of meals. Did you see Jill's face when she ate that real whipped cream on top of the apple cobbler? We made them happy, Hadley."

"It was easy to do. I can see why you enjoy helping. Maybe *enjoy* isn't the right word, but you find satisfaction in it."

"I usually enjoy it, too. Purpose is everything."

"Purpose?" she asked.

"Sure. Your purpose is getting up each day and helping as many animals as you can, right?"

"I suppose it is," she said thoughtfully. But then she wondered if that was enough of a purpose for her life.

She was still thinking about that as Eli drove her back to the boardinghouse. After he pulled up in front, he cracked a window and let the heater run along with the engine. "Are you ready to have that conversation now?"

She knew exactly what conversation he meant. But, no, she wasn't ready to have it. Still, she knew she couldn't avoid it.

"Eli, what do you want me to say?"

"This has nothing to do with what I *want* you to say. I want to know how you *feel*. There's chemistry between us, maybe even something more than that. But if it's all one-sided, you can hop out of this truck and I won't call you or expect you to visit Amber and Coco or the cats ever again."

When she thought about not seeing Eli again, she had a sick feeling in her stomach. Worse than that, her heart hurt a little. Oh, no. Her heart couldn't be involved.

"Eli, I'm not going to be here much past Thanksgiving."

He shrugged. "It's not like Bozeman is that far away."

No, it wasn't, she supposed. But long distance was no way to start a relationship. What was she even thinking? She didn't *want* a relationship.

Eli turned fully toward her and gently clasped her shoulder. As he nudged her toward him, he said, "I enjoy your company, Hadley."

She swallowed hard. "And I enjoy yours. This afternoon was pleasant." Better to stay on safe territory.

Even in the dim light from the dashboard she could see his small smile. "I was thinking more about the intimate time we shared in the barn."

"We didn't have any intimate time. We both had our clothes on," she pointed out.

"Do you think clothes make a difference?" he joked.

"I know clothes make *all* the difference in the world."

He suddenly grew serious. "I suppose that's true. If we'd taken off our clothes, we would have really found out what intimacy was."

"Eli," she warned.

"Does the idea of being intimate with me make you want to back away?"

Actually the exact opposite was true, but she couldn't admit that.

"Why are you so afraid to give in to this attraction?"

"Maybe attraction has gotten me into trouble before," she blurted out.

Although she suspected he might drop the subject, he didn't. "Do you want to tell me about it?"

"No, I don't. I just mean attraction is limited and sometimes doesn't go anywhere."

"But it could be a lot of fun finding out exactly where it's going to go," Eli protested.

Eli always seemed to carry the scent of leather and soap about him. It drew her to him, almost as much as anything else about him. Though she did like his eyes and his heavy brows and the jut of his jaw and the set of his lips. She was crazy for even thinking about becoming more involved with him. Not that she *was* involved. She could put the brakes on at any time. She could leave Rust Creek Falls and forget all about him.

But right now, sitting in his truck, so close to him, inhaling that soap and leather, inhaling him, watching his expression, feeling the electricity that ricocheted between them when they were in a confined space, she couldn't deny she was very attracted to him. If she could just take a moment to think… However, she didn't. She acted on impulse.

She reached up to his face and ran her thumb over the dent in his chin. He clasped her hand and did something she totally didn't expect. He kissed her fingers, one by one. Then he slid his hand under her hair at her neck, pulled her close and kissed her.

There was no doubt she was kissing him back this time. There was no doubt they were both involved in this kiss up to their eyeballs and down to their boots. Eli seemed to have the expertise and the power to make her feel more like a woman than she'd felt in years. She felt sensations deep inside that pushed her closer to him. Her fingers ached to touch him. They tunneled into his hair, knocking his hat off.

He didn't seem to mind because he kissed her harder, longer and wetter. The windows steamed up, and she decided breathing was overrated.

Suddenly the porch light went on and blazed through the car windows. They both became aware of it, blinked and slowly ended the kiss. Hadley felt embarrassed that she'd gone from zero to ten on the passion scale in a matter of seconds.

She mumbled, "I wonder if that thing's on a timer, or Old Gene is turning it on intentionally."

Eli's voice was husky when he said, "It could be Melba. She'll want you to know you have backup if you need it."

Hadley could have used backup three years ago… backup against her own foolishness. Backup to sit her down and explain what the wise thing to do would be. But she'd been besotted with Justin, and wisdom might not have entered into it either.

Before she could pull completely away, Eli stroked

her cheek. "Hadley, there's nothing wrong with what we did."

"I know that. I'm still not sure it's wise."

Even though Hadley said it, she was reluctant to get out of the truck. Eli didn't seem eager to move away either. She racked her brain for something to say, something to bridge the silence. "So you'll be having a big Thanksgiving dinner on Thursday?"

"We will. It hasn't been decided yet where the celebration will take place—at the Circle D or at the Dalton family ranch, Uncle Ben's place. But it will be big and noisy with more food than even the Dalton clan can eat. They'll all be there, except for Kayla. She'll be spending Thanksgiving with you Stricklands. I suppose your celebration will be huge, too."

She nodded. "Melba and Old Gene will be in their glory having everybody. It will be noisy with lots of food and lots of teasing."

"You don't like the teasing part?"

Apparently Eli was beginning to know her, the nuances in her voice. She supposed her expression gave her away, too. "Maybe I'm just not a crowd person. Give me a litter of puppies and I'm fine. But give me a crowd of people, and I'd rather be holed up with one person, talking."

"I can relate to that," he said, with a smile in his voice. "Especially if that one person is the pretty lady in the truck with me."

He leaned over to give her another kiss, but she braced her hands on his chest. "I think I'd better go in." She unfastened her seat belt and moved over to the door.

"If I don't see you before you leave, Hadley, well—"

He paused a moment before he added, "I have your phone number and you have mine."

She had it. But when she went back to Bozeman, she wouldn't use it, would she?

She nodded, murmured, "Yes, I have your number," then opened her door and left the truck. She already felt as if she missed Eli. That was a sensation she was just going to have to get over.

On Thanksgiving Day, Hadley felt a bit nervous about the announcement she was going to make. Brooks Smith was complicating her life, and she was letting him. But the real complication could be her family's reaction to all of it.

Her parents had arrived from Bozeman last night along with her uncle and aunt Jerry and Barbara Strickland. Her mom, Melba and Barbara had had their heads together going over recipes since then. The smells emanating from the kitchen today were worth all of their planning. The boardinghouse was practically bursting at the seams. Somehow they'd all managed to sit in one room for dinner.

There was her grandmother and grandfather, of course, along with her sister Claire, her husband, Levi, and daughter Bekka. Her sister Tessa, her husband, Carson, and their twins, Declan and Charlotte. Jerry and Barbara and their son Trey and his wife, Kayla, and little Gil, too. All Hadley had to do was look at Kayla and she saw her brother Eli's features, the sparkling eyes and the wide smile. Around the table were also Jerry and Barbara's four unmarried sons, Drew, Benjamin, Luke and Billy.

The male cousins talked sports, while the females

shared gossip and Old Gene joked with Carson and the twins. The conversation was lively and loud, but it didn't stop Hadley from hearing the question that she dreaded. The one that was always bound to come up when a group like this gathered.

"And who's going to get married next?" her sister Tessa asked.

Old Gene shook his finger at Tessa. "The bigger question is—who's going to produce the next grandchild?"

Luke gave Benjamin a shove in the ribs, but Benjamin just shook his head. Everyone seemed to take the ribbing in stride until Drew said, "Miss All-Business Hadley is more likely to give us grand dogs than grandbabies, don't you think?"

Hadley flashed back to a time when she'd planned to announce her Las Vegas wedding to the whole family. She had been so happy. But her dreams and her hopes had all been a terrible delusion.

Now smiling at everyone, she said, "Grand dogs or grand kitties I can produce. I can probably find one of each for all of you to adopt."

There were groans around the table. Billy said, "As if there's room for an animal in this house."

"There's always room for a pet," Hadley insisted.

Kayla nodded and backed her up. She held up her hand and said, "Even my brother has adopted a cat and a kitten. Who would have thought? That was all Hadley's doing."

"She can be persuasive when she wants to be," Old Gene said with a wink at her.

Before her family entered territory where she and Eli were lumped together, or before anyone else mused about her romantic life, she passed the serving dish of mashed potatoes to Drew and said, "I have an announcement to make."

"You're engaged," Carson joked.

"Nothing like that," she was quick to assure them all. Then she thought of something. Maybe she should have talked to Old Gene and her grandmother before she announced this to everybody. But it was too late now.

To Melba she said, "I probably should have asked you about this first. Do you mind if I stay a little longer?"

Her mother gave her a look. "Longer? Why would you do that?" Donna Strickland asked her.

Melba, on her other side, patted her hand. "Of course we don't mind if you stay. *If* there's a good reason," she added.

"I think it's a good reason, but you can judge. I think you know Brooks Smith's dad is recovering from knee-replacement surgery. After Dr. Wellington left, Brooks thought he could handle the practices on his own, but it's become overwhelming at times. So he asked me if I'd stay on the next couple of weeks to help him out. His dad's recovering slowly, and he doesn't want him to rush it."

"But what about your job at the clinic in Bozeman?" her dad asked.

"I spoke with them last night. They tell me as long as I'm back there mid-December, they're fine with me staying here and helping. They brought on a new vet tech, and she's working out well."

"She can't replace you," Hadley's mother insisted.

"True, but it will do me good to get more experience here with horses and cattle. So, Grandmother, if you don't mind my staying—"

Old Gene cut in. "We don't mind at all. It's a shame you can't stay for Christmas."

"Oh, but we'll be glad to have her back in Bozeman," Hadley's mother assured them. "We have to share her, you know."

Everyone around the table laughed. On her other side, Drew leaned close to her and said in a low voice, "I was talking to Derek Dalton at the Ace in the Hole."

"And?" Hadley asked, with a lift of her brow.

"And he said you and Eli Dalton got cozy. You stayed overnight there, and you two were alone in the barn."

"In a cold barn in a blizzard," she reminded him. "We were practically strangers, Drew. Nothing was going to happen overnight. Derek's imagination is too vivid."

"And maybe you're protesting a little too much."

Maybe she was protesting because she could still remember the feel of her head on Eli's shoulder as they cuddled together for warmth. Maybe she was protesting too much because the touch of Eli's lips on hers was more than a memory.

Drew gave her a curious look, then shrugged. "Did Derek ask you on a date and you turned him down?"

"No, we never quite got to that. He approached me at Kayla's wedding and tried to charm me."

"But you can't be charmed?" Drew asked.

"Not by Derek."

"Ah. Could that leave an opening for his older brother?"

She elbowed Drew in the ribs. "Fill your face with that turkey and stop making up scenarios about my life."

Drew behaved for the most part after that, and the conversations jumped around to other things besides marriage and grandchildren.

As she was helping Melba clear the table, Melba said, "You know you're welcome here whenever you want to stay, especially in the winter when we don't have many guests."

Hadley was still smiling at that when the phone on her belt buzzed. In Bozeman she was used to it buzzing all the time—either a client calling or one of the other vets or one of her friends. But here, her phone had mostly been quiet except for texts between her and her sisters.

When she checked the screen now, her heart sped up. It was Eli.

"Hey," she said when she answered, trying to sound casual.

"Hey, yourself. Happy Thanksgiving."

"Happy Thanksgiving to you, too." After she said it, she mentally groaned. How lame could she get?

"You probably have a houseful there at Strickland's."

"We do," she said, sounding a little weary of it.

He chuckled. "A little too much family?"

"I love them all," she reminded him.

He chuckled again. "How would you like to drive over here and have dessert with me in my cabin?"

"I'd like that," she said. "Believe me, nobody here will miss me."

"I doubt that. About half an hour?"

"See you soon." After she ended the call, Hadley wondered what she'd just done. Agreed to a date of sorts?

Tessa was passing by her on the way to the kitchen when Hadley snagged her arm. "I'm going out for a while."

"Out where?" Tessa asked.

"To the Dalton ranch."

"Checking on that foal?" Tessa asked with a twinkle in her eye.

"Sure am," Hadley said with a straight face.

"I'll cover for you," Tessa agreed, then added, "Say hello to Eli for me," and disappeared into the kitchen.

As Hadley went to fetch her coat, she wondered if Eli would be glad she was staying longer in Rust Creek Falls.

She'd soon find out.

Chapter Nine

Eli watched for Hadley's SUV. When she drove up and parked near the cabin, he opened his door. He'd debated about calling her. Should he or shouldn't he? He'd asked himself more than once if he wanted more than a casual relationship with her. Hadley was different from any woman he'd dated. She was natural, no fake airs. Animals were more important to her than makeup. Not that she needed makeup. She had a natural beauty that drew him to her. Yes, she'd be returning to Bozeman, but did that really matter if they wanted to see each other?

He'd thought again about Elaine…about her leaving. Was he really going to let that affect his relationships for the rest of his life? The failure of his first serious relationship had kept him from becoming involved for years.

He'd told himself that today could be the last chance

to see Hadley before she left Rust Creek Falls. That conclusion had led him to pick up his phone and call her.

Now Hadley hurried up the walk, saying, "Aren't you afraid the cats will run out?"

"They're sleeping up in the loft," he said, pointing in that direction. "I just got back from the barn checking on Amber and the foal. Come on in."

After Hadley stepped inside, he closed the door. "Are you interested in dessert or sitting in front of the fire?"

"Both sound nice," she admitted.

He went to the fireplace, where he'd laid kindling. Pulling a log from the carrier on the hearth, he placed it in position. "Did you have a nice Thanksgiving with your family?" he asked as she shrugged out of her jacket.

He went to her, and as he took her jacket from her, his fingers brushed hers. When both of them stopped and gazed into each other's eyes, Eli felt the world spin a bit. To find his bearings again, he carried her coat into the kitchen and hung it over one of the chairs. Returning to her, he waited for her answer.

"It was nice," she said, not giving any further explanation.

He never knew how much to prod her, so he said casually, "That doesn't sound like an endorsement for a big family gathering."

With a sigh, Hadley sank down onto the sofa. "The truth is, I needed an excuse to get away."

He could take that as an insult, but he chose not to. If she felt he was a haven of sorts, so be it.

She must have realized what she said. "I'm sorry. I didn't mean to make that sound— I mean, I wanted to come here and have dessert with you."

If he went to her now, he might just take her in his arms and kiss her. That could send her driving back to her family. Instead he put another log on the fire, then he took the can of long matches from the mantel and plucked one out.

"So tell me why you needed an excuse to leave."

"When I'm sitting there with everyone, I feel the pressure of family expectations," she explained.

Eli glanced at her over his shoulder and saw the serious expression on her face. Whatever was bothering her seemed like more than just the typical irritation of family poking into private lives. He kept quiet to see if she'd tell him more.

By the time he'd lit the fire, she'd started talking again.

"I'm aware that my grandmother and my mother think I should settle down and start a family. And maybe that *is* on my mind, too. But that doesn't mean I should want to date every eligible bachelor. That doesn't mean I should jump at the chance of marriage."

A quaver in Hadley's voice alerted Eli, but there was hurt behind her words. He wished she'd confide more in him. However, he saw her lips set perfectly now, and he sensed she was already regretting she'd said too much. He was glad when the cats chose that moment to descend the stairs from the loft. Both of them came running over to Hadley and wrapped around her legs.

Her smile was back as she picked up Winks. "You are such a cutie." She snuggled her until the kitten started squirming.

When she put her down, Winks scrambled over to Eli and, as before, started climbing up his jean-clad leg.

He caught her at his knee and lifted her into his arms.

"She's a character. It's a good thing I don't have curtains on the windows or she'd be climbing them." There was just a Western-patterned valance over each window that had been Kristen's idea. Now he was glad of it.

"You'll have to get them a scratching post and train them to use it, then they won't bother your furniture."

"I'll do that," he said. "So tell me what kind of dessert you'd like. Mom didn't take it all along to Uncle Ben's."

"Why are you here when they're all over there?"

"I just came back to check on the horses and the cats. Believe me, there are enough people there that they won't miss me. Anyway I have apple and pumpkin pies."

"Your mom made you two pies?"

"My cousins drop in. Besides, she knows I like late-night snacks."

Hadley looked up at him and then at the table in the kitchen. "Do you want me to come to the kitchen?"

"No need. We can sit here and enjoy the fire."

She peered into the fire as if she was looking for answers to a question. But then she nodded to him. "I'd like a slice of apple."

"Coming right up. Coffee with that?"

"Sounds good."

From the kitchen, Eli watched her. She was dressed in a green sweater with a black turtleneck underneath. Her slim-cut black jeans showed off her legs above her shoe boots. He saw that she busied herself with the cats while he cut two slices of pie and poured coffee into mugs. He brought it all to the coffee table.

When he sat beside her, they ate. He noticed their silence was companionable and not at all awkward.

After Hadley was finished, she set her dish on the coffee table and let out a sigh. "You know, this is the first I've really relaxed since I got here. The boarding-house is more like a dorm with everybody in and out of each other's rooms. There's lots of company for meals, and generally speaking I like that."

"Except, sometimes you want private time," Eli guessed.

"Exactly. Private time with no one butting into my business or asking where I'm going or what I'm going to be doing. You'd think I'd be used to it with two sisters. But somehow I thought once we were adults on our own, that would change."

"That's why I built this house," Eli said with complete understanding. "It was time. My mother gives me the same lecture that your grandmother gives you. That look and a wink that says she wants grandkids from me. And I tell her that will happen when it's supposed to happen."

Somehow while eating their pie and drinking their coffee and talking about family issues they both understood, they had leaned closer to each other. Eli was reading the signals from Hadley that she was glad to be here and glad to be close to him. Yet he sensed her reserve also and wondered if he could break through it.

So instead of wondering, he asked, "Are you going to run if I kiss you again? Or will you stay for a second cup of coffee?"

He thought she swallowed hard. He thought the color in her cheeks pinkened. She hesitated only a moment before she answered him. "I'll stay for the coffee."

He didn't rush and he didn't move too quickly. He realized in some ways he was treating Hadley like a skittish colt. But what other way was there to gentle somebody you wanted to care for? He laid his hand on her shoulder, then he leaned in and rubbed his cheek against hers.

It must have been the right thing to do because she turned her face up to him. When he took her lips, they were soft and welcoming, and he felt as if they'd been building to this since the first moment she'd stepped into his barn. Their other kisses had been impulsive and maybe even considered mistakes by Hadley. But this one was fully consensual.

In no time at all, with his arm wrapped around her, he'd brought her over onto his lap, where kissing was easier. She seemed as lost in him as he was in her. She ran her fingers in his hair and along his jawline. He'd learned restraint in his thirty-plus years, but Hadley's response made him want to break free of all restraints. He'd moved his hand to her breast and was about to take them a little farther when suddenly Whisper jumped up to the back of the sofa.

Eli could tell Hadley was aware of it. Her hand suddenly went to his chest, and she leaned away from him.

In a husky voice, he asked, "Too much?"

"Too fast. I'm not going to let attraction sweep me away into regret."

He had a feeling there was more to those words than the subject of their kiss.

Where they hadn't been awkward before, now they were. He wasn't sure the best way to handle Hadley or the situation.

She slid from his lap back onto the sofa. As he tried to convince his heart to slow, Hadley righted her clothes. But then she turned toward him, one leg up on the sofa, purpose on her pretty face.

Uh-oh. He had a premonition he wasn't going to like what was coming.

Earnestly, she asked, "Why did you stop traveling and rock climbing?"

He'd been right. He didn't like the question, or the answers it brought with it. On the other hand, he realized in order to earn Hadley's trust, he needed to give his. To give himself a moment to pull his thoughts together, he reached up on the sofa to stroke the cat. "I was serious about a woman once…maybe too young to know what serious was or simply too young to read character well. I suppose I ignored things I shouldn't have because she liked to go rock climbing with me. We traveled together. I suppose it was her adventurous spirit I liked. But it was her adventurous spirit or her wanting something bigger that took her away from me. I didn't realize until it was too late that she had no desire to stay in Rust Creek Falls. I didn't realize that what I considered an adventurous spirit in Elaine was really ambition. I thought we were happy. I was wrong. She informed me she felt trapped. So we broke up and I lost the traveling bug."

"And the rock climbing?"

With a shrug, he explained, "I poured that energy into the ranch, making it a success, making sure no one could fault the fencing or the upkeep on the barn or feeding the cattle in winter or making sure the horses had the right feed. Derek might think he's a rancher, but he's not about ranching. Do you know what I mean?"

Her eyes sparkling with empathy, she told him,

"I know some vets who are great clinicians, but they don't have a bond with animals."

"I feel the ranch in my blood, just like my father does."

Suddenly there was a loud rap-rap-rap on Eli's door. The next moment the door opened and Derek strode in.

When he saw the two of them on the sofa, he grinned. "Am I interrupting something?"

Before Eli could give him a gruff *turn around and go back outside*, Hadley motioned to their coffee and plates. "Just having dessert."

Derek had never been good at taking hints, and now he didn't take the one that the two of them possibly wanted to be alone. He said, "You have the pies Mom baked." He crossed to the kitchen as if he might steal one.

"You didn't get enough dessert at Uncle Ben's?" Eli asked him.

"I got dessert, but Mom's apple pie went first, and I see you still have some left. Coffee, too. I'll just join you."

There was a retort on the tip of Eli's tongue, but Derek was his brother. He wouldn't get into a spat with him in front of Hadley.

In no time at all, Derek had cut himself a big slice of pie, poured a mug of coffee and sat in the armchair across from the sofa. He said to Eli, "Anderson wanted to know if you want to meet up tomorrow night at the Ace in the Hole. I told him you would."

Eli's cousin Anderson was probably his best friend. Meeting up with him to share a beer and talk sports would be good. "I'll text him later," Eli said. "But that should be okay."

In between forkfuls of pie, Derek asked Hadley, "Are you going to the holiday dance at the community center on Saturday night?"

"I haven't decided," she said.

"I'd be glad to take you," Derek offered.

"Not necessary, bro. Hadley said if she goes, she's going with me."

Derek looked from one of them to the other. Then he waved his hand across the coffee table. "So this isn't just *we're going to have dessert together.* This is, *we might be dating each other.*"

Eli didn't want to put Hadley in the position she didn't want to be in. "I think this is none of your business," Eli said firmly.

Hadley turned around to Winks, who'd fallen asleep on the back of the sofa with her mom. She said, "The cats look great. You're taking wonderful care of them." Then she got to her feet. "I'd better be getting back. My mom and dad will be leaving in the morning, and they'll want to visit while they're here."

That sounded odd to Eli since Hadley would be going back to Bozeman soon. But he'd let her use the excuse. He went to get her coat and helped her put it on. The touch of her hair on his fingers reminded him how soft it was, how much he liked running his fingers through it.

He pointed to Derek. "Don't eat all the pie. I'm going to walk Hadley out."

His brother gave him a thumbs-up.

As soon as they were outside, Hadley turned to him. "You don't have to feel obligated to go with me to the dance. I know you were just protecting me from Derek."

"Nope, I wasn't. I know you don't need protection. Asking you to go with me has nothing to do with him."

"You didn't exactly ask," she teased.

"Well, I'm asking you now. Will you go to the dance with me?"

"I will," she said with a wide smile.

He couldn't help it then. He had to kiss her again.

They created enough heat to ward off the cold, but once again Hadley pulled away. "I really do need to get back. The reason I need to spend time with my parents tonight is that I won't be seeing them again for a couple of weeks."

He waited for her to explain.

"Brooks asked me to stay and help him, and that's what I'm going to do. I cleared it with my practice."

"So the dance at the community center might not be our first and last date?"

"Might not," she said coyly. Then she gave him a wave and went to her SUV.

Eli felt as if he'd just been handed an early Christmas present. Now he just had to figure out what to do with it.

On Friday, Eli pulled a hay bale from the back of the buckboard and laid it out for the cattle. His mind was on another viewing party tonight at the Ace in the Hole. He was going to meet his cousin Anderson there. Would Hadley be there, too? He couldn't wait for the dance tomorrow night to see her again.

Thinking about holding her in his arms, he came back to earth when his dad asked from the driver's seat of the buckboard, "Need a hand?" His father had a weathered face and dark brown hair heavily laced with gray. He usually wore his hat, so not many people noticed he was going bald on top. Eli had looked up to him all of his life and liked working beside him.

"I'm fine," Eli called back. This wasn't like him not to keep his mind on what he was doing. After he finished with a few of the bales, he climbed back in the buckboard to take the feed a little farther. This was a good time to talk to his dad about something.

"What do you think would please Mom for Christmas?"

His father just shook his head. "She insists she doesn't need anything, so I don't know what to tell you. Maybe you should get some advice from that woman you have your eye on."

Eli was surprised his dad had noticed.

Surprising him again, his dad went on, "Your mom thinks that girl has her head on straight."

"Hadley's a very caring vet."

"Um," his dad mumbled, "that's about her job. What about *her*?"

Eli and his dad talked straight when they talked serious. "I think somebody did a number on her."

"You mean like Elaine did to you?"

There again Eli didn't think his dad had paid all that much attention. After all, Eli had tried to hide his feelings about the breakup, about the disappointment he felt in not having the future he'd envisioned. Apparently his father saw more than Eli realized.

"Yeah, just like that," he answered. "The other thing is—she's college educated. She's getting her pilot's license. I think she wants to own her own practice someday."

"And you mind you didn't go to college?"

"No, it's not that I mind. I didn't want it. I didn't think I needed it."

"You feel less than her?" his dad asked perceptively.

"You know, if you want a college education you can do it on that computer of yours."

Eli had thought about that, too, getting a degree that way. Something in business management, maybe, that would help him run the ranch.

His phone inside his coat pocket vibrated and buzzed. It was the signal that a text had come in. Cell service could be spotty out here but texts usually made their way through. Slipping it from his pocket he saw that it was from Derek. The text made fear grip Eli's chest. 911.

Eli knew Derek had gone out snowmobiling on the other side of the ranch. Keeping his voice as calm as he could, he said to his father, "We've got to head back. Derek could be in trouble."

As Hadley entered the boardinghouse, bags in hand, she realized she hadn't gone dress shopping in way too long. She actually had had fun, and she'd found something for the dance that might make Eli take a second look tomorrow night, and maybe even a third.

She entered the kitchen to hopefully pull Claire upstairs with her so she could show her the dress. But then Claire's husband, Levi, came clomping down the stairs and into the kitchen, his cell phone at his ear, worry on his face. Into the phone he said, "I'll load up Old Gene's snowmobile on his truck. Be there in ten."

"What's wrong?" Claire asked.

"An alarm has been sounded for anyone with a snowmobile."

"What happened?" Hadley asked.

"Derek is missing. He went out snowmobiling and texted Eli a 911 message. Nothing since then."

Levi grabbed his jacket from the peg near the door but Hadley called to him. "I'm going with you." She dropped her bags on the counter and asked Claire, "Will you take these up to my room?" Then she was hurrying after Levi, praying nothing serious had happened to the brother Eli loved.

At the Circle D, Hadley raced into the house while Levi unloaded the snowmobile and spoke to other ranchers who had gathered there. In the kitchen Rita Dalton was busy making sandwiches while two coffeepots brewed.

Hadley shrugged out of her coat. "What can I do to help?"

"They started the search about an hour ago. Eli's been out there the longest. The searchers are going to need sandwiches and coffee to keep them going. Can you fill those thermoses? Just add a touch of milk. Most of the men like it that way."

"You've done this before," Hadley guessed.

"I had lots of experience after the flood. Now once in a while we get a lost hiker. Before I've never had to worry that one of my own was out there, possibly hurt." Rita's voice cracked.

Hadley went to her and put her arm around the woman's shoulders. She didn't say anything because she realized Rita was a realistic woman who didn't want platitudes. They didn't know what had happened to Derek or what would happen next.

After a moment, Rita pulled away. She continued to assemble sandwiches. Then she said, "A rancher's wife has to be prepared for anything." Her gaze met Hadley's, and there seemed to be a message in that. She went on. "All I ever wanted was to be a wife and a mom.

That single focus has driven my life, and there hasn't been room for much else. But now that my children are grown, my girls and Jonah married, Eli with his own house, I respect women with careers even more. They have something else to occupy their thoughts when their children are on their own. That might make for livelier conversation with their husbands."

Hadley said, "It's never too late to have other interests."

"Oh, Charles and I are set in our ways. But you might have a point. I might stop in at the community center and see if anyone's interested in organizing a book club or something like that."

Hadley had poured coffee into the thermoses and was making sandwiches with Rita when Charles tramped in the door. "Eli found Derek. He's bringing him home."

"Is Derek hurt?" Rita asked.

"We don't know what condition he's in," Charles answered her. "Eli didn't say. I've called the paramedics just in case. Even if the boy is on his feet, something happened out there and I want him checked out."

Rita nodded her approval at that.

The paramedics arrived before Eli. Hadley went outside to wait. The revolving red light on the paramedic's van cast an eerie glow over the snow. She heard the sound of a snowmobile before she saw it. Then she saw the machine and the man driving it, and Derek holding on behind Eli. If he was holding on, he had to be all right. At least that's what she told herself, though she didn't know for sure.

She stayed back as Rita and Charles crowded around their sons. The paramedics took control, spoke with Eli and handled Derek as if he were glass. They laid him on a board, put a collar around his neck and then loaded him into the ambulance.

They were backing out, when Eli saw her. "What are you doing here?"

"I had to know if you were okay...if Derek was okay."

The features of his face softened a bit. "I have to follow the ambulance to the hospital."

"I'll go with you," she said impulsively. "Let me grab coffee and a couple of sandwiches for you."

"No need," he said, raising his hand. But she didn't listen. She ran to the house, grabbed the items and ran to Eli's truck that he'd already started up. She hopped inside before he could protest.

"Hadley, there's going to be a lot of waiting."

"I know that. Don't you need someone to wait with you?"

He cut her a glance and turned up the heater.

She realized he had to be freezing from being out in that weather for the time he'd been searching. It probably hadn't been easy finding Derek in the snow, getting him on the machine and worrying through the ride back.

Without being asked, she poured coffee into the top cup of the thermos. "Take this," she said, "and drink it."

He didn't argue. After he swallowed about half the coffee, he handed it back to her.

"Just tell me if you want more. How about a sandwich?"

He shook his head. "Maybe later."

"Do you want to talk about it?"

Eli seemed to mull that over. "I was never so scared as when I got that text from him. It was just '911' then it cut out. I tried calling him back. I tried texting him back. But there was no answer. I think he passed out. He probably has a concussion and maybe a broken arm. I don't know how he held on to me on the way back, but he insisted that we do it that way. I wasn't going to argue. I just wanted to get him warmed up."

"What happened?"

"I think he hit an ice patch. I found him pinned under the machine. But once I moved the snowmobile off him, he insisted he was perfectly capable of riding back with me. I'm still afraid I made the wrong decision. But with the snow and night falling, I didn't have any choice."

She reached over and touched Eli's arm. If he had more to say, she'd let him get it out.

"I'd had some first aid training. I checked his breathing and took his pulse. But nothing prepares you for an emergency like that. Absolutely nothing."

"Your mom was worried sick about both of you, but she didn't let it show much."

"That's Mom. I'm so thankful for everyone who came out to search. I think every man in town who had a snowmobile came to the ranch."

"Levi included. That's how I knew what had happened."

"That's the emergency alert chain. One person calls the next."

"Rust Creek Falls is really a tight-knit community," she mused.

"Yes, it is. Neighbors really care about each other."

"Not just neighbors," she said lightly.

Eli cut her another glance.

What had she just admitted? That she cared about Eli Dalton?

As if he wasn't sure what she'd meant either, he said, "I'll take more of that coffee now."

She added hot coffee to what was already in the cup, handed it to him and watched his large, capable hands as he drank the coffee and expertly steered the truck. When she couldn't tear her gaze from him, she knew then without a doubt she was falling for Eli Dalton.

What was she going to do about that?

Chapter Ten

Hadley didn't try to make conversation as she and Eli sat in the hospital waiting room for over an hour. Eli had alternated between pacing, sitting and brooding. Talking would have been too much of a burden at a time like this.

Finally she looked at the thermos that she'd brought inside with her. "How about another cup of coffee? I'm sure it's better than what's in any vending machine here."

Eli glanced over at her as if he were seeing her for the first time. "Thanks for coming along and waiting with me. If I don't call Mom and Dad with some kind of report soon, they're going to be here, too."

"Evaluation and tests take time," Hadley reminded him.

"I'm sure this isn't the way you expected to spend your evening," he muttered.

"I've learned life often takes twists and turns I don't expect." She couldn't help but think about what happened with Justin and what a scoundrel he'd been. She'd been a terrible judge of character because she'd been blinded by attraction. She'd sworn to herself that would never happen again. This attraction to Eli had thrown her into a tizzy because she needed to see through it to the real man underneath.

Suddenly the doctor appeared in the doorway. Eli stood and so did Hadley.

The doctor nodded to Hadley. "Is she family?"

Eli didn't hesitate to say, "Close enough."

The doctor didn't question him. "Your brother has a concussion. His arm is badly sprained but not broken. He'll have to wear a sling. He's protesting that he wants to leave. He can, of course, sign himself out, but it would be better if you convince him to stay overnight for observation."

"I'll try to do that," Eli said, looking somewhat relieved. "But he can be stubborn."

"Young men his age often are. Come on, I'll show you to his cubicle."

"Do you want me to come?" Hadley asked.

Eli didn't hesitate. "Yes. We might need two against one."

Their gazes met, and Hadley saw more than a common purpose in Eli. She felt her nerve endings light up. Even in these circumstances, the attraction between them pulled like a strong magnet. Eli might have his brother on his mind, but when he looked at her, she could feel the bond that had formed between them. And not only the bond. She couldn't deny the fact that she wanted to be held in his arms again, wanted to feel another kiss, wanted to kiss him back and maybe more. She'd guarded herself for so long, but somehow Eli had broken through that guard, not forcefully, but gently and persuasively.

He reached for her hand then as they walked toward Derek's cubicle. Seeing the man underneath the sexy rancher, she realized that there was so much strength in Eli. She could feel the calluses on his fingers from hard work. But more than that, she felt his warmth. She felt the energy that invigorated her in a way she hadn't been invigorated before. Just what was it about this tall rancher that made her rethink her past and maybe even her future?

As she walked into Derek's cubicle with Eli, she didn't know what to expect. Certainly not what she found. A pale Derek talking to one of the nurses, smiling at her with that twinkle in his eyes.

The nurse moved away, and he saw them. "Why are you two looking so serious? I'm still alive and I'm ready to go home."

Eli strode over to his brother's bed and Hadley followed him, knowing this could be a battle.

"Don't make light of what happened to you," Eli warned his brother.

"I have a headache the size of the state of Montana. I'm not making light of it," Derek told him. "But my brush with that snowmobile isn't going to make me an invalid either."

"You've got to stay the night," Eli said firmly.

"I don't," Derek protested. "All I have to do is sign a paper and I'm out of here."

Eli threw a glance at Hadley and she stepped into the situation, even though she didn't know if she wanted to. She sank down onto the chair beside Derek's bed. "Let me tell you what happened, Derek."

"I was there. I know what happened," he said, his smile fading.

"You know what happened to *you*, but let me tell you about the rest of the people who care about you. When the call went out that you were missing—"

"I wasn't missing," he mumbled.

"Well, apparently your cell phone was because it didn't answer when Eli or your mom and dad repeatedly tried to call you. Anyone in Rust Creek Falls with a snowmobile rushed to the Circle D, including my brother-in-law. That's how I found out about what was happening. When I arrived, your mom was fluttering around the kitchen like a busy bee trying to hide all her worry. But she couldn't. She was worried sick, and so was everyone else who was gathering for the search. She and I made sandwiches and coffee to distribute to the searchers as they took breaks. You know it *is* cold out there. You're fortunate you didn't get frostbite."

When Derek started to protest, she held up her hand. "Eli was searching the longest, so of course your mom and dad were worried about him, too. With spotty cell phone reception, they couldn't stay in touch. Can you imagine worrying for that hour or two?"

Derek's face showed that, yes, he could.

"As soon as Eli reports to your parents, your mom and dad are going to drive here to make sure you're all right. You're going to prove you are by staying overnight and letting the doctors and nurses fuss over you. Just consider this your chance to acquire a few more females' phone numbers." She arched her brows and waited for Derek's reply.

He glanced at his brother. “She's good.”

Eli placed his hand on her shoulder. “I know she is. Why do you think I let her come along?”

She eyed Eli and then Derek. “He didn't *let* me come along. I jumped into his truck before he knew what was happening. He needed the coffee.”

Derek laughed out loud. “So you two are a couple. Who would have thought!”

Neither of them responded to that comment.

Eli said, “I want to make that call to Mom and Dad. When I tell them you're going to stay the night, they'll be here as fast as they can.”

Derek seemed to regroup, and some of his bravado faded away. “All right,” he said in a resigned tone. “Make the call. I'll stay.”

Once Eli had called his mom and dad, it seemed like Charles Dalton must have put the pedal to the metal. They arrived at the hospital in record time. Once Rita was fussing over Derek, Eli gave his brother a wave, took Hadley's arm and said, “I'll let Mom take over now.”

On the return drive to Rust Creek Falls, they didn't talk much. Eli switched the radio on to a country channel. As they neared town, Hadley said, “I came to your ranch with Levi. You'll have to drop me at the boardinghouse.”

But when Eli reached town, he didn't drive directly to the boardinghouse. He turned off into the parking lot for Wings to Go. He parked in a back corner where the lights weren't too glaring and let the engine idle.

“What are we doing here?” she asked.

“I didn't want to park in front of the boardinghouse and be interrupted by the porch light going on.” He unfastened his seat belt and then unfastened hers. "Thank you again for what you did with Derek. I don't think I could have convinced him to stay at the hospital overnight."

"Sure, you could have. You're an older brother. You would have bribed him."

Eli laughed out loud at that one. "Maybe I could have, but he's as stubborn as my dad."

"And probably as stubborn as you."

"I'm only stubborn when I'm right," he insisted.

"I'm sure Derek and your dad think the same thing."

She could see only the shadow of Eli's face, but she thought she saw his lips twitch up.

"We still have a date tomorrow night, don't we?" he asked.

"We do. I even bought a dress."

He tilted his head. "That isn't a weekly occurrence?"

"I haven't had much occasion to get dressed up lately."

"Sometime, Hadley Strickland, you're going to tell me what you're *not* telling me."

Panic assaulted her. She certainly couldn't tell Eli what she'd never even told her family. And what good would it do if she was going back to Bozeman? He certainly wouldn't be leaving Rust Creek Falls.

"Do you think you know me so well?" she asked lightly.

"Oh, I'm beginning to know you well. Very well," he murmured as he leaned closer to her. Suddenly she realized she didn't want to be interrupted by a porch light either. She wanted Eli's kiss. It wasn't like they could do more than that here in the parking lot in the cold. At least not very much more.

When Eli nudged her chin up, she felt him wait a beat as if asking if she wanted this, too. Yes, she did. As he bent his head and set his lips on hers, she knew this wouldn't be a simple kiss. Whenever Eli kissed, he was all male, all passion, all masterful intensity. Their kiss took her thoughts as easily as it took her breath.

As his tongue searched her mouth, she felt the fire. He kissed her deeply, and she felt as if she were flying solo into the wild blue yonder. There wasn't any other exhilaration like it. His arm dropped down to her back to bring her closer, and closer was what she wanted to be. She ran her fingers up the nape of Eli's neck and felt him shudder. Apparently she had the same power over him that he had over her. A kiss or a touch, and she could go up in flames. Did he feel that way? Even with Justin, she hadn't felt this kind of sexual hunger. It almost shocked her. But then she realized how selfish Justin's lovemaking had been. After the fact, she realized how selfish his life had been.

Why did the thought of Justin always have to interfere?

Eli deepened the kiss, and she almost forgot where her thoughts had been going. Why couldn't she just give in to this?

Because she was too scared to trust her own judgment?

He pulled back and said huskily, "Not a porch light this time."

Although for a while conscious thought had fled, it had returned with a vengeance. Eli had realized her mind had gone somewhere else. She saw it on his face.

"I'm sorry," she said.

He gently touched her cheek and ran his thumb down

her chin. “There’s nothing to be sorry about. This is a two-way street. And speaking of streets, I’d better get you home before the whole town closes down for the night.”

He was treating the end of their kiss nonchalantly, and she didn’t know if she wanted him to. Before he could fasten his seat belt, she leaned over and kissed his cheek.

“What was that for?” he asked.

“For not pushing.”

“I’m pushing for our date tomorrow night. I’m looking forward to it. Pick you up at seven?”

“That sounds good.”

He shifted his truck into Drive and drove out of the parking lot onto the deserted streets. When he pulled up in front of the boardinghouse, the porch light was already on.

“Somebody wanted to give you a guiding light home,” he said.

“Levi’s been home for hours. I texted Claire from the hospital, but that doesn’t mean they all won’t worry.”

When she reached for the door handle, Eli leaned toward her much as she had done to him. He gave her a gentle kiss on the temple. “Sleep well, Hadley.”

After she hopped out of his truck and started up the steps to the boardinghouse, she looked back over her shoulder and could see his shadow there. She had a feeling she’d sleep a lot better in his arms.

When Eli came to the boardinghouse to pick up Hadley on Saturday evening, he absolutely took her breath away. He was dressed in a Western-cut sports jacket with a white shirt, bolo tie and black jeans and boots.

His black Stetson was cocked at the angle she liked best. She was immediately taken back to their phone conversation that morning. She'd called him to find out how Derek was doing. He'd responded with, "Do you know how many girls have called to ask how he is?"

She'd laughed and said, "I'm just inquiring because I know you'll feel better when he's home. Any word from the hospital?"

"Derek should be discharged this afternoon. Mom will cluck over him until he can't stand it. Then he'll escape to my place to get away from her care."

"I bet she'll bake extra goodies for both of you."

"There *are* some benefits," he'd said with some amusement, and his voice had gone husky when he said again, "I'm so looking forward to dancing with you tonight."

Now here he was, looking at her as if he'd never seen a woman in a dress before. She'd bought the dress because she felt pretty in it. It had tight long sleeves, a slim waist, a floaty short skirt and, above all, it was red. She didn't know how long the two of them stared at each other.

All of a sudden Old Gene appeared and clapped Eli on the back. "Melba and I thought about going to the dance, but we're taking care of the young-uns."

Melba had slipped up beside Hadley and now she handed her her coat. "You're going to need this, I think." Hadley felt foolish, like a schoolgirl lost in a dream or her first date.

Eli took the coat from her hands and held it for her as she put it on. When she turned to face him, he said in a low voice, "You look beautiful."

She'd heard those words before from another man's

lips. But this was Eli, and the look in his eyes said he meant them.

He held her arm as they descended the steps, then helped her up into his truck. On the short drive to the community center, he asked, "So your sisters will be here tonight?"

"Tessa and Carson are busy. Claire and Levi are coming. Ever since they solidified their marriage and renewed their commitment to each other, they try to get out more."

"And Old Gene and Melba help with that?"

"They do. It's nice to see."

"I guess after kids come, still maintaining date nights keeps a marriage strong."

"I suppose it does."

At the community center, Eli parked and then came around the truck for her. He helped her down and made sure he held her arm tightly in case there were any icy spots to walk over. She hadn't wanted to wear her boots with this dress, opting for heels.

Once inside, he took her coat for her and hung it on the rack. They wandered into the main room, where the dance was being held.

Brooks and Jazzy waved to them from one of the tables. "Would you like to sit with them?" Hadley asked.

"Sure, let's."

She could feel Eli's hand at the small of her back as he guided her to the table. She liked the feel of his strength and his tall figure beside her.

After they were seated, Brooks said to her, "Just the person I wanted to see."

Jazzy nudged his arm. "You're not going to talk business, are you?"

"I thought we might as well get it out of the way first, then we can enjoy the rest of the night."

Hadley looked at him with questioning eyes. "What business?"

"I just want to say again how glad I am you're going to stay to help out with my practice."

"I'm glad to do it. But I have to be back mid-December to cover for my boss. Especially on Christmas Day."

"I understand," Brooks said, shaking his head. "But I wanted to tell you that my dad's made a decision. He's going to put his practice and his property up for sale. I wanted you to be the first to know."

"Are you sure this is a good time for him to make that decision?" Hadley asked. "Maybe he's just frustrated he's not getting better quicker."

"I said the same thing," Brooks admitted. "But he seems pretty sure of himself. He says he'll continue to help me however he can, but he won't have the administrative headaches. He won't have the ranch to care for. I think he's found he likes being under the same roof as we are. It gives him a feeling of security. Going forward, that's important for him."

"When is he going to close his practice?"

"He won't do anything official until spring, but I just wanted you to know."

So now she knew. But she wasn't sure what it meant for her, if anything.

A DJ up at the front of the room had started the music. A buffet line was forming, and Eli asked, "Do you want to get something to eat?"

"I do," she said, not wanting to think about the future tonight.

During the meal of pulled pork, barbecued beef, twice-baked potatoes, raw veggies and more, they easily chatted with Brooks and Jazzy.

Jazzy filled them in on what had happened on *The Great Roundup* episode last night.

Jazzy explained, "Brenna and Summer were paired up. They had to get two cows and calves off of an island in the middle of the pond! And then, after they swam back to shore, Summer, who's a flirt, attacked Brenna for being *little miss perfect.* They actually had a girl fight in the mud!"

Brooks was grinning. "I wish I could have seen that."

Hadley knew Brooks had taken his snowmobile to the Circle D to search for Derek, too. Eli's arm brushed hers, and their eyes met for a brief second.

Eli broke the eye contact first and asked Jazzy, "So who won last night?"

With a wide smile, Jazzy proclaimed, "Brenna did. Not only the fight but the challenge."

"And what did she win?" Hadley asked.

"A romantic night for two at the lodge with dinner. She took Trav as her date," Jazzy answered.

Although there was lightness on the surface of their conversation, Hadley felt the undercurrent every time her arm brushed Eli's, every time they glanced each other's way, every time they reached for a dish and their fingers touched. There was a raw sexuality surrounding Eli that drew her closer without him saying a word or moving a muscle. But when they touched... She imagined Brenna's night at the lodge with Travis and knew that's what she wanted with Eli.

When they'd all finished eating, Eli asked her, "How about a dance?"

Just the idea of being held in Eli's arms made her heart flutter erratically. She said *yes* because this was an adventure she wanted to go on. Nothing too improbable could happen on the dance floor. She'd be safe from her own impulses and his.

Nevertheless, once he took her into his arms, she rethought that idea. Nothing about being this close to Eli was safe, not when he smelled like a pine woods, not when he looked at her with that smoldering passion in his eyes. Their bodies were just grazing each other, and that was enough to tease her silly.

"I could use your expertise," he said.

At that she studied his face. "My expertise in what?" she asked cautiously.

He grinned. "How about going shopping with me tomorrow to find a Christmas present for my mom? My dad has no idea what she'd like. She says she has everything she needs, so I need a woman's point of view. Maybe you can come up with something I can't."

Looking into Eli's eyes, Hadley almost couldn't think straight. But his words penetrated, and she realized he really was asking her for a favor. She didn't have much opportunity to go shopping, but she enjoyed it when she did. "Sure, I'll go with you," she said. "Just make sure your wallet's full."

He laughed and clasped her a little closer. His fingers encircled hers as he brought her hand to his chest. She took in a breath, suddenly filled with the desire to do more than dance. That desire made her notice everything about him, from his clean-shaven jaw, to his hair dipping over his brow, to the lines around his eyes that came from squinting into the sun…or from laughter. She had a feeling there had been lots of laughter in

Eli's life with his brothers and his sisters. He enjoyed his life now, that was obvious.

They navigated around other couples on the dance floor, including Levi and Claire, but Hadley didn't really notice them. She and Eli seemed to be moving in their own world to music soft and sultry meant only for them. At this moment Hadley couldn't imagine being anywhere else.

One dance faded into two, and they molded to each other even more closely. He brushed his cheek against hers, and she wanted to kiss him right then and there. As the dance ended, Eli did place a light kiss on her lips. It was a promise of more to come.

He said close to her ear, "I like dancing with you, but you know what I'd like even more?"

She could hardly get the word out. "What?"

"I want to be alone with you. Will you come back to my place with me?"

She said the only word that was in her head. "Yes."

An hour later, back at his cabin with Hadley, Eli realized all his experience with women hadn't taught him how to handle tonight with Hadley. As they'd danced, he'd been sure she wanted the same thing he did. But she'd gotten very quiet on the drive here. Not that he'd been a chatterbox himself. After all, they knew what they were going to do, didn't they?

Once they'd come inside, he'd taken her coat from her and told her to make herself comfortable. Now she was sitting on the sofa with Winks and Whisper, giving all of her attention to them. She seemed fidgety to him.

Earlier, he'd laid the fire in the fireplace, ready to be set with a flick of a match. Now he did that and watched as the flames took hold. Maybe a little conversation would go a long way. Maybe he could coax her to open up. If she did, he'd know she was ready for whatever tonight brought.

Going to the sofa, he sat beside her. The kitten ran back and forth between their laps, and they both smiled. He settled his arm around her shoulders and brought her close. She didn't resist.

"I read the signals right tonight, didn't I?" he asked. "You wanted to come back here with me?"

She looked up at him, but there was a slight furrow in her brow. "I did want to come back here with you. That's why I said *yes*."

"You don't seem comfortable, though. Are you having doubts? We can just sit by the fire and talk."

She nodded, seeming to agree with him about that. "What do you want to talk about?"

Momma cat and baby settled in a corner of the sofa watching them.

He brushed his fingers down Hadley's arm. He knew what he wanted to ask her. "Why are you willing to work on Christmas, which is a family time?"

That brought a deeper furrow to her brow. She was quiet so long he wasn't sure she was going to answer him. But then she said, "It *is* a family time, and I do enjoy that part of it. But ever since—" She stopped.

"Ever since what?"

"For me the holidays have become associated with disappointment and shame."

He wasn't sure what to say to that. So he stroked her arm again and listened.

"I broke up with my ex the day before Christmas."

"Oh, Hadley, I'm sorry." He couldn't imagine why a

man would break up with her. Or had *she* broken it off? "Do you want to tell me what happened?"

"I met Justin at a veterinary convention in Las Vegas three years ago. He swept me off my feet. He was a pharmaceutical rep with a lot of charm, and I guess I fell for it. It didn't last long," she said.

Being around Hadley as much as he had been, especially having her sleep in his arms with complete vulnerability, Eli realized she still hadn't let her guard down completely. He didn't think she'd given him the whole story, but that story was hers to tell when she trusted him.

"Any man who would walk away from you or let *you* walk away from *him* would have to be some kind of fool," he assured her.

Her cheeks reddened a little, and he saw her eyes tear up. "It was complicated."

"And you still hurt from it."

She nodded.

He held her closer then and swiped away the single tear that was rolling down her cheek. He couldn't keep from kissing her. He knew she wanted that kiss, too, when her arms rounded his neck and her fingers laced in his hair. He'd been anticipating the kiss and longing to take it somewhere else. Yet he knew he couldn't hurry her. He couldn't hurry this. When he leaned back, she moaned a little. He smiled and used his tongue to outline her lips. He could feel her tremble and knew she liked it. He was certain of it when her hand went under his shirt placket and she touched bare skin.

"Hadley," he groaned.

"What?"

"Do you want to take this up to the bedroom?"

She nodded again against his chest. That was the only signal he needed. He swooped her up into his arms, strode to the stairs and carried her up to the loft. They were in a big, king-size bed in no time, and all he wanted to do was strip her clothes off her and rid himself of his. But, again, he didn't want to rush. He didn't know how he could keep from rushing, but that was the plan.

Hadley didn't hesitate now. Her hands went to the buttons on his shirt. She pulled his shirt out of his slacks, and he figured it would give her a measure of confidence for him to disrobe first. So he let her take off his shirt and skim it down his arms. He couldn't help but suck in a breath when she leaned forward and kissed his chest.

He said huskily, "We've got to get your clothes off, too."

"Mine are easier," she said simply. And he had to laugh. He could see what she meant. There was one zipper down the back of her dress. He didn't even have to turn her around to reach it and pull it down. The dress slipped from her shoulders, and she was standing before him in a bra that seemed a filmy bit of nothing and panties that were the same. They were under her pantyhose, but he could tell. Had she anticipated tonight, too?

"Shoes," he whispered before he peeled them down her hips and then her legs. She held on to his shoulder as he pulled off one foot and then the other and tossed the pantyhose aside.

"The rest of your clothes," she breathed.

Once she had unbuttoned his belt buckle, ridding himself of the rest of his clothes didn't take long at all.

In a matter of seconds, they were in his bed and he'd laid a condom on the nightstand.

"Are you on the pill?" he asked.

"No," she said simply, and he suspected what that meant. She hadn't dated recently. She hadn't seen anyone seriously recently. But still he wanted to know. "Have you been involved with anyone since your ex?"

"No."

That meant he was right about going slow. He was right about taking precious care of her. And he did. Although Hadley was impatient, he kept it slow, and she soon fell into the experience with him, making it more sensual. He kissed her cheek. She kissed his. He kissed her jawline. She kissed his. He kissed her collarbone. She kissed his. And so it went until she was at his waist and he couldn't take it any longer.

Applying the condom first, he rose above her. He stroked her thighs apart and could tell she was ready for him. "I want you, Hadley."

"I want you, Eli."

And so they had each other until he saw stars, she shouted his name…and the whole universe seemed to explode.

Chapter Eleven

Hadley awakened in Eli's arms. This experience was so different from when they'd awakened in the tack room with all their clothes on. He was cuddling her close, and his chest hair brushed her nose. She felt the tips of his fingers along the crest of her shoulder, and she shivered, remembering everything from last night.

"Are you cold?" he whispered, close to her ear.

"Anything but," she assured him, burrowing her nose into his chest. She'd been free with him last night and so hungry for him. That embarrassed her a bit now.

"What's wrong?" he asked, giving her a look that said he wanted the truth.

"Last night was wonderful." She hurried to explain, "But I've never been quite like that. I just feel a bit embarrassed this morning, that I was so—"

"Sensual? Hungry for me like I was for you? There's

nothing wrong with that, Hadley. In fact, that's what made it so electric and…fun."

She poked him in the ribs. "Fun?"

He laughed. "Don't you want to have fun in bed?"

When she thought about Justin, she didn't think about fun. She thought about lust. She thought about chemistry and where that had gotten her. She had chemistry with Eli, that was for sure. But there was more, too, and that's what puzzled her. Her feelings for him were becoming so much more expansive than a simple attraction.

"Your mind's going. I can hear the wheels turning," he teased.

"Stop them from turning," she said.

"Gladly."

When his lips came down on hers, pleasure seemed to fill every bit of her. As his tongue stroked her mouth, she passed her hands down his back, felt the strong muscles there as well as his spine. She raked her nails across his skin, and he groaned. His caresses were more than touches. They were embedded with caring. She felt that as well as the desire to arouse her.

When she stroked his hip, he said, "I have trouble restraining myself around you."

"Maybe we shouldn't think about restraints this morning," she suggested. That caused another groan.

She found herself wanting to look at him as well as touch him. But that was hard to do when he was determined to make her melt. When both of them were panting and glazed with desire, he prepared himself, stretched out on top of her and slowly let their lower bodies touch. It was a teasing ritual that made her frantic to have him. But he wasn't ready to take her yet. He concentrated on her breasts. His mouth on them made her dizzy with need.

She'd never ever felt like this. Last night they'd been seriously sensual and seriously hungry for each other. But this morning, they both tantalized and teased, having some of that fun Eli had mentioned. Finally, finally, he entered her. She took him in, glorying in every sensation. They seemed to melt into each other as heat wrapped them in an embrace. Before she knew it, she was reaching for the same stars she'd claimed last night, only this morning she seemed to reach higher and farther until she felt their glimmer through every nerve ending. Her climax rocked her. She felt his rock him.

Just what did this mean for either of them?

She wasn't going to think about that now.

She decided not to think about it two hours later, either, after they showered together, dressed, looked after the horses and driven to Kalispell. The mall was bustling with pre-Christmas activity. They stopped at Santa's Workshop in the middle of the mall, where children and parents lined up so their kids could sit on Santa's knee.

"How many do you want someday?" Eli asked.

She gave him a quick look, but his question had seemed nonchalant as if he was just gathering information.

"Kids? I haven't really thought about it," she said. "I always thought I'd have pets sooner than kids. How about you?"

"Two or three," he answered reasonably. "Enough that they'd have each other, not too many that they don't get enough attention."

That was a well-thought-out answer. Eli had spent

time thinking about it, whereas she hadn't. Because she thought it would never happen? Because trusting a man again had seemed so impossible? When they walked away from the line of children and parents, she had a lot to think about.

They wandered in and out of shops until Hadley spotted something that might be the perfect gift for Rita Dalton. She took Eli's arm and pulled him toward a display of wooden keepsake boxes. One had a beautiful carving of a horse on the lid.

She asked, "Do you think you could coax your brothers and sisters to do something special for your mom?"

"That depends," he said warily. "What would they have to do?"

"What if each of you put a note or letter in here about what she means to you. I can't think of a Christmas gift that would be more appreciated."

Eli first discriminately studied the box. He opened the lid and saw its blue velvet-lined interior. Then his gaze fell on Hadley. "You haven't known my mother very long, but you're right. That would be a very precious gift to her."

"To any mother," Hadley assured him.

"You've found the perfect gift. Now all I have to do is make sure my family cooperates."

"I don't think you'll have a problem with that."

Eli was a leader, and she expected that his brothers and sisters respected him enough to see the wisdom in what he asked.

Hadley's cell phone buzzed. She'd texted Claire this morning and told her where she was and what she'd be doing…for the most part.

Eli said, "Go ahead and answer it. I'll take this up to the counter."

As he carried the box up to the sales clerk, Hadley stepped to a quiet corner and checked the screen on her phone. It wasn't Claire. However, she knew the name on the caller ID. She just hadn't heard from him in a few months. Greg Fordham had gone to vet school with her. The last time she'd heard from him this summer, he'd still been practicing in St. Louis.

She answered, "Hadley Strickland here."

"Hadley, it's Greg."

"Hi. It's been a while." She waited, wondering what he wanted.

"I'm flying into Kalispell tomorrow and I'd like to have dinner with you."

"Dinner? Why?"

He laughed. "That's what I like about you, Hadley. You ask the tough questions. I want to consult with you about something."

"I see," she said, though she really didn't. "I'm working with a vet in Rust Creek Falls while I'm in town."

"I can drive *there* if it's more convenient for you."

She thought about Eli and whether they'd be spending more time together, maybe tomorrow evening.

"There aren't many food choices here, but there's a great rustic place called the Ace in the Hole."

He laughed. "Will I get into a bar fight?"

"Not if you behave yourself."

"All right. That sounds like a plan. What time should I meet you there?"

"About six?" she asked. "If I'm going to be tied up, I'll give you a call back."

"You have my number. I should be getting into Kalispell around noon. I'll text you where I'm staying in case you need that."

"Are you sure you don't want to tell me what this is about?" she asked, still puzzled by his call.

"No, I'd rather discuss it in person. I'll see you tomorrow at the Ace in the Hole."

The call ended and Hadley once more belted her phone. Just what did Greg Fordham want with her?

When Greg walked into the Ace in the Hole, he looked totally out of place. But that wasn't a surprise to Hadley. He was wearing an expensive suit, which he usually did. He came from money and he had a trust fund, but he'd become a veterinarian because he loved animals. Because of that, they had connected.

She stood and waved to him, and he spotted her easily. There weren't that many people at Ace in the Hole right now.

As soon as Greg sat down, a waitress came over to their table. Hadley ordered a cranberry spritzer. He ordered an expensive shot of whiskey.

"Same old Hadley," he said, teasingly.

"Same old Greg."

Hadley happened to look up at the door when the next person strode in. That person was Derek. She thought about waving to him but then considered not doing it. If he came over to the table, she'd be friendly. But she and Derek mixed like oil and water.

The waitress soon brought their drinks, and she and Greg ordered from the menu. It was obvious Greg was waiting until they didn't have interruptions to speak with her.

"You were right about no gourmet food," he said. "Tell me it's the best burger in Montana."

"It's the best burger in Montana," she said with a straight face.

He laughed. "That's another thing I like about you, Hadley. You make me laugh."

She was tired of waiting and wanted to know why he'd come. "So tell me, why this visit to Rust Creek Falls?"

"I have a proposition for you."

She studied him. There had never been anything romantic between them. Greg had preconceived ideas and could be a bit of a snob. But he'd always been kind to her and they agreed on veterinary medicine practices.

"But first I have one important question for you," he said.

"Shoot."

"Haven't you always wanted your own practice?"

"Sure, I want my own practice."

"How about having it right now? How about a partnership? How would you like to come to St. Louis and form a successful practice with me?"

"You're serious?"

"I know you, Hadley. You're interested in more than a practice in Bozeman. Think about the cultural advantages of St. Louis and a chance to see and live in another place. Big-city life would be an experience for you."

It certainly would. Hadn't she wanted to experience big-city life someday? But a practice with Greg?

She hadn't even had time to wrap her head around the idea when Derek spotted her. All smug smile and twinkling eyes, he strode toward their table, his arm in a sling.

Greg raised a questioning brow as he watched the cowboy approach.

Derek stopped at their table. “Hi, Hadley. I didn’t expect to see you here.”

“Hi, Derek. Just having dinner with a friend. Derek Dalton meet Greg Fordham.”

Derek eyed Greg suspiciously. Maybe it was the cut of Greg’s suit or the glimmer of his gold watch that caused that wary look in Derek’s eyes. “I’m meeting Eli here for drinks.”

Hadley could have groaned. She’d really never expected that, or this…to have to give some sort of explanation. On the other hand, she didn’t owe *anybody* an explanation. This was her life, and she was going to live it as she saw fit. Eli hadn’t asked her if she wanted to get together again tonight. Obviously he’d had plans with Derek.

She didn’t have to involve Derek in conversation because at that moment Eli walked into the Ace in the Hole. He saw the three of them, frowned and came over to the table.

“This town is full of cowboys,” Greg said, loud enough for Derek and Eli to hear.

Hadley did have the right to live her own life, but what she and Eli had shared *did* mean something. She didn’t want him to think she had taken it lightly.

So she went through introductions again, ending with, “Greg and I went to veterinary school together.”

Derek rolled his eyes. “I can see the three of you are probably going to be talking about horses. I think I’ll just mosey over to the bar.”

When Eli looked at Hadley and said politely, “Enjoy your dinner,” she couldn’t let him walk away. Impulsively she asked, "Won't you join us? You haven't eaten yet, have you?"

He waved at their burgers. "You've already been served."

"That doesn't matter. You know they'll bring another burger out here quick. Please join us."

Eli slung a chair around from one of the other tables and positioned it between Hadley and Greg. "Where are you from?" Eli asked, because it was obvious Greg wasn't from here.

"At present, St. Louis," Greg said formally.

Eli shed his suede jacket onto the back of his chair, revealing a plaid flannel shirt and jeans.

"So you and your brother handle steers?" Greg asked, looking as if he really wanted to know.

"We handle steers, feed horses, see to everyday workings of a ranch."

"Do you have a big spread?" Greg asked.

"It's a family spread," Eli answered truthfully, then signaled to the waitress and pointed to the burger at Hadley's place. She got the idea and nodded.

"So you all live in one big ranch house?"

Now Hadley spoke up. She didn't like Greg's tone or his questioning attitude. Eli wasn't someone to put under a microscope, even though he showed no signs of being bothered by Greg's questions. Still, she sensed the squaring of his shoulders and the straightening of his spine that said he was on guard.

"Eli and his brothers and sisters each received a parcel of land. Eli built his house on his. It's beautiful," she said. "The finest workmanship I've seen."

Greg looked from Eli to Hadley then back at Eli. "That sounds as if you worked on it yourself."

"I did. My brother's an architect, so I consulted with him."

"An architect," Greg said with a nod, as if that was something he could understand. "And where did you go to school?"

Hadley shifted in her seat as a look crossed Eli's face that was much like a shadow. She didn't understand it.

"I decided against a formal college education," Eli told Greg.

"I see," Greg said, obviously not seeing at all. "Hadley and I attended one of the best veterinary schools there is. That's why I was so surprised when she decided to practice in Bozeman."

Eli shrugged. "It seems logical she'd want to be close to home."

"After an education, home is where life takes you," Greg protested. "I've just invited her to join me in a practice in St. Louis. It would be a wonderful life experience for her. She'd be able to break out of the constraints of small-town life."

Hadley was totally surprised by that comment. "I never said I was constrained by small-town life," she said.

"You don't have to say it. It's obvious. Your mind has a much greater reach than you give yourself credit for. Once you're in a setting with culture, amenities and a more eclectic lifestyle, your horizons will broaden tremendously."

Was it true? Would her horizons broaden? Maybe. Would she be gaining rather than giving up? Or would she be losing connections she found dear and miss them so much that no experience would be worth that? Hard to know without thinking on it, without discussing it with Claire and Tessa, and maybe even her mother and grandmother.

Eli was giving her an odd look, as if Greg were unveiling a side of her that he'd never seen. Would she change if she moved to St. Louis? Did she want to change?

Greg kept talking about St. Louis as she picked at her burger. She seemed to have lost her appetite. Eli ate his with a distracted look, but every once in a while he glanced from her to Greg as if he were puzzled. She had the sudden urge to touch him, to put her hand on his forearm, to have a conversation just with him. But Greg was rattling on, and she could see Derek sitting over at the bar, watching all.

Finally, Greg wiped his mouth with his napkin and then set it on the table. "I know you need time to think about this, and also to see if you can come up with money for the investment. I wanted to present this to you before the new year. I'll email you the details." He stood. "I'd better be getting back to Kalispell. I have an early flight in the morning." He nodded to Eli. "It was nice meeting you."

Then Greg gave Hadley a cursory hug. "I'll give you a call after Christmas and we can talk about this further. If need be, maybe you could fly to St. Louis and see what I'm planning."

"I'll think about all of it," she said because she would. She sat down again slowly as Greg left the Ace in the Hole. She felt a little bit shell-shocked by the whole evening.

She hardly had a chance to catch her breath when Eli moved his chair closer to hers.

He asked, "Did you and that guy once have something going?"

"No," she protested. "At least not in the way you mean. Greg and I had classes together. We have the same philosophy about veterinary medicine. But the closest we got was the same study group."

"You've been in touch since college?"

"Sure. Emails, catching up on what the other's doing. We're friends, Eli. Not close friends, but friends."

Eli looked as if he wanted to say something but seemed to think better of it.

"What?"

"Maybe he has a torch for you and that's why he wants you to come to St. Louis."

"You don't think this is a purely professional reason he came to see me?"

"I don't know. *You* tell *me*."

"I'm telling you. It's purely professional." Could Eli be jealous? Was that what his questions were about?

"You said you weren't serious about anyone since that Justin."

"I haven't dated since Justin," she said a bit defensively.

"For some reason Greg thinks you'd want to move to St. Louis. Is that the kind of life you want? A big city, traffic, noise?"

"A broader experience, theater, a different lifestyle?" she countered.

"A partner who thinks he knows best about everything?"

Eli had that right. But for the moment, her concentration wasn't on Greg. It was on Eli, and she didn't like where this was going. "He's given me much to think about, maybe even an opportunity. I've always wanted to have my own practice or be a partner in a practice."

"You can do that anywhere."

"Yes, I could. But why shouldn't I want more than what I have? Don't you want more than what *you* have?"

"I'm satisfied."

"Are you? Is that why you don't travel anymore? Is that why you don't rock climb? Would you even give a different kind of life a chance?"

Eli's face was stony with resolve. She wanted to shake him or get a rise out of him. She wanted to see him as other than dependable, reliable and stoic. "Maybe I want a chance to change my life. Didn't you break off your engagement because you couldn't change yours?"

As soon as she said the words, she wished she hadn't. But the harm was done. Eli's expression told her that. He was closed down to her.

She reached for his arm. "Eli, I'm sorry."

Apparently Eli didn't want to hear any apologies from her. He didn't brush her off, but he easily broke her grasp and stood. "I'll pay for my burger at the bar. I can't criticize you because you want to experience something new. But don't tell me how I should live *my* life."

Hadley thought about going after him as he strode toward the bar, but that would be just too humiliating. She wouldn't be humiliated by a man again. However, as Eli left the Ace in the Hole and Derek followed him out, she wondered exactly what she had just done.

And if she'd ever see Eli Dalton again.

Eli wanted to ram his fist into something, but he knew that wouldn't do any good. Besides, his brother was close on his heels. They were on the street now, headed toward Eli's truck.

Eli called over his shoulder, "See you back at the ranch."

But Derek didn't stop. He kept coming. "What was that about?" his brother asked.

"None of your concern."

"It looked like it should be *somebody's* concern. Did you two have a fight?"

"Hadley received an offer to join a friend in a practice in St. Louis."

Derek whistled low. Then he muttered, "I can only imagine how much that guy's suit cost."

Eli suddenly rounded on his brother and asked, "Do you think I'm inflexible?"

Derek's mouth opened in surprise. Then he studied Eli. "Inflexible? You mean because you know what you want?"

"Yeah, something like that. Was I being inflexible because I wouldn't move to Chicago to be with Elaine?"

Derek shrugged. "I don't think that whole situation was about moving."

"No? Then what was it about?" Eli demanded to know, feeling frustrated and unsettled.

"I don't think you loved her enough to change your life."

Derek's observation hit home. As Eli thought about what he'd felt for Elaine, he said absently, "I used to enjoy rock climbing."

"Yeah. So?" Then a lightbulb seemed to go off in Derek's head. He held up a finger. "Oh. So you don't do it anymore because you did it with her?"

Eli felt shaken by that thought. "Something like that."

"And you didn't find a new hobby."

"Maybe I didn't need a hobby anymore. I had the ranch."

"And is that all you have?" Derek wanted to know.

Up until Eli had met Hadley, he'd thought the ranch was enough. Oh, sure. He'd thought about the future sometimes and having a wife and kids to share it. Maybe even buying his own place. Or maybe starting up a breeding business on the Circle D. Yet he hadn't felt in any hurry to decide.

"Do you think she's going to move to St. Louis?" Derek asked. "Her family probably won't be too fond of that idea."

"Maybe she doesn't care what her family thinks. Sometimes I get the feeling she wants to get away from them." Yet he wasn't sure exactly why.

After a few beats of silence, Eli asked, "Do you think you'll ever get married?"

Derek pointed to his chest and flashed Eli a wide grin. "Me? Why should I get married when I'm having so much fun?" But then his younger brother turned serious. "You, on the other hand… You'd make a good husband and dad."

At this moment, Eli wasn't sure whether he would or wouldn't. But he did know one thing. He now had to entertain the idea that he couldn't find a life partner because maybe he was too rigid!

Chapter Twelve

The following Saturday, Brooks stepped into the exam room that one of his patients had just vacated. Hadley was cleaning up.

"How did the yearly physical go with Nancy's cat?" he asked. "She can be a handful."

"Just fine. Treats are a great distraction."

He smiled. "Not only for cats. I can't tell you how much I appreciate your being here, mostly because it takes the worry from Dad that we're not overbooked."

"We're good for the next hour or so. I told Anne I'd help her decorate the office this afternoon."

"I'm sure you don't want my help with that. I'll be at the computer for a while."

Brooks had just left the exam room when Hadley's phone buzzed. Her heart skipped when she saw the number. Eli.

She'd been debating with herself all week about calling him. She'd wanted to call him. But on the other hand, with her life in such a state of flux, was there a point?

After she answered, Eli asked, "Are you speaking to me?"

"If you're speaking to me."

"I shouldn't have left like I did on Monday night."

"And I shouldn't have said what I did," she admitted.

"You were feeling defensive because I was at you about St. Louis. And maybe, just maybe, you hit the mark with me."

A man who could admit to something and apologize, too. She hadn't run into many of those.

"Are you free? Can we meet for lunch?" he asked.

She hesitated for one reason. She was falling hard for Eli. She said, "I probably shouldn't. I promised Brooks's receptionist I'd help decorate the office."

"I see," he said thoughtfully. He obviously suspected she was putting him off, and she was.

"Maybe we can coordinate our schedules another time," he suggested.

"Another time," she agreed. After goodbyes, she ended the call, feeling deeply disappointed and even sad.

A half hour later she was helping Anne Lattimore attach a garland around the reception counter when the front door to the clinic opened. To Hadley's surprise, Eli strode in.

"Need help decorating?" he asked with a smile, taking off his Stetson and hanging it on a hat peg.

Just looking at Eli made Hadley feel as if she'd received an early Christmas present. His gaze swept over her violet sweater, leggings and her practical boots. She suddenly wished she'd taken care with makeup this morning.

They were still gazing each other's way when Brooks came into the reception area. "Hi, Eli. I don't have you on my schedule."

"I came to see if Hadley would put me on *her* schedule," Eli teased. "Face-to-face seems to work better with her."

Hadley felt herself blushing. They'd been more than face-to-face, and he was referencing that.

"She doesn't have to stay," Brooks said. "Anne and I can finish up. Our appointments are done for the day unless I get an emergency call."

In a glance, Eli took in the boxes of garland and the ornaments ready for hanging wherever a critter couldn't reach them.

"I'll help," he said. "Then you'll all get done faster."

Hadley wasn't sure what to say to that. Anne was looking back and forth between them, her eyebrows quirked. She said, "I'll go fetch the twinkle lights."

Brooks disappeared, too, and Hadley was left with Eli. He took a hammer and a tack from the counter and tapped it into the door frame. "Can you spare some time if we get this finished?"

"What did you have in mind?" she asked, her heart beating way too fast.

"How about drinks at Maverick Manor? We can talk uninterrupted."

Just what were they going to talk about? But she didn't ask that question.

He took a step closer to her. "Are you running away from me?"

"Not right now," she said with certainty. "And, yes, I'll go to Maverick Manor with you and have drinks."

He came even closer. "Ever since the other night, all I want to do is touch you."

She glanced over her shoulder. "Eli," she warned.

"I think Anne and Brooks left us alone on purpose. They seem pretty savvy about those kinds of things."

Maybe they were, but Hadley wasn't sure *she* was. She knew exactly what Eli meant. She wanted to touch him, too. After all, they'd made love. They'd been naked with each other. They'd spoken in low whispers and called each other's name at the height of passion.

Eli reached out and ran his thumb over her cheek. "I remember everything, Hadley, don't you?"

She nodded because she couldn't speak, not with Eli looking at her like that, not with him touching her this way. The brush of his thumb went deeper than skin. It went to her heart. When he bent his head and gently nibbled on her lower lip, she wrapped her arms around his neck. His kiss was prolonged and deep, and she responded to it with all of her being. She didn't know how long they kissed. She just knew all of it was romantic and heart-melting and just what she needed.

Finally, they both came up for air. He said in a husky voice, "So you have to decorate in here, huh?"

She smiled. "I do."

"Then let's get to it," he said with determination. "The faster we get done, the faster I get you to myself."

An hour later, when they left the veterinary clinic, Eli suggested they drive their own cars. It made sense to him since Hadley seemed to be in a skittish mood. She hadn't been in a skittish mood during that kiss, but other than that, he could see she felt almost awkward with him. How could that be when they'd made love so passionately?

While they'd decorated, they'd made small talk about what had happened on *The Great Roundup* last night. He'd watched the show at the Ace in the Hole again while Hadley had caught the program with Claire and Melba.

Eli wanted to erase the awkwardness. There were so many things they needed to discuss. Maybe today they would. Maybe today they'd move forward so they both knew where they stood.

Maverick Manor was a rustic hotel that had a gorgeous view of the Montana wilderness. He met Hadley in the lobby, in front of the stone fireplace that was big enough to stand in. They went into the restaurant that had been added on. It was after the lunch hour, and most of the seats and tables were empty. Eli was grateful for that, as the hostess showed them to a private table in a corner alcove. When the waitress came to take their drink orders, Eli held up the extensive wine list.

"Wine?" he asked.

But Hadley shook her head. "No, I think I'd better stay clearheaded for this conversation."

"How about an Irish coffee?" the waitress asked. "Easy on the Irish."

Hadley glanced at her. "That does sound good."

"I'll have the same," Eli said.

Once the waitress had scurried off, Eli reached across the table and took Hadley's hand. "I don't want to put you on the defensive, Hadley," he told her. "But I do have a question."

"If you're already warning me—"

"It's just that I might not have any right to ask it."

"Go ahead."

"Why didn't you tell me about the offer for the job in St. Louis? We were together the day before."

"It just came up. Remember when I got the call when we were shopping? That was Greg, and I didn't know what he was going to ask me then. He just said that he wanted to meet, that he had a proposition for me. I had no idea what that meant."

Eli studied her face and decided she was telling him the truth. He'd come to expect honesty from Hadley. "And you tried to avoid seeing me today because you thought it would be awkward?"

"Yes, it would be awkward. I never should have poked into your personal life. I shouldn't have said anything."

"You were right on the money."

Hadley looked startled for a moment.

"I don't know if rigidity was my problem, but I thought Elaine and I were building a life here. She thought she'd make a grand move and I would go with her. I was never anything but clear that my life was in Rust Creek Falls."

"Did you know she wanted more?"

"I knew she had ambition."

"If you knew she had ambition, why didn't you see the rest?"

"I don't understand."

"Just how far could ambition get her in Rust Creek Falls? She had to take it to the next level, Eli. Was she unhappy here?"

"I didn't think she was unhappy when she was with me."

"Other than you. Was she happy in her life here?"

He looked troubled. "No. She complained about a lot."

"That was the red flag that you didn't want to see.

You thought you could be everything to her, and that wasn't so."

As he thought about it, he realized Hadley's conclusion was credible. He squeezed her hand. "How did you get so smart?"

"You don't want to know."

However, he *did* want to know. But he had the feeling Hadley wasn't going to tell him today. "Do you think I rigidly just don't want to move away from Rust Creek Falls and that's why I broke off the engagement?"

"Isn't that the reason?"

"No. I like my life. I like being close to my family. I like knowing what's going on with them as much as I can, and having their support and my giving mine. Tell me about your family. Don't you want to spend time with them?"

At that moment the waitress brought their Irish coffees. This gave Hadley the chance to stall, to taste the whipped cream, to stir the coffee with her spoon. But finally she looked him straight in the eye. "My family is paired off. I'm already long-distance from Tessa when she's in California. If I move away, they won't miss me."

"You're wrong, especially if you move to St. Louis. You and your sisters are close."

"We can talk on the phone and text."

"That's not the same thing as talking face-to-face, and you know it. What about your grandmother? And I'm sure your parents want you close." He let up the pressure, took a sip of the coffee and then set it back down, intending to change the subject. He didn't want to put more barriers between himself and Hadley. He wanted to break them down. "You know we're both very lucky to have large extended families. Rust Creek Falls is overrun by Daltons of late, and I couldn't be happier about that. But not everybody is so lucky."

"Are you thinking of someone in particular?"

"I'm thinking about the Stocktons. Bella and Hudson have found happiness, but Bella and her brother Jamie have been through a world of hurt because they were separated from their siblings."

"I know some of their story," Hadley said. "They were torn apart by a car accident ten years ago, right?"

"Yes. Jamie and Bella went to live with their grandparents. The older children left on their own because they were eighteen. The younger ones were adopted. Jamie and Bella had no idea where any of their brothers and sisters were. I can't imagine what it would be like to grow up not knowing where my brothers and sisters were. Just think about that hole in your heart every day, not knowing if they were okay or thriving."

"But the Stocktons recently reunited with two of their missing siblings."

Eli nodded. "Daniel and Dana. And they're still looking for the rest. They're hoping to have them all back by the time Dan marries Anne Lattimore at Christmastime."

Soft piano music had begun to play in the background, and they listened for a while as they sipped their coffee. Staring at Hadley, realizing her beauty, remembering their night together, his mind wandered off. There was a huge Christmas tree at the side of the room. It stood for everything he wanted, and maybe hadn't realized it until this moment. Staring at that tree, its glistening ornaments and its lights, he could see Hadley and himself standing there in front of it with children of their own. His mind veered on a detour to Christmas morning where they were all gathered around the tree opening presents. There was a little Eli Junior, all excited about a fancy fire truck. And a little girl who looked just like Hadley clutched a teddy bear. When Hadley entered the scene, she was rounded with child. His child. His children.

"Eli?"

Hadley had asked him a question and he must have missed it.

She asked, "Where did you just go?"

He'd taken a trip into the future, maybe the exact future he wanted. He'd looked for a woman like Hadley for a long time. Now that he'd found her, he didn't want to let her slip through his hands.

"So where did you just go?" Hadley asked him again.

He couldn't scare her off. That would defeat every purpose. And she'd been hurt before. He needed to proceed with caution. "Are you really sure you can't stay through Christmas?"

"I can't let my boss down. I told him I'd be back to cover for him by December 11."

"All right, then. If you won't be here on the twenty-fifth, then I'd like to celebrate Christmas with you ahead of time."

"I don't understand."

"I'll create Christmas just for the two of us. We'll have our own celebration before you leave."

"I don't know, Eli. There's a lot to do between now and then—"

Leaning forward, he took her hands in his and pulled them up to his face. "Say you'll let me create a celebration for the two of us...a private celebration." He kept his gaze on hers and wouldn't let her look away. She didn't.

In fact, she said, "This *could* be a Christmas celebration to remember."

"As soon as I figure out the best way to celebrate, I'll let you know. I'm thinking Friday evening would be good. Are you free?"

"I can be free."

"Then Friday evening it is. And how about we seal the deal with a kiss?"

"We're in public," she whispered.

"And no one's watching," he said, as he kissed her and she kissed him back with all the enthusiasm of their earlier kiss. He'd better come up with the best before-Christmas celebration ever and make it memorable.

Eli looked around the suite at Maverick Manor and knew everything was perfect. Hadley would be meeting him here shortly. They'd managed to meet at his cabin only twice since their drinks at Maverick Manor. Both times had left him wanting more. The problem was they'd both been a little on guard there in case they were interrupted. His family didn't always respect his boundaries.

He could have set up this Christmas celebration at his place, but he hadn't wanted to take any chances. He didn't want any interruptions. He wanted a secluded place where he and Hadley would be undisturbed. No ranch. No relatives. And if he had his way, no phones.

Understandably Hadley's memories of Christmas weren't good ones. He was going to change all that tonight. Maybe they couldn't spend Christmas Eve or Christmas Day together, but they'd have their holiday tonight—and he'd make sure it was memorable.

At the knock at the door, Eli went to answer it. When he opened it, he found Hadley, who had a puzzled expression on her face. "That was an enigmatic text," she said. "'Meet me at Maverick Manor, Room 333.' Here I am. Did you have a business meeting here or something?"

He took her hand and led her inside. "No business meeting. I decided we needed a change of venue."

Hadley's eyes widened as she gazed around the room. First she spotted the Christmas tree with its ornaments, garland and lights twinkling at her from almost every branch. A fire burned brightly in the fireplace, sending a glow throughout the room. She took a few more steps inside. Beyond the sitting area and fireplace stood a king-size lodgepole pine bed all dressed up for Christmas with a red-and-green spread. Beside it on one of the nightstands was a cooler with a bottle of wine. Flameless candles glowed here and there, adding to the holiday charm. And last, but not least, her eyes took a path back to the fireplace and its mantel. From that mantel hung a huge red stocking emblazoned with Hadley's name. The stocking was filled to overflowing with little wrapped presents.

"Eli, what did you do?" She turned to face him, her eyes glowing bright.

"I told you I wanted to celebrate Christmas with you. This is my idea of it. I ordered room service, so dinner should be here in about fifteen minutes. How about a glass of wine to start off the evening?"

She took off her scarf and jacket, and Eli took them from her. After he laid her coat over a chair, she agreed, "A glass of wine would be lovely." She motioned to the tree and the fire. "I still can't believe you did all this."

Going to her, he wrapped his arms around her and brought her in for a kiss.

Afterward, when they were both breathing heavily, he asked, "Now do you believe it?"

She laughed. "I do. I feel like a kid on Christmas morning."

"Exactly what I was going for," he said lightly.

He'd no sooner poured the two of them a glass of wine and put the bottle back in its cooler when there was a rap on the door. It took him only a few seconds to sign for the food. He had the busboy set it up on the coffee table by the sofa.

When they were alone again and seated on the sofa, Hadley said, "I can't wait to see what you ordered."

He took the lids from both of their dinners to reveal prime rib and lobster tail, mashed potatoes, green beans almandine and crème brûlée for dessert.

"Oh my gosh, Eli. This is decadent."

"Just wait until you have butter dripping from your lips and I kiss you. Now *that's* decadent."

The look in her eyes told him that she agreed. They talked and laughed throughout their meal, but more often their eyes met and so did their lips. Buttery kisses seemed like their new best idea ever.

They fed each other crème brûlée, letting the creamy texture linger on their tongues and tasting the dessert from each other. Their kisses were becoming longer and hotter until Eli broke away, took a deep breath and said huskily, "You have to look in your stocking."

Hadley blinked at him. "Now?"

He nodded, rose from the sofa and unhooked the stocking from the mantel. He brought another package along, too, a Santa bag with a mound of white tissue. He lay the stocking on her lap. "Start with these."

As Hadley unwrapped each small package, her

smiles grew broader. There were chocolate bars and gummy candies, a toy dog and cat, and a figurine of a foal with the same coloring as Coco. Hadley ran her fingers over it lovingly. "It's beautiful, Eli. Thank you. I'll never forget that moment when the foal was born, or being with you when it happened."

She'd said the words that were important for his heart to hear. Being with him had mattered. He knew being with her mattered. He handed her the bag next. "Something for tonight."

"Should I guess?" she asked with a sexy look in her eyes.

If she was expecting red or black lace, she was going to be surprised, he thought.

And surprised she was. Her eyes widened, her cheeks grew rosy with delight, and her smile blessed his soul. She carefully unfolded a cozy fleece nightshirt embroidered with a puppy wearing a Santa hat. Hadley laughed, and Eli knew he had hit just the right note.

"Stay here tonight with me?" Eli asked, knowing her answer could tell him everything he needed to know.

"This could be our last night together," she murmured.

"Don't think about that," he suggested, still waiting for her answer.

"Yes, I'll stay." Then teasingly she asked, "Are we going to watch *The Great Roundup*?"

"Not tonight," Eli murmured as he took her into his arms and kissed her.

That kiss fueled their passion. She couldn't seem to rid him of his clothes fast enough nor he hers. They dropped their clothes on the way to the bed and hardly made it there. Eli's groans seemed to quicken her hands as she stroked his muscles, his skin, every part of him. When his tongue drove into her mouth, she took him, tasted him, nibbled at his lips, too.

They seemed to burn for each other. The curve of Hadley's neck was perfect for his kisses. Her shoulders were creamy pink, so feminine yet so strong, too. She was the type of woman who could face adversity and win. As Hadley sifted her hand through his chest hair, she made him crazy with need. Wherever Hadley touched him, it wasn't only pleasure but torment. He wanted satisfaction as much as she did, but he wasn't willing to rush to get there. She might be arousing him, but each brush of his hand on her skin aroused her, too. Her breaths were shallow, her pulse was racing and his name was on her lips.

He'd never felt before what he was feeling with Hadley, and that's what drove him on. He coaxed sighs from her. He kissed her until all of her skin had a rosy glow.

Finally, Hadley seemed to be at her limit. Her hands gripped his shoulders, and she said, "Let go, Eli. I want you. Can't you see that?"

"I see that," he said with some satisfaction. "And I want you, too."

She arched toward him, but still he wouldn't hurry. He entered her with a slowness that drove them both crazy. And then, finally, they found the pleasure they were seeking. The release, when it came, seemed to shatter them both.

Hadley held on to Eli as if she'd never let him go. And that's what he wanted. He didn't want her to ever let go. That was almost his last conscious thought. Almost. Because there was one other, and he knew exactly what he was going to do.

Chapter Thirteen

Hadley had never had a more perfect night. She'd never been loved the way Eli had loved her—with care, with passion, with gentleness. She'd worn her nightgown with the puppy in the Santa hat as they shared a midnight snack. And then he'd removed it and they'd started all over again. Now they were dressed and having the full breakfast he'd ordered for them from room service. Sitting next to him on the couch, she couldn't stop smiling as they drank orange juice, ate scrambled eggs and croissants, and sipped coffee. She hated to leave, but she knew she had to. She'd told Brooks she'd be in this morning.

All of a sudden, Eli said, "I want to ask you something very important."

She thought he might ask when she'd be back after Christmas. She thought he might ask if they could see each other again before she left tomorrow. She thought…

Suddenly Eli pushed their breakfast tray back on the coffee table. Then he stood. He was towering over her, looking a little uncertain. And she had no clue as to what he was thinking. She had no clue until he pushed the coffee table away and got down on one knee in front of her.

Taking her hand in his, he said, "I'd like to wake up every morning the way we woke up this morning. I hadn't planned on doing this just yet. I know you might have doubts, but I don't, and I need you to know that. I want you to stay in Rust Creek Falls and start a future with me. I'd like you to marry me. Will you, Hadley?"

Hadley had never had a panic attack in her life. But right now, her breaths were short and shallow, her chest felt tight and she didn't know if she could suck in another lungful of air. She was looking at Eli and the hope in his face. She felt joy that he wanted to marry her. Yet she also felt panic and so much fear. Could this possibly be the real thing? Just asking that, her thoughts went back to that Vegas chapel and how hard she'd fallen the last time, and how badly it had all turned out. Justin had impulsively proposed, too!

Eli was still on one knee, gazing at her, waiting for an answer.

She wanted to say yes. Oh, how much she wanted to say yes. But she knew she couldn't. She had to let him down easy. She had to make this easier for both of them.

Finding her voice, she murmured, "We hardly know each other."

He squeezed her hand. "I know this is fast. Yet I feel like I *do* know you. And I think I know you very well.

I know you like cream in your coffee with a dab of sugar. I know secretly you like cats more than you like dogs. I know that although you complain about them, your family is important to you, and that Claire is probably your best friend. I know that you like to cook, and you like to be kissed on the nape of your neck. I know you can drive a stick shift, and you prefer boots with a fleece lining."

He was still smiling, and she knew she had to wipe that smile away. She knew she had to disappoint him, and that by disappointing him, she might be turning away a future with him. But what choice did she have? No one knew her secret. Absolutely no one. But she had to tell Eli and hurt them both.

She cleared her throat and tried to take all emotion out of her voice. "You do know those things about me. But you don't know *everything*."

"What else could I possibly need to know?" he teased.

"You need to know that I've been married before."

Eli's smile faded into a frown. His brows drew together, and she knew he was trying to decide what to say. Finally, he asked, "Why didn't you say anything before now?"

Feeling defensive, feeling as if the bottom were falling out of her world, feeling as if everything she'd hidden for so long was going to be made public, she said tersely, "We haven't known each other all that long. I didn't feel it was necessary."

At that Eli got to his feet and sat on the sofa beside her. He went silent.

She knew what he was thinking. He disapproved. Maybe he thought she'd never been seriously in love.

Possibly he thought she was still in love with her ex. She could certainly disabuse him of that notion, but what good would that do? He disapproved, that was obvious, and he didn't even know the worst of it yet. But why tell him the whole sorry tale? Why humiliate herself further? How could she ever admit to Eli how badly she'd been duped by Justin? He'd know then she was a poor judge of character. He'd know then that her impulses had gotten her into a peck of trouble. He'd realize even further that she wasn't the woman he thought she was.

Sparing herself the indignity of admitting all of it, she rose to her feet. Her coat was still lying over the chair where he'd put it last night. She went to it, picked it up, then pulled her purse from the end table.

She knew her voice was stilted when she said, "Eli, thank you for my Christmas celebration. I do appreciate it. I really do." Then she swung around, headed for the door and left. She practically ran down the hall, and she knew she was going to keep running until she reached Bozeman.

When the door closed behind Hadley, Eli felt as if he were in shock. She'd been married?

Restless, unsure what to do next, he paced around the suite studying the remnants of the night they'd shared—the tousled sheets, the condom wrappers on the nightstand, the empty wineglasses.

Then he spotted what made him saddest of all. Hadley had left the nightshirt that he'd bought for her, the one embroidered with the dog in the Santa hat.

She'd been so cool when she'd left. Had he imagined last night?

His mind raced. Part of his mind had told him she

was too good to be true. This was like the other shoe dropping. This was like Elaine saying she was moving to Chicago. This was like—

This was like he'd fallen and Hadley hadn't. Maybe she was still in love with her ex-husband. Maybe he was a fool for thinking he'd really known her. Worse yet, maybe he was just plain stupid for making her into something she wasn't. Did she even care for him? That blank expression when she'd left—

He'd never seen her look like that before. An ex-husband? How long had she been married? Was this the guy who had dumped her? Had he served her with divorce papers on Christmas Eve?

Eli had questions, and he needed answers. But first he had to figure out what was real and what wasn't.

Hadley had put in the morning with Brooks, going through the motions, letting her training and experience guide her, doing all the right things at the right times. But she'd really just been biding her time until she could leave. When she made a promise, she kept it, professionally and otherwise. So she hadn't wanted to let Brooks down. But when he'd said she could leave at noon, she'd taken the opportunity to do just that.

At the boardinghouse, she was so glad that everything seemed quiet. Everybody was busy doing Christmas errands, all except for her grandmother, who was working on reservations for the new year.

She told her grandmother she had to get going today instead of tomorrow and she'd be down to say goodbye as soon as she'd packed. It didn't take long. As she said goodbye, her grandmother tried to delay her with a question. "Is everything all right?"

Hadley assured her it was and made her way out, till she ran into Old Gene. He took one look at her and asked, "What's the matter?"

"I'm fine. I just want to get back to Bozeman and take care of things since I've been away."

Gene scrutinized her more carefully. "You were gone last night. How's Eli?"

She couldn't prevaricate with her grandfather. "Eli is fine."

"Too much *fine* going around," Old Gene said. "Why are you rushing off today instead of tomorrow if both of you are fine? Shouldn't he see you off or something?"

All right. So she had to tell him. "Eli and I probably won't be seeing each other anymore. Now I really have to get going, okay?"

"Your sister is going to be calling you," he warned her.

And she knew what that meant. He was going to tell Claire exactly what she'd said and Claire would probably tell Tessa. But for now, she just had to escape. So she gave her grandfather a kiss on the cheek, climbed into her SUV and headed for Bozeman.

The drive didn't do much to calm her. Too many times she found tears rolling down her cheeks and she swiped them away. At her apartment, she gathered up all the mail that had accumulated on the floor when the postman had slipped it through the mail slot in the door. She sorted through it to give herself something to do. Nothing of importance there. She unpacked in sort of a daze, still thinking about Eli down on one knee…still thinking about last night…still thinking about the way he'd held her and kissed her and touched her.

So she was startled when her cell phone buzzed. She

saw the caller was Tessa and thought about letting the call go to voice mail. But she'd have to deal with her sisters eventually.

After she answered, Tessa asked, "What happened with Eli?"

"We…broke up," Hadley said lamely. Then she murmured, "It was never that serious."

"I don't believe you."

"Not my problem," Hadley shot back.

"Yes, it is if you aren't being honest with yourself," Tessa said. "Every relationship has bumps. Work things out with him."

"There's nothing to work out," she insisted.

"What did he do?"

"He didn't *do* anything."

"Then why did you break up? You know, Carson and I faced troubles, and we got through them. Claire and Levi have certainly had theirs. But their marriage is stronger than ever. You and Eli are a perfect couple."

"Tessa—" Hadley's voice broke.

"Tell me," Tessa prompted.

Eli knew now. Maybe it was time everybody knew. "Three years ago I got married."

"You *what*?"

"I met Justin at a veterinary convention in Las Vegas. He was a pharmaceutical rep. We had a few meetings together, sat in on workshops, had lunch together every day. More than lunch. We were so attracted to each other. I came back to Bozeman, but we were on the phone together every day. We were just so hot for each other, so I flew back out to Las Vegas. We got married in one of the wedding chapels. I should have known something was wrong when Justin convinced me we shouldn't tell our families until we could meet them in person."

"So you were secretly married," Tessa repeated slowly.

"Yes, and it was thrilling. The sex was phenomenal. But when I said we should fly back together to tell all of you the happy news, Justin just kept postponing that. Finally, one night after he'd made another excuse, I went online and searched him."

"You Googled your husband?"

"I should have done it before he became my husband because then I would have found out he was already married to someone else."

"Oh, Hadley. What did you do? Did you press charges?"

"Press charges? All I wanted to do was curl up in a ball and die. I couldn't understand how I'd been so *stupid*. But I had a life to live and a job to keep, so I hired a discreet attorney and was divorced. But I haven't trusted a man since. You know, I keep suspecting they're not what they seem. At least I didn't trust anyone until Eli."

"Are you sure you don't want me to beat up this jerk or have him arrested?"

Hadley knew Tessa was probably only *half* kidding. "No, it's over and done."

"Sis, you can't let your past determine your future. What did you tell Eli?"

"All I told him was that I'd been married before. That seemed to be enough of a shock for him. I couldn't tell him the rest. And I don't even know if he really loved me or just said he did."

"He told you he loved you?"

"Well, not in so many words, but he asked me to marry him."

"Hadley. You've got to tell him *all* of it."

"No, I don't. It's embarrassing and it's humiliating. It's bad enough it was a shock that I told him I was married before. To tell him I was married to a bigamist?"

"Mom and Dad don't know about this?"

"No one knows about this. No one. And I want to keep it that way. Promise me you won't say anything to Eli or the rest of the family."

"It's going to come out, Hadley."

"Maybe, maybe not. Please, just don't tell anyone."

"I can't promise."

"You have to promise."

"Let me tell Claire."

"If you tell Claire, she'll tell Levi. If you tell Claire, she'll let it slip to Grandmother."

Tessa was silent for a few moments. Then she said, "I'm going to give you a few days to think about this. But I hope you'll change your mind. I hope you'll let me bring it all out into the open because that's really what you need to do."

"I'll think about your advice," Hadley said, knowing she would. And that's the way they left it because they were sisters...because they trusted each other... because they would always have each other's backs.

Eli checked the app on his phone the following Friday evening. The map said he was here. According to Tessa, Hadley rented the first floor of a two-story Federal-style house in Bozeman. He'd been miserable since she'd left...since he hadn't stopped her from leaving. And why hadn't he?

Because he had a past, too, and apparently, just like Hadley, it was affecting his future. Tessa's call had made him bump up right against that. They hadn't had a long conversation, but essentially she told Eli if he wanted a future with Hadley, he had to fight for it.

He'd done a lot of thinking over the past week. He hadn't been wrong about his feelings for Hadley. And he suspected she had feelings for him but was afraid of them. Tessa had said as much. She hadn't told him any more of Hadley's story. She said that was for her sister to do. But if he'd judged Hadley from the moment she'd started to tell him that she had been married before, that's why Hadley had run.

Had he been judging her or himself? He hadn't meant to judge her. He'd just been so shocked. But before making this drive he promised himself he would not be shocked again, no matter what Hadley told him. Because whatever her romantic history was, it simply didn't matter. He loved her, and he had to make her see that. He had to make her see that they both had to fight for what they wanted.

As he strode up the walk to the door, he realized she could still be at the veterinary clinic where she worked. After all, she said she was covering for her boss.

He rang the bell, not knowing what to expect. When Hadley opened the door, her eyes went wide and her mouth rounded in an O. She was wearing a red sweater and green leggings with black boots and looked delicious.

"I didn't know if you'd be home," he started.

"I just got home," she said.

"May I come in?"

She looked embarrassed for a moment, but she backed up and motioned to her living room. It was comfortably furnished in blues and tans and yellows. But as he looked around, he got the distinct feeling Hadley didn't spend much time here.

"Tessa called me," he said.

Hadley turned and walked away from him. "So you came because Tessa called? I'll strangle her."

"No need to do that. She just decided to give me what-for, that's all."

"I don't understand," Hadley said. "She doesn't know you."

"No, but she wants to get to know me because she asked me a very important question."

"Which was?" Hadley inquired.

"If I love you enough to fight for you."

At that, Hadley's whole body stilled and her gaze set on his. She studied his face as if she'd never see it again.

"You look as if you haven't gotten much sleep," she noticed.

"I can say the same about you. Maybe we've both been suffering needlessly. I tried to let you go because I thought I made another mistake. I thought you didn't care like I did. Your sister didn't say much. She just said we needed to talk face-to-face, and I realized how true that was."

"Let's sit," Hadley said, going to the sofa. "Or do you want something to drink first?"

He followed her and sat. "Nothing to drink. I want you to tell me whatever you need to tell me."

She must have been nervous about doing that because she inhaled a very deep breath. "All right," she agreed, blowing it out. "For three years I've kept this secret. My family doesn't know. I just told Tessa everything, and she probably told Claire. Next I'll have to tell my parents and my grandparents."

"Hadley, nothing can be that bad. They love you."

"Yes, they love me, but I didn't want them to think less of me. I'm humiliated and embarrassed by what happened."

Eli unbuttoned his jacket and shrugged out of it. He wanted to give her the plain message that he wasn't going anywhere, no matter what she had to tell him. "I'm listening," he said, reaching for her hand and holding it.

But she pulled away, obviously unsure of what his reaction would be. Somehow he had to reassure her that he loved her. That would come.

"It's not really complicated," Hadley said. "I married a bigamist. He was already married when he married me."

That wasn't something Eli had expected. "Is he in jail?" he asked angrily. "How could he do that to you?"

"I don't know," she admitted.

Eli fought the urge to reach for her hand. Instead, his eyes pleading with hers, he said, "Tell me what happened."

And she did. She ended with, "So we kept up a long-distance marriage until…until I finally got suspicious… until I did some research…until I found out he was married."

Eli couldn't help reaching for Hadley now. He took her hand and wouldn't let her pull away. "What did you do?"

"I just wanted out. I found an attorney who handled it all discreetly. Actually, I think he threatened Justin with public humiliation and jail time. I didn't care. I just wanted to be free of him. And I was. And nobody knew about it. I'm sorry I didn't tell you earlier. I'm sorry I didn't trust you enough to tell you. But I didn't know where we were headed…or how you felt."

"That's my fault. I can't even imagine how much pain the whole thing caused you. Because of it, I can certainly understand why you turned down my impulsive wedding proposal. I can wait as long as you need me to wait to be convinced we have staying power. I'll move to Bozeman or St. Louis if that's what you want."

She looked totally shocked, totally amazed, totally radiant. "Oh, Eli, you don't have to move to Bozeman or St. Louis. I already turned down the partnership with Greg. That just wasn't right for me. But I did something yesterday."

"What?" Eli asked, because she sounded hopeful.

"I spoke to Brooks about coming on staff in Rust Creek Falls permanently. Or there is another option. I could buy his dad's practice. I don't know if I can pull together enough money."

"Yes, you can, because I'll help you if that's what you want. Are you sure Rust Creek Falls is where you want to be?"

"It would be great to be near Tessa and Claire and my grandparents. And I'm not that far from my parents in Bozeman. And, of course, I need to be near you. I love you, Eli. I really do."

Eli drew her into his arms then. As he kissed her, he realized all of his dreams could come true.

When he carried her to her bedroom and made slow, sweet love to her, he knew they could live anywhere and it would be home. Would Hadley feel that way, too?

After a storm of passion they both fervently gave in to, they lay face-to-face in the bed. Eli pushed Hadley's hair away from her face. "If you bought Brooks's dad's practice, would you want to live in his house?"

"I don't know. I want to be with you."

He nodded. "And I want to be with you. I was just thinking, my place is more of a bachelor pad. I'm pretty sure Derek would like to move into it. Barrett Smith's place is more of a family house. We could raise a family there."

"I can see little Elis running around the property," she said with a laugh.

"And I can see little Hadleys learning how to ride a horse, wanting maybe too much freedom too early."

"You'd really give up the house you built?"

"It's a house, Hadley. I want a *home* with you. So I'm going to ask you again, and you can take all the time in the world to answer. Will you marry me?"

"I don't need time, Eli. Yes, I'll marry you!"

He kissed her again, knowing this Christmas would be one to remember for a lifetime.

* * * * *

Don't miss the next installment of the new
Mills & Boon Cherish continuity

MONTANA MAVERICKS:
THE GREAT FAMILY ROUNDUP

After over a decade away from his family, Luke Stockton has finally returned to Rust Creek Falls. Beautiful baker Eva Rose Armstrong warms his hardened heart with her honesty—and those yummy homemade treats! But can the loner cowboy crack the barriers he's built—and start the New Year with a new love?

Look for

THE MAVERICK'S MIDNIGHT PROPOSAL

by

Award-winning author Brenda Harlen
On sale December 2017, wherever Mills & Boon books and ebooks are sold.

MILLS & BOON®

EXCLUSIVE EXTRACT

With just days until Christmas, gorgeous but bewildered billionaire Max Grayland needs hotel maid Sunny Raye's help caring for his baby sister Phoebe. She agrees – only if they spend Christmas with her family!

Read on for a sneak preview of
THE BILLIONAIRE'S CHRISTMAS BABY

'Miss Raye, would you be prepared to stay on over Christmas?'

Oh, for heaven's sake…

To miss Christmas… Who were they kidding?

'No,' she said blankly. 'My family's waiting.'

'But Mr Grayland's stranded in an unknown country, staying in a hotel for Christmas with a baby he didn't know existed until yesterday.' The manager's voice was urbane, persuasive, doing what he did best. 'You must see how hard that will be for him.'

'I imagine it will be,' she muttered and clung to her chocolates. And to her Christmas. 'But it's…'

Max broke in. 'But if there's anything that could persuade you… I'll double what the hotel will pay you. Multiply it by ten if you like.'

Multiply by ten… If it wasn't Christmas…

But it was Christmas. Gran and Pa were waiting. She had no choice.

But other factors were starting to niggle now. Behind Max, she could see tiny Phoebe lying in her too-big cot. She'd pushed herself out of her swaddle and was waving her tiny hands in desperation. Her face was red with screaming.

She was so tiny. She needed to be hugged, cradled, told all was right with her world. Despite herself, Sunny's heart twisted.

But to forgo Christmas? *No way.*

'I can't,' she told him, still hugging her chocolates. But then she met Max's gaze. This man was in charge of his world but he looked...desperate. The pressure in her head was suddenly overwhelming.

And she made a decision. What she was about to say was ridiculous, crazy, but the sight of those tiny waving arms, that red, desperate face was doing something to her she didn't understand and the words were out practically before she knew she'd utter them.

'Here's my only suggestion,' she told them. 'If you really do want my help... My Gran and Pa live in a big old house in the outer suburbs. It's nothing fancy; in fact it's pretty much falling down. It might be dilapidated but it's huge. So no, Mr Grayland, I won't spend Christmas here with you, but if you're desperate, if you truly think you can't manage Phoebe alone, then you're welcome to join us until you can make other arrangements. You can stay here and take care of Phoebe yourself, you can make other arrangements or you can come home with me. Take it or leave it.'